heart of FROST and SCARS

PAM GODWIN

Interior Designer: Pam Godwin
Cover Artist: Pam Godwin
Editor: Fairest Reviews Editing

Visit my website at pamgodwin.com

The books in the **FROZEN FATE** trilogy
are not stand-alones.

They must be read in order.
Hills of Shivers and Shadows #1
Cage of Ice and Echoes #2
Heart of Frost and Scars #3

Hills of Shivers and Shadows - Links and Content Warning

My Dear Readers,

Welcome to the conclusion of the Frozen Fate trilogy. Before you dive in, I want to set your expectations.

Frankie and her snow cabin boys no longer grapple with wolves, bears, starvation, and blizzards. They face new fears and obstacles, and I felt it was crucial to honor their journey by not rushing their transition.

Adjusting to a world so vastly different from the hills is neither quick nor easy. It's goddamn frustrating. But I wanted to give their experiences the time and depth they deserve without the relentless, heart-pounding action that defined the first two books.

In other words, your poor heart will get a breather.
If only for a while.

You followed them through their harrowing survival in Hoss. As they claw, snarl, and fight their way through this new world, I hope you find their struggles as compelling and poignant as their past adventures.

Thank you for continuing this journey with them.
Happy Reading,

"My! People come and go so quickly here!"
Dorothy, The Wizard of Oz

leonid

ONE

Frost-laden shock clings to my heart as Monty parks the car on the tarmac.

An early spring fog casts a haze over the runway of Anchorage's airport, the last vestiges of the blizzard lingering in dirty slush along the edges of the pavement.

The weather might have cleared, but the storm still rages inside me, its blinding flurries of resentment and distrust obscuring the path forward, numbing my senses, and leaving only a sharp, cold determination to protect Frankie from this new danger. Whatever the fuck it is.

She sits in the back seat, pressed tightly against Kody, her face ashen, her voice seemingly frozen in her throat. She barely breathes, her shoulders rigid and lips bloodless.

I hate seeing her like this, the fearless spark she usually exudes snuffed out, replaced by a dull, haunted look.

Kody's arm wraps around her, holding her close to his side, his expression dark and brooding.

None of us have spoken since we left the lawyer's office, the gravity of Denver's revelations suffocating the car.

Beside me, Monty stares at his private jet through the

windshield.

I don't know the man, but I bet his hand doesn't normally tremble like that.

He clenches it and reaches for the door handle, his face glowing with the shiner I gave him at the hospital.

"You said my reappearance made national news," Frankie whispers. "But I haven't seen a reporter since we left the hospital."

"I took care of it."

"How?"

"My public relations team is providing controlled, regular updates and exclusives, eliminating the need for invasive reporting. It only buys us a day or two. Long enough to fly to Sitka. Once we're on the island, we'll be out of the public eye, secluded, safe, and impossible to access. I also have security measures in place here and when we land to stop anyone trying to approach us." He opens the door. "I'll check on the plane. Stay here."

He exits the car like he can't escape our unbreathable air fast enough.

The door clicks shut as he strides away, a dark silhouette against the overcast sky.

I may not grasp the full scope of his influence over the media, but I understand the outcome. He's shielding Frankie, protecting her from public scrutiny.

It's an uncomfortable reminder of the power he wields.

Montgomery Strakh.

My uncle.

Kody's half-brother.

Wolf's father.

Frankie's husband.

The part that I'm really struggling to wrap my head around is that Kody, the guy who's been my little brother my entire life, is actually my uncle.

And we share the same woman.

Shit doesn't get more tangled than that.

I don't trust Monty, and he shouldn't trust me. Yet the dumbass left the car running.

leonid

I've never driven before, but I can figure it out. The controls can't be more complicated than flying a plane.

"Let's get out of here." I twist in the seat and find Kody's eyes. "We don't need him."

"You sure about that?" He stiffens, his voice low and rough. "You heard what he said about the reporters. We can't have them broadcasting her location. She's in danger."

"Apparently, being in danger is my new normal." She curls her fingers on her lap, her words clipped. *Angry.*

Outside, Monty gestures animatedly as he converses with the crew beside the jet, preparing to carry us off to his estate in Sitka.

"This threat against you..." I soften my tone, not wanting to scare her more than she already is. "It's worse than wolves and blizzards and starvation. You know why? Because we don't know who or what it is. We won't see it coming until it's too late." I thrust a finger at the man who is far too eager to help us. "The threat could be Monty."

I expect her to react, to argue, to defend him. But she doesn't. She glances in his direction, where he huddles into his coat and talks to the crew.

Then she nods. "We can't rule him out. Denver said this...*admirer* is from my past, yearning for me in a way far darker than his own affection." She shudders. "Maybe it is Monty. But he had me for three years. He had endless opportunities to do what he wanted. I mean, I lived with him. Married him. *Trusted* him." Emotion builds in her tone. "My brain says to run. I can't trust him. But my gut...I don't know. It's just a twisted, hard knot of fear. It doesn't tell me anything. I don't know what to do."

"You're upsetting her," Kody snarls.

"It's not Leo." She slumps. "It's everything else. We need a fucking break, you know? It's like we escaped, only we didn't."

What have we gained by leaving Hoss? We traded starvation and cold for what? A monster worse than Denver?

I shift uncomfortably, the stiffness of new denim chafing my skin. Every layer of fabric on my body carries a scent I don't recognize. An unwelcome, chemical stench that isn't found in nature.

Monty bought our clothes, our boots, even our goddamn underwear. The suede coat envelops me, its edges precise, each stitch meticulous, so different from the worn, practical clothing I shared with my brothers all my life.

I run a hand along the soft, luxurious material. It may have come from an animal, but it's been crafted into an unrecognizable pelt meant to shield me from the cold in a way that seems too gentle for the life I've lived.

Frankie pulls her coat tighter around herself. A white puffy thing, similar to the first one she wore when she arrived at Hoss. The memory of that day flashes in my mind—her strength, her vulnerability, as she stepped into a world so brutally different from anything she knew.

She despises the cold, and that coat doesn't look warm enough.

I remove mine and pass it to her.

"What are you doing?" She pushes it back.

"You're shivering."

"I'm not cold, Leo. I promise. Put your coat back on."

Despite her assurances, I make a mental note to find her something warmer, something that feels more like us. Something less like this new, polished existence and more like the survival and warmth we've found in each other against the raw cold of the Arctic.

Kody's new coat, similar to mine, hugs his frame awkwardly, as if it's unsure of its place on his body. The fabric, though fine and expensive, seems to constrain him, like he's wearing someone else's skin.

"What does *your* gut tell you?" he asks me, tugging at the collar, his fingers rough against the velvety material, pulling it away from his neck like he's trying to escape it. "Do we fly to Sitka or cut ties and run?"

I shift my gaze back to Monty, churning with suspicion, confusion, and an unbearable acknowledgment that, for now, we could use his help.

"I don't like it," I finally murmur, glancing back at Frankie.

Her pale skin, tight expression, each breath strained and shallow—she's a far cry from the woman I know, the woman I love.

A fresh wave of worry crashes over me. "Maybe we should stay in Anchorage for a bit, give ourselves time to adjust."

"And do what?" Kody stabs a hand through his hair, setting the black strands in disarray, an unconscious rebellion against the refined look he's been forced to adopt. "I'm not disagreeing with you, but we need a plan. Where would we stay? How would we survive?"

I don't have an answer, and he knows it. Our options are limited, dire realities pressing in from all sides. The thought of staying in an unknown city, where threats lurk unseen, without money or shelter to protect her, makes my hackles bristle.

We need time to process everything—the tangled family ties, the looming danger, Denver's haunting words.

I look out at Monty again, watching as he climbs into the cockpit, his conversation with the crew concluding.

For all my distrust, Monty's right about one thing. We need to go somewhere safe, somewhere isolated. The offer of his island, the privacy of his guest house, seems a small solace amidst the madness.

The engines of the plane roar to life, the deep hum vibrating through the tarmac, through my bones.

I turn back to Frankie, her hand clutching Kody's arm, her knuckles white.

"Say the word." She sits taller. "I'll climb into the driver's seat and drive us away from him."

If that's what she wants, she would've already done it.

She certainly didn't ask my permission before stealing my snow machine and crashing it into a hill.

"What's stopping you?" I narrow my eyes.

"If Monty is the danger Denver warned us about..." She swallows. "He'll find me. Doesn't matter where I go or how long it takes. He'll hunt me down. Stealing his car and driving to another city won't stop him."

"He didn't find you in Hoss."

She makes a noise in her throat, her face collapsing. "I can't—"

"You're not going back there," Kody growls, spearing me with a threatening glare.

"We'll go to Sitka then." I pull on my coat, my voice as steady as I can make it. "We don't have a choice."

She gives a slight nod, her eyes glistening. I reach toward the back seat, gripping her free hand, finding her fingers ice cold.

She's fucking shaking.

Something else is wrong. My gaze flies to Kody.

He directs his eyes to the plane.

The plane...

Fuck.

"You're not ready to fly again." I close my hand around hers, trying to warm it. "That's what this is about?"

"It's fine." She blinks rapidly. "I'm fine."

"Bullshit." I stroke my thumb across her knuckles. "Don't lie to me."

"It's everything. All of it. I'm trying to be brave. I swear. It's just a lot all at once." She clings to my grip, her gaze pleading. "I haven't even processed Denver's video or what Monty's role might be in it. Right now, I can't think past the immediate danger, which is boarding that plane after...after...watching you and Kody get ripped away in the cockpit and the sound of twisting metal, the terror—"

"Shh." Kody pulls her onto his lap. "We won't fly. We'll find another way."

"No." She scrambles off him and slides across the back seat, putting her arm out. "If you two can fly, I can, too. I won't let fear control me. I'm just acknowledging it, okay? Let me voice it. Let me face it."

Kody's nostrils pulse.

Maybe the plane crash should've affected me more, but I don't remember much of it. I recall Kody's calming voice in the headset, the blinding whiteout of the blizzard, then...nothing.

"What about you?" I ask him.

"I don't fear the plane."

No, I suppose he's more worried about Monty and his plans for Frankie. Same as me.

"Come here." I reach for her.

She scoots forward, leaning between the front seats until our arms entangle and our foreheads connect. My lips find hers on instinct, my breath guiding hers, slow, steady, and together.

"How does he already have a plane waiting here?" I slide our noses together.

"Money." She sighs. "He has chauffeurs and pilots everywhere. Someone brought his plane here, and someone else will drive this car away when we leave."

"Back to Sitka?"

"If he owns it." She shrugs. "It's probably a rental."

"How do you not know?"

"He owns a lot of shit. I never cared about that."

"But you care now."

"What do you want from me, Leo?" She pulls back, separating us.

"I don't want you to be dependent on him."

"I'm not. I have my own money saved, but it's not enough to support all three of us. I can't help you the way he can. Whether you like it or not, he's your family, and he's willing to assist—"

"At what cost?"

"He's coming." She watches him exit the plane, rushing her words. "Let's say he *is* taking advantage of our situation for some malicious purpose. If this is a trap, we'll set a trap right back and use him in the process."

"Keep your enemies close," I grumble. "Your logic is terrifying."

"Fear has never stopped us before, and we're going in with our eyes wide open. Are you afraid to exploit him and the help he's offering?"

"Not if you promise to remain with Kody or me at all times."

"I promise. If we do this, we do it together. I'm in if you guys are. Decide."

Kody's our hunter, the silent predator. His watchful strength and feral intuition, honed by a lifetime of survival, reassures me, even as I grapple with my swirling doubts about what lies ahead.

Frankie's our healer. Her intelligence and medical skills saved us more times than I can count, and now she faces an even greater challenge. We need her to keep us intact through the psychological scars we bear. Her ability to see the best in us, to push us toward healing even when it's the last thing we think we need, is more critical than ever.

I'm the brawler, the fucking enforcer. In the wild, my boiling temper and leadership often made the difference between life and death. Here, I need to find better ways to channel my protective fire. Not just against physical threats, but against the psychological, insidious dangers that might sneak up on us.

Our strengths complement one another, creating a force of solidarity. Whatever happens, we'll face it as a team, a partnership forged in blood, survival, and unbreakable love.

A renewed sense of purpose cements itself inside me. We're not just survivors of the past. We're warriors for our forever.

"We need to keep our senses sharp and learn fast." I look at Kody.

"Together." He takes her hand.

"Together." I shake off my unease and open the door.

leonid

TWO

My protective instincts leap into overdrive as Kody and Frankie join me on the tarmac, their faces grim.

The chilly air nips my skin, but it's a familiar cold, one I've battled all my life. Right now, it's the only thing I relate to amid the sights and sounds of our surroundings.

Monty may know these places, these routines, but for Frankie, I trust no one.

My protection isn't passive. It's an active, constant thing as I probe the sprawling expanse of concrete and snow, the distant mountains, and the few private jets scattered across the field.

"Stay close." Kody grips her hand, scanning the area, too.

She's used to this—the commotion, the people, the world beyond the wilds of Hoss. This may be a controlled environment, but the openness of the space, the shadowed areas beneath the planes, all of it triggers my vigilance.

Her safety is my responsibility, a weight I shoulder willingly, fiercely.

Together, we trudge toward the sleek jet, its wings slashing against the gray sky. We slow our steps to maintain Frankie's stiff pace, refusing to rush her as she works through her rising panic.

With Kody's focus on her, mine remains razor-sharp on the less visible corners of our path, the places where someone could hide, the angles of approach a stalker might use if they're watching.

The crunch of our boots on the lightly frosted ground, the clatter of a cart being loaded, the hum of engines, the muffled conversations of the ground crew—every noise is cataloged and analyzed for its threat level.

A ground worker passes too close for my liking, and my body tenses, ready to act. But he moves on without giving us a second glance, and I force myself to relax.

I note the positions of the cameras on the hangar walls and the faces of the crew. I commit everything to memory. Every detail matters, every observation could be the difference between safety and danger.

Monty meets us halfway, halting us mid-step as his eyes narrow on Frankie. "What's wrong?"

I grit my teeth, biting back the *fuck you* that surges, resenting how keenly he sees her, how intimately he understands her.

"I'm fine." She fidgets, glancing at the plane.

He follows her gaze, his forehead knitting. Then his lips part, and he drags a hand down his face. "Shit. I didn't think." His gaze softens as he steps closer. "We don't have to fly. We can drive to Sitka. It'll take a few days by car, but it's an option. Or a yacht. It'll take longer, but we can manage."

"No." She shakes her head vehemently, her chest hitching in shallow, uneven motions. "I can do this."

But her eyes are wide, her pupils dilated. She's panicking.

Everything inside me screams to grab her and carry her away from this. From him. But she doesn't want to be sheltered. She wants to be brave.

If she only knew how goddamn brave she already is.

Monty's hand twitches at his side as if he wants to reach out and comfort her, too. It makes me burn with jealousy, my face stinging with heat.

"Fuck that." He removes his phone and taps on the screen. "I'll make other arrangements. Go back to the car."

"Don't." She reaches for his device.

He holds it above her head and continues typing on it. "It's been a tough few days, and we have other options. I won't force you to endure any more hardships."

She stiffens, her eyes darting between Monty, Kody, and me, a flicker of resolve flashing across her striking features.

"I need to get this over with, Monty." She sets her fists on her hips, the tension in her posture betraying her struggle. "I need to go home."

Home.

Fuck if that doesn't punch me in the gut.

Kody and I are her home.

Monty's expression gentles, the muscles in his jaw loosening.

"All right." He steps back, pocketing his phone. "But if you change your mind at any point, let me know."

She nods, glancing at Kody and me, her lips pressing into a tight line.

Did she just manipulate him to get what she wanted? I don't know whether to be impressed or pissed off. I don't want her leading him on for any reason.

We resume our march toward the jet, my heart pounding in my chest, the jealousy gnawing at me.

As we approach the stairs, Monty's gaze lingers on her, his eyes dark with unspoken emotion. It takes all my willpower to check my temper, to resist the urge to confront him, to reclaim her from his blatant affections.

She's ours now. We'll overcome this like everything else. Together. Even if it means sharing her in a way that feels both necessary and impossible.

Our journey is only beginning, and despite the chill of the tarmac beneath our feet, we can only press forward, each step heavy with the burden of what still lies ahead.

Monty boards first, turning back with an extended hand to assist her. Before she can move, Kody steps between them, a flash of defiance flaring in his eyes.

He looks at me, and a wordless agreement passes between us. The cold wind whips around us, carrying the tension of our decision.

Monty goes rigid, setting his jaw. "What's the problem?"

He's used to controlling everyone around him, but he'll quickly learn that he can't control us.

No amount of fine clothing can smooth out the rugged edges of our souls, shaped by years of survival against harsher elements than these.

"In Sitka, Frankie will share a room with Leo and me," Kody says clearly, each word deliberate, marking our territory in no uncertain terms.

Monty's face turns to stone, his hand still outstretched, hanging in the air like an unanswered question.

Awkward.

His expression slowly empties, donning a mask of composure, but the frost in his blue eyes shows his true feelings—cold, cagey, dangerously aggressive.

"There are plenty of bedrooms." He lowers his hand, too calm. "The guest house has two, and the main estate has five. No one needs to share."

"We're not boarding that plane until you agree to the sleeping arrangements." I take a stance beside Kody, forming a solid front.

"For fuck's sake. It's cold out here. We can discuss it in—"

"There's nothing to discuss." Frankie inches forward, squeezing between us. "You read my journal, Monty. You know I've been sharing a bed with them for months, and it's more than for warmth. It's comfort. It's safety. We need to maintain some semblance of what we had. It's crucial for us during this transition."

His expression fractures, the image of a composed, controlled man cracking under the agony of what he lost.

His wife, the woman he loves, aligns her comfort and safety with two other men. This isn't a battle he can win. Nor is it one he can afford to fight right now.

He wants us on that plane.

With a heavy sigh, he slips a hand into his pocket.

"You can sleep wherever you feel most comfortable." His gaze flits between Kody and me. "I know you don't trust me. Hell, you probably think I'm the stalker Denver talked about, the one hunting Frankie." His voice lashes in the wind, his anger breaking through. "Denver put that suspicion into your heads on purpose. He wanted us divided and distracted, warring against one another as the real threat moves in. Don't team up against me. We'll be stronger together. I understand I have a long way to go to earn your trust, but until then, give me a chance to right my wrongs and prove myself."

Frankie peers up at us, seeking our reactions.

Kody ascends the stairs and stands toe-to-toe with him. "We'll hold you to that. Our priority is Frankie's safety and happiness."

"And my priority"—she grabs my hand—"is them."

"Let's board then." Monty oozes confidence, arrogance even, but an undercurrent of defeat rests in the pinch of his mouth, a bitter pill swallowed.

As we climb into the jet, I'm hit by an overwhelming sense of opulence that makes the Turbo Beaver feel like a tin can in comparison. The interior gleams with polished wood and chrome, oversized leather seats inviting us to sink into luxury we've never known.

A crisp, clean scent permeates the air, far removed from the musty, fuel-tainted confines of our last desperate flight.

The cabin feels less constricting than the vast, unprotected landscape we're leaving behind. In this enclosed space, flying toward a new life, the lines are drawn, roles defined, and alliances solidified.

Whatever we're about to face, be it the shadows of Denver's threats, Monty's obsession with Frankie, or the task of assimilating into a foreign society, it's a little less daunting when I consider the bond we share.

The importance of our unity can't be understated. In the hills, where the world tried to crush us with ice and starvation and hungry beasts, our trust in one another kept us alive. Now, facing a world of concrete and excess and unknown predators, that trust is our greatest asset.

We are each other's protector.

In the cabin, Monty's attention zeroes in on her. He moves with that distinguished grace of his, drifting close enough to her to make Kody growl.

A warning Monty ignores.

"If you need anything during the flight, don't hesitate to come to me." He reaches to touch her hand.

She jerks away and lowers into the closest seat.

A faint shadow of pain darkens his face before he quickly covers it with a practiced smile. "The flight attendant will be available as well. Whatever puts you more at ease." There's a stiffness to his posture now, a hint of her rejection stinging him as he turns to me. "If you're interested, you can join me in the cockpit. I can give you some pointers on flying this bird."

I nod, wary but curious. "Might take you up on that."

If I ride up front, it isn't just about learning aviation. It's strategic. I need to learn everything I can about this man and his world.

With a final, longing glance at Frankie, he slips into the cockpit, leaving us to settle in.

As the door closes behind him, the space feels charged and tense. She looks shaken, the quick withdrawal of her hand not lost on me.

"Talk to me." I crouch before her.

"I don't like hurting him." She squeezes her eyes shut for a moment before meeting my gaze. "I know that's naive after everything he's done. But what if his help is genuine? What if he's a victim in this, just like us? I'm not trying to be mean—"

"You don't have a mean bone in your body." Kody crosses his arms, towering over us.

"We'll get to the bottom of Montgomery Strakh." I cup the back of her head and pull her face to mine. "In the meantime, there's nothing wrong with being cautious and setting boundaries. He has no right to touch you, and when we land, we'll make the rules clear for him."

"My snow cabin boys have rules?" She quirks an eyebrow.

"Snow cabin boys?" I scowl. "When it comes to you and him, you better fucking believe your *men* have rules."

"There is no me and him."

"Exactly." I kiss her lush mouth, savoring the soft, sensual glide of her tongue against mine, groaning into the heat. "I think I'll stay back here with you."

"No." She fans her fingers over my braids, kissing me again. "Fly with Monty. Ask him about the plane, about what to expect in Sitka. Find out everything you can."

"Okay, but if you need me—"

"She has me." Kody grunts.

I glide my thumb along her bottom lip. "If Monty's flying lessons are worth anything, I'll be up there learning something useful for us."

"I know." She manages a small smile. "I love you."

"My forever." I look her over for any sign of distress, reluctant to leave.

"I've got her." Kody clamps a hand on my head and shoves me away.

I lunge to my feet and grip his neck. "You need anything, you call for me."

"Yep."

"Keep her safe."

"Always." He swats me away, but the look he shoots me echoes the concern pulsing through my veins.

Her fear of flying could materialize into a full-blown panic attack.

He'll alert me if that happens.

Bending down, I steal another kiss from her. Then I turn and make my way to the cockpit.

Even though I'm leaving her in Kody's capable hands, my role as her protector never leaves me.

"Frankie." I pause with my hand on the door. "I'm putting my trust in Monty to get us there safely. But make no mistake. If he looks at me wrong or if this becomes too much for you, I'll turn this plane around myself."

My words are a vow, carved from the depths of my savage commitment to her.

kodiak
THREE

As Leo disappears into the cockpit, I swallow my nerves and keep my attention on Frankie.

She clutches the armrests of her seat, her fingers stiff and pale.

The plane hasn't even started its taxi to the runway, and her eyes already dim beneath ghosts of anxiety. She tries to hide it with a brave smile, but it's not working.

The distant tinkling of glass and subtle movements from the nook in the front signal the presence of a crew member.

They haven't closed the air stair door yet. I can still carry her off.

"Hey." I crouch beside her, meeting her stark gaze with a steady one of my own. "Give me one good reason not to throw you over my shoulder and haul you out of here like a caveman."

"Because I secretly enjoy the caveman act and might start thinking it's the only way to travel."

"Woman, I'll always be your caveman."

A small, nervous breath escapes her, wrapped in curved lips.

Stunning.

I need to strap her in, but the seat she chose puts her back to the cockpit.

"Is this where you want to sit?" I glance around, counting. "There are five other options plus that three-person divan."

"If we crash, no seat is safe."

"The chance of crashing twice in three days is extraordinarily rare, verging on statistically improbable. For once, the odds are in our favor."

"Good answer, handsome." She runs the backs of her fingers along my jaw. "Even so, will you sit across from me so I can look into your eyes when we become an improbable statistic?"

Christ. My chest constricts.

Her fear is instinctual, a deep-rooted dread that even the bravest can't easily shake off.

"I know it's hard, but I need you to try something for me." I take her seat belt in my hands, beginning the familiar ritual of securing her in. "Focus on the here and now, not on what could happen. You control this moment, not your fear."

"Okay." She squares her shoulders. "I'll try."

As I straighten the straps across her lap, every little flinch and tense breath she takes has me scrambling to lighten the mood. A tactic Wolf excelled at.

"When I buckled you in on the Turbo Beaver, I checked it about twenty times. Bet you thought I was just being overprotective."

"There was another reason?"

"I was making excuses to stay close." I peek at her face. "To get into your pants."

"Stop." She laughs, the sound warming my skin.

I continue my routine with the buckle, deliberately fumbling and drawing out the task. "I might need to check it another twenty times, just to be sure. You know, safety first."

Brushing my thumb against the waistband of her jeans, I deftly release her button and hook a finger in the opening, teasing her zipper.

"Kody," she whispers.

"Or maybe I just like coming up with excuses to touch you."

"You never need an excuse to touch me." Her smile widens, and her grip on the armrests loosens as she watches my exaggerated concentration on the buckle.

"That right?" With one hand, I blunder my attempts with the latch while my other hand sinks deeper into the heat behind her zipper.

"If you play with it much longer, I might think you're doubting your handiwork."

"Never." I click the buckle securely and with the hand I still hold in her pants, give the latch and her zipper a tug. "See? Just had to make sure it's as strong and resilient as the person wearing it."

Her laughter, more genuine this time, fills the cabin, easing the stiffness from her shoulders. "I know what you're doing, you wicked man."

"Tell me." I shift forward, wedging my hips between her legs.

"You're trying to make this less terrifying."

"Tell me it's working."

"You know it is." She leans closer.

"Sorry to interrupt." The female crew member, dressed impeccably in a navy uniform, approaches with a polite smile.

With a growl, I remove my hand from Frankie's jeans and keep it tucked against her waist.

"We're about to take off. Please, take your seat." The pretty Black woman blushes as she meets my eyes. "My name is Tanya. Can I get you anything to drink?"

"Bourbon for her. Vodka for me."

"Please and thank you," Frankie adds.

I grunt.

Tanya nods and moves on.

"We need to work on your manners, caveman." Frankie taps my lips.

I bite her finger, making her yelp. "Trying to tame me already?"

"Wouldn't dream of it." She zips up her pants, shutting down my advances. "You're supposed to be in your seat."

"I'd rather be in *your* seat."

"Sir?" Tanya calls out. "Where are you going?"

I glance up and find Leo stepping out of the plane.

"Taking a leak." He's already unzipping.

"Outside?" Tanya gasps. "There's a lavatory on board." She points to the rear.

"Fine." He ambles toward us, pausing to caress Frankie's cheek. "Want to hold my cock while I pee?"

I catch Tanya's wide-eyed stare. "We found him in the wild. He's not potty trained."

"Fuck off." He continues toward the back. "What the—? How am I supposed to fit in here? How does it even work?"

"Figure it out." Frankie laughs.

He proceeds to piss with the door open, bumping around and cursing over the sound of his stream.

"Wipe off the seat," she yells.

"What seat?"

"Oh, God." She covers her face.

At least he washes his hands before returning to us. "The bathroom is a no-go, but that divan is the perfect place to fuck like animals." He glances at the cockpit. "We have a few minutes before—"

"You're a barbarian." She smacks his abs, grinning. "Get out of here."

"Love you." He winks his one gold eye and stalks back to the cockpit.

I can't fault him for being an ass. Everything he did was an attempt to calm her down. Most of it, anyway. I'm certain he meant to piss on the tarmac.

"Feeling better?" I brush a strand of hair from her face, my movements tender.

"Yeah."

Our eyes lock, and the world outside the plane, with all its threats and uncertainties, falls away. It's just the two of us, connected and safe in the knowledge that our bond is the constant we can rely on.

I test the connection points where her seat belt bolts to the frame with a focus born of a crash that still haunts us both. Then I check the latch once, twice, three times, each click a reassurance that I silently whisper to both of us.

As Tanya closes the air stair door, my gaze stays on Frankie, searching for any trace of fear, ready to soothe it away.

"Brave, beautiful thing." I inch closer, my lips finding hers.

I pour all my love and devotion into the kiss, all my promises of protection. She's going to make it. We all are.

When our mouths part, the heat lingers, suspended in the electricity that travels between us.

Until I look up.

Monty stands just inside the doorway to the cockpit, his features twisted into a barely contained rage. His blue eyes sharpen into lethal blades, his body tense as if ready to spring into a fight. The dark bruises that Leo gave him only add to his manic appearance.

But he catches himself, his jaw clenching as he battles his fury. Then, with visible effort, he reins it in, his face smoothing into the cultured facade he wears so well as he turns and closes the door.

My heart thuds against my ribs, the encounter lifting the hairs on my nape.

"What's wrong?" She twists, glancing at the door to the cockpit. "What happened?"

Nothing.

The lie sits on my tongue. I'm trying to comfort her, not add more stress.

But I'll never lie to her.

"Monty watched me kiss you." I move to the seat facing hers. "Pretty sure he wants to disembowel me."

"He'll have to go through me first." She sets her cute little jaw.

"He doesn't scare me." I latch my seat belt and reach for her, fitting our hands together. "This will be an adjustment for him as much as it is for us."

I can't imagine losing this woman's love and watching her

move on with other men. I can survive anything. But not that. It would hollow me out, cleave me apart, and turn me into dust. No coming back from that.

The engines roar with a surge of power, the vibration seeping into the cabin.

At first glance, Frankie seems composed, but subtle signs creep in—the twitching of her hand in mine, the hitching of her shoulders, and the way her breath catches as the plane begins to taxi.

Her momentary calm fractures before my eyes.

The jet picks up speed on the runway, and her fingernails dig into my hand. Her jaw flexes, and a fresh layer of fear clouds her eyes. No doubt every motion of the plane reminds her of what could go wrong.

I scoot forward as far as my belt allows and wrap my hands around her thighs, marking the tension there.

Our gazes hold as I soften my voice just for her. "You're safe. I've got you."

Her breath shudders.

"We'll make it through this, just like we always do." I squeeze her thighs gently. "Focus on me."

"That part's easy. You're really nice to look at." She tries to smile but not quite managing it. "I thought I could handle this."

"You are handling it. Being scared doesn't mean you're not strong. It means you're human. We're all a bit shaken." As the plane lifts off, ascending higher and leaving the ground behind, I keep talking to distract her. "We're rising above it all. Just like we planned. Nothing can touch us up here, not while I'm by your side."

Her eyes dart to the window before meeting mine again. "I don't want to feel this way, so scared, so out of control."

"Fear is just...it's like the cold we faced in the hills. You acknowledge it. You respect it. But you don't let it stop you. You taught me that. We adapt. We survive."

"I taught you that?"

"Yeah, you did. You also taught me kindness. And forgiveness." I caress my hands along her legs. "You taught me how to be with a woman. Not just sex. But the truest form of love I've ever known. A woman's love."

"Your mother loved you."

"I don't remember. I don't even know what she looked like."

"Maybe Monty has photos of her." The plane bumps with turbulence, and she chokes. "If we make it to Sitka."

"I won't let anything happen to you." I grip her hands, stilling her shaking. "Just like we always had a plan if a storm hit or the ice cracked beneath our feet, we have a plan now. You're not alone. You've got Leo up there, giving Monty hell. Anything feels off, he'll take care of it."

The muscles in her face relax, the fear not gone but somewhat abated by the reassurance. "Thank you. For understanding. For talking me through it."

"Always." I feel the heaviness of my promise, not just in the words but deep in my bones. "You focus on breathing. Control what you can. Let us worry about the rest."

She sways closer, her grip loosening as she listens to my voice.

"Remember the wolf you took down? And the bear you outran? And the psychopath who hurt us for thirty years?" I keep my gaze steady but fierce, imbued with my pride. "You annihilated our greatest enemy within months. You're a force to be reckoned with."

"I nearly starved you to death in the process."

"We survived. Nothing has beaten you. Not going to start now."

With our fingers intertwined and the world receding below, the threats and shadows of our past might linger, but together, we're untouchable.

We fall into silence until the speakers overhead crackle with static.

Leo's voice fills the cabin.

"Ladies and feral men, welcome to cruising altitude. If anyone's thinking of joining the Mile High Club—I'm looking at you, Frankie—give me the signal." He laughs. "The pilot doesn't like that. You should see his face right now."

Rustling and scraping sounds over the intercom.

"I hope they're not fighting." Her complexion pales.

"Just a reminder," Monty cuts in. "My plane, my rules. This is a family flight. Keep it PG."

She snorts.

I glance back at the divan, and my thoughts plunge into darkness. "Have you and Monty...?"

She goes still, her lips pressed in a line.

Of course, he's fucked her on his plane. And on every surface of the estate we're about to share with him.

A hot ember burns in my stomach.

"Kody..." She grips my arm.

"It's smooth sailing from here," Monty continues. "If you feel a bump, it's just me teaching my co-pilot a lesson."

"Try me, old man." Leo's voice comes at a distance, barely audible over the intercom before it clicks off.

"Well then." Frankie sinks back into her seat with a sigh. "We're off to a roaring start."

kodiak

FOUR

I shift restlessly, feeling stiff and out of place in these new clothes. They're sharp, clean, and nothing like the rough and ready gear I've always worn.

Every so often, I look down at myself, startled to see the perfectly sewn seams and unstained leather that feels so strange against my skin.

"How's the leg holding up?" Frankie's gaze drifts to my knee, her nurse's instincts overtaking her anxieties.

I can tell she's compartmentalizing her fear to focus on me, something she's always been good at.

The friction burn I got during the crash throbs persistently. It's been three days, and the skin still feels tight and hot, the damaged layers sensitive to movement and touch.

If I adjust my position too quickly or the fabric of these new jeans rubs against it the wrong way, a sharp sting pulses through the area.

The pain isn't just physical. It's a nagging echo in my muscles, reminding me of every jolt of that crash.

Thankfully, the surface scratches that Leo and I received on our faces have already healed.

"It's manageable." I don't want her worrying about me more than she already is with everything else going on.

"Make sure to keep it clean and watch for any signs of infection."

It's not just the injury and the new clothes making me uneasy. My eyes flicker to the window, drawn to the unfamiliar world speeding by. It's all so different from the open, wild landscape where I spent my life. The change isn't just around me. It's on me, and it's a lot to take in.

I lean back, my gaze grabbing hers again, making sure she feels every bit of my presence.

"What?" She flutters those long, sexy lashes, raising my body temperature.

"You're beautiful."

"You don't have to say that anymore."

"Why the fuck not?" I frown, not understanding.

"I know those months in the cabin took a toll." She smooths a hand over her hair, catching a red lock between her fingers. "But I'm no longer starving. My confidence will improve as I gain the weight I lost. I'm working on it."

Anger flares in my chest. Not at her but at the thought that she might believe her worth or beauty has anything to do with her condition.

"Woman." I bend closer so she can see the sincerity on my face. "You've always been beautiful to me. Not because of how you look but because of who you are. Even when things were at their worst, it didn't change how I saw you." I reach out, grazing a thumb along her jawline. "You are strength and courage in a world that was falling apart. You're the fire that warmed the coldest nights and the light in the darkest times. Your beauty isn't just in your appearance. It's in your spirit, your resilience."

She's quiet for a moment, staring at me. I know she's processing my words, maybe not fully convinced but affected by them nonetheless.

"Every time I looked at you, even when you were struggling, I saw the woman who challenged the wilderness with me, who fought through every day with a heart full of hope. Do you know how attractive that is? You're hot as fuck, and I will keep saying it as long as I live because it's the truth."

Her eyes soften, moisture gleaming. "Thank you," she whispers, "for seeing me like that."

"Why are you thanking me? Resting my eyes on you is a goddamn privilege."

"I totally want to hump you right now." She bites her lip.

My cock jerks as I recline in the seat and pat my lap. "Hop on. Or..." I jab a thumb over my shoulder. "We can move to the divan."

"Not here. But soon." She lifts a booted foot and nudges it between my legs. "I promise."

The jet banks, and we turn to the windows.

Below, Anchorage stretches like an intricate, tangled web of concrete, the buildings rising in clustered columns toward the sky. And green. So much green. Not just trees but fields of vegetation I've never seen before.

I grip her ankle and remove her shoe. Lifting the other, I remove it, too. With her socked feet on my lap, I massage her delicate arches, feeling her tremble, her anxiety rolling off.

"It's like watching a living map unfold." I turn my face toward the window. "Everything is so interconnected. So designed."

"It's a different kind of wilderness. One made by humans."

As the plane cruises higher, I'm mesmerized by the transition between untamed landscape and the structured chaos of civilization. Roads carve through forests. Buildings cluster like flocks of resting birds. Gleaming threads of rivers wind through it all.

I trace the curve of her ankle. "Makes me feel small."

"Small but not powerless. Part of something bigger."

The scenery is vibrant, like her eyes, pulsing with life and movement in a way that both thrills and terrifies me.

"We need to learn a lot quickly," I say, thinking aloud. "Driving, using phones, getting IDs."

"And therapy." She lowers her feet and reaches for my hands, her fears momentarily forgotten as she considers our needs. "We've all been through so much. We can't ignore how it's impacted us. That includes Monty, too."

If Monty is dangerous to her, he won't live long enough for therapy. I don't care that he's my brother. I'll kill him myself.

Tanya returns with our drinks. "Vodka and bourbon." She folds down a table between our laps and sets the glasses on it. "Lunch will be served shortly. May I take your coats?"

We shed our outerwear, and I nod my thanks, not used to this level of service.

Frankie unlatches her seat belt.

"What are you doing?" I reach for my belt, ready to go to her.

She moves with a fluid grace that belies her nerves, slipping around the table to where I sit. Crawling onto my lap, she folds into me with the intimacy of a hundred nights curled together for warmth.

I wrap my arms around her, pulling her against my chest, unable to ignore the sharpness of her bones beneath her skin.

Knowing she'll have access to proper nutrition and regular meals fills me with immense relief. I imagine her health returning, her figure filling out to its natural, womanly state.

I want to see her not just surviving but thriving, laughing, and lively, her soul as nourished as her body. To see her more freely, without the shadow of hunger darkening her eyes, fuels a deep, burning hope inside me.

You're going to get better, Frankie. I'll make sure of it. We'll have food, shelter, warmth, happiness, and each other. Everything we need.

She peers up, choosing me as her view instead of the sprawling scenery beyond the window. Her presence in my arms, so light yet so profoundly significant, reaffirms my need to watch her flourish, to reclaim the vitality that the harsh life of Hoss stripped away.

Slowly, her breathing grows shallow and even. As I indulge in the sweet scent of her hair against my nose, her eyes drift shut.

Within minutes, she's asleep.

Careful not to disturb her, I take a sip of the vodka, the

clear liquid cool against my lips.

As it glides down, I instinctively critique its profile, comparing it to the batches I distilled under conditions far less ideal than any commercial distillery.

This vodka, likely expensive and well-regarded, hits my palate with an initial smoothness that's promising, but it quickly reveals its shortcomings.

Swirling the liquid in my glass, I watch it catch the light. It lacks the depth that comes from the meticulous filtering process I used with mine. I always allowed the spirit to mellow through natural charcoal—sourced from peat, wood, and other organic materials—stripping away the harsh notes while enhancing the vodka's character.

I set the glass down, cataloging the adjustments I would make, the personal touches that would elevate this vodka from merely good to memorable. It's not just about distilling. It's about crafting a story in each bottle, a story of survival, of ice, wilderness, and hardship. A story this vodka, for all its refinement, doesn't tell.

After a while, the faint aroma of heating food drifts through the cabin, stirring something primal within me. My stomach rumbles.

What would they serve on a flight like this? Gourmet meals or something simpler? Certainly not the stark survival fare we've been hunting and scraping out of cans all winter.

My mouth waters at the prospect of enjoying a meal I didn't have to kill or gather myself.

I glance around, detecting movement in the alcove toward the front. It must be a small kitchen area. The scent grows stronger, a blend of savory and unknown spices that are entirely new to my senses.

Leo must smell it, too, because within minutes, he slips out of the cockpit. But he only has eyes for the sleeping woman on my lap.

He approaches quietly as if the very act of walking could disturb her peace, his eyes scanning her features, searching for any hint of pain or fear.

That tenderness in his gaze is new, a softness that didn't surface until he met Frankie.

Whenever I look at her, I know my face does that melty thing, too.

As he edges nearer, her eyelids flutter open, and a gentle smile spreads across her lips.

"Hi." Her drowsy voice, barely a whisper, fills the space with warmth.

He bends in, his hand brushing a stray lock of hair from her forehead. His touch lingers, fingers trailing lightly down the side of her face as if memorizing every detail all over again.

Leaning closer, he kisses her in a careful melding of lips that speaks of missed moments and relief at being together.

"Hi, love," he whispers against her mouth.

Rather than pulling away, he hovers closer, his forehead resting against hers. In a moment of quiet connection, his hand cradles her face, his thumb gently caressing her cheek. His eyes, when they meet mine, thank me for taking care of her.

"How'd it go with Monty?" I ask.

"We talked about jobs." He moves away, taking the seat she vacated, his posture relaxed but alert.

"Jobs?"

He steals my vodka and swallows a healthy slug, his mismatched eyes on Frankie as the flavor slides over his tongue.

"Doesn't taste right." He pushes the glass back. "What's missing?"

"You tell me."

"Wild berries, wood smoke, snow..."

"The essence of the hills." She rests her head on my shoulder.

Nodding, I kiss her brow.

I always infused something from the Arctic in my recipes. Those subtle undertones give complexity, making each sip an experience rather than just a drink.

Maybe it's the pure snowmelt water I used, which this commercial brand could never replicate. Theirs leaves an oily residue on the tongue, probably from being rushed through mass filtration processes that prioritize quantity over quality.

"Monty brought up your vodka recipes." He sprawls in the seat, a nerve twitching along his jaw. "Read about them in Frankie's journal. He thinks you should open a distillery, maybe even a bar. Said he would help if you want to pursue it."

Suspicion, protest, and a million ways to say *fuck no* pound through my head.

Until I think back to those long winter nights in Hoss that were filled not just with survival tasks but with dreams.

Dreams fueled by the extensive reading I did.

I always imagined turning my makeshift distillery in the cellar into something legitimate, even when I believed I would never set foot beyond those frozen hills.

Among the tattered pages in our library, I learned about the complexities of establishing a distillery, the bureaucracy of obtaining permits and licenses, and the stringent regulations governing the production and sale of alcohol.

An entire manual on the regulatory hurdles explained the need for health inspections, environmental compliance, and safety protocols. Another book covered the capital investment, market analysis, and the economic forecasts necessary for sustaining a business.

I absorbed every word, procedure, and potential stumbling block. Those books weren't just manuals. They were windows to a world I longed to be part of. I studied them not just out of curiosity, but with fierce dedication, underlining passages, making notes in the margins.

It was theoretical knowledge, gleaned in isolation. Yet I treated it as a blueprint for a future I never dared to hope for.

Now, soaring above concrete cities on a private jet, that knowledge feels less abstract. The possibility of applying it, of navigating the red tape with Monty's backing, transforms my lofty dreams into tangible goals.

It's thrilling.

And overwhelming.

"A distillery would be a lot of red tape." I glance at Frankie, seeking her input. "Why would he help with that?"

"He owns a global consulting firm." She straightens on my lap, taking the conversation seriously. "They specialize in business development, handling everything from market analysis to regulatory compliance. Helping you set up a business is right up his alley."

"He mentioned the challenges." Leo drums his fingers on the table. "Zoning, health regulations, getting a liquor license...It's a lot, but he's willing to invest the capital and handle the legal stuff. He would be a silent partner, letting you run it and focus on the product."

Monty's offer is a chance to use what I know to build something worthwhile. It could give us something that's ours, not just a shelter from threats but a real footing in this world.

But it would mean laying down roots in Sitka.

It would make us more dependent on him.

I stare at my unfinished vodka.

His offer sounds promising, but it leaves a bad aftertaste.

Kodiak

FIVE

I stab a hand through my hair, my thoughts tangled as tightly as my fingers.

"It's just an offer." Frankie turns on my lap and cups my face. "Not a demand. You can say no."

An itch crawls between my shoulder blades, a prickle of suspicion that won't ease.

It's clear Monty's playing at something deeper, something more than mere familial support.

The clothes, the food, a place to live, and now a job. Not just any job. My dream job. He's putting his fingers in everything, pressing a little too hard.

It's a show of kindness, maybe, but it feels like a claim, like he's marking territory. I know, deep down, it's not about me at all.

It's about her.

My jaw tightens.

He wants her back, but there's more to it. I need to find out what before it costs us more than we can afford.

"Why would he help me?" I put my mouth at her ear. "I'm fucking his wife."

She goes rigid, her gaze darting toward the cockpit where Monty steers us through the skies, holding our fate in his hands. "I'm not his, Kody. Not anymore."

Leo snorts, glancing out the window at the clouds racing past. "Monty doesn't believe that."

"You're his brother." She meets my gaze.

"And Denver's brother. Let's not forget they assassinate and rape their brothers."

She sucks in a breath. "I'm sorry. You're right."

"Don't apologize. Always speak your mind with me."

"It's just...he knows we're facing a tough transition, and he's offering a bridge to help us get established. It's not just about the vodka. It's about giving us a means to stand on our own."

"The sooner we stand on our own," I say, "the sooner we move you out of his house. He doesn't want that."

"Okay, fine." She sighs. "It's more than an investment for him. But it could also be an extension of trust, a way for him to make amends for hurting me."

"Or a way to keep us under his control." Leo folds his arms on the table, regarding her. "To bind you further to him."

She nods, her hand finding mine and squeezing tightly.

"Nothing needs to be decided now." I relax in the seat, tucking her against my chest. "We'll talk it over later."

This isn't a decision I can make on my own. It affects all of us.

"What about you?" She tips her head at Leo. "Did you discuss your dream job with him?"

Before he answers, Tanya rolls in a cart loaded with more food than three people can eat.

She places the dishes on the small fold-out table between us. Gleaming silver trays covered with assortments of cheeses I can't name. Slivers of smoked salmon that look like they've been cut with a surgeon's precision. Tiny glasses filled with creamy soup topped with green herbs.

"Another vodka?" She smiles at me.

I decline, and she turns to Leo, who shovels in food like he's still on rations.

"Water for everyone." Frankie unfolds a napkin. "Thank you."

"Would you like to move to the rear?" Tanya gives her a pointed look on my lap. "It would be more comfortable—"

"We're comfortable." I lock an arm around Frankie's waist, holding her in place.

As Tanya pushes away the cart, Frankie plucks a wedge of cheese from the platter and arches a brow at Leo.

He meets her gaze, a half-smile breaking through as he inhales several slices of salmon. "Yeah, Monty brought up my career goals. It's like he memorized your damn journal."

"His mind is sharp and misses nothing." She gulps down her bourbon. "Remember that."

"He offered to help me get my pilot's license."

"You should." I sample the soup, groaning at the burst of flavor. "Then what?"

"Then I have some decisions to make. Do I want to be an aviation mechanic? Run a pilot school? Own a seaplane base in Sitka? Or a private airport somewhere else?"

"All of the above." She winks at him.

"You bet your sweet ass." He winks back and pops the last of the salmon into his mouth. "Watching him fly this bird, seeing everything from the co-pilot's seat, it's a different kind of freedom."

"More freeing than winging it out of the hills?" My lips twist.

"I risked your lives." His expression hardens. "I almost lost you."

"You saved us." She reaches across the table and grips his hand. "No matter what you decide to do, you'll be fantastic at it. You've always been good at fixing things and explaining how everything works. You taught me so much at Hoss."

"But starting from scratch in an unfamiliar world? That's different. It's daunting."

"I get it. Not too long ago, I was a fish out of water in your world, remember?"

"I remember, love." His eyes soften.

"Kody and I will be with you. If Monty's willing to help, take advantage of it. Or don't, and we'll find another way. You can make this happen. I believe in you."

I watch him closely, trying to appraise his feelings about it. He's intrigued, maybe even excited by the prospect, but there's an uneasiness in his posture. A holdover from our trauma with Denver.

Trust doesn't come easy for us, especially where Monty's concerned. Like she said, he's sharp. Perhaps as calculating as Denver. We can't forget that.

Tanya returns, bringing out plates of steak, the pieces so tender they nearly fall apart under the prod of her serving fork, alongside heaps of golden buttery potatoes.

A basket of warm, crusty bread permeates the cabin with a pleasant, familiar scent.

Frankie explains what everything is, showing us how to eat it. Like the chocolate fondue set. Tanya places it on the table across the aisle with fruits and marshmallows for dipping and a separate plate piled high with assorted macarons in pastel colors.

Every dish is a statement, not just of wealth but of a world where food isn't just survival. It's an art, a luxury.

I'm not sure what to make of it all, but it's obvious Monty is trying to impress us, reassure us, or weaken us into complacency.

Frankie puts away more food than I've ever seen her eat. And her moans. The pure bliss on her face. The only time she looks this satisfied is during sex.

I can't help it. Watching her eat makes me hard as a rock.

Of course, she knows. Sitting on my aching cock, she twists around to peek at me, her eyes wide and mouth full.

"Stop wriggling." I swat her hip.

With a laugh, she presses a piece of steak against my lips and wriggles again.

"It's so good," she says around another bite of meat.

It really is. Best fucking meal I've ever had.

I feed her a forkful of potatoes, just to hear her moan again, which she does exquisitely.

Leo's in his own world, caught in the thrall of so much food.

"Look at him." I nibble on her neck. "Diving into this spread like he won a Willy Wonka golden ticket."

"Let's hope he doesn't turn into a blueberry or get mauled by squirrels."

He stares at us with a straight face, his jaw working as he chews. "You know the moral of that story?"

"Greed is bad." Her bright eyes stray to the chocolate fondue.

"Not as bad as denying you whatever you want." I reach across the aisle and snatch a plate of dipped strawberries for her.

"The moral is..." He props an elbow on the table. "Billionaire CEOs can be crazy and diabolically cruel in ways the rest of us can't."

"And they can get away with murder." My gut clenches.

"Exactly. We're all in agreement we don't trust Monty. Even if he plies us with meat and..." He devours a huge hunk of steak. "*Fuck.* This shit melts on my tongue."

Leaning across the table, she dabs his beard with a napkin. "You were saying?"

"His island will give us a place to figure things out, but we can't forget that behind that smile is a..."

"Murderous CEO in a top hat?" I lift a brow.

"I was going to say a man hellbent on reclaiming his wife."

"That, too." I squeeze her thigh.

"I love that you guys know that movie." She picks at the uneaten strawberries on her plate.

"But?" I touch her chin, capturing her gaze.

"It doesn't fit." She shrugs. "I mean, I'm not defending Monty's bad behavior. But he's not a murderer."

We don't know that.

"He's a wildcard." I rest my chin on her shoulder. "He has motives. Don't know if they align with ours."

"We keep our eyes open and stay sharp." Leo eyes Frankie's dessert.

She pushes it toward him. "When we land, we have a lot to sort out."

"First thing," I say, "we get IDs. Can't do much until we're legal."

"Yeah, and we need to learn how to drive." Leo finishes off her strawberries. "Cars, boats, whatever gets us around."

"Phones." The word tastes strange in my mouth. "Gotta communicate in this world, right?"

"And we train." His voice rises, that aggressive fire always near the surface. "Self-defense, survival in this urban jungle. Ain't getting caught off guard."

"All essential." She leans forward, her earlier fear gone. "But therapy is our priority. We heal. Then we learn."

I grunt, not at all interested in sharing my story with a stranger. Frankie won't let this go, and her reasoning is sound. But the primal part of me, the part that's guarded my survival for so long, resists.

The scowl on Leo's face sums up our thoughts on the matter.

"You guys." Impatience laces her tone. "Therapy is non-negotiable. I'll look into the best options for you." She sips her water. "I loved my therapist in Sitka."

"Hold up." Leo straightens. "You had a therapist?"

"Yep. When my mom died, I struggled. A lot. The sessions really helped. So I kept going after I was healed. Until..."

Until she was abducted.

The plane rocks gently, the motion sending a shudder through her.

"Here." Leo stands. "Let's buckle you in."

"That's okay." She curls into me. "I'm good here. Kody can do my seat belt when we start the descent."

"I should head back to the cockpit." He studies her features. "Unless you want me to stay."

"Go." She surveys the table. "Should we send some of this food to Monty?"

"He said he'll eat later." He catches her hand and kisses her knuckles. "If you need me..."

"I know where to find you."

As he heads to the front, Tanya returns to collect the dishes, asking if we need anything else.

"All set here." Frankie pulls her feet up on my lap, settling in.

"We'll touch down in about two hours. Press the button if you need me."

As she strolls away, I recline the seat back, taking Frankie with me.

Our earlier conversations play in my head, everything we need to do, the plan forming. A checklist of survival in this new wilderness.

Sitka.

A fresh start on Monty's island.

My chest clenches at the thought.

She sighs, sensing my tension. "You're thinking about Monty."

"So are you."

"I know it's not ideal. But he's offering us a place, security, things we desperately need right now."

"Yeah. His house, his rules. That's the game he's playing."

"So we set some ground rules of our own, carve out some space for independence. Like you did with the sleeping arrangements." She scratches her fingers through the scruff on my jaw. "We'll make it clear we're there on our terms."

"If he steps out of line or tries to control us, we walk. We're survivors. We'll find a way, like we always do."

"We're not captives anymore. No one will trap us, imprison us, or chain us down. Never again."

Christ, I love her feisty conviction. It steadies me, reinforcing the resolve that's been the backbone of my existence. Her unbreakable will draws me in, binds me to her more than any chains ever could. The way she digs in and doesn't give up ignites a fierce pride.

And an even fiercer desire.

My hand follows the curve of her hip, her upper thighs, fingers sliding between her legs, sinking into her sexy heat. The urge to pull her onto my cock, smell her everywhere, and fuck her brains out thrums powerfully within me.

I lean closer, my breath chasing hers. “I want to be inside you.”

The plane cuts through the sky, the murmur of the engines a backdrop for her husky response. “We shouldn’t.”

She’s right. This isn’t the time or the place.

Yet her breathing doesn’t slow. Her eye contact doesn’t waver.

She smirks. “But we should totally make out.”

Her words are barely out before my lips crash against hers, a kiss laden with all the hunger, reverence, and raw adoration I feel for Frankie Novak.

That night, I step off the yacht in Sitka and tread across the familiar dock. In the rain. In the dark. In the grip of overwhelming memories.

The stone mansion I shared with Monty looms ahead like a beautiful ghost from my past. Every towering tree and winding path on the island bring back flashes of my life.

Before everything changed.

Kody senses the direction of my thoughts and tenses, turning into an impenetrable shield at my side, as if he can fend off the past with sheer will.

"Need a minute?" The look of concern in his eyes cuts through the rain.

I nod because, dammit, the memories are vivid, too vivid, as I'm thrown back to the night I was bound by rope, gagged, and abducted from my bedroom.

Denver carried me to this dock, tripped, lost his grip, and I plunged into the icy water, the darkness enveloping me.

That chill runs through me now, a shiver that's part dread, part defiance. I thought I knew fear then, but the horrors that awaited were beyond my wildest nightmares.

"The night Denver took me, he dropped me right there." I point to the churning black water beside the dock. "My arms and legs were tied. I couldn't swim. I thought I was going to drown."

"Fuck this." Leo paces behind me, a caged animal not suited for the confines of the narrow dock. "We don't have to stay here. It isn't worth it."

His instinct to fight often overrides his logical mind. I don't fault him for it. His instinct saved my life more than once.

"Frankie." Monty approaches with caution, trying to erase the gap with words that no longer reach me. "If you need—"

"My needs aren't your concern anymore." I straighten, meeting his icy blue stare. "You invited us here, and for that, I'm grateful. But I'm doing this at my pace, on my terms."

His reaction is subtle, a faint tightening of his eyes, a nod of acceptance that doesn't quite mask the hurt. He steps back, giving me space, respecting the boundary I've drawn.

"We're here with you." Kody's hand finds mine, his fingers strong and reassuring. "For whatever you need."

Leo stops pacing and looks back at the mansion, then at me. "Whatever you decide."

With a deep breath, I push forward, the rain a curtain parting as we walk through it. I lead the way, toward whatever remains of the past, ready to fight for a future where fear no longer holds dominion over us.

We advance toward the house, the path slick under the downpour. Kody moves with a predator's agility, scanning the thick brush and shadowed corners of the estate.

He positions himself slightly ahead, his body angled to shield me, every muscle coiled, ready to spring into action at the first hint of danger.

On my other side, Leo matches his vigilance, his eyes darting to the treetops, the hidden alcoves, and back along the path we just traversed.

Then he freezes, his hand moving to his back, a subconscious check for a rifle he no longer carries.

"What is it?" I follow his line of sight, my pulse redoubling.

"We're not alone." The ferocity in his gaze burns with

bicolored flames as he presses into me, sandwiching me against Kody.

"There's no need for alarm." Monty breezes past us, gesturing vaguely into the shadows. "It's my security team."

"What security team?" I run a hand down Leo's stiff spine, trying to relax him.

"After the video..." Monty turns back to face us, raindrops clinging to his black lashes. "Seeing Denver sitting in our house, I took no chances and hired the team before we left the lawyer's office." His gaze locks with mine. "To ensure your safety."

"You didn't think to mention this before?" Leo squints into the rain, the droplets drumming a relentless beat against the path, echoing my racing heart.

"I wanted to tell you when we arrived, Frankie." His eyes darken with regret and longing, a silent apology hanging between us. He starts to move forward, an impulse stopped by his better judgment. "One less thing for you to worry about."

His restraint hits hard, reminding me of everything we've lost, of every wound not yet healed.

"Thank you." I squeeze Kody's hand.

He squeezes back. "Let's keep moving then. The sooner we're inside, the better."

Monty takes the lead, his back straight despite the tension in his shoulders.

His concern is evident, his actions respectful, yet the distance between us feels awful. Even if I'm the one enforcing that distance.

As we approach the grand doors, the sense of foreboding grows, but so does my resolve.

Leo glances over his shoulder one last time before we maneuver inside, his profile chiseled with sharp lines. His hand shifts to rest on my lower back, guiding me in. Kody's grip on my fingers never wavers.

Warmth greets us at the threshold, our footsteps loud in the vast foyer, making the space feel empty despite its opulence.

We shed our wet coats, hanging them in the entryway.

"I'll introduce you to the security team later." Monty strides ahead toward the kitchen. "For tonight, make yourselves at home. There's plenty of food. Frankie and I can show you around in the morning."

"I'll start now." Leo takes off, charging through the main sitting room, his untamed physique casting a beastly shadow against the elaborate decor.

His braided hair, wild and drenched, clings to his rugged face as he opens every door he passes—closets, cabinets, even peering behind curtains and framed art.

Veins stand out on Monty's neck, his jaw clenched. He's not thrilled with Leo's invasion of privacy, but when our eyes connect, he says, "Let him explore."

Oh, Leo's not exploring. He's hunting for cameras, secret spy holes, implements of torture, anything to confirm his suspicions about Monty's true intentions.

We trail behind him, drifting from room to room, water dripping from our clothes and forming a path on the polished floors.

The estate looks exactly how I left it, spotlessly maintained as if a full staff lives here. But Monty is too private for that. The chef, housekeeper, primary chauffeur, and landscaper don't reside on his island.

He always lived alone.

Until me.

In the dim glow of the hallway, he stands like one of his many sculptures, carved from mystery, old money, and power, his presence as commanding as a tsar in his imperial palace.

"When was the last time you were home?" I watch Kody wander the room, his interest piqued by the Soviet-era statues.

"Months."

Because he was looking for me.

After he cheated on me.

The agony of his betrayal surges anew, tangled with a grudging gratitude for his search.

It's hard to look at him. The purplish-black marks left by Leo's violent beating stand out against his pale skin.

Seeing him like this stirs unwanted things inside me. I hate that he's in pain, even after he caused me so much. It's fucked up, this tenderness for a man who hurt me.

As I discreetly examine his swollen cheek, the anger I harbor wars with the instinct to reach out and comfort him.

I wish I could trust his reasons for helping me when I've clearly moved on.

But I can't trust him.

He catches me staring, his eyes shadowed with guilt and something else. I quickly avert my gaze, not wanting him to see the conflict in my expression.

I don't want him to think I've forgiven him, because I haven't. But I can't deny the empathy and old feelings that well up at the sight of him bruised and underweight.

"You should get those looked at." I keep my distance, arms crossed defensively over my chest.

"You're looking at them. That's all I need."

"Stop."

"Stop what?"

"You know what."

We stand there in awkward silence, the air oppressive. It's confusing, frustrating, the lines between love and hate blurring beyond recognition.

Leo's heavy boots thud against the ornate rugs, his suspicious nature propelling him into the main room with high painted ceilings and intricate moldings. Kody follows closely, pulling me along while observing every luxurious detail with a feral wariness.

They both pause when they recognize the couch.

The one I handpicked when Monty and I married.

The one Denver occupied when he made the video.

"No one will break in here again." Monty's eyes, like chips of glacial ice, assess us with unsettling intensity. His carved, clean-shaven jawline gives him a stern, intimidating allure that only heightens the air of authority that clings to him. "No one will step onto this island without me knowing about it."

I believe him. But that doesn't protect me if the danger is

already here.

He strolls toward the couch, circling it, his body a study in controlled strength. Lean muscles flex beneath a tailored suit that hints at the boardroom and clandestine deals made in quieter, darker corners.

Rich, inky black hair rakes back stylishly from a forehead that's too smooth for a forty-nine-year-old man.

Wait.

He had a birthday since I saw him last. We both did.

"You turned fifty." I follow Leo and Kody around the room, watching them snoop through every nook and cranny. "How did you celebrate?"

"I was on my way out of Whittier after..." He straightens the cuffs of his sleeves with jerky movements as if trying to distract himself from a memory. "It was a long weekend of bad news. I wasn't in the mood to celebrate."

"Because you learned that Denver lived."

"Yes." His shoulders hunch, a subtle inward collapse of a man burdened by his own decisions. "That's when I came to the horrifying realization he'd taken you."

I'm sorry.

The apology sticks in my throat. I won't say it because I'm not to blame. None of this is my fault.

"Did you celebrate your thirtieth birthday?" He cocks his head. "It wasn't mentioned in your journal. You were with him." His gaze settles on Kody, who releases a low growl.

"I was?"

"I tracked thc timeline in your notes. You turned thirty the day after you died in the lake." Monty's gaze drills into me with an edge of accusation undercut by a cloud of regret.

I had sex with Kody the day after I drowned. It was our first time together, Kody's first time ever, and Monty knows it. He read every detail.

In the tense silence, his stare is heavy and aggressive. His hands clench and unclench at his sides as if wrestling with the urge to reach out or pull back.

Every aspect of him oozes refinement and manners, but I'm well-acquainted with the vicious possessiveness simmering beneath the surface. It's what drew me in and kept me at arm's length. A constant paradox wrapped in primal, sexual energy.

As he stands there, looking all stoic and arrogant, I don't miss the subtle quiver in his jaw, a twitch he can't control. A silent scream against the pain of losing me and the role he played in our unraveling.

My chest tightens, a knot of confusion and hurt that I struggle to ignore.

How do I reconcile the man who sought me across the Arctic with the one who kept family secrets and wandered from our vows?

"Back off, asshole." Leo, missing nothing, steps between us.

All I see is his broad back, effectively severing my eye contact with Monty. I exhale a held breath.

"Back off?" Monty asks. "We're having a conversation."

"You know exactly what you're doing." Leo crosses his arms, his posture imposing.

"You missed her birthday."

"So did you."

I can't breathe through the fog of testosterone as they puff their chests and mark their dominance with their potent scents.

Too many alphas in the room.

"That's enough." I slip around Leo before he escalates this to another fistfight. "There were no birthdays in Hoss, Monty. No holidays, no celebrations, no joy." I brace my hands on my hips. "But that's in the past. We're moving forward."

I keep my posture rigid, my shoulders firm, but my eyes flit through the room like a captured bird.

The air presses against me, thick with the aroma of rain and old wood, stained with memories, good and bad.

Monty doesn't blink, his lips pressed into a thin line, the corners downturned in a frown that holds a world of things unsaid.

"Do you still employ a chef and housekeeper?" I ask, changing the subject. "Oliver and Aurora?"

"Yes." He inclines his head. "And Kai and Greyson."

The chauffeur and landscaper.

"Until we get on our feet," I say, "are there any jobs around here we can do?"

"No." His fingers tap a silent, impatient rhythm against his thigh, a display of controlled annoyance. "No wife of mine will do domestic work."

"I'm not your—"

"The answer is no, and that's final."

"Well, then I guess I'll be returning to the hospital sooner than—"

Three snarling objections slam into me.

"You're not going anywhere alone," Kody growls. "Not for work or otherwise. Not until your life is no longer threatened."

"Let's be clear." I thrust my chin. "No one tells me what to do."

Kody releases another growl that has Monty smirking.

"But..." I sigh. "I agree with you on this, which is why I asked about jobs around here."

"You'll have plenty to keep you busy." Monty looks me up and down. Then he gives Kody and Leo a cursory perusal. "You need to rebuild your strength, eat a healthy diet, exercise, get good sleep. We all do."

"He has a home gym," I say to Kody and Leo, heating at the thought of their sculpted bodies straining beneath weights. "I can show you how to—"

"I'll show them." Monty turns to them. "When you're ready, we can start training together."

"Where?" Leo heads toward the hallway that leads to the garage, den, and gym.

"That way." Monty directs him with a flick of his finger.

The air changes as we enter the exercise room, charged with something different. Curiosity. Fascination. Awe.

Leo and Kody sweep their gazes over the sleek, modern equipment, whose purposes are a mystery to them.

Monty steps in, turning on his charming host demeanor. "This is the treadmill." He gestures at the machine. "It simulates walking or running. You can adjust the speed here." He powers on the digital panel.

"Why would anyone run on this," Leo asks, "when there

are running trails on the island?"

Monty chuckles, his too-familiar eyes imprisoning me.

"Exactly." I cross my arms and lean against the wall of mirrors. "I've never used that thing."

Moving on to the rack of weights, Monty lifts a dumbbell and hands it to Kody. "This is the best way to build strength and endurance."

Kody thrusts it over his head like it weighs nothing. "Feels lighter than the logs we lifted back home."

"There are different sizes for different exercises." Monty offers him a heavier one.

Eyes widening, Kody grunts as he lifts it. "Fuck." He sets it back on the rack and grabs another. And another.

Monty tests his strength, too, while showing him some curling techniques.

"Great. Maybe I should leave you alone to bond with your new best friends." I can't help but smile at their boyish competitiveness. "They seem pretty heavy."

Leo circles the punching bag, grinning and bouncing on his toes.

"This is where it's at." He throws a few experimental punches, the bag swinging wildly.

Monty nods, watching him. "Use any of this whenever you like. It's here to help you guys get back in shape."

Kody puts the weights away and steps onto the large mat where I used to spend hours doing Pilates and yoga.

He exchanges a look with Leo, and I know they're thinking about self-defense training.

"We'll start this week." Leo strides toward me, his steps lighter, clearly impressed with the gym. "That includes you, love."

"I prefer the running trails in the fresh air." I follow him into the hall and up the stairs to the second floor.

"And the rain?"

"Maybe not the rain."

Upstairs, he gives all the guest bedrooms the same thorough search. Kody joins him, speeding things along.

"What are they looking for?" Monty lingers in the hall, his hands resting casually in his pockets.

"If you were in their positions..." I lean against the doorframe. "What would you look for?"

His eyebrows climb together, his jaw working. "Sedatives, rope, latex gloves, weapons, incriminating photos, recording devices, basically anything that might point to me as a stalker."

"If you have any of those things in your possession, I know you're too smart to leave them where they can be discovered. But they don't know you. They need to do this so they can sleep tonight."

"Fair enough."

Leo ambles out of the final guest bedroom and pushes open another door, revealing Monty's dimly lit study.

Pausing on the threshold, he sniffs the air like a tracker, his tall, rugged frame contrasting sharply with the delicate antiques and gleaming surfaces of Monty's world.

It feels unnerving, watching the wild men I've come to love prowling the halls of my previous life. A life so meticulously curated by Monty.

"Go ahead." Monty follows at a safe distance, his hands clasped behind his back. But his voice lacks warmth. "My home is open to you."

Leo stops before a seascape painting by Ivan Aivazovsky, his head tilted. He has no idea he's admiring a piece of art worth millions. Nor does he care.

I catch the reflection of our group in the gilded mirror beside Monty's desk—so out of place yet so irrevocably entwined. My past and present are colliding in the heart of this grand estate, under the watchful eyes of a man I once vowed to love forever.

As evening shadows creep through the windows, I wonder how we can weave these fragmented parts into a new whole.

Will my history with Monty prevent him from building a relationship with Kody and Leo? Does he intend to hurt me worse than he already has?

His eyes flicker away before meeting mine again, a dance of avoidance, necessity, and something else.

"It's like a museum here." Kody bends to peer closer at a glass cabinet filled with Fabergé eggs. "How did you ever live in a place like this?"

"It was another life." I meet Monty's cool gaze. "One that no longer appeals to the woman I am now."

I'm not trying to be cruel. It's the hard truth, and Monty needs to understand.

We're finished.

Rather than backing down, he stares right back, his lips quirking at the corners.

Goddammit, I know that wry, challenging smirk. It's the same one he wore when I repeatedly turned down his advances during his year-long pursuit to date me.

He's still the master of the game.

A man who refuses to be beaten, even by his own mistakes.

Monty's bedroom is the last stop on Leo's security patrol. He and Kody wait at the doorway, refusing to enter before me, as if it's a restricted crime scene.

It's just a room.

No longer *my* room.

"You guys go ahead." I wave them on.

They don't move, don't speak. I might've heard a growl.

Their battle-ready postures suggest they're prepared for any reaction I might have. As if I'll be triggered into violence.

I don't have triggers, do I?

Jesus, I hope not.

I can't even look at the man standing beside me. I feel Monty everywhere, in my space, under my skin, breathing, watching, analyzing.

My hesitation only makes this a bigger deal than it is.

"Fine." Heart pounding, I push past them and step inside.

The large bed that Monty and I once shared sits in the center, immaculately made, as if it hasn't been touched since that night.

The table on his side holds a clock, a bottle of sleeping pills, and chargers for his devices. The table on my side has the one thing I left on it.

The glass of bourbon I never drank, the liquid partially evaporated, leaving behind decomposed cherries.

What the fuck?

"Where have you been sleeping?" Unnerved, I keep my back to him.

"When I'm home, I sleep in our bed. But I already told you. I haven't been home in months."

He also said there were no other women after Aubrey.

Do I believe him?

A man with his insatiable sex drive and stamina wouldn't abstain. Especially not with the way women throw themselves at him.

Do I care?

Nine months ago, I did.

I turn to the window with the view of the dock, the scene of that terrifying night reflecting back at me. The burn of rope against my skin. The scent of latex gloves. The rumble of Denver's raspy voice.

Don't struggle. This will only hurt a little.

"I was standing here, waiting for you to come home." The memory chokes me, tightening like Denver's restraints. "I thought when I heard movement behind me..." I spin, startled to find Monty right there, too close. I step back. "I thought it was you."

"It should've been me." His face tightens, remorse rolling off him in waves. "I made an unforgivable decision that night, one I'll regret for the rest of my life. I'm sorry."

Leo barrels toward us, his bearing rigid. I shake my head, and he huffs, his anger directed at Monty. But he stays back.

I glance at the fire detector above the bed. "Denver removed a camera from there."

Monty follows my gaze. "I've had the entire estate swept for bugs and recording devices. It's clean." He looks at Leo. "Go ahead. Check this room, too."

Leo bares his teeth at him and returns his attention to me, waiting to jump in if I need him.

frankie

"Everything is just as you left it." Monty watches me wander through the room, his presence evoking nostalgia for the whispered dreams, tender cuddles, and wild sex we shared here.

Until I'm hit with the memory of our last fight. As I circle the bed, I stare at the spot on the floor where he crushed the pregnancy test beneath his cruel shoe, the echo of the crunch splintering in my ears.

As if reading my thoughts, he stiffens, struggling between his desire to draw closer and the knowledge that he lost the right to reach out.

Swallowing hard, I make my way to the walk-in closet and push open the door.

Inside, everything is disturbingly familiar. My clothes hang exactly how I left them, untouched and organized by seasons. My running shoes lie on the floor, one flopped on its side, where I kicked them off nine months ago.

"I don't understand." I trace the rows of hangers holding my garments, my fingers coming away with dust.

But Monty's clothes hang freshly cleaned.

Aurora, the housekeeper, must have been given orders not to touch my things.

Charging out of the closet, I head to the en suite bathroom.

Seeing my personal items still lined up on the counter is even more unsettling. My favorite perfume sits beside my cleansers. My hair products and body wash still hog the single shelf in the shower.

In the drawers, I find my collection of soaps, lipsticks, and razors organized by my own hands. Even my hairbrush, with a few strands of red hair tangled in it, lies next to the sink.

Why keep these reminders of me as if waiting for my return? It's both touching and troubling, smearing the lines of his feelings and intentions.

Returning to the bedroom, I make a beeline to the dresser and pull open the drawers one by one. Each is filled with my folded clothes. Leggings, bras, underwear, camisoles—everything is here, arranged with my go-to pieces on top.

These things weren't put back in anticipation of my return today.

They've been here the whole fucking time.

Everything is just as you left it.

Except...there, on the surface of the dresser, I spot the items I wondered about the most.

My phone, plugged in and fully charged, sits beside my wedding rings on a crystal tray.

Like a goddamn shrine.

"Why?" Turning sharply, I find Monty's watchful gaze, my voice tight with anger. "Why would you keep all this? It's like walking into a time capsule of the worst day of my life!"

He steps forward, his timbre low, filled with an emotion I can't decipher. "I thought—"

"You thought what? That I'd slip back into our marriage like nothing happened?"

Kody's hand appears on my lower back, grounding me, while Leo's presence looms close.

Monty looks between them, his composure airtight. "Calm down."

"Calm down?" I lean forward and level a searing glare at him. "It's fucking creepy, Monty. Like I was just here yesterday. Like I never left. The glass of bourbon? The hairbrush? My phone on the fucking charger? Explain it to me."

He lowers to the edge of the bed and stares at the floor between his feet.

"I couldn't let you go." He lifts his head, his eyes pained. "I couldn't remove your things and accept you were gone."

"Didn't stop you from fucking someone else."

A dark, thunderous fury breaks over his expression. "Judge not, lest ye be judged for the same."

His response stuns me into silence, but anger quickly wells up again.

He strayed first. He rejected his child. He gave up on us.

He broke my fucking heart.

If he felt a fraction of my pain, he would understand my reaction.

Before I can say something I'll regret, Kody's firm grip on

my chin forces my eyes to him.

"Woman." He puts his face right into mine. "Time to call it a night."

Leo's tense posture by the door signals his readiness to haul me out of the room.

I pull away from Kody and storm to the bedside table, snatching the stale bourbon.

"This isn't reassuring, Monty." I shove the glass into his hand and walk to the door. "You kept my life on pause here, but I wasn't paused. I was living a nightmare."

"I know," he murmurs. "I was living one, too."

His words turn my stomach to ice. My feet stop moving. My breath strangles, and oh, hell, here come the tears, the hurt.

And the rage.

I whirl, my voice rising with the surge of my pulse. "It was hard for you, was it? Was it hard to cast off our baby? Was it hard to go to work and leave me here after you broke my heart?" I thrust a hand out behind me, warding off the protective shadows at my back. "You should've been here. You should've come home that night. You should've told me your real fucking name!"

He stares at me, his eyes stark and glassy. Mute.

I won't cry. He's taken enough from me. I won't give him the satisfaction of seeing me break. Again.

"You want me to believe you're not the unhinged admirer in Denver's riddle? That you're not *the silent ache, the shadow that lingers, the present from my past, the knife in my heart?"* I shiver and motion around the chilling, carefully preserved room. "This doesn't help build your case."

His jaw sets, the muscle ticking in irritation.

The only response he gives me.

I turn on my heel and walk out, just as he did the day everything changed.

But I'm not alone. With the warmth of Kody's hand on my back and Leo's vigilant gaze flanking me, I feel the strength that comes not just from surviving but from being truly seen and understood.

We descend the stairs and move through the house.

No one speaks.

Silence between us once meant a storm of survival thoughts—how to stay warm, what to eat, whether we'd see another sunrise. But those fears are gone, and in this new quiet, I don't know what they're thinking.

Are they concerned about my mental state? Disappointed by my crazy behavior? Troubled about the tension between Monty and me?

I let my memories and emotions get to me.

I overreacted.

That's all. They have nothing to worry about.

We slip outside through the back door, the rain tapping against the covered walkway that connects the main house to the guest house.

Paths branch off through the dense woods, leading to the infinity pool, helicopter pad, gear shed, boathouse, and docks. It's beautiful here, secluded, the darkness thick and impervious beneath the tree cover.

I can't shake the chill that settles over me, nor the sense that every corner we turn might reveal something that tries to break us apart.

Leo and Kody flank me, forming an armor of muscle against the oppressive night.

Halfway there, the snap of a twig shatters the silence.

We freeze. Our eyes dart to the shadows, hearts pounding in unison.

Something's out there.

The press of menacing eyes rakes against my skin and penetrates my bones.

I stop breathing, frantically searching the inky blackness. The steady patter of rain smothers all sound. Whatever it is, I won't hear it coming.

Then a shape takes form. A tall, dark figure among the silhouettes of the trees.

"Do you see that?" I whisper, trembling.

"See what?" Leo scans the darkness.

"There, in the trees." I point a shaky finger at the shadowy figure, trying to adjust my vision to the murky gloom.

It's there, then it's not, fading in and out like an apparition.

Fear tightens its grip on my throat, squeezing the breath from my lungs.

Kody steps into the rain, his posture predatory and intent. He charges in the direction I pointed, moving with the lethality of a predator.

I swallow my gasps, every muscle tense as he disappears into the shadows.

The rain intensifies, drumming against the leaves and the roof of the walkway. Leo and I stand together, waiting, the minutes threading into eternity.

I strain my ears, listening, my pulse thudding in my stomach.

"Kody?" Leo calls, his voice a low rumble.

No answer. Terror plucks at my nerves, whispering unbearable possibilities.

At last, Kody emerges from the shadows, his black eyes unreadable.

"Nothing." He shakes his head, droplets of rain flying from his hair. "There's nothing out there."

"I saw something." My shoulders creep up, and I force them down. "I know I did."

"Probably a security guard." Leo places a kiss on my brow. "You're safe."

It's been a long day. We only left the hospital this morning. Then there were the revelations at the lawyer's office, the flight from Anchorage, the stressful interactions with Monty...

No wonder I'm seeing things. I'm not thinking straight.

When we reach the entrance of our temporary housing, I realize too late that I should've grabbed my phone and a change of clothes.

I enter my code in the keypad, surprised it still works.

Inside, I give them the code and flick on the lights.

"Kitchen and sitting room." I gesture, indicating the open floor plan. "There are two bedrooms upstairs. I'm going to take a shower."

Maybe it will relieve the ache in my chest. I'm wound so tightly I can't breathe.

As I veer toward the stairs, Leo moves quickly, transforming from a calm breeze to a raging gale in three powerful strides.

His hands capture my hips and sweep me off my feet. Turning, he sets me on the nearby kitchen table and dips his head to clamp his teeth on my neck. He pins me there, his eyes closing as he inhales deeply.

I tangle my fingers in his braided Viking knots and pull him closer. Over his shoulder, I share a look with Kody, who regards me with questions in his liquid black eyes.

"I'm okay." I kiss Leo's temple, breathing in his smoky cedar and mechanic scent. "I'm just...emotional."

Leo inches back to see my face. "You're human."

"I'm a mess."

"Messy like a river crashing through the mountains. Like a bonfire, flickering wildly, sparking into the night. Like the rain—"

"Stop." My eyes burn and start to leak as I melt in his arms. "You're making me cry."

"Every tear is a sign of your infinite worth." He runs his thumb across my wet cheek. "In you, my universe lies."

"And you, my poetic savage, are a dark vine reaching."

"Better to wrap around the soul that mirrors mine."

"Cute." Kody grunts.

"To think..." I sigh, smiling. "You had me at *human*."

"I'd rather have you in the shower."

"What are you waiting for?"

"Got my eyes fixed on eternity with you. There's no rush."

When I start to argue, he shoves three fingers into my mouth and pumps them, gently at first. Then his touch becomes rougher until I'm sucking, gagging, and gasping for more.

He replaces his hand with his lips and, with forever on his breath, he slowly, passionately seduces me with his mouth.

Stroking that sinful tongue against mine, he licks and savors with a reverence that owns me. His deep, inveigling kiss fills me with an ache so raw I forget where I am and why I needed this so badly.

Outside, the rain ceases to fall, leaving a serene hush when he finally pulls away.

Kody is there, arms reaching, as Leo plucks me from the table and hands me over.

Like the whole thing was orchestrated.

"Nice and docile." Leo brushes a wayward curl from my face and meets Kody's eyes. "I'll be right behind you."

As Kody carries me up the stairs, I hug his corded neck and watch Leo stalk through the sitting room, checking windows and doors and searching for cameras. As if he didn't just kiss me into a boneless puddle.

Nice and docile.

He catches my gaze and winks.

Motherfucker.

All those sensual words and toe-curling kisses were just a ploy to get me out of my head?

I bite down on my smile.

Well played, Leonid Strakh.

frankie

EIGHT

As it turns out, I didn't need to grab clothes from Monty's room.

Standing in the largest of the two guest bedrooms, Kody and I stare at the walk-in closet in disbelief. Clothes for every season fill the huge space, with two sections for the guys and one dedicated to me.

"How?" He rummages through the built-in drawers, pulling out men's shirts, pajamas, and underwear. "We didn't agree to stay here until after we left the hospital this morning."

"One text to his staff, and they drop everything to do what he asks." I open more drawers, finding women's clothes, things I would pick out for myself, all in my sizes, styles, and favorite colors.

Everything we could need.

The attention to detail disarms me.

Overwhelms me.

Shakes me to my core.

During those final months at Hoss, we wore the same stitched-together clothes for weeks. When it came to survival, fashion and style were never a consideration.

It's just nice to have something clean and appropriately sized.

But this…

This is too much.

The clothing, the food, the security team, the private island with all its luxuries—everything about Monty clashes with the simplicity and brutality of our recent lives. I can't help but feel torn between these worlds.

Not only did Monty invite us into his home, his sanctuary, but he's going above and beyond to make us comfortable. It's out of character.

He's not a man who rescues and adopts wild animals. He sets traps to keep them out.

My temperature rises, forming a bead of sweat on my forehead.

The room feels suddenly too hot, suffocating, as if all the windows have been sealed shut on a summer day.

"Is it just me, or did it get really warm in here?" I fan myself with a hand.

Kody pulls at the collar of his shirt before peeling it off entirely in a clear surrender to the swelter, leaving him in the sexiest pair of low-slung jeans. "Not just you."

A wave of stifling heat envelops us, the air from the vents blowing as hot as a coal stove.

I nod toward the French doors leading to the balcony. "Open those and maybe the windows. I'll check the thermostat."

As I head into the hall, he flings open the French doors, welcoming the cooler outside breeze.

The climate control panel shows the upstairs temperature on the highest setting. An easy fix. I make the adjustment and return to the bedroom.

"What's this?" He holds up a shiny new phone and gestures to another on the desk.

"Those must be for you and Leo." A shallow breath escapes me, too quick, too sharp. "I'll teach you how to use it tomorrow."

He lowers to the bed, instantly engrossed with the device.

Within minutes, he figures out how to power it on and navigate through the set-up guide.

Guess he doesn't need my help.

"Kody?" I kick off my boots.

"Mm?" He doesn't look up.

I've lost him.

The fact that he's taking to technology this quickly is a good thing. Hard to maneuver through the modern world without it. I just hope it doesn't change him.

I'm rather fond of his feral nature.

A trickle of sweat runs between my breasts.

Time for that shower.

In the attached bathroom, I find all the same items I left behind in Monty's bathroom. Shampoo, conditioner, perfume, skincare—all my favorite brands are here, including razors and hygiene products for the guys.

It's been so long since I've moisturized. My skin will probably soak up a full bottle of lotion.

Staring at my reflection in the mirror, I touch my gaunt face. I look haggard, pale, weathered by harsh conditions and stress. *Older.* My cheekbones protrude sharply, making the hollows beneath them more pronounced.

Monty should've taken one look at me in the hospital and moved on. He can have any woman he wants.

When Leo and Kody start venturing out in public, they'll turn heads and attract female attention just like Monty. It will only worsen after they take advantage of the gym and return to their beefed-up, chiseled physiques.

Once the world sees how potent and irresistibly sexy they are, they'll be propositioned, chased, objectified, and idolized. How will they handle that?

Adultery runs in the family.

My face burns, and my ears pressurize.

Oh, the irrational fears of a scorned woman.

I have a long way to go to rebuild my confidence, but I will, despite the hard truth staring back at me.

I'm not the sweet, healthy, fresh-faced girl I was nine

months ago. That girl died in the hills, and a battle-hardened, half-starved, bloodthirsty woman rose in her place.

A woman with a lot of baggage.

Which makes Monty's obsession with me suspicious and worrisome.

He kept all my things in his bedroom like some love-sick widower, only to set up a room for me to share with my lovers.

I can't make sense of it.

The man I married is an over-the-top, jealous, possessive male who always gets what he wants.

Evidently, he wanted me on that plane badly enough to agree to our sleeping arrangements.

I'm no longer his to share, but that's precisely what he's doing.

He's sharing me with his brother and his nephew.

It's fucked-up.

Deep down, I hope his intentions are genuine. If his generosity is steeped in a need for atonement, or even if it's a harmless obsession with the woman he lost, I can deal with that. Or rather, a therapist can help *him* deal with it.

But if there's something else driving him, something malicious and evil...

No. I can't accept that. The man has his faults, but he's not Denver.

Among the bathroom supplies, I don't find any condoms, lubes, or performance enhancers. Thank God. That would cross the line of acceptance and make it really fucking weird.

In the drawer, I find the ointment that Kody needs for the burns on his leg.

Overwhelmed once again by Monty's thoughtfulness, I reach for the perfume and spray it on my wrist.

The scent explodes in my memories before it reaches my nose—a balance of sweetness and tartness, fruity and floral, with a bloom of cherry as the top note.

Cherry perfume might be the sexiest fragrance in existence, and Monty loved to inhale it from my skin.

As I return the bottle to the counter, a click snaps my head to the doorway.

Standing just outside the bathroom, Kody holds his phone low, the camera lens angled at me, with his coal-black eyes focused on the screen.

"Did you just take a picture of me?"

"More than one, woman. You're my favorite feature on this thing." He turns the phone, revealing a photo of me bent over the bathroom sink. It's a picture of my ass.

"Delete that."

"Never." He pockets the device and prowls toward me.

Those jeans cling to his hips, accentuating the leanness of a man who survived for months on rations. His bare chest ripples with defined muscles honed by the physical demands he endured. Every sharp line and sinewy curve represent his raw, wild resilience.

What a gorgeous, compelling creature. With mussy, finger-raked hair and a dark shadow of stubble covering his jaw, he strikes an imposing silhouette.

His boots, heavy and untied, add a ruggedness to his gait. And the way his body moves, fluid yet powerful, hints at the fiercely controlled violence that snarls inside him, waiting to be unleashed.

The bathroom is too small for him, especially with all that lethal energy he's packing.

A thrum ignites across my skin as he crowds me against the counter. Gripping my hips, he spins me to face the mirror. His hand goes to my hair, gathering it over my shoulder as he buries his nose in my neck.

The rock-hard inferno of his towering frame licks along my back. He leans closer, letting me feel the heavy, fully erect beast between his legs.

I flatten my hands on the counter, bracing for whatever he has planned.

He sucks on my neck, deliberately leaving hickeys before brushing that hot mouth along my shoulder and down my arm. When he reaches my elbow, he lifts my wrist and brings it to his nose, scenting the mist of perfume.

"You smelled like this when you came to Hoss." He lowers

my arm and releases a slow breath. "You still have feelings for him."

"Not on purpose." I meet his intimidating gaze in the mirror. "Please, don't look at me like that. They're not good feelings, okay?"

Those eyes, broody and black as night, hold mine with a penetrating intensity that borders on intrusive. I can't hide from this man. Not that I want to, but dammit, it's exhausting to be so exposed and open to scrutiny.

"You're entitled to have feelings." He slides his hands around my waist. "Three days ago, you were starving in the Arctic, and Monty was a cheating husband with a fake name who rejected your baby. Now you're in his house, and his side of the story makes everything more complicated."

"I don't want to be this angry. But I'm afraid to *not* be angry because that means I feel other things for him, and that's a betrayal to you." I swallow. "I won't betray you, Kody."

"I know. I can feel you." His fingers dip beneath my waistband and free the button. "I see you, all of you, and I'm still here, not to judge but to protect and love. I find deep beauty in the parts of you that others can't see." He pushes his fingers inside my undies, cupping me. "I'm addicted to your strength."

"I long for a day when I don't have to be strong. Strength has drained me. I don't want to be praised for enduring. I want tenderness and peace. I crave a softer path, a gentler life, that asks nothing of my toughness."

"You think that's what you want, but you won't settle for it. You'll go to sleep tonight and wake rested tomorrow, ready to fight again. Not because you must but because that's who you are. You don't give up."

"Maybe. But I'm tired, Kody. Tired of being scared. Tired of fighting every day. I'm ready to fast-forward to the epilogue where we live happily ever after."

"And miss out on our adventurous life together?"

"I think we've had enough adventures for several lifetimes."

"Epilogues are boring."

"Not ours." I wriggle my ass against his erection. "Ours will be nonstop sex."

He rumbles a deep, vibrating sound in the most arousing, primal way. I tremble in the echo of it.

The reflections of our gazes hold fast as he slowly opens my zipper.

"How's your leg?" I ask.

"The pain I'm feeling isn't in my leg." He caresses his hands along my hips and beneath the denim, guiding my jeans and underwear down, down, down my legs, and off, taking my socks, too.

He lowers to his haunches behind me, his nose trailing up between my thighs until his teeth close around my ass cheek in a claiming bite.

The pain awakens me, setting me on fire. My legs shake. My back arches. Then his nose is there, buried between my legs, smelling me. Of course, he is, and I'm fucking here for it.

I whimper as he tongues me from behind, delving past swollen flesh, parting me, and sinking deep with languid circles. Each curling lick feels like worship. Every thrust of that strong tongue focuses on my pleasure.

His fingers join in, slowly massaging my clit as he feeds. I squirm and gasp, my inner thighs slick with my arousal.

Another gasp, drowned by a masculine groan against my pussy. Then he devours me with vicious indulgence as if desperate to swallow my climax.

I give it to him, crying out and flooding his tongue as I peak.

Warm, shimmering waves crash over me as he rises and spins me to face him.

Rough hands yank off my shirt. My bra hits the floor next.

Once I'm completely naked, his mouth crashes over mine, the taste of my pussy on his tongue. He kisses me the way he kissed me to orgasm. Intimately. Aggressively. Hungrily.

When we come up for air, the room spins. My lips throb, and my body drips with desire.

"Fuck." I grip his hips for balance. "Goddamn, Kody."

"Hold on." He moves me to the wall between the counter and the doorway.

I slump against it, nude and buzzing with the remnants of my release. He takes one step back and reclines against the opposite wall.

At some point, he opened the zipper on his jeans, making room for the unnatural creation between his legs. A bead of precome clings to the tip.

With his shoulder blades braced against the wall, his boots planted wide, and his massive cock jutting from the open *V* of his jeans, he runs a hand through his rumpled hair, looking for all the world like a sculpted, immortal sex god.

Mine.

I'm going to fuck him until he can't move.

He smirks, and Lord Jesus help me, it's such a rare thing to see on those gorgeous, pouty lips. I could come again just from the sight of it.

I let my hand fall to my pussy, my fingers caressing the ache.

He wags his head. "Let me look at you. Spread your legs."

I widen my stance, and my God, does he look. There isn't an inch of me he doesn't touch, caress, and violate with the phantom fingers of his gaze.

My blood sings. "I love you."

"Know what happens when you say that to a caveman?"

I laugh.

He scowls.

As if our very lives rest upon that question, he closes the distance and shows me.

Holy hell, Kody's kiss is flammable. It's incendiary. It's the spark before the blaze that burns down the world.

I writhe in the flames as he drags his searing tongue along my throat, my collarbones, teasing the hollow dip between them before trailing to my breasts.

They're small. Smaller than they were a year ago. But when he draws one into his mouth and sucks, I've never felt so feminine, so desirable.

He nips and licks, palming one breast as he flicks his tongue possessively over the other.

Restless and wanton, I grasp the back of his head, fisting his soft hair and holding him to me.

Clamping his mouth over my hardened tip, he sucks so greedily his teeth nearly break my skin.

"I need you." My mind spirals, focused on one thing. "Inside me now."

"I know what you need." He returns to my mouth, lapping into my gasps and swallowing my breaths.

His hands continue their assault, kneading my breasts and tweaking my nipples. I moan into his kiss, dueling my tongue with his as he thumbs my sensitive buds, sending jolts of pleasure through every nerve ending.

My fingers claw at the front of his jeans, fumbling to free him, to hold all that hard, heavy virility in my hands.

He brushes my arm away and shoves a powerful thigh between my legs, lifting it until I'm riding pure muscle.

"Oh, fuck." My breath snags, and a rush of wetness soaks his leg.

With his hands on my waist, he guides my body into a feverish dance, undulating my hips, rocking my pussy against his thigh, pulverizing me.

I burst into a thousand tingling embers. The release hits so hard it feels like my bones are disintegrating, and I'm floating like ash in the wind.

His arms, so strong and vascular, hold me upright until I catch my breath.

"Can you stand?" He peppers kisses on my bruised lips.

"I might've blacked out there, but yeah." I strengthen my legs and prop myself against the wall. "Carry on."

He chuckles and makes an unhurried descent down my body, leaving a fresh trail of desire in his wake. Closing my eyes, I bask in every tantalizing nip and devoted touch.

When he's tasted and caressed every inch, he kneels before me, positioning one of my legs in between his. He hoists my other over his shoulder, pressing my foot against the wall behind him.

The stance leaves me balancing on one leg, with the other bent at the knee and anchored against the opposite wall above his head.

Okay, I'm not as fit as I used to be. But I got this.

I flatten my hands and spine against the wall for support. The position opens me to him, exposing every wrinkle and fold of my pussy, putting it all out there, level with his face.

And what does the animal do?

He licks his lips.

A sure sign he intends to torment the hell out of me.

My head falls back at the first touch of his breath on my thigh. Then the torture begins.

He wraps himself around my leg, his hands roaming, mouth teasing, fingers swirling over throbbing flesh. The way he plays with my body spreads lava through my bloodstream.

Just when I think he's ready to get his dick wet, his palm slams down on my cunt with a sadistic smack.

A strangled cry escapes my lips. "What was that for?"

"You fell in love with a caveman." He slaps my pussy again. "What did you expect?"

"I expected sex." I wing up a brow. "In this century."

"If you want a quick fuck over a desk, you should've stayed with the other guy." A trace of jealousy rumbles through his voice.

Monty was never quick with me. He saved that particular selfishness for his office manager.

I shut my eyes and bury the thought, focusing on the path of Kody's mouth on my thigh.

Until I hear the sound of another click.

I glance down as he snaps more photos of my pussy.

"You did not just do that." I drop my leg and dive for his phone.

"Sure did." He flings his new toy out of the bathroom.

My gaze follows its trajectory, but it doesn't land on the floor.

Leo catches it and stares at the screen, his eyes hooded and mouth parted. "This is the hottest thing I have ever seen."

"Nice. Now delete it. All of them."

"No way, love. Look at this." He holds a second phone in his other hand and turns the screen toward us.

The photo was taken from his position outside the bathroom seconds earlier. It shows my leg raised above Kody as he kneels for me and snaps pictures of my pussy with a look of reverence on his face.

Sweet Jesus, it really is hot.

Inhaling through my nose, it pains me to say this. "You can't keep those pictures. We don't know who can access your devices, what apps are connected to the photo gallery, or if they're being uploaded elsewhere." I wince. "Monty could see them."

"You fucking serious?" Leo taps on the screen as if it'll disprove my claim.

"I'm sorry." I hold out my hand, gesturing for the phones. "I'll put some security measures on them, but I'm a stickler about this. Never store nude pictures on your phone. Someone might steal them."

"Dammit." With a scowl, Leo hands over the devices.

I quickly delete the photos, empty the archived trash, and set them on the counter.

"Did I kill the mood?" I recline against the wall.

"Impossible." Kody shifts forward, caging me in. "You're exactly how I want you—naked, dripping, and delicious."

Leo leans a shoulder against the doorframe, shirtless like Kody, his body a map of jagged scars and veiny muscles, glistening beneath a sheen of sweat.

"It hasn't cooled down out there?" I ask him.

Distracted, he shakes his head, his gaze slowly traveling over my nudity.

"Won't be cooling down anytime soon." He sheds the rest of his clothes and looks at Kody. "Shower first or sex first?"

"Sex in the shower." Kody noses the shell of my ear. "And sex after the shower."

"Good plan." Leo pushes into the cramped space, sliding between me and the wall.

The addition of a third body smashes mine against Kody, our chests heaving as we squeeze together. The temperature of the room rises to nuclear, and I'm crushed between two hotblooded men, swimming in testosterone and heat. Blistering, coiling, delirious heat.

Leo reaches into the walk-in shower and starts the water while Kody strips down to nothing.

A wordless conversation passes between them. Then we're moving into the shower stall.

I go where they direct because, damn, I love when they take control. Nothing turns me on more than when they work together, shut off all their inhibitions, and surrender to the burn between us.

They're all business at first, scrubbing away the long day from our bodies. Shampoo, conditioner, body wash, rinse.

As Leo finishes with his hair, Kody lifts me against the wall and hooks his arms around my thighs to balance me. With foreplay out of the way, he doesn't waste time.

Notching himself at my entrance, he impales me.

Fuck!

Too big. Too big. Too fucking big.

I squirm and whimper as he works himself in, kissing me through the stretch. His lips press against mine with such ferocity, every sweep and clash of his tongue leave me breathless and bruised.

The feral essence of his mouth seeps into my tastebuds, his sharp teeth catching tender skin, engulfing me in familiarity.

I would recognize him in the dark by taste alone. And his scent. His earthy, wildfire scent is the elixir that transports me to a little hunting cabin in the Arctic, surrounded by snow, hearth smoke, and masculine skin.

Thrusting into me, he grabs my hair and chases his pleasure. His impossible size scorches between my legs. I'm nothing but need and sensation as I open myself wider and do my best to take him as deeply as I can.

But it's Leo's voyeurism that cranks my arousal to the next level.

Eyes fixed on where Kody and I are joined, he flexes his hips, gripping himself and stroking in sync with Kody, lost in the moment.

The honesty in his expression, how blatantly hungry he is for me, how accepting he is, sharing me with the only brother he has left—I'm addicted to it.

I'm addicted to the three of us.

"You love what he's giving you." Leo hisses past clenched teeth, working his uncut cock harder, faster.

Sex with Kody is always a soulful experience. But sex with him in this new freedom? Freedom to fuck without freezing exposed skin? Without worrying about using precious calories? It elevates our intimacy, blazing past physical limits and making space for rabid, possessed, fiendish fucking.

"Only one thing missing." I reach down and grip Leo's hand on his cock. "Stop strangling that thing and put it inside me."

"No room." Kody grunts.

"If I can push a baby out, I can fit two dicks."

"That thing he's ramming inside you..." Leo angles closer, panting heavily. "It's the size of a baby."

Not quite. But Kody's girth makes things more challenging.

"Can we *not* talk about babies right now?" Kody flexes his hips.

"I have another hole." I climb up his frame, clinging to him as he buries himself deep. "Show him, Kody. Let him see where he can fit."

A deep, guttural sound parts Kody's lips as he palms my rear and strokes my back entrance with eager fingers. The idea must excite him because he drives his hips harder, sinking deeper. Then he shifts, peeling me off the wall to lean his back against the other.

So Leo can see his options.

The thought of taking them both at once sends a jolting thrill through me.

Leo plasters himself against my back, trapping me against Kody. His hardness jabs against me as his fingers slide down my crack to join Kody's hand.

"Christ." Leo groans against my shoulder.

Together, they caress and tease my tight ring of muscle, wetting it with my arousal, relaxing me, opening me up.

Then a thumb presses in. Leo's thumb. Kody's hands shift back to my waist as he continues to plough my pussy.

"I feel him." Leo breathes, plunging two fingers into my ass. "I feel him moving inside you."

"Imagine how that would feel on your cock." I clench around his digits, making him hiss.

"I think..." He pumps his hand, stretching me. "It would feel incestuous."

"That's not us."

"What's not us?"

"Labels. Limits. Rules made by a society that's quick to judge. They don't know us or what we've been through."

"Don't stop." Kody drops his head back, readjusts his grip on my hips, and pounds into me with the desperation of a man on the brink.

"Don't stop what?" I hold on, riding his brutal thrusts.

"Whatever he's doing. His fingers…stroking you…Oh, fuck. Fuck. Fuuuuuuck!"

He roars, his hips bucking with his release, the heat of it spurting inside me and triggering my own.

I scream and flail, choking and struggling to hang on as he empties himself, milking every drop from us both.

My Lycan prince. My sulky hunter. My grizzly lover.

His undoing is glorious.

Insatiable lust saturates his eyes as he stares at me. His lips, swollen and wet, separate to accommodate his rapid breath.

He hooks his thumb over my bottom teeth, calloused fingers cradling my chin, capturing me in a hold that feels more like possession than restraint.

Claimed. Loved. *Theirs.*

Still seated inside me, he doesn't pull out as he drops his hand and shifts his attention to Leo over my shoulder.

I can't decipher their wordless conversation, but something's happening. I feel it in the air—the crackle, the challenge.

"Pull out." Leo's hot breath coats my neck, his fingers easing out of my ass to clutch my hips, to tug me back.

"She wants us both." Kody gives me a teasing thrust.

Yep. Still hard.

I'm in so much trouble. "You guys…"

As the words leave my mouth, Kody shoves past Leo, lifting me off his cock and over his shoulder as he stalks out of the bathroom.

Leo shuts off the water and prowls after us with a battle in his eyes.

In the bedroom, they both slam to a stop, dripping all over the floor like savages.

The heavy desk now sits in front of the door, barricading it. Leo's paranoia.

The French doors remain open, airing out the stuffy room. It's too high to climb, but anyone can see in and, by anyone, I mean Monty.

If we close the doors, we'll suffocate in this infernal heat.

"The lights." Hanging awkwardly upside down, I gesture at the switch.

Leo's already on it.

As darkness drenches the room, the last thing I see is his beautiful, angry hard-on.

In the pitch-black, Kody unerringly finds the bed and sets a knee on the mattress. Before he can lower me from his shoulder, Leo pounces.

His strong hands capture my hips. Not to pull me away but to hold me in place as he spreads me open and shoves his face between my thighs.

Oh.

My.

Fuck.

My legs weaken, falling open to welcome his possessive mouth.

Kody's head turns, his whiskers scratching my hip as he sinks his teeth into the curve of my ass.

My breath severs, the pain all-consuming. But the next touch of his lips is lavishing, smothering the hurt.

Draped over his shoulder, I cling to his scarred back as Leo plunders me with his wicked tongue, raiding and ravaging and lapping up my come. Mine and Kody's.

A moan slips from me as Kody's fingers part my folds for Leo's mouth.

But Leo jerks away, suddenly angry.

Shit. Did Kody push him too far?

My lungs deflate.

Kody sets me on the bed and turns to him, emitting a throaty, inhuman sound that shivers down my spine.

The air thins, taut with violence, straining to snap.

Teeth bared and growls rumbling from their chests, they

circle each other in the dark.

Raw, ferocious aggression overtakes Kody's usually calm and strategic demeanor. And Leo, the unpredictable firebrand, meets him head-on, every bit as feral and intimidating.

I squint, trying to adjust to the absence of light.

Their eyes are engaged, communicating in that way they do with unspoken dialogue. As much as I want to interfere, I know they need to work this out their way.

As long as they don't bleed.

The turbulence in the room intensifies, spitting static across my skin. They move like predators in the wild, their silhouettes tense and poised to strike, each waiting for the other to make the first move.

Then they pause.

Oh, fuck.

All at once, they lunge for the bed.

For me.

In a blur of muscled limbs and snapping jaws, they move too fast to follow. I roll onto my stomach and scramble across the mattress, giving them the chase they crave.

A hand captures my ankle, halting me. Another fists my hair, wrenching my head back.

Kody's earthy scent penetrates my senses, his grip shooting pain along my scalp as Leo wrenches my legs apart and presses his hardness against my center.

I thrash and squeak like a mouse trapped beneath a lion's paw, no match for Leo's brute strength.

Muscles coiled, he hauls my hips to his groin and slams inside me, taking me from behind.

"Fuck!" With a strangled groan, he collapses on me, giving me his weight as he fucks and snarls and pins me down in a claiming rage of animalism.

The carnality of the act amps my pulse and melts my bones. Frenzied desperation tramples my lungs.

Kody's huge hand collars my neck, craning it at an awkward angle while aligning his dick to fuck my mouth.

Leo seethes, hungry and possessed, as he drags me away

and pounds me into the mattress.

Unrelenting, Kody stays with us and grabs for my mouth. He's aggressive, matching Leo's madness, and in the next breath, they're at each other's throats, more beasts than men, lost in a mindless need to rut and mate.

They're not hurting each other or me, but the intensity of their clash walks the line of brutality. Feral like wolves, they nip and snarl and bite at the air as if they could tear each other apart with the sheer force of their dominance.

I don't sense hatred or resentment. The love between them runs deep, but it's not sexual. Leo has boundaries and jealousy issues, and Kody wants to crash through them.

Leo just wants to fuck me to the edge of my life.

With impressive strength, Kody rolls us, shoving Leo onto his back. For a breathless moment, they struggle for the dominant position. Their grunts fill the room, a haunting din of animalistic hunger that makes my inner muscles throb.

With Leo beneath me, he can't win this without hurting me.

So he relents, going still with me lying face-up on his chest and Kody mounting us, his knees planted between our legs.

Hard to believe that less than three months ago, he'd never touched a woman. The man hovering over me now radiates savage sexualism and male confidence as he presses my knees to my shoulders. The position changes the angle of my pussy, and Leo's cock springs free from my body.

I don't know what Kody's doing, but I'm certain it involves pushing Leo's horizons.

Right now, all it does is incite his rage.

He gnashes his teeth beside my ear, one arm banding around my chest while the other lashes out at Kody.

This isn't an argument. It's a full-blown eruption of primal hunger.

Carnal combat.

I'm not afraid. I understand their instinctual pack behavior and battle for dominance. It's in their nature. Two alphas, locked in a struggle to establish a pecking order, their conflict as old as time itself.

Caught between them, I draw in a breath, heart pounding, but with calm acceptance. This is who they are—untamed, vicious, and fiercely alive. They're fucking beautiful.

Kody puts his face in mine, his pupils blown and eyes wild, as he dips his fingers into my cunt.

"Take her ass, you stubborn fuck." He shifts, spits on my back hole, and shoves his thumb in it. "She's fucking throbbing for it."

Leo rotates his hips, horny and belligerent. "Fuck you."

"Not me. *Her.*" With gritted teeth, Kody slowly removes his thumb and holds me open.

Leo's restraint breaks. With my legs still bent against my chest, he guides himself between my cheeks and feeds his length into my ass.

Full. I'm so fucking full. With Leo's cock in one hole and Kody's fingers in the other, I instantly, shockingly, violently come on the first thrust.

Then they really move, stroking in tandem, setting a diabolical rhythm, and turning my already used body into a pile of flayed muscles and woolly bones.

"Woman, you're making me so hard." Kody squeezes my breast with one hand and fingers me with the other. "I can't wait to fuck you again."

Fuck me now.

I want to beg for their elusive double penetration, but Leo's not ready. I'm surprised he's allowing Kody's hand so close to his balls.

The guttural sounds of his groans, the crazed flex of his hips, and the way his fingers savagely dig into my thighs indicate he's deep in the throes of carnal bliss.

And Kody's right there, sliding his fingers along my inner walls. I know Leo can feel him.

It's hotter than the fires of hell. Filthier than my most depraved fantasies. I'm leaking all over them, trembling and pulsing and tumbling from one orgasm to the next.

"Goddamn." Leo quickens his pace. "You feel so fucking good. I can't control myself. You're going to make me come."

"I love when you come in my ass." I clench around him, making him roar.

"Uuuuuhhhhh! Fuck! Fuck! Just like that." He grips Kody's hand, trapping it between my legs, as he curls his fingers inside me, thrusting them alongside Kody's.

My back bows. My breath seizes. I meet Kody's eyes and go off like a bomb, shaking and gasping in the shrapnel of splintered pieces.

"Jesus Christ, I'm coming." Leo jerks erratically, his mouth open and heaving against my neck. "I'm coming so fucking hard."

"With my fingers tickling your dick." Kody removes his hand and smacks those wet fingers against Leo's cheek. "Now I know how perverted and incestuous you truly are."

"Kody!" I shove his chest.

My God, he's rotten. Deliberately trying to rile the beast.

A breathless howl of laughter vibrates against my back. Satiated, pleasure-soaked laughter.

With a surge of strength, Leo pushes Kody off me, flips me onto my back, and grins down at me.

"I don't even care." He kisses me passionately, still winded, still smiling. "That was fucking amazing."

"Yeah." Listless and happy, I roll to my side.

With a swat on my ass, he leaves the bed.

As his glorious, naked form moves to the bathroom, a stream of moonlight shines a spotlight on all that is holy. That fine, sculpted ass flexes with hard muscle, taking my breath away.

Speaking of asses...

Kody presses up against me, chest to chest, looking pretty proud of himself. Despite the pouty lips and broody brow, a smug smile lurks in the dark, sparkling in his midnight eyes.

"Did you get your pecking order worked out?" I poke the bear.

"I won this round." He pokes back.

With his stiff, overfed cock.

Taking him in my hand, I stroke the veiny length as he lowers his mouth over mine.

In the bathroom, the water runs and shuts off.

We should sleep. But I'm not ready to relinquish this feeling. This, right here, is what we worked so hard to obtain. Our freedom. Our happiness. Our forever.

Pulling my leg over his hip, he doesn't hesitate to enter into my body. I coil my arms around his neck and lazily roll my tongue against his. Lying on our sides, we move together and sink slowly, languidly into the pleasure.

Leo returns and breezes past the bed to check the balcony and the steep, mossy slope far below it.

"No one's getting in," I murmur against Kody's lips.

Seemingly satisfied, Leo joins us, climbing in behind me to nuzzle my neck.

Either my eyes have adjusted to the dark or the moon is now brighter because the bed is alight, pale and shimmery, making us glow like magical creatures as we rock and writhe to the beat of our hearts.

Maybe the light I see is just our own, an illumination of our own making.

I give myself over to it, to the perfect iridescence of watching them love me.

monty

TEN

Every muscle in my body clenches as I watch them kiss her. Touch her. Fuck her over and over.

I drag a hand through my hair, fisting and ripping at the roots. Desperate to scrub the images from my mind, I try to turn away.

But I can't.

I can't fucking stop.

Darkness surrounds me, churning inside me, broken only by the moonlight filtering through the grimy, arch-top window.

I've never ventured into the unfinished attic space in my estate. Never had a reason. Until now.

Old furniture and forgotten belongings scatter around me, draped in sheets like ghosts in the gloom, with shadows looming in every corner.

I'm one of those shadows.

Hovering in the window with the cobwebs, I can't look away from the open French doors of the guest house. Through them, I watch my wife. My young, vivacious, beautiful wife, spreading her legs for another man.

Two other men.

The night vision goggles make everything green and eerie, but all I see is red. I seethe. I claw at my head, grinding it against the window frame and gouging my scalp on the jagged edges.

Still, I can't look away.

My phone is in hand, the thermostat app open. I adjust it again, making their room unbearably hot, forcing them to leave the doors open.

It's ruthless and wrong, and I know it. But I thought it would make them go to sleep, so I wouldn't have to watch. So I wouldn't have to torture myself with the sight of her taking one dick after another.

Reading about it in her journal was a special kind of hell. But the night vision goggles add details she didn't include, letting me see every graphic position, every moment of eye contact, every gutting thrust.

I see her erotic expressions as she takes them into her body, the way she blooms for them, glistening in the heat, unaware of my gaze.

Right now, Kody's licking her face like an animal, uncouth and degrading. She climbs over him, straddling him. He wants her. I don't have to look at the monstrosity between his legs to know how badly he fucking wants her.

I dig my fingernails into the windowsill, unable to breathe as he flips her onto her back and shoves her legs open.

It's quick. Frantic. There isn't a thought between them. He fucks her into the mattress while Leo watches. Not ten minutes after Leo finished in her ass.

The dirty, unfinished walls close in on me, the sense of isolation overwhelming. Suffocating. I hate myself for doing this, for needing to see her even if it's from a distance, even if it's like this.

My surroundings reflect my state of mind—dark, cold, filled with malicious shadows—trying to suck me in.

Kody puts his mouth at her ear and says something that makes her laugh.

The silence presses in on me.

When he finally rolls off her, she pushes herself up, wiping sweat from her forehead. Leo brushes the hair from her face and kisses her shoulder.

My heart aches with longing. I want to be with her, to hold her, to be the warmth beside her while she sleeps. But she doesn't want me there.

She doesn't want me.

I press my palm against the cool glass, trying to suppress the rage that threatens to turn me into my brother.

But I'm not him.

This devil doesn't bargain.

I take.

I'm a monster on the cusp of insanity. A stalker in the night. Her silent ache, haunting her from the darkness.

But beneath the horror of my actions, there's a man who's just lonely, broken, and desperately in love. A man who wishes more than anything that things were different, that she still wanted him the way he wants her.

Fuck.

What am I doing?

I rip off the goggles and pace through the attic, stirring up dust. The floorboards creak underfoot, the sound amplified in the stillness.

Cobwebs drape the rafters, and an old, musty smell dangles in the air, mingling with the sharp, metallic tang of cold. The temperature hovers just above freezing, unlike the sweltering heat in the guest house.

Why am I here?

What am I doing?

A chill seeps into my chest, but my heart is already cold. Split-open. Scarred beyond recognition.

What am I fucking doing?

She's humiliating me. Controlling me. Fucking two men—*two Strakh men*—while I watch from the shadows. She's a goddamn cockhold.

I have banged more women than there are days in a year. I fucked them in twos and threes. Sometimes five or six at a time. Before I met Frankie, I had a penthouse in Anchorage just to host sex parties. Women-only invites, and they came by the dozens.

I have more stamina than a horse, even at my age. My sex drive is legendary. No one can satisfy it.

Except her.

I don't know what kind of succubus-level magic she's wielding, but with her, the sensations are different. The chemistry, the orgasms, the connection—everything with her hits differently. Her sexual magnetism is so fucking intense it terrifies me and makes me insanely hard.

The first time I sank into her body, I knew.

I didn't need a bed full of women to get off.

I only need one woman.

Her.

My life before Frankie had no flavor, no meaning, no purpose. It was sex without feeling. A book with blank pages.

I cannot go back to that.

I won't.

Leo and Kody aren't going anywhere. They're addicts like me. But I have something they don't.

Money. A lot of it.

She needs me.

Feeling calmer, I return to the window, set my phone on the ledge, and slip on the goggles.

A shroud of stillness cloaks the guest house. Two unmoving male bodies sprawl on the bed, passed out.

Where is she?

Moments later, she emerges from the bathroom, exquisitely naked, carrying tubes of something.

She kneels on the mattress, squirts ointment from a tube, and smooths it on Kody's injured knee. He doesn't stir.

When they were released from the hospital this morning, I compiled a list of everything they might need. My employees have been running around all day, gathering every item on that list.

Providing for Frankie brings me great pleasure. Providing for Leo and Kody is an extension of that, despite my desire to kill them. They're my family, and as much as it sickens me, she loves them.

She moves to the edge of the bed and extends a slender leg. I lean closer to the window as she rubs the contents of another tube into her skin.

Lotion.

I used to watch her do this every night, greedily tracking the paths of her hands as she moisturized every dip and curve of her body. Like now.

When she spreads the cream across her perky little tits, my insides tighten. My cock hardens, and all my blood rushes south.

I came here directly from my shower, wearing only a pair of sweatpants. Shoving my hand inside them, I fist my eternal ache.

How many times have I masturbated to visions of her? Nine months of self-pleasure has done nothing to take the edge off. But seeing her in the flesh? I might actually enjoy this release.

I spit in my hand and curl it around my length, stroking from root to tip.

As she glides lotion down her arms, her face looks so peaceful, so content, not caught in the lines of the anger that plague her when she sees me. Like this, her beauty is stunning, mesmerizing. She leaves me breathless.

After all the weight she lost, she's too thin but still painfully, unjustly, indescribably gorgeous. The natural radiance that shines from her is still there, surrounding her like an aura.

My fist tightens, jerking harder on my straining cock.

I need those lush cherry lips wrapped around me. Fucking hell, she knows how to suck a dick. Never shied away from taking me deep. When I hit the back of her throat, I nearly blacked out. Every. Fucking. Time.

Hers is the only mouth I'll ever fuck again.

Finished with the lotion, she stands and walks to the open doors, looking out into the night.

I step back into the shadows, heart thundering, fucking my fist, groaning with desperation and despair.

Look at me, wife. Give me those gorgeous eyes. See me. Come to me.

She searches the darkness, gaze roaming, each sweep never quite snagging on the small attic window.

Is she looking for me? Hoping to catch a glimpse of me staring back? Why else would she be standing in the open doorway, fully nude and on display?

Deep down, I know you still want me, Frankie. You still love me. You're just too angry to see it.

The thought sends me into a tailspin of frenzied hunger. I kick my hips, thrusting and stroking, my love for her twisted into this dark, obsessive need.

I come with a strangled gasp, squirting all over my hand and abs, dripping the last drops into the shadows slithering at my feet.

"Fuck!" I heave, squeezing my dick, drawing out the release, chasing the high.

But it doesn't last.

It doesn't compare.

Nothing rivals the real thing with the only one I want.

I need her. I need to feel her mouth on mine, her eyes staring into my soul. I just...need her.

She lifts her heavy mane of hair off her neck and rolls her head from shoulder to shoulder, stretching those delicate tendons, letting the breeze caress every angle.

She's hot.

Hot as fuck.

But also burning up.

That's why she sought the open doors. She's trying to cool down.

I'm a bastard. A creepy fuck with my dick hanging out. And I can't even scrounge up a sliver of regret about it.

Stuffing myself away, I wipe my hand on my sweatpants, grab my phone, and lower the thermostat in the guest house.

Sleep, my beautiful girl. Dream of the life we had. The life we can still have together.

She retreats from the doorway and crawls into bed between Leo and Kody.

Resting her cheek on Leo's chest, she drapes a leg over his hips and stares out the doors.

I should go. I've already lingered long past disturbing. But my infatuation glues me in place.

Her eyes grow heavy, and within minutes, the graceful curves of her face soften with sleep, drawing attention to the perfect bow of her lips.

Her long hair cascades around her, a fiery halo against Leo's chest. Her pale skin and slender figure make her look ethereal. Otherworldly. A delicate, celestial creature too perfect for this harsh world.

Every ounce of me wants to drag her away from them and lock her in our room. In our bed. To feel her softness against me, to breathe in the cherry scent of her skin, to taste her mouth again, it would be my salvation, my deliverance from this damnation.

She's the only one who can rescue my black soul.

Christ, I miss her smile against my lips, the feel of her body relaxing when I grab her hips, and the way she looked at me with *mine* in her eyes. Now there's only hurt and anger, a barrier that keeps us apart.

She left a fierce ache in my chest, a burning need that never fades. Every time I look at her, I want to bend her over my knee and spank the resentment out of her. I want to choke her, bruise her, tie her to our bed, and fuck every hole in her body until her heart finds its way back to me.

But she's too far away for that, even when she's right here. The distance between us is a chasm that can't be crossed until I earn her trust again.

Until that time, I'll remain her devoted shadow, following her, watching her, never leaving, if only to feel close to her even when I'm not.

I despise what I've become and the lengths I'll go to get her back.

Guilt festers in my gut, turning sour and foul. It morphs into something darker as the images of tonight replay in my mind, taunting me, unraveling me.

Every time she lets them touch her, she inflicts another wound, another scar inside me. The pain is ungodly, making it impossible to keep a clear head.

I start to turn away until I catch movement in their room. The bed stirs behind her. Kody rolls against her and buries a hand between her legs, groping her while she sleeps.

That's all it takes. My boiling veins erupt, spewing venom and rage. Unable to contain it, I toss off the goggles and swing my fist, sending it into the half-moon window.

A crack splinters across the glass as pain shoots through my knuckles and shatters up my arm, making me angrier.

I lose my fucking mind, overturning furniture, the heavy wooden chairs crashing to the floor with a satisfying thud. Boxes go flying, the contents scattering across the room.

She was pregnant with our baby. A baby she lost because of me.

A son or daughter I'll never meet.

My breaths come in ragged gasps. My vision fogs with fury. I grab a small table and hurl it against the wall, the wood splintering on impact. I attack old paintings, tearing the canvases with my bare hands.

I had a son. *Wolfson.* A son she loved and lost because of me.

A son I'll never meet.

Because I refused to accept him.

I kick over a trunk, the tumble of books echoing in the room. The sound of destruction fuels my anger, pushing me further into madness.

All the money in the world won't bring them back.

They're gone.

Panting, seething, I collapse to my knees, surrounded by the chaos I've created.

I need to get out of here. Away from this house. Away from the memories. Away from the woman who's driving me insane.

My body trembles as I force myself to stand and head for the door.

Moving on autopilot, I slip out of the crawl space, into the guest bedroom closet, and cover the opening with the shelving unit.

In my bathroom, I wash my hands, gritting my teeth against the hot sting of broken skin.

I pull on running shoes, grab the boat keys, and bolt outside.

The rain stopped, leaving the air fresh and crisp. Shirtless and out of breath, I sprint into the night, following the running paths away from the guest house, away from the torment of watching her with them.

The scent of damp earth fills my lungs as my feet pound the ground, my mind a bleeding mess of heartache and desperation.

The dock comes into view. One of the men on the security team stands at the entrance. He looks at me funny but doesn't say anything. He only nods as I pass, recognizing the violence in my eyes.

I jump into the yacht and start the engine, the roar of the motor shattering the silence.

Water churns beneath the hull as I speed off into the Sitka Sound.

Richness and extravagance surround me in comfort. Polished exotic wood, stitched Italian leather, custom artwork, and handwoven carpets—all crafted by renowned interior designers.

The best that money can buy.

Yet I've never felt more alone.

None of it means a goddamn thing without her.

The wind whips through my hair, and the salty tang of the sea melds with the smell of diesel.

As the island fades into the distance, the dark expanse of the Sound stretches out before me. I push the yacht faster, slicing through the waves, but the speed and fresh air bring no pleasure.

My chest cracks with each crash of the bow against the water. Doesn't matter how much distance I put between her and me, I can't escape the pain.

As I steer into the night, it starts raining again. Pouring.

The droplets hammer down, the darkness swallowing everything, leaving an expanse of sorrow and isolation.

I slow the yacht and pour a glass of the finest whiskey, but the burn does nothing to warm the cold ache. I turn on music to drown out my thoughts, but every note feels hollow. I pace the deck, the rain soaking my sweatpants, the wind lashing at me, but nothing eases the torment.

The image of my wife fucking two men invades my mind, a relentless torture hellbent on destroying me.

I'm consumed.

My bloody knuckles turn white as I squeeze my hands around imaginary necks, the rage transforming me into something unrecognizable.

With no one around, I stop the yacht and kill the engine.

Stepping out onto the deck in the pounding rain, I raise my face to the sky and scream into the storm. A primal, guttural sound tears from my throat. I scream until my voice goes raw, until the agony pulls my legs out from under me.

I drop to my knees, my cries echoing across the empty sea.

"Frankie." My voice breaks, my body shaking, my sobs lost to the downpour.

The loneliness crushes me. I can't breathe.

I miss her with every fiber of my being, the longing a physical pain that rips through me.

The night closes in, the darkness hovering like a reaper. I collapse, my strength gone, my spirit shattered, and reach for the only thing that can numb the pain.

I drink until I pass out.

leonid

ELEVEN

I wake in a heap of warm limbs and tangled sheets. Every muscle aches. My cock is sore. My head swirls with fuzz, and it takes a minute to remember where the fuck I am.

Beside me, Frankie is curled up on Kody's chest. She's so much smaller than him, like a child sleeping on a giant, hugging his bicep with both arms as he holds her in place.

And the legs entwined with mine? Yeah, those are his.

Better his legs than the fully erect limb between them.

I have no interest in going near that thing. Not purposefully. Not accidentally. Not even when it's inside the hole I want to be in.

Last night, what we did together...I didn't want it, fearing it would trigger my demons and resurface memories with Denver I don't want to ever relive.

But it didn't.

It was fucking incredible.

Do I have sexual thoughts about Kody? Fuck no. I'm *not* my father.

But the pressure of Kody's fingers inside her while I fucked her? That was different. It was unreal. We were connected—

the three of us—in a new way, and I loved every fucking second of it.

Doesn't mean I want to rub dicks with him, but I wouldn't mind a repeat of last night.

As if I said all that aloud, he cracks open an eye and aims it at me.

I roll out of bed. "Nice morning wood, Uncle Kody."

"Don't ever call me that."

"Someone needs to make it uncomfortable since Wolf isn't here."

I feel like Wolf this morning—sarcastic, offensive, playful, and ready to fuck things up.

The temperature in the room finally dropped through the night. The desk still barricades the door, and my fiery little redhead is so full of come it'll be leaking out of her for days.

I reach toward the heavens in a full-body, naked stretch, feeling like a goddamn stud. With a satisfied groan, I step outside through the open French doors and soak in the first light of dawn.

Floating toward the railing, I grip my cock.

"Leo," Frankie says sleepily, "don't you dare pee off that balcony."

Busted.

I drop my hand. "Wouldn't dream of it."

The brisk morning air gives me an invigorating rush, the breeze chilly and refreshing, not lethal. I take a deep breath, savoring the rich scents of pine and loam.

The balcony hangs over a steep ravine of moss, facing the secluded side of the main house. Frankie was right. No one can climb this high, not even with a ladder.

The estate's primary living areas and bedrooms are located at the other end. No windows on this side. Except one. A cracked half-moon window sits beneath the eaves of the roof.

Is that an attic? I didn't see access to it during my walk-through.

From my vantage point, I can see directly into that window. If I were standing in there, I would have a perfect view of the bed behind me.

Good thing I turned off the lights last night.

I return my attention to the island landscape and all its lush, green vegetation. Everywhere I look, life bursts forth in every direction, vibrant and full of energy.

The melodious calls of songbirds echo through the trees. The underbrush rustles with the movement of critters. Squirrels scurry along branches, and somewhere nearby, gentle waves lap at the shore.

This place is surreal.

Surrounded by the feeling of growth and renewal…I can get used to this.

The Arctic is beautiful in its own way, with its endless horizons and the silent majesty of icy hills. But it's cruel and unforgiving.

Here, there's a sense of possibility, of *more.*

I turn back to the room and catch something at the edge of my vision.

A cold, prickling sensation spins me back around, my eyes narrowing, focusing on the shadows beyond the tree line.

Still and silent, a man-shaped silhouette stands there, staring back at me.

I squint, trying to make out details, but the figure is too far away, too shrouded in the dappled shade of the trees.

Fucking unnerving the way it just stands there, like a goddamn ghost.

Or is it moving?

My heart gallops as the thing shifts, almost imperceptibly, floating backward, retreating into the deeper shadows of the forest. The way it moves, so fluidly yet deliberately, chills my blood.

What the ever-loving fuck?

I lean closer to the railing.

Slowly, it fades into the tree cover, becoming one with the shade, until it's gone.

Did I imagine that?

Fuck.

I scrub a hand over my face. It must've been one of the

many security guards on the island, doing their rounds. I'm just being paranoid.

But something about the way it stood, the way it watched me, lingers like a cold fist around my heart.

Dismissing the unease, I turn away, lock the door behind me, and follow the trail of discarded clothes to the bathroom.

Frankie and Kody watch me with heavy-lidded eyes, not ready to leave the bed. Bite marks and hickeys cover her tits from Kody's barbaric mouth. More hickeys discolor her neck.

She looks well fucked and deeply loved.

After I shower and get ready for the day, I return to the room to find them both asleep.

Slipping into the closet, I pull on a T-shirt and jeans, loving the fit more than I should.

Being dependent on the Strakh family patriarch makes my skin crawl. It feels too much like the life we just escaped.

Quietly, I push the desk away from the bedroom door.

"Where are you going?" Kody's gravelly voice drifts from the bed.

"Need to walk the outside perimeter of the guest house."

"Thought you did that last night before you came up here."

"I did, but it was dark. I need to see it in the daylight, make sure I didn't miss anything." I open the door, reengage the lock, and step out. "Then I'll head to the main house."

"No fistfights, assfucker."

"No promises, cocksucker. Don't let her out of your sight." I shut the door on his grunt.

After my perimeter sweep, I stroll along the paths through the island's interior with the image of that shadowy figure in my mind. I look for it amid the vibrant life around me, glancing back at the trees, half-expecting to find those haunting eyes staring back at me.

The few security guards I pass make themselves known, stepping out of the shadows to nod at me.

Their presence eases my trepidation, and eventually, I find my way back to the covered patio behind the main house.

Sitting beneath the overhang, Monty sips from a mug and types on his phone.

His head lifts as I approach, and his expression takes me aback.

Rage.

It twists his features and leaks from his rigid posture. A leak he's struggling to contain.

His eyes, bloodshot and bruised from my fists, sink into his face like he hasn't slept in days. But holy fuck, that glare cuts into me, cleaving and hacking with murderous intent.

The scent of alcohol clings to him, heavy and pungent, despite the presence of aftershave and cologne. He slumps over a cup of coffee, his hand trembling as he pours more whiskey into it, the amber liquid swirling in the dark brew.

His freshly washed hair clumps across his brow, still damp. His suit hangs askew on his hunched shoulders.

A mess of cuts and bruises covers one hand, his knuckles swollen and raw, adding to the image of a man who's losing a battle with himself.

A man on the brink of self-destruction.

And hungover.

Last night was long for Montgomery Strakh, and I don't have to guess why.

How many punches did he throw in a jealous rage? How many bottles of whiskey did he escape into?

Nothing will bring her back to him.

I feel a twinge of compassion as I engage his venomous stare. Just a twinge. Nothing more.

He hurt my girl and deserves every stab of guilt and pain that torments him.

Pulling out the chair across from him, I settle in. "You look like shit."

He drags his angry gaze over my tied-back hair, beard, and clenched teeth in my feral smile. "You look like you're ready to raid a village and rape its women."

"Already pillaged and plundered this morning. Met my quota for the day." I rest my elbows on the table, leaning in. "Let's cut the bullshit. I see the temper you're trying to conceal beneath that suit. I recognize it." I hold up my hand, letting him inspect the scarred skin across my knuckles. "Guys like us can't exorcise our demons without breaking things." I tilt my head. "What are your demons?"

"I think you know."

"I know one of them. I lived with him for twenty-seven years."

He bends his fingers, stretching the broken skin as he broods and ruminates. The forced casualness in his movements doesn't hide the ticking time bomb in his eyes.

"Do you see that sick fuck when you look at me?" I ask.

"You *are* his son."

"That's not an answer."

"No." His gaze fixates on me, his tone biting and cold. "I don't see him in you. Your eyes are…fucking strange."

"Strange is better than evil."

"You look like your mother. Tia."

"Tell me about her." My breath quickens at the thrill of that discovery. "Did she have my eyes?"

"I don't remember. Never paid attention to her. Never talked to her."

"Because she was the lowly help? The groundskeeper's daughter?"

"No. Because she was a *child*."

"That's fair." I sit back and drum my fingers on the table. "Let's talk about why you didn't sleep last night."

Since I know Frankie is the reason, I expect him to either shut down or blow a fuse.

He does neither.

"I haven't slept in nine months." He clears his throat, his jaw flexing. "I failed her. I won't gloss over my mistakes with generic words. I fucked up, and I own it."

"You have the knuckles of a man who's unraveling. You own that, too?"

"Takes one to know one."

"Considering the things my father did to me and my brothers, I'm entitled to some unraveling."

He shuts his eyes for a moment, breathing deeply. Then he meets my gaze. "I don't talk about my feelings. I push it all down and pack it away until I break. Or break something." He glances at his hand. "I'm not afraid of vulnerability. So if you think I'll slink off with my tail between my legs rather than face what I've done, you're wrong. I'll show up for her, one hundred percent, even on my worst days when I'm stripped and gutted with my jealousy and guilt hanging out of the holes in my chest."

Well, that was...candid.

Part of me wants to believe him. The other part hopes he's lying, so I can justify rearranging his face every time he looks at Frankie.

Denver camouflaged his evil beneath a charming smile and composed demeanor.

Is Monty a monster like my father? Or is he just a miserable pantywaist with no ill intent? If it's the latter, she'll eventually forgive him. She's too compassionate to hold onto her resentment for long.

But will she trust him again?

God, I fucking hope not.

We sit in a stifling standoff, neither of us speaking, until the back door creaks open.

A man with a wrinkled scowl steps outside. He's older, distinguished, with a judgmental look in his eyes that immediately makes me uneasy.

He strides toward us with a sense of purpose, chin held high, his gait ceremonious and deliberate.

"You must be Leonid, Monty's nephew." He bows his head in a formal gesture, his silver hair meticulously combed back from a stern brow.

My eyes narrow. He knows who I am?

"I'm Oliver." His voice carries a faint accent, tinged with an old-world courtesy that feels out of place. "I'm responsible for making Monty eat, though I've done a terrible job as of late." He gives Monty's thin frame a disapproving once-over.

The man's tailored navy suit seems too courtly for the casual setting. A gold watch chain peeks from his vest pocket, glinting in the early light.

Weird.

"Are you the butler?" I ask.

"The chef." He sniffs. "Would you like coffee? Juice? Something to eat?"

"Sure. Coffee, food, and..." I flick a hand at the whiskey. "Some of that."

"I think we're finished with that." With lightning speed, Oliver snatches the bottle before Monty can stop him. Stepping out of reach, he continues as if he didn't just cut off his employer's drinking. "Will Frankie and Kodiak be joining you?"

"In a while." I glance back at Monty, whose glare hasn't softened.

"Any food allergies or special diets, Leonid?" Oliver's pronunciation of my name is a bit too precise in that accent, hinting at a past that likely began in Russia.

"It's Leo. And I'll eat anything you put in front of me."

"Very well." He shoots Monty another glower before marching back into the house.

I shift, making the chair groan. "I get the feeling your chef spits in your food."

"He's a pompous old prick who doesn't know his place."

"Why don't you fire him?"

"He makes the best Eggs Benedict in Alaska."

"Or could it have something to do with his history with your family?"

Monty's head snaps up, eyes wide, before he quickly refastens the scowl. "*Our* family."

"Sure. Your father. My grandfather. Whatever. Oliver worked for Rurik."

"What makes you think that?"

"The accent."

"His accent is too subtle for the untrained ear." He absently traces the rim of his cup, studying me.

"I heard it."

"Denver trained you well. Did he teach you Russian?"

"He didn't know Russian."

"Yes, he did. We were both taught at a young age."

"Well, he kept that from us. Nothing new there. What's Oliver's story?"

He adjusts the cuffs of his sleeves, a peculiar habit that surfaces whenever he's stalling. "Oliver was Rurik's butler in Russia." His gaze darts to the back door. "When my father fled to America, I was an infant, and he never spoke to Oliver again."

"Yet here he is, working for you."

"I keep track of Rurik's known associates. When Oliver immigrated to Alaska many years ago, I hired him."

"Why?"

"To find out if he was a threat against my family and to ensure he didn't know who I was. When I cut ties with my parents and changed my name, I didn't want anyone to find me."

"You fear Rurik's enemies?"

"I don't fear them. But I like to know if someone is hunting me."

"What about Frankie?" Air catches in my lungs. "Would they go after her?"

"Not without me knowing."

"Considering she was abducted from your house, I don't have a lot of faith in your awareness or security."

His eyes blaze, and his fingers flex and release, a rhythm of barely restrained aggression.

For a moment, I think he might try to rip my throat out. Instead, he takes a long breath, his shoulders sagging.

"You're right. I was complacent, overly confident in my handle on things, and too focused on my career to see the danger lurking on my island." His voice drops to a deadly snarl, each word a weapon aimed at himself. "My failures put her through nine months of hell and caused her unfathomable pain. I can't undo what I've done, and it's eating me alive."

He pauses, looking away as if gathering his composure.

When he focuses on me again, steely determination draws his features in harsh strokes.

"I made changes to the security protocols on the island. All new equipment, motion detectors, outdoor cameras, and a rotation of vetted guards with twenty-four-hour surveillance. I also hired a self-defense instructor to train her." He straightens. "This is not the same place she was abducted from. I won't let anything happen to her again."

"Neither will I." My breath steadies as I consider the security weaknesses I found during my tour of the estate. There aren't many. "Frankie gave me a passcode for the door to the guest house. Is that a code she had before?"

"Yes. I reactivated it last night so she could get in. I'll assign new ones today for all of you."

"What code did Denver use to get in?"

"He figured out my personal code."

"How?"

"It was the date of his assassination."

"That's fucked up."

"Yeah."

I see the torment in his expression, the anger at himself for failing, and the determination to make things right.

In that flicker of vulnerability, he appears to fight with himself to say something, his jaw working and his eyes flaring with conflict.

"I'm sorry." He pushes the apology past his teeth, the words rough and strained with angry pain. "I should've killed your father when I learned what he was. Running to Rurik was cowardly. If I'd done it myself, Denver wouldn't have been able to ruin your life."

Dark hatred burns in his gaze. Even though some of that loathing is for me, his guilt makes me reconsider my harshness.

"You were nineteen. No one faults you for not wanting to murder your own brother." I choke on a mirthless laugh. "If anything, *my* existence is to blame."

Denver said as much in the video.

A twist of fate spared me when I confessed to my father that same week that I would be a father. I got sweet, little Tia Langston pregnant, and that revelation stayed my father's hand.

"No." Monty winces, his guilt deepening. "The mistakes

were mine, and I've paid dearly for them." He stares at his busted knuckles, the malice in his voice softening into regret. "I won't let Frankie suffer for my failures any longer. I'll do whatever it takes to protect her, to make things right."

"There's a crack in the arched window that faces the guest house." I gesture in the general direction.

His eyes lock onto mine. Then he blinks. "I'll let Greyson know."

"The landscaper?"

"He's also the handyman."

"Does he wear a suit and gold pocket watch, too?"

"No."

"So the window…Is it attic space?"

"Yes."

"I want to see it."

"It's a mess up there. Just a bunch of old furniture and—"

"Then you won't mind me poking around."

"Of course." His eye contact holds steady, his anger and hatred of me just beneath the surface. "It's important that we keep certain conversations between ourselves. The guards, Oliver, Greyson, Aurora—there are too many ears, always listening. Be mindful of what you say in front of them."

"What do you mean?"

"No one knows our full story. Only the four of us and Melanie Stokes have the details."

"Do you trust the lawyer with this information?"

"I don't trust anyone. Melanie was hired by Frankie."

"Hang on. So Oliver doesn't know anything? Does he know you're Rurik's son?"

"He didn't learn I'm a Strakh until he saw it in the news. He didn't even know Rurik had a second son."

"Or a third son." I grimace at the reminder of how Kody was conceived. "Does he know Kody's your brother?"

"I told him yesterday when I informed him you would be staying here."

"How long has Oliver worked for you?"

"Twenty-five years."

"And you didn't trust him enough to tell him your real identity?"

"I don't trust anyone," he snaps, short-tempered. "I kept him on my payroll because I wanted him close and..."

"He makes the best Eggs Benedict."

"Yes."

"But he knows everything now?"

He shifts his eyes back to the door, his voice low. "He only knows what I'm feeding to the press. While I was in Whittier, news of Frankie's disappearance and my brother's possible connection to it exploded in the media. Oliver didn't know about Denver's existence until he saw it on TV. No one did. When the story hit, I controlled the narrative as much as possible. I'm still controlling it."

"What's the narrative?" My mind spins.

The door opens, and Oliver emerges, balancing trays in both hands.

The aroma hits me first—a rich blend of coffee and the savory scent of meat, lemon, and eggs.

"Eggs Benedict." He sets the trays down before us, revealing two perfectly plated servings.

Poached eggs rest atop slices of Canadian bacon and English muffins, all generously covered in a glossy, golden sauce. On the side, there's a mound of crispy hash browns and a steaming cup of dark, fragrant coffee.

The sight mesmerizes me, each element artfully arranged. The smell is even better, a mouthwatering smack of butter, eggs, and tangy vinegar from the yellow sauce.

I dig in without hesitation, and the flavors burst in my mouth. "Holy fuck."

The creamy richness of the yellow stuff blends perfectly with the runny egg yolk. The smoky saltiness of the Canadian bacon, the crunch of the toasted English muffin...

"Christ." I chew greedily, savoring each mouthful, my taste buds reveling in the experience. "This is fucking amazing."

I glance up to see Oliver watching me with a pleased expression, his grin softening his stern features.

As he turns to pour Monty's coffee, the smile vanishes,

replaced by cold, simmering anger.

He drips coffee over Monty's eggs with deliberate rudeness, his lips pressed into a thin line. The silent fury in his eyes chills the damn air.

When he steps back, his expression returns to that of a stoic servant. He gives me a final nod before leaving, the door closing behind him with a soft click.

As I look at Monty, who remains sullen and unresponsive, I realize why he tolerates the old man's blatant insubordination.

Guilt.

He didn't trust Oliver or Frankie with his identity. If he'd told Oliver who he was, he might've had a much-needed friend for the past few months rather than sharing this massive estate with an employee who resents him.

Then again, I'm a stranger in a strange land. Maybe Monty's distrust in everyone is what's kept him alive.

Still, I can't help but point out the obvious. "That man is harboring some deep-seated animosity toward you. Might want to check your eggs for rat poison."

"He wouldn't dare."

"What about the animosity you're harboring toward me? Should I check my food for poison?"

"Yes."

A swallow of eggs sticks in my throat.

"I want you dead." He pitches forward, his breath a surging tide of wrath. "I want to fucking bury you."

There it is. The venom that's been boiling beneath every glance, every word since I sat down. He's about to pop a blood vessel.

"Why?" I smile, provoking him.

"Why?" His eyes go wild, and he slams his injured fist onto the table, unleashing his rage with a roar. "You're fucking my wife!"

My nostrils flare with the fire of each labored breath. I stand from the table, seething with images of last night's fuckfest.

Leo launches to his feet, meeting me head-on.

"I can smell her on you." My voice vibrates with fury.

"If you had Kody's nose, I'd believe you. But you don't. I doubt you can smell anything past the reek of your hangover."

"I will destroy you. You hear me? I will tear you apart for touching what's mine!"

"She's not *yours*." He jabs a finger at me, carving it through the air and slicing invisible wounds. "But go ahead. Come at me. See what happens."

If I hurt him, I would never win her back. Killing him or Kody would break her irreparably, and that's the last thing I want.

But I'll make damn sure he feels my wrath.

It's a molten river inside me, threatening to overflow. My chest tightens, and every muscle coils, ready to snap. Heat rises up my neck, and my vision narrows to a tunnel focused solely on his face.

"You think you can fuck her, and I'll just sit back and

watch?" I step into his space, so close I glimpse the spark of uncertainty in his strange blue and gold eyes. "She's everything to me! Everything!"

"And now you have nothing." He stands with feet firmly planted, a solid foundation of aggression.

If he swings first, all bets are off.

"Hit me, motherfucker. Do it." My body trembles with the effort to restrain myself as I delete the final few inches between us, putting us nose to nose. "What are you waiting for? Take that fucking punch, you little bitch."

He doesn't flinch, doesn't blink. He just stands there as if nothing happened, as if he didn't spend the entire night balls-deep inside my wife.

"Nah." He holds his position, neither swinging nor backing down. "I won't hit you, old man. She's not a possession to fight over. She's a person who deserves better than your twisted control."

"You think you're more deserving than me?" I roar, my voice echoing across the patio. "That you're worthy of her? If you touch her again, I swear, I'll make you fucking regret it."

He smiles, throwing kerosene on my swarming rage. I shove him hard, sending him stumbling back, but I stop short of actually hitting him.

"You don't scare me." He straightens, rolling his neck. "If you loved her, you'd be fighting for her happiness, not trying to own her."

"Stay away from her." I shove him again, harder this time. "Or I'll make sure you wish you had."

"She deserves to be with people who love her, not someone who's obsessed with controlling her."

My fury peaks, and I grab his collar, wrenching him close. "You have no idea what you're talking about. I love her more than you ever could. But if you keep pushing, I'll make your life a living hell."

"Good thing I'm an expert at surviving hell." He lets out a laugh, heated and unhinged. "How ironic that, not so long ago, I stood where you're standing now. I was possessive, angry, and willing to kill anyone who touched her. You read her journal, so you know how that worked out." His lips curl back from his gnashing teeth. "I was wrong to try to own her. She deserves better, and I'll be damned if I let you ruin her life any more than you already have. So back the fuck off."

The air between us writhes with violence, both of us breathing hard, our faces inches apart. The urge to eradicate him rides me hard. My fingers clench in his shirt as my other hand rears back to strike.

A shadow blurs in my periphery, like a predator, silent and undetectable. I have no time to register the movement before someone materializes behind me and snarls in my ear. "You heard him. Stand down."

I freeze, shocked that Leo's brother sneaked up on me so easily.

No, not Leo's brother.

My brother.

If he's here, so is she.

Fuck.

Forcing myself to let go, I shove Leo away one last time.

In the next breath, Kody's in my face, engaging me with an open stance, poised to pounce.

"Can't be left alone for ten minutes." Her sultry lilt caresses my skin, calming me instantly and pulling my entire being into her orbit.

She's all I see as she strides toward us, delicate like porcelain, impossibly petite, and glowing with a passion that matches all that red hair.

"Sit. Both of you." Stepping between us, she pushes all of us apart with a strength that doesn't fit her small hands.

"This isn't over," I bark at Leo. "Not by a long shot."

"No, it's not." His eyes bore into mine. "But remember. This isn't about you or me. It's about her."

The truth of his words stings, but I refuse to show it.

She needs to know she's safe with me. To earn back her trust, I must proceed carefully, gently, and take my time to reconnect her heart with mine. I need to present the most protective and tender aspects of my masculinity rather than the dark, volatile corners.

I step back, and the tension disentangles as Leo and I lower into our chairs.

"You, too." She narrows those huge green eyes at Kody.

With a grunt, he lumbers around the table and takes the seat across from her.

"Are you ready to talk like adults?" She crosses her arms, standing behind the remaining chair.

I feel Leo's glare. Neither of us speaks.

Her presence has me in a chokehold.

She's here, inches away, safe and *home*. I'm no longer searching for her. No longer haunted by thoughts of never seeing her again.

I may not have her back in my arms, but having her here, despite the circumstances, is enough to keep my head in the game and my eyes on the prize.

"I started it." I force my gaze to Leo. "I was out of line."

His nostrils pulse as if sniffing for trickery. "Does that mean you didn't have my breakfast poisoned?"

"It's safe to eat."

"Thank you." He wastes no time, forking eggs down his gullet and speaking with his mouth full. "Thank you for the food, the clothes, the place to stay…everything." He gestures around until he awkwardly lands on Frankie.

The shithead better not be thanking me for her.

A muscle bounces in his cheek as he stares at me.

"It's no problem." A vein throbs at my temple. "Just my sanity at stake here. It's the least I can do." I harden my voice. "Seriously, the least."

The sound of laughter, soft and musical, snaps my attention to Frankie. A hand comes up to cover her mouth, unable to contain her amusement.

Fucking breathtaking.

"Sorry. It's just…" Her eyes twinkle. "That was the most uncomfortable exchange I've ever heard, and I enjoyed it immensely."

"Happy to entertain you, love." Leo pulls out her chair and slides his plate toward her. "Eat."

How easily he offers his meal to her. A meal he clearly savors.

It's a painful reminder of how they survived the winter—rationing, scavenging, sharing the scraps between them, and building a bond I have no hope of breaking.

"I'm not eating your breakfast." She pushes it back and glances at the door. "I'll get..."

As if on cue, Oliver steps outside, and his gaze goes directly to her.

Just like that, all the coldness he reserves for me is gone. Nothing but tenderness in his eyes for Frankie.

"Oliver." She melts when she sees him, her smile sad and full of affection.

He doesn't move as she walks to him and wraps her arms around him. My wife is a hugger. Oliver is not. But he tolerates it, maybe even secretly loves it. The old fuck has a soft spot for her.

What I wouldn't give to feel her arms around me again.

"Frankie, you look well." He steps out of her embrace, polite and professional. "Though it seems you could use a good meal. What would you like?"

She glances at the table, at our half-eaten plates. "Kody and I would love your Eggs Benedict. I've been dreaming about it for months."

"Yes, of course." With a crooked smile, he turns to Kody. "You are Rurik's youngest son."

"That's what I hear." Kody frowns.

"It's a pleasure, Kodiak. I'm Oliver, at your service." He bows deeply, either to piss me off or to hide whatever emotion sneaks onto his face.

Probably both.

When he takes his leave, Frankie sits at the table between Leo and me.

"What did you break?" Her gaze goes to my busted hand.

"A wall."

"A wall is better than a face." She purses her lips. "What did we miss?"

I catch them up on the relevant parts of the conversation. Then Leo picks up where we left off, asking me about the narrative I'm feeding the press.

"I'll show you." I remove Frankie's phone from my pocket and launch one of the major media websites.

Pressing play on the headline story, I slide the phone to them.

They hover over the screen as a well-known news anchor informs the nation that the wife of billionaire mogul Monty Novak was abducted by his estranged brother last year. The brother, Denver Strakh, held her in a cabin in the Arctic for nine months, where he also kept his son and younger brother, whom he kidnapped and raised in isolation. Over the winter, the food ran out, and Denver didn't survive. Half-starved, the survivors found a way to escape on a plane and crashed near Fairbanks. They were released from the hospital this morning.

Frankie's eyes close briefly. Kody remains unreadable, taking in the information.

"You told them Denver died of starvation?" Leo's gaze grabs mine.

"I led them to that conclusion without outright stating it. The details surrounding his death haven't been disclosed. But because abduction was involved, the detectives want to meet with each of you."

"They want to interrogate us." Frankie sits back.

"They'll ask questions, yes. I held them off as long as I could and pulled strings so we could deal with it here in Sitka. But they're growing impatient. I expect them to show up here today or tomorrow. We need to corroborate a story before that happens."

"Melanie has my journal." She rubs her temple. "The whole story is in there. Denver's murder, Wolf's suicide, the abuse that we all endured..."

"No crimes have been reported outside of the kidnappings. If you want it to remain that way, keep the story as is. If you want Denver's crimes exposed, be prepared for a long, messy, and very public investigation."

"No." Kody stiffens. "Denver is dead, appropriately

punished, and will never hurt anyone else again. The abuse he inflicted...that stays among us. No one needs to know about our history."

"Except your psychiatrist." She cocks a red eyebrow.

He scowls.

"Psychiatrists are mandatory reporters." I tap my fingers on my knee, thinking. "But in your case, the crime isn't active, and your kidnapper allegedly died of starvation. Your psychiatrist won't need to report the information to law enforcement. That said..." I take a steady breath. "The press is speculating that there's more to the story. Kidnapping implies assault and abuse. Since they don't have evidence, they're digging for it. We don't want them digging."

"So you promised them an exclusive." Her shoulders bunch up.

I can almost hear the echoes of Denver's abuse ringing in her ears, and I fucking hate it.

"I'm sorry." The impulse to reach for her twitches through my hand. "We must deliver exclusive interviews within the next few days. This bought us a little reprieve, but not much."

"How does it work?" Leo sips his coffee. "We corroborate the narrative you crafted by providing details that satisfy their curiosity without exposing too much?"

"Yes."

"We have to be careful with what we reveal and how we frame it." She nibbles on her lip. "The focus should be on our survival and the loss of Denver, painting him as a tragic figure rather than a villain."

"Fuck that." Leo glances at her, concern evident in his eyes. "What if they dig deeper? What about our mothers?"

"You were too young to remember them, right? And no one reported them missing." I shrug. "Let the world believe a different outcome for them. Maybe your mothers gave up on finding their missing sons and now live across the country with their new families."

"Won't someone investigate that?" Kody asks.

"That's a risk we would have to manage. But they won't

find anything. You were abducted over twenty-five years ago. The crime is old. The perpetrator is dead. They'll keep the case open, but I don't see them putting much effort into locating the cabin or hunting down your mothers. Especially if you don't push them to do it." I take a breath. "How do you want this to play out?"

"I want it to go away so we can fucking move on." Kody pushes back his shoulders with the strength of his conviction.

"Then we stick to the story I gave them and prepare for any questions they might throw our way."

"What about Wolf?" Leo looks at me.

"If we don't mention him, no one will know of his existence except us."

"And Sirena. She knows." Frankie's expression darkens, her voice sharp and demanding. "Why haven't you fired her?"

"Why would I?" A surge of satisfaction courses through me. Her jealousy makes me unreasonably happy in a twisted way, but I keep my face neutral. "She's the reason I discovered Alvis Duncan, which led me to learn about Denver. She's too good at her job to let go."

"So her skills are worth more to you than how I feel?" Her eyes flash with sudden, vicious anger.

"If you want me to fire her, admit you're jealous. Say those words, and she's gone."

"Jealous?" Her face contorts with fury. "This isn't about jealousy, Monty. It's about trust. She's dangerous, and I don't trust her."

"She's dangerous because she makes you jealous."

And seeing Frankie jealous makes me hard as fuck.

She pulls herself up, bristling all over. "You arrogant, controlling, narcissistic, arrogant—"

"You already said arrogant."

"I know I already said it, you dick."

"Sirena has done nothing but help us."

"And try to fuck a married man."

"Tried and *failed*. If anyone can find Wolf, it's her. But if you truly want her gone, say it. Your trust means more to me than anything."

"Frankie." Leo grips the back of her chair, leaning over her. "Let it go."

"Why? So you can stare at her tits again?" She pushes him away, her anger boiling over.

"Keep it up." He pushes right back, crowding in and growling low, "I'll bend you over my knee right here at the table."

My lungs slowly empty, but the exhale does little to calm my own raging jealousy.

For a moment, I worry she might explode and take me right along with her. Instead, she sucks in a deep breath, her eyes still blazing.

"Fine." She grits her teeth, glaring at me. "Keep her. But don't expect me to trust her. Or you, for that matter."

"Do you trust her?" Leo asks me.

"I don't trust anyone."

"Right." Leo huffs.

Frankie doesn't respond, just turns away.

Emotions are wrung out, and tempers are tight. We sit in strained silence, each of us lost in our own thoughts.

Eventually, Kody rests an arm on the table and brings us back around. "If we don't mention Wolf, no one will know of his existence except us and the investigator. What happens if we mention him?"

"If you mention him, he'll be known only as a victim of abuse and suicide." The thought makes my stomach turn, but this isn't my decision. I lost that right when I dropped off his mother at the abortion clinic. I clear my throat. "Which would he prefer?"

"He had a flair for dramatics." Leo traces the edge of a butter knife. "He would choose negative media attention over nothing at all."

"Wolf is ours to protect." She grips Leo's hand on the table. "Then and now. So that's what we'll do. We'll protect him from this, even if that means keeping him a secret."

Everyone mumbles their agreement.

I can't look away from her hand where it entwines so

casually with Leo's. She's pissed that I employ a woman I haven't touched. Yet she's fucking my nephew and my brother under my roof.

She's not just fucking them. She *loves* them.

They share so many things that exclude me, including my son.

It's fucking crushing.

The worst part is I only have myself to blame. My mistakes put me in this position.

Frankie gives me a sad smile, and for a span of several heartbeats, a flicker of understanding passes between us.

But a dark shadow remains, hovering over our fragile peace.

Leo and Kody exchange uneasy glances, knowing the battle between my wife and me is far from over.

monty

THIRTEEN

Oliver delivers breakfast to Frankie and Kody while we discuss the safest location to do the exclusive. All four of us would be questioned by the media, so it's crucial we get this right.

"We should hold the interviews here." I motion at the main house. "That way, I can control the security and ensure we aren't caught off guard."

The conversation pauses as Oliver collects empty dishes from Leo and me and returns to the house.

When the door closes behind him, I reiterate the importance of discretion around the guards and household staff.

"We need to stay united and consistent with our story. No mention of our ties to Rurik Strakh. No mention of any crimes beyond the abductions. When they ask, you claim ignorance."

"What about Frankie's relationship with Kody and me?" Leo raises an eyebrow.

"That's none of their business."

"So we let them believe you're still married?"

"We are still married."

"You know what I mean."

"Who I'm with and not with has no bearing on our abductions and captivity." She rests her forearms on the table. "Our relationship status stays between the four of us. Let the world think what they want. Do not engage in those discussions."

"The more controlled the environment, the better we can manage the narrative." I meet the eyes of the bastards who are fucking my wife. "Is everyone in agreement?"

They nod, glowering.

Fuck them.

"What about the crate we had on the Turbo Beaver?" she asks. "Where are Wolf's personal belongings?"

"Melanie is shipping everything here. Except the items that would be used as evidence if a homicide is reported."

"You mean the bones." Leo threads a hand through his hair.

"Yes." I can't help but think about Kaya's death. When I glance at Kody, I see my sadness reflected in his eyes. "The media cannot get wind of it." I pull out my phone. "I'll message Melanie to get an update on the crate and the investigation."

As I type out the message to the lawyer, I also send a quick text to Greyson. I need to make sure the attic is cleaned up.

I talked to him early this morning, so it's probably already done. But when Leo goes snooping around up there, all evidence of my breakdown last night must be gone.

Seconds later, my phone buzzes with an all-clear from Greyson.

I breathe a silent sigh of relief. "The lawyer will get back to us soon."

"What about the plane we saw in the hills?" Leo watches me, his eyes sharp and suspicious. "We built an SOS for it, but it never returned. Do you know anything about it?"

"It was mentioned in the journal, and I made the same assumption you did. Trophy hunters. But I didn't see anything like that during my searches on the ground or in the air while looking for Frankie."

"So you have no idea who it was?" His frown darkens with distrust.

"No, but we need to find out. With Denver's threat and Rurik's criminal history hanging over us, we can't afford to leave any stone unturned."

"Do you think someone was watching the cabin from the air?" She searches my expression.

"It's possible."

"If someone was watching us," Kody says, "they know the cabin's location. They could be a threat. They could be watching us now."

All eyes fall on me.

"Let's not get ahead of ourselves." I finish my coffee, thinking through our options. "I'll have Sirena look into flight traffic during that time. Maybe we can identify the pilot."

"Why Sirena?" She squints.

"She leads my investigative team."

"And she's the best?"

"She hasn't failed me yet."

"Oh, good. You should let her handle your other problem, too."

"What other problem?" I lean forward, daring her to cross that line.

"You know..." She twists her lips. "Those urges that aren't being satisfied."

I lower my voice to a silken pitch. "Only one person can satisfy those urges."

She grabs Leo's arm, stopping him from lunging.

His unbridled fury blasts in my direction, and a snarl pitches from Kody, the sound vibrating with raw power.

I don't look at them. My eyes are solely for my wife.

She lets out a slow, heavy sigh. "You'll be waiting a long damn time."

"Haven't you heard? Waiting is my thing now. Every second without you is a second spent waiting for you. Even if you don't want me in your life, you're the constant in mine. Always here." I tap my temple. "And here." I touch my chest. "Doesn't matter how long it takes. My feelings for you are timeless. I'll wait forever."

A harsh noise shoots from Leo's lips.

She gives his arm a warning squeeze. "Monty, please, don't make this harder than it already is."

"Harder for whom? You or me?"

You, her eyes assert sadly.

She's right. It would be so much easier to let her go and move on. I can have any woman I want.

But I already tried that.

Seven unsatisfying minutes with Aubrey was all the confirmation I needed.

Seven minutes that I'll regret for the rest of my life.

There's no walking away, letting go, or moving on from Frankie Novak. She's it for me, and that's a goddamn shame. Because earning back her heart after I stomped it to pieces? It'll be the hardest thing I ever do.

"I hear you." I edge closer. "But pushing through the hard shit is where we excel. I'm not backing down."

Her stare shoves into mine, frustrated and intimate.

She's so painfully gorgeous. Her knitted top and jeans fit her perfectly, accentuating every faint curve of her beautiful figure. Even in her anger, she possesses an effortless grace that hypnotizes.

When she looks away, something shifts in the air around her.

A deep furrow etches itself into her brow. She removes a hair-tie from her wrist, her movements sluggish. As if gathering her thick mane of hair requires immense effort. As if invisible chains burden her arms as she secures those red tresses in a high ponytail.

The action exposes her delicate neck, and that's when I see them.

Hickeys.

They cover every inch of her nape.

She runs her fingers over them, ensuring I don't miss a single bite.

My jealousy is instantaneous—a dark, seething beast climbing the rungs of my rib cage.

Burning heat surges through my veins, my vision

narrowing on those maddening marks on her skin.

The world around me fades, leaving only a crimson haze of possessive rage.

My hands curl into fists, knuckles turning white, as I scan her body, guessing what lies beneath her clothes.

"Where else did they mark you?" I spit the words like shards of ice, cutting through the tense silence. "Tell me where!"

"None of your business." She glares at me, defiant.

I glance over at Leo and Kody, sensing the violence brewing between us. Leo's eyes flash with a feral intensity that mirrors my own. Kody, ever the calm one, shifts forward, his gaze unyielding.

Refocusing on Frankie, I drop my voice to a menacing whisper. "Everything about you is my business. They're touching you, fucking you, and marking what's mine."

Her eyes go wide, but she holds her ground. "Goddammit. I'm not yours. You have no right to—"

"You think I don't see the way you look at me? The way you try to provoke me?" I reach out but stop myself from touching her, my hand hovering inches from her neck. "These marks are a challenge. A test of my patience. A punishment for my mistakes."

"They have *nothing* to do with you."

"You showed them to me, darling." I sit back, my pulse jagged and bloodthirsty, each exhale a strike against the air. "I told you I would wait forever, and that terrifies you. So you exposed your neck, hoping to provoke my jealousy and turn me into a liar."

"I need you to understand." Her expression softens, but her voice remains firm. "While you are waiting *alone*, I will not be. Listen to me, Monty. This jealousy...it's going to destroy you. I've been here one day, and it's already happening."

"I'm not destroyed." I grind my molars, my gaze falling to her neck. "Seeing those marks feels like a knife in my soul, but I'm still breathing. I bleed, and I breathe to protect you."

"You can't protect me from everything. You have to let me

live my life."

I nod slowly, the jealousy inside me still raging but well hidden. "Just...be careful. And know that I'm always watching. Always ready to fight for you."

"I don't need another savior."

"You have one anyway. When you need me, I'll be there. I'll fucking show up with every muscle of my beating heart."

Her lips twitch.

"What?" I narrow my eyes.

"The heart has just one muscle. The myocardium."

My chest expels a huff of surprise.

Christ, her brain is sexy as fuck.

"The marks weren't meant to hurt you." Kody meets my eyes, his voice quiet but firm. "We love her."

"I know." I roll back my shoulders, freeing the tension, and shift my attention to her untouched breakfast. "Your food is getting cold. Eat."

She exchanges glances with Leo and Kody, who watch her with the same intense obsession that I do.

Fucking Strakh men. We're cut from the same controlling cloth.

"Look at us." She forks up a bite of eggs. "Conversing like adults. There's hope for us yet."

Kody grunts.

Leo looks like he wants to pee on her.

I fantasize about dumping their bodies in the Sitka Sound.

She wraps her sexy lips around the fork, closes her eyes, and moans.

I go still, my groin tightening at the sound. Leo and Kody don't move, either, which reignites my anger.

Her eyes widen, recognizing our reactions and zeroing in on me.

"Oh no." She sets down her fork. "I didn't mean...Shit. I can't do this. Me being here...It's too much."

"It's not."

It is.

She's under my skin, in my head, and infecting my bloodstream. She's everywhere, all around me, yet completely out of reach. The agony is too much.

But it's my pain to bear.

"You're safe here." I keep my face relaxed, my voice soft. "You're safe with me. In your heart, I know you know that. Even when your anger makes you forget."

"Safe?" Leo huffs. "You hurt her—"

"Leo." She touches his arm without breaking eye contact with me. "Let him finish."

Our gazes clash like midnight thunder, and fuck me straight to hell. I *crave* her.

I hunger for every beat, drip, and whisper of her pure, unfiltered goddess essence. I want to devour her soul with my kisses until she remembers the depth of my love and adoration. She's captivating and introspective, a treasure far beyond what any man could ever deserve.

And so fucking strong.

She's been abducted, drugged, raped, starved, frozen, drowned, cheated on, and attacked by wild animals. She lost her baby, watched her friend commit suicide, and survived a plane crash. And here she sits, with her chin held high, radiating a raw, sensual, feminine power that no amount of fear or trauma can diminish.

With each passing day, she'll heal a little more and break another shackle. But she doesn't have to do it alone.

"Everything I have is yours." I search her face. "My energy, my presence, my heart—all of it exists for you, to support you and keep you safe."

"She has what she needs." Kody's neck turns red. "She has us."

The impulse to lash out at him slams my teeth together.

She doesn't deserve my rage. She deserves the things that are the hardest to give.

Like my humility.

That's what I owe her.

Even though it hurts, even though it feels like I'm swallowing glass.

"She needs *all* of us." The words come out hoarse, strained, like they're being dragged out of me against my will.

My pride takes a hit, a sharp sting that burns in my gut.

I hate admitting it, hate the vulnerability it exposes. But I can't deny it. She does need all of us. And despite the resentment, there's a stronger force at play. My love for her, my commitment to see her through this, no matter the cost.

As her stunned silence pressurizes the air, I stare into her eyes, letting her see the depth of my devotion. "I'm here in whatever capacity you require. Whatever you need. Name it, and it's yours."

She sits back, lips parted. Then she blinks.

"Okay. I need you to accept them." She tilts her head at Leo and Kody. "*Really* accept them."

Leo starts to interrupt, and she holds up a finger, stopping him.

I frown, my resistance flaring.

"Family isn't about control or cruelty." She softens her tone. "It's not about tearing each other down or causing pain. Family is about love and support. It's about being there for each other, no matter what. It's about caring for one another, lifting each other up, and creating a safe space where everyone can grow and thrive."

Her words hit me hard, and I find myself torn. She's asking me to love the men in her bed.

I don't know how to love anyone. Except her.

"They need a healthy family dynamic, and so do you." She sits taller. "One that's filled with kindness, respect, and understanding. You should be able to rely on each other, trust that you have each other's best interests at heart. When someone falls, the others are there to pick them up. When someone succeeds, the others celebrate with them. It's about being a team, working together through thick and thin."

"I'm not the right person for that. My family was—"

"*They* are your family." She points at their glaring faces. "Embrace them. Build something better together. It won't be easy. It'll take time and patience, but dammit, Monty, you built a fucking global enterprise from the ground up. I *know* you can create a home where everyone feels valued and loved. I want that for you. For all three of you."

"What about you?"

"Did you move my things from your bedroom? Your closet? Your bathroom?"

I press my lips together and blow out through my nose.

"Monty." She sighs. "Let me go."

"Can't do that, Frankie."

"You returned my phone." She gestures at the device on the table. "Thank you for that. Now I need you to sell my wedding rings."

"What?" My fists clench. "Fuck no."

"I want a divorce."

"Never." The objection rips from me like flayed skin, making me roar in pain.

"You must." Her shoulders slump. "It's over."

"No. Anything but that." My ears ring. My lungs collapse. I bend forward, my body folding in on itself. "Anything else. Anything."

"Okay, okay." Her hands hover around me, reaching but not touching. "Shhh. It's okay."

Touch me. Please, put me out of my misery and fucking touch me.

"Will you guys give us a minute?" she asks quietly.

"Absolutely not." Leo scowls.

"Then behave." A beat of silence passes between them before she scoots her chair closer to me. "Monty. Look at me." She tentatively places a hand beneath my chin, lifting it. "Please."

The touch is light, but it sizzles through my nerve endings and electrocutes my blood like a goddamn thunderbolt.

I let the exquisite warmth of her fingers guide my face upward. Then I fall. I fall right into her gaze, knowing she sees the devastation in mine.

"I can't." I clasp her wrist, lowering her hand from my jaw to my chest. "I won't survive it."

A low, comforting hum slips past her lips, a sound of shared solace.

"What happened last night?" She presses closer, giving me her full attention. "Did you sleep?"

"I took the yacht out."

"You got drunk." Her nostrils pulse as if scenting it on me. "And broke a wall."

"Not in that order."

"Okay." She presses her palm against my chest, directly over my heart. "You said anything else. Anything but a divorce."

"Anything."

"Get help."

"Help?" My hand twitches around hers.

"Therapy. Talk to someone. You need counseling. We all do."

"Fine."

"No, not fine. You have to want this, to *want* to get better. That means sharing your feelings and opening up."

"I'll try." I release a shaky breath. "For you, I'll try."

"Starting immediately. Like this week."

"All right."

"Thank you." She inhales sharply. "One more thing."

"I'm listening."

Her nails dig into my shirt, fisting the starched fabric. "Don't fucking hurt me again."

"I won't. I promise."

"I don't believe you."

"I'll prove you wrong."

"I hope you do." She untangles our hands and leans back, regarding me.

Gratitude. Relief. Hope. It's all there in her striking eyes, the change of her breath, the drop of her shoulders, and the chambers of her heart inviting me in.

Fucking finally.

Let this be a lesson to you, little girl. Never invite a monster into your heart. Because it renders you powerless.

monty

FOURTEEN

The next three days bleed into a grind of finalizing details and rehearsing our story until it's woven tight. Every word we practice is a carefully placed brick in the wall we're building to protect Frankie.

Meetings with detectives come first. They interrogate us separately, poke around for cracks in our wall, and leave with the promise to find the two mothers who lost their sons.

They won't.

Then the press arrives, vultures circling for scraps, starving for a juicy story, demanding their pound of flesh.

They're the hardest to convince.

To satisfy them, we agree to separate interviews and spend two days moving from one engagement to the next within the estate.

We only need to give them enough to answer their questions. If there's nothing scandalous to report on, they'll pack up and go away.

After my final interview, I wander the main house, searching for my wife.

My mind races, constantly scanning for potential threats,

calculating risks, and mapping out contingency plans if our story doesn't stick.

The most pressing topic in every interview has been the location of the cabin. If I only knew. It's the catalyst that can set the whole thing on fire.

Denver never told them its location, and the storm disoriented Leo during the flight, leaving him unsure of the exact direction they came from. Frankie's convinced it lies in the hills of the Brooks Range, but we have no way to confirm this without sending a massive search party. Which could draw unwanted attention.

The Turbo Beaver's Hobbs meter indicates it was within a four-hour flight from Whittier, which matches Leo's recollection.

I sigh, feeling the prick of every stake. The flight data recorder was destroyed in the crash, and without GPS or navigation systems, there's no way to track the flight path.

If we can't find it, neither can the media. The last thing we need is an ambitious journalist discovering Denver's body or any of the others left behind.

But if we can't find it, we may never find my son.

The gravity of it all presses down on me. Sleep is a distant memory, replaced by caffeine and adrenaline. My body moves on autopilot, driven by the singular goal of getting my wife back.

Her eyes, shadowed with fear and determination, haunt my thoughts. I can't let her down. I won't let her fall. We've repeated our lines, refined our alibis, covered every angle, and tied every loose end.

So far, none of us has slipped up.

Turning the corner, I find Frankie in the kitchen.

Alone.

She stands at the sink with her back to me, the sound of running water masking my approach.

My heart hammers, and my breath quickens.

She's never without Leo and Kody. They must be stuck in their interviews.

The opportunity is too perfect, my longing to be close to

her too overwhelming.

I pause, hanging back for a minute, just watching her.

Her naturally red hair glows in the sunset light from the window, cascading to her waist like a fiery waterfall. She shifts her weight from foot to foot, swaying those slender hips. I know every curve and dip by memory. I could draw her shape with my eyes closed. She's so soft. So feminine and dainty. But her petite frame belies the strength she possesses.

She's always been meticulous about her health, eating right, running, and taking care of herself. The nurse in her demands a healthy lifestyle, and it shows in the way she moves, every gesture filled with unconscious sensuality and allure.

She leaves me breathless.

I miss her so much it hurts. I miss holding her in my arms, feeling the warmth of her body, spreading her out beneath me, and fucking her for hours every night.

Her pure, compassionate heart is almost as addictive as her filthy, sexual mind.

The sight of her standing in my kitchen transports me back to when she lived here happily, before the abduction, when everything was right in our world. It feels natural to stroll up to her, wrap my arms around her, and rest my chin on her shoulder.

I do it without thinking, drawn in by the rightness of it, drugged by the scent of her cherry perfume.

The instant my hands slide around her waist, I'm a slave to the familiar feel of her. My skin heats. My mouth dries, and my cock stiffens against my zipper.

She freezes. Chokes on a cry.

My stomach clenches, and I drop my hands. Too late.

She whirls, slashing out a knife from the butcher block. The blade catches my throat, the blinding pain making me gasp.

Fuck! How did she grab a weapon so fast?

"Frankie." I press my hand to the wound, unable to stop the flow of warm blood through my fingers. "I'm sorry. I didn't think."

Her eyes widen in horror. Her face pales. Her hand trembles, and the knife clatters to the floor.

She stumbles away, her breath coming in ragged bursts. Her pupils dilate, and her eyes dart around the room as if trapped somewhere else.

Caged in a nightmare.

"Frankie, it's okay." I take a step toward her, reaching. "It's not your fault."

She flinches violently, her whole body recoiling as if I'm the threat, cutting me deeper than any knife.

"No, no, no, no." She blinks rapidly, tears spilling from her eyes and breaking my heart.

"Hey, hey, shhh." I can't touch her. She despises me, and I'm covered in blood. I don't know what to do.

Her hands cover her head, fingers tangling in her hair as she rocks back and forth.

"Stop! Stop! Let me go!" Her eyes are wild, lost in a memory I can't see.

Is it the trauma of her abduction? Or the sexual assault? Her journal described everything in detail. Denver took her from behind when he kidnapped her and later when he forced himself on her.

A shudder tears through me, and my thoughts scatter, unable to grasp the magnitude of what I've done.

The helplessness, the fear—I brought it all crashing back, hitting her like a tidal wave and pulling her under.

"Breathe, baby." I flutter my hands around her, not touching, utterly useless. "Listen to my voice. You're in Sitka. You're home. Safe. No one can hurt you here."

She lowers to the floor and curls into a ball, her quick, shallow gasps flooding me with panic.

Fuck, fuck, fuck!

I remove my phone, my fingers flying over the screen, smearing blood with the urgency of my message.

Leo, Kody: Come to the kitchen now. Be calm. She's scared. PTSD?

I hit send and pocket the device, unsure if they know how to open a text. They've only had their phones for three days.

Sinking to my knees beside her, I reach out a hand, then pull it back, afraid to touch her. I'll only make it worse. But my mind screams at me to do something, anything, to bring her back from the edge.

Her chest heaves as she struggles to breathe, each inhale a desperate gulp for air. Her skin takes on a clammy sheen, beading with sweat, and she shakes uncontrollably in the grip of a full-blown panic attack.

"Frankie, please," I whisper, heart pounding. "You're safe."

She can't hear me. She's too far gone, lost in the depths of hell. The sight of her like this, so vulnerable and broken, it shatters me. It makes me realize just how deep her wounds truly go.

"Frankie," I say again, hoping somehow my voice can reach her, bring her back to me. "I'm here. You're not alone. You're safe."

She doesn't respond, her eyes wide and unfocused, still caught in the throes of panic. Her breaths come in rapid, shallow gasps, and she clutches her head, rocking in the fetal position.

I can't fucking bear it.

Footfalls approach from the hallway, heavy and determined. I release a sigh of relief.

Leo bursts into the kitchen, his eyes instantly locking onto her trembling form on the floor. His expression hardens, and he rushes to her side, kneeling beside me.

"What happened?" He glances at my bleeding neck, reaching for her.

"Wait. Go slow." I stop him with a hand on his chest. "I triggered something, a memory, and she pulled a knife on me. How often does this happen?"

"Never." He looks shocked, his brows knitting. "Kody does this sometimes, but not her."

"How long does it last?" I whisper. "With Kody?"

"Sometimes minutes, sometimes hours, depending on the

severity and trigger." He bends over her, his movements slow and deliberate. "Frankie, it's me. I got you, love. You're safe."

He leans in close to lift her.

"Don't touch me! Don't touch me!" She screams over and over, sobbing and scrambling away until her back hits the pantry door. "Please, don't hurt me again."

He looks stricken, sitting back on his heels and grabbing his head. "What the fuck? What the fuck?"

"Hey." I snap my fingers in his face, halting his mini-freak-out. "How do you pull Kody out of it?"

"We don't. I mean, she did once. But I don't know how."

Kody rushes in, his posture taut like a bowstring drawn to its limit. His black eyes sweep over her, and he steps closer, his presence an oppressive shadow that consumes the light.

He crouches beside her, his expression blank as he gently cups the back of her head.

"Frankie, it's me, Kody." His voice, though gruff, holds a note of desperation. "Snap out of it."

Her eyes remain wide, unseeing, as she coughs and wheezes, hyperventilating.

He tries everything—commands, firm touches, stern reminders of who she is—but nothing breaks through.

Leo paces back and forth, unable to stand still. His fists clench at his sides, every exhale a snarl of distrust aimed at me.

"Frankie, look at me." Kody crowds her without making physical contact. "He's dead. Gone. He can't hurt you anymore. Look at me, goddammit. See *me*."

"No needles. No needles. Please, no more needles." Her panic escalates. Her feet kick out, and she fights her way across the floor, putting distance between her and us.

I watch helplessly, my own anxiety rising with her terror. Measuring my breaths, I try to calm my growing anger—at myself, at the situation, at the lack of control.

"What the hell did you do to her?" Leo strides over, his temper unraveling. "What triggered this?"

Fuck, this isn't helping. *They* aren't helping. But I'm desperate, so I give him the truth.

"She was at the sink. I didn't announce myself. I came up

behind her and put my hands on her hips. I thought…" I shake my head. "No, I wasn't thinking. My touch, my presence, something triggered her. She grabbed a knife and…"

I gesture at the cut on my neck.

Too bad my ferocious girl didn't have a knife the night Denver took her.

Leo's eyes narrow, his expression dark. "You fucking sneaked up on her?"

"I didn't know it was a trigger." I narrow my eyes right back. "That would've been an important fucking thing to tell me, don't you think?"

"We didn't know." Kody hovers over her, his frustration boiling over into barely concealed rage.

Before any of us can say more, footsteps echo down the hall.

Reporters.

Some of them are still on the island, and if they walk in on this…

The knife on the floor. The blood leaking from my throat. Frankie curled up like she was attacked.

"Fuck!" I tear off my shirt, sending the buttons flying, and use it to sop up the red mess coating my hands and chest.

"I'll deal with them." Leo storms off, leaving me and Kody with Frankie.

I draw in a steeling breath and move closer, lowering beside her. Kody glares but doesn't move to stop me. My hand trembles as I reach out, brushing her hair away from her face.

She doesn't react, doesn't seem to hear or see anything around her. Her mind is somewhere else, somewhere horrific and unfathomable.

I close my eyes, searching for something, anything, that might help her escape.

Then it comes to me. A song. Our song. The one we danced to at our wedding. I start humming softly, the familiar tune shaky at first but gaining strength with each note.

"Frankie, it's me," I whisper between the verses. "It's Monty. I'm here. Come back to me."

I keep humming, the melody wrapping around us.

Memories flood back—our wedding day, her radiant smile, the way we swayed together under the twinkling lights. My throat tightens, breaking the rhythm. But I push through, focusing on the music.

Slowly, ever so slowly, I notice a change. Her breathing, rapid and shallow, begins to steady. Her eyes, wild and unfocused, start to clear.

She blinks, her gaze darting around before landing on me. Recognition pulses in her eyes, and a small, fragile connection forms.

My shoulders droop as a thousand-pound mistake lifts from them.

"Monty?" Her voice is brittle, faint, but it's there.

"I'm here. I'm right here, baby." I keep humming, holding her gaze, willing her to trust me.

Gradually, the tension in her body melts away. She uncurls from her fetal position, extending a trembling hand to grasp mine. I squeeze it gently, offering her my strength, my love.

"You're okay." I brush a tear from her cheek, the echoes of our song lingering in the air. "You're safe."

She nods, a tiny, shaky movement, but it's enough. The panic recedes, leaving us both drained but connected.

I haven't forgotten Kody, his stormy presence looming behind me, his eyes boring into my back. Slowly, I turn to face him, still holding her soft hand.

Surprise and wariness war in his expression, his usual confidence shaken.

"Didn't know you could sing..." He stares down at her, then back at me, cruelty frosting his eyes. "Like a goat."

"Kody," she whispers, her breathing now even as her body sags over my lap.

Within seconds, she's asleep.

His bearing softens into something more complicated—reluctant gratitude, residual distrust, and relief.

"Guess it worked," he mutters, his tone grudging as he runs a hand through his hair. "Thank you."

His gratitude is stiff, strangled. I can tell it cost him.

I incline my head, acknowledging the truce, however temporary it may be.

Leo returns, sprinting into the kitchen, out of breath and sweating.

"Reporters are taken care of. Everyone's gone except the security team." He glances between us, assessing the situation quickly. "Is she…?"

"Better." I keep my voice low. "For now."

First thing tomorrow, I'm lining up a therapist, psychiatrist, whatever she needs.

He nods, his gaze sharpening where her head rests on my thigh. If he picks a fight with me about this and disturbs her sleep, I'll know exactly where his priorities lie.

His eyes shift to Kody, and in one look, they seem to hold an entire conversation. It's not the first time I've seen them do that.

"He did good," Kody finally says, the words surprising in their sincerity. "He calmed her down, brought her back to us."

Leo turns to me, letting his unnerving, dual-colored stare linger several beats too long. "We need to keep her stable."

Silence descends in a twilight of acceptance.

We may not trust each other, but we all want the same thing.

And right now, she's stable with *me.*

kodiak

FIFTEEN

The adrenaline wears off, but the lump in my throat remains. Even though this crisis has passed, it's only the beginning of a long road to recovery.

For all of us.

It's not just Frankie's nightmares that twist me into knots of protective fury. It's Monty's hands on her. It's his fingers stroking her hair.

It's him.

I can't believe she passed out with her head on his lap. Does that mean she trusts him?

No fucking way. She was panic-stricken and not in her right mind before exhaustion took her.

Every fiber of my being screams to rip her away, to shield her from the man who's caused her so much pain. But a territorial pissing match isn't what she needs right now.

Leo and I stand at the kitchen counter, uncertain how to proceed. We need her off the floor and settled somewhere comfortable, but the state of her fragile mind is worrisome. How will she react when she wakes?

Monty looks up at me, his expression creased with guilt

and concern. It infuriates me that he has the power to affect her like this, to send her so deeply into a panic attack with a touch of his hands.

Hands that are still touching her.

I swallow my anger, knowing we must work together for her sake.

Teamwork. Fucking yay.

"We need to move her." The pulse in Leo's neck stands out, a rapid beat of turmoil. "She can't stay on the floor."

With a tight jaw, Monty nods.

"Let's get her to the couch." Leo bends down to gather her in his arms.

"I'll carry her." Monty shifts, careful not to disturb her.

I want to protest his involvement, to intervene, but I know it would only cause more chaos. For now, I have to let him lead, no matter how much it burns.

He slides his arms beneath her, lifting her with a tenderness that momentarily softens my anger.

We maneuver as a unit, a fragile alliance forged by necessity. Monty escorts us out, holding my entire world against his bare chest.

Leo and I follow, our eyes never leaving her. I watch Monty's every move, ready to break his teeth if he causes her more distress.

The maze of hallways, excessive living spaces, and outdoor trails took a couple of days to memorize, but I know the layout of the property now. The next turn leads to the front entrance and...

A hint of cigarette smoke. The creak of wood flooring. Footsteps so light they aren't meant to be heard.

I grab Monty's elbow, silently halting him. His eyes dart to mine, and I hold a finger to my lips.

Leo, already sensing my alarm, stalks ahead and creeps around the corner.

The instant his hands relax, I do, too.

"What do you want?" he asks whomever lurks out of view.

"I'm looking for Mr. Novak."

"You have an update, Carl?" Monty remains beside me, not

showing himself.

Given the stab wound on his neck, it's a smart move.

"Yes." Carl clears his throat. "All media personnel and visitors have been escorted off the premises, and the island is now secure. We have completed a thorough sweep of the area and will maintain a vigilant presence throughout the evening. You can rest assured that there will be no further disturbances tonight."

Frankie stirs in Monty's arms, a soft whimper escaping her lips.

My protective instincts flare immediately, and I place a hand on her thigh.

"Thank you." Monty dismisses the guard, tucking her closer.

As the sound of the front door shuts behind the guard, she looks around, disoriented and confused.

The clarity in her eyes isn't there yet. She's still fuzzy, trying to piece together where she is. I've been in her position. It's a terrible feeling.

"What happened?" She doesn't notice Monty's bleeding wound, her focus too scattered to catch details.

My heart aches for her, and I know we need to be gentle.

"You had a panic attack. But you're safe now. We're all here." I meet Monty's eyes and shape my lips around a command. *Couch.*

She blinks, trying to absorb the information. Her lips tighten, and her hands shake as she grips his shoulders. The fear hasn't fully dissipated.

When we reach the living room and she sees the couch, her body tenses.

"No…not the couch." A sharp, panicked cry cleaves from her chest. "Not the couch."

The fucking couch in Denver's video. It needs to be set on fire.

"Okay, okay." Monty turns away and steps in front of me to catch my attention. "It's dark outside."

He thrusts his chin at the nearby window.

Carrying her to the guest house after nightfall could trigger another panic attack, as it might remind her of the night she was abducted.

I exchange a quick glance with Leo. The distrust we feel for Monty is mutual, but right now, she needs safety and rest.

"Plenty of beds upstairs." Leo veers toward the staircase, motioning for us to follow.

As we ascend to the second floor, I stick to Monty's side to stay in her line of sight.

"I don't remember...I don't remember anything." Her eyes dart around, trying to anchor herself to the present.

"It's okay." I lean in, softening my tone despite the frustration boiling underneath. "You don't need to remember right now. Just focus on me."

"Where are we?"

"You're home." Monty adjusts his hold on her and follows Leo into the first room. "You're in the guest bedroom." He sets her on the bed and brushes the hair from her face, taking too many goddamn liberties with his hands. "You're safe. Just try to relax."

I recognize the effort it takes for her to calm down, her breathing still uneven. It tears at me, especially since he's in the damn way, hovering over her.

His presence is a necessary evil since I can't kick him out of his own house.

"We're here for you, Frankie." I push down the resentment, keeping my voice soft. "Just take it easy. We've got you."

Her gaze finally meets mine, and I see the gentle easing of recognition and relief. It's a small comfort, but I'll take it. We've been through hell and back, and we'll keep fighting, no matter what it takes.

Slowly, she relaxes as she takes in her surroundings. But when her eyes drift back to Monty, she gasps. "Monty! You're hurt!"

"It's nothing." The pain he's ignored now pulses with renewed intensity, trickling fresh blood and twitching his eyes.

"That's *not* nothing." She reaches for him, gaining strength. "It's a deep cut. What happened?"

He grimaces and looks to us for help.

We can't lie to her. At the same time, we want to protect her from the truth.

"That's a stab wound." She climbs to her knees and positions him to sit beside her as she examines the injury. "Who did this?"

Her glare goes straight to Leo.

He coughs and stares at his boots.

I empty my expression.

She shoves back her shoulders. "I swear on the fires in hell, if you don't tell me what happened, I'll make sure you end up on life support, begging for every breath while I control the plug."

"She's back." Leo's lips twitch.

I grunt, hiding my amusement.

Goddamn, I love her viciousness.

"Woman, listen..." Stepping forward, I try to formulate the best way to tell her.

But Monty saves me from the task. "I sent you into a panic attack. It might've been a PTSD episode."

"I don't have PTSD."

"We don't know that." Pressing his palm against the cut on his neck, he walks her through what happened in the kitchen.

When he finishes, she sits back on her heels, looking stunned, embarrassed, and ashamed.

"I'm so sorry." She cups a hand over her mouth and slowly shakes her head. "I don't remember. I don't know why I would've—"

"Shhh." Monty tugs her arm down, uncovering her face. "It's not your fault. I triggered it. I shouldn't have crept up on you. Blame me."

"No. I won't blame you." Shadows of sorrow cloud her eyes as she peers closer at the wound. "You need stitches."

He nods, knowing better than to argue with her in this state. "All right, but no hospital. We can take care of it here. There's a first aid kit—"

"I know where it is." Leo fixes me with a look, a wordless

order to watch her, before leaving the room.

He's familiarized himself with every inch of this estate, every item in every cabinet, including the attic space.

"I don't remember any of it." She stares at her hands on her lap, her eyes hazy and unfocused. "It's a blur except for this feeling of…of being trapped."

"Hey." Monty sets a knuckle beneath her chin, lifting her face. "We'll figure it out. I'll call some psychiatrists in the morning and find someone who can make house calls to the island. We'll get you the help you need."

"I want Doyle." She moves his hand. "No one else."

"Who's Doyle?" My brows knit.

"The psychiatrist she saw when her mom passed." A muscle ticks in his jaw. "I don't like him."

"You don't like him because he's attractive." Her eyes flash with annoyance.

"Now I don't like him." I frown.

"Great," she mutters.

"I don't like him because I don't *trust* him." Monty straightens. "He's too friendly with you, too eager to make you dependent on him."

"God forbid I have a friend." She throws her hands in the air. "You don't trust anyone. Doyle knows my history. He understands me. And he doesn't keep my unfinished drinks on his nightstand for nine months."

He flinches but quickly recovers. "This isn't about me. It's about finding someone who can genuinely help you, not someone who wants to fuck you."

"What?" She clambers from the bed, eyes on fire. "You think everyone with a dick wants to fuck me."

"They do."

"Are you hearing this?" She turns her anger on me.

If this Doyle guy wants to fuck her, I'm taking Monty's side. But for now, I withhold my judgment and say nothing.

That only incenses her more, and she whirls back on Monty. "You're so damn controlling. I need someone who can actually connect with me, not dictate what's best for me."

"I'm trying to protect you, darling."

"I'm not your darling."

"I want what's best for you." He grinds his teeth. "Even if you can't see it right now."

"And what do you think is best for me?" She pins him with the force of her glare. "You?"

He glares right back.

The room vibrates with the intensity of their argument, both of them too stubborn to back down.

Time to defuse the situation.

"You, back in bed." I grip her arm, steering her there. "And you." I point at Monty. "Shut the fuck up."

He growls.

"Focus on getting through tonight." I stand over him, folding my arms. "The rest will wait until morning."

Leo returns with the first aid kit, instantly sensing the tense atmosphere.

"What's going on?" He hands the kit to her.

"Nothing." Her shoulders slump, her anger giving way to exhaustion. "Just Monty being...*Monty*."

Monty releases a slow breath and pushes off the bed. "I'll do this myself." Grabbing the medical kit from her, he charges to the door.

"Wait." She sits up, her movements shaky but resolute. "Stop. Please. I'm sorry."

He reaches the threshold, not stopping.

"Always walking away from me," she whispers under her breath.

At that, he pauses.

Turning back to her, he looks like he's about to explode. "Frankie, I'm not—"

"Don't be so dramatic." She pats the mattress beside her. "Sit."

Long seconds pass before he returns and sits beside her. "No stitches. Use the butterfly closures."

"I disagree, but whatever." Bracing a hand on his shirtless chest, she leans in with an intimacy that makes my skin crawl.

Her attention on his wound is all business, but her face

drifts too close to his. I don't like the way his lips part or how intensely he studies her.

I don't like any of this.

Leo watches them with mayhem in his eyes, restlessly chewing on his thumbnail.

I know he's waffling on whether to stay out of it or throw Monty through the wall. I'm leaning toward the latter, even if I can kind of understand Monty's side of the argument.

I'm out of my element here. Emotions like this, the rawness of the fight and the need for comfort, are foreign to me. I only know abuse, fear, and manipulation. There was nothing normal or sane about my upbringing.

The only healthy relationship Leo and I have experienced is with her, and we'll kill anyone who threatens it.

Sensing our unease, she looks up and quickly lifts her hand from his chest. "Everything is fine. Monty and I just have different ways of seeing things."

"He upset you." I crack my knuckles.

"Okay, but I upset him, too. Our disagreements don't involve kin punishment or any kind of violence." She makes a face. "The hole in his neck notwithstanding."

"Yeah, I get that." I feel a pang of something I can't quite identify.

Respect, maybe. They butted heads without drawing blood.

"Emotions are all over place." Her hands are steady as she opens the kit and gathers the supplies. "We've been dealing with detectives and reporters for three days. I haven't really faced what happened over the past nine months, and I guess..." She shrugs. "I freaked out."

"You had a panic attack," Monty says quietly yet firmly.

"Hold still. This will sting." She applies the antiseptic.

He lets out a sharp hiss.

"Butterfly bandages won't work on this." She cleans the cut with gentle precision, her laser-sharp focus telling me she compartmentalized her own pain to deal with Monty's. "It's still bleeding. The edges are jagged, and it's so deep I can see down to your shriveled-up heart."

"Then you can see the scars you left there."

"Not through all the ice around it."

His face hardens. "Use the bandages or fuck off."

"Watch the way you talk to her." Leo stalks forward.

"No." She points at him. "Stay back. We're just bickering."

"You don't need this, love." Leo takes another step. "You took a huge emotional hit downstairs. You can barely sit up. You're white as a ghost, and he's fighting with you."

"We're *arguing*." She sighs.

"Same thing."

"No, it's not."

Monty glances at Leo. "The woman loves to argue."

"I do not."

"See?"

"Arguing is a productive form of communication." She takes a breath. "As long as there's respect on both sides, it helps everyone express their differing perspectives and clear up misunderstandings." She meets Monty's eyes. "And maybe find one thing we agree on."

"Was any of that directed at us?" Leo asks me.

"No." I cross my arms. "That was her passive-aggressive way to keep arguing with him."

She flips us off.

Monty chuckles.

"Laugh it up, jackass." She tosses aside the butterfly bandages and snatches the medical kit. "You're getting stitches."

The tension in my chest constricts as I watch the energy slowly drain from Frankie.

She's been through too much today, yet here she is, stitching the stab wound in Monty's neck.

Her fingers move with practiced ease, guiding the needle with swift, sure motions. She bends in close, her breathing stable, her focus unshakable. Pulling the wound's edges together, she places each stitch with a gentle touch.

"I was only a few millimeters off from nicking your carotid artery." A shiver runs through her, leaving goosebumps on her arms.

"But you didn't." Monty angles his head, making the wound more accessible to her. "It's like some part of you didn't want to kill me."

"Monty..." She lines up the next stitch. "No part of me wants to kill you."

"The letter you wrote to me disagrees." Eyes closed, jaw clenched in silent endurance, he remains still under her careful ministrations.

An impressive effort, given his apparent aversion to

needles.

"I wrote that letter the night Denver...the night he raped Wolf." Her fingers brush over the edges of his bruised face, lingering on the features that look so much like Wolf, as though she's imagining him instead of Monty.

"I know." Monty's voice cracks. "I'm sorry."

She blinks, sucks in a shaky breath, and adds another suture.

Despite the conversation and circumstances, there's undeniable beauty in her dedication. It's in the way her brow furrows in concentration and the murmur of reassurances she offers Monty as she works.

Flexing my hand, I stare at the scar that runs through it. She didn't trust me the night Denver stabbed me. She didn't trust any of us. Rightfully so. Still, she stitched my wound with a kindness I didn't deserve.

She's so strong, so capable, so damn caring, even after everything. It's something I've always admired about her, even if it makes me insanely protective.

There's a raw, unspoken bond between healers and protectors.

She's a hellion on the outside, full of fire and fight. But beneath the ferocity, she's a tender-hearted soul, drenched in empathy, her heart forever open, giving away her healing power to anyone in need. She bleeds energy, tangled in the pain and need of others until she's hollowed out.

If she's not careful, she'll lose her life force in that endless give.

That's why she needs protectors, warriors of her heart, standing guard and warding off the takers who try to steal her. She needs us to be her sanctuary, to give her a place to recharge and breathe life back into her weary soul.

Leo and I stand watch, connected in so many ways, but especially in this. In our admiration and love for her. And in our undying need to keep her safe.

She finishes the final stitch and ties it off with a knot. Leaning back, she exhales slowly and rests her fingers against Monty's throat as if to reassure herself that he's okay.

He's fine, woman. You can stop touching him.

"Thank you." He opens his eyes, staring up at her with unsettling adoration.

"Just...be more careful next time." Her bottom lip trembles, and she looks away, lowering her hand. "No more sneaking up on crazy people."

"You're not crazy."

"Aren't I?" She heaves a sigh. "Monty, I need to be honest with you."

He gives her a single nod, his eyes sharp.

"If I find out you aren't a danger to us," she says, "I'll feel really fucking shitty about the way things turned out." She swallows. "I haven't been kind. I've been too angry for too long, and you don't deserve that."

"Frankie..." He holds up a hand.

"Let me finish. If straying from our vows is your greatest sin, I'm a sinner, too." She gestures at Leo and me, producing a snarl in my throat. "But...*but*...if you end up hurting us, then I'm a colossal, certified idiot for moving into your house and depending on you to help them. Do you see the position I'm in? You understand what I'm saying?"

Working his jaw, he inclines his head.

"Why are we here?" She glances around as if noticing her surroundings for the first time. "In this room?"

"We thought..." I rub the back of my neck. "If you went outside in the dark so soon after your panic attack, it might make it worse."

"I see," she whispers. "The thing is...I don't have triggers. I mean, I didn't. I wish I could remember what happened."

The few times I had a similar episode, I was sleeping, stuck in a nightmare, and reliving traumatic events. I always remembered the details.

I wish I didn't.

"It's okay." I crouch before her and take her hand. "Your mind is protecting you."

"Why? Nothing has happened to me that hasn't happened to you."

"That's not true. When you came to Hoss, you were trapped with four men twice your size, and we didn't exactly roll out the welcome mat. We were cruel to you. Kept you at a distance. We all went through hell, but I always had my brothers. Those first few months, you were completely alone."

Her lips purse in a pensive frown. "Denver trapped me against his kitchen counter. I'm talking about the day he held a hypodermic needle to my neck, and Wolf..." Her hand twitches in the cradle of mine. "Wolf was there."

"I remember." I lift her fingers to my mouth, warming them with my breath.

"Maybe that's why..." She nibbles on her cheek. "Maybe that's what triggered me."

I don't have to wonder if she wrote about that day in her journal. One look at Monty confirms it. He stares at the floor, his eyes unblinking, scourged with the knowledge of what happened.

"I'm tired," she admits, her voice softening. "Can I just rest for a while? By myself?"

"Of course." Monty pushes to his feet, giving her space. "We'll be within earshot if you need anything."

Then, because she's Frankie, she looks him dead in the eye and asks, "Are you the threat in Denver's riddle?"

He holds her gaze, his fingers splaying open and his hands falling limply to his sides. "I don't know."

"How do you not know? You're either going to hurt me, or you're not."

"I already hurt you. Maybe he believed I would hurt you again." He rubs his temple. "That's not my intention."

"Are you hiding secrets from me?"

"I love you. More than I've ever loved anyone or anything. But you already know that."

"That's not an answer. Are you hiding anything from me?"

"Not on purpose. I don't share every thought in my head. But if you ask, I'll give it to you. I'll give you anything you want."

"I want to trust you."

"Tell me how to earn it." He slides his hands into his

pockets.

"I don't know if you can." She lifts a shoulder.

"Do you need anything?" Leo prowls forward, ending the conversation. "Water? Something to eat?"

"I want to drink tea with no pants on."

"Good answer." I adjust the pillows behind her, ensuring she's comfortable.

Leo removes her sneakers and socks and reaches for the button on her jeans.

When he glances over his shoulder at Monty, she doesn't wait for their impending argument. She unzips and shimmies the denim down her hips.

"Here. Let me." Leo adjusts his body to block Monty's view as he eases the jeans down her legs.

A tightness forms around Monty's mouth, carving deep lines of jealousy and discontent.

I brace to intervene as Leo pulls the blanket to her chin and kisses her lips.

Monty turns away, hands fisted on his hips.

Leo steps back, giving me room to lean in. My forehead rests against hers in a silent connection. I taste her mouth, caress the graceful shape of her face, and reluctantly pull back.

As we leave the room, I take one last look at her, searching for an excuse to stay.

"I'll be fine." She waves her hand. "Go. Keep the peace."

"What peace?"

"Touché."

Downstairs, Leo heads to the kitchen to make tea. I lean against the wall in the living room and scowl at the couch.

"It'll be gone tomorrow." Monty nods at the thing and takes the chair across from it, the exhaustion finally catching up with him.

"She's tougher than she looks."

"You don't have to tell *me* that."

My lip curls. "Don't touch her again."

"I'll give you the same warning."

"My touch doesn't trigger her."

A vein visibly throbs in his neck, right beside the stitches.

Leo returns with a mug of tea and jabs a finger at us. "No fighting."

That's rich, coming from him.

I grunt.

Monty closes his eyes.

While Leo delivers the tea to Frankie, we sit in silence, lost in our thoughts. The only sound is the ticking clock on the mantle, marking the passage of time.

After what feels like hours, Leo joins us, sprawling on the hated couch. "How do we help her?"

"She has a psychiatrist." I take in Monty's sudden rigidness. "Who is he?"

"Dr. Doyle Whitaker." Monty rises from the chair, instantly agitated.

"What's his deal?"

"He has some kind of hold over her." He paces the room, his erratic movements and tight circles reminding me of Leo.

With all that anger buzzing under the surface, waiting for an outlet, pacing must be a coping mechanism for him, too.

"Look, I get it." He swipes a hand down his face. "Doyle has all the credentials. Prestigious medical school, over a decade of experience, and a reputation for helping patients through tough times. But he's too smooth for a doctor, too magnetic with that damn smile. It makes it easy for him to win people over, especially Frankie."

"Is that how *you* won her over?"

He pauses, meets my eyes. "Yes."

I'll give him this. He doesn't shy away from hard questions. His honesty makes me want to side with him.

Good thing I don't.

"There's something about him." He strides to the window, staring out at the dusky landscape. "He's the type of asshole who crosses ethical lines and manipulates his position for his own gain. He helped her through her mom's death, and because of that, she values him like a friend."

"Do you have proof of him manipulating her?" Leo asks.

"No. Their interactions are always behind closed doors, as

expected, given the privacy laws. But I can't shake the feeling that he's exploiting her when she's vulnerable. He's not in this for her. He's in it for himself."

Monty is so twisted up with jealousy and possessiveness that it may be clouding the truth. Not that I judge him for it. Leo and I suffer from the same affliction.

Maybe Frankie's irresistible pull affects all men. Or maybe it's a Strakh thing. Are the men in my family inclined to latch onto a woman with their fangs and claws and never let go?

Despite everything, Monty has known her the longest. If he thinks Doyle is a threat, I can't ignore the warning.

Doing something about it, however, is another problem. I saw the way she reacted to Monty's accusations about Doyle. I need to find a different approach.

"She wants us to see a psychiatrist." My stomach hardens at the thought. "Let's bring Doyle in as the family doctor. Each of us can meet with him and formulate our own opinions. Kill two birds with one stone. We get help while getting to know the man helping her."

"I hate that fucking idea." Monty grimaces. "But it's brilliant. I'll call him in the morning."

As Monty paces off down the hall to use the bathroom, I turn to Leo. "How's she doing?"

"Sound asleep." His smile carries a tenderness reserved only for her.

"Good. She feels safe then."

"But is she?" Leo flicks his gaze in the direction that Monty went.

"I go back and forth on that. His guilt and concern feel real, but so did Denver's at times. What do you think?"

"His face gives my middle finger an erection."

"That's mature," I mutter.

"We need to treat him as a threat until we know with one hundred percent certainty that he's not."

"Agreed."

If Monty isn't the lethal hunter Denver warned about, who is it? Maybe there isn't a stalker at all, and the riddle is just another way for the devil to fuck with us. We haven't seen any indication to support his claim. No ominous shadows or suspicious behavior.

But we've only been out of the hospital for three days. We haven't left the privacy and security of the island.

Time will tell.

When Monty returns, his eyes probe, searching for something in our expressions, trying to read us like he knows we were talking about him.

I keep my face neutral.

"How did the interviews go?" He reclines in the chair.

"As expected." I roll my neck, ready to put the past few days behind me. "I stayed with the narrative. Didn't give away anything that would cause suspicion."

"Same." Leo nods. "They had a lot of questions about our family dynamic. How happy we must be to have finally found each other."

"Are you?" Monty smirks.

"Thrilled," Leo deadpans.

"How did you handle those questions?" I ask.

"I played along."

I make a noise in my throat. "So basically, you showed your teeth and said nothing."

"Pretty much." He props a boot on the coffee table. "Did you tell them how much you love your new big brother?"

"Kept that to myself." I stare into Monty's eyes, the depths as blue as a cold sea, reflecting no warmth or invitation. "They asked about the reunited couple. I didn't comment, letting them believe the marriage is still intact."

"Good." His jaw twitches. "No one cares about a perfect marriage. It makes a boring news story. They won't spend any time on it."

"You know," I say, my voice dropping, "all that will change when we start going out in public. I won't hide my relationship with her, nor will Leo."

"Discretion is the goal here. The story we created is delicate. We don't want to give them anything to squawk about."

"I understand the need for caution. But I won't pretend forever."

"We all want what's best for Frankie." Leo taps his fingers on his leg. "We just need to find a balance between protecting her and being honest about our relationships."

"We need to stay united on this," Monty says. "No surprises."

The distrust lingers on both sides like a shadow that doesn't fade. But we need to push through it. We have no choice.

I take a deep breath, forcing the next words. "Thanks for sending the message about her panic attack."

Monty nods, his expression guarded. "How are you doing with the tech? Any trouble with the phones?"

"It's been harder than I care to admit," I say. "I never thought I'd be struggling with something as simple as making a call or sending a text."

"Actually, I have a question." Leo pulls out his device. "I was trying to look up something earlier but couldn't figure out how to switch between the screens."

"The browser tabs?" Monty scoots forward on the chair, gesturing at the empty spot on the couch. "May I?"

Leo makes room for him and hands over his phone.

After a few swipes on the screen, Monty passes it back. "See this icon here? Yeah. Tap that. Now you see all your open tabs. You can switch between them or close the ones you don't need."

That prompts a string of more questions, which leads to a full-on tutorial. I find myself pulling out my phone and following along.

Frankie showed us the basics of what these little electronic bricks can do, but we've only scratched the surface. I'm starving for more knowledge.

All I've ever known was a life of solitude and silence, broken only by the howl of the wind and the crunch of snow underfoot. Denver raised us to be tough, to rely on nothing and no one but ourselves.

Now I find myself on this lush, green island with comforts I never thought possible. The biggest change, the one that thrills me the most, is the technology. I went from no Internet or outside communication to holding all this power in a tiny computer that fits in the palm of my hand.

This phone opens up worlds I never knew existed. I can connect with Leo and Frankie anywhere, at any time.

The first time I browsed the Internet, it felt like magic. Information at my fingertips, answers to questions I didn't even know I had. I can spend hours wending through the dark forest of videos about everything and nothing at all, diving into the endless sea of knowledge and entertainment.

Of course, I have my share of frustrations. The sheer volume of information overwhelms me quickly. When the constant connectivity is too much, I long for the simplicity of the tundra.

Then I remember the loneliness, the abuse, the endless hardship, and yeah...

Fuck that place.

The climate here is milder, the air saturated with the scent of saltwater and evergreen. Bustling towns wait nearby, with people and noise and activity. I can't wait to explore them.

I also dread leaving the safety of the island. Without my crossbow or a grasp on the dangers out there, I don't know how to protect her the way I could in the hills.

As the night wears on, the strain between Monty and us eases, if only for a short while. I find myself glancing at the time on my phone, the minutes ticking by with agonizing slowness.

Finally, I can't take it anymore.

"I'm going to check on her." I stand and stalk toward the stairs.

The need to see her, to reassure myself that she's safe, is a physical ache.

Monty and Leo rise as well, pocketing their phones and trailing after me.

We head upstairs, the house quiet and still. I push open the door to the guest bedroom, my heart pounding.

The bedside lamp casts a gentle glow on her stunning

features. Deep in sleep, she looks so peaceful and untroubled.

Relief settles over me.

"Beautiful," Leo whispers.

I grunt, spellbound.

Monty hovers in the doorway, wearing the stony expression of an overlord as we get ready for bed. As we prepare to sleep beside the woman he still considers his wife.

I strip down to my underwear, Leo doing the same.

We can shut him out and lock the door, but that would only lead to a brawl and disturb her rest.

She'll be safe, sleeping between Leo and me. We'll wake if anyone intrudes.

Careful not to disturb her, we slip in on either side of her. The warmth of her body instantly grounds me, her presence a balm to my frayed nerves.

"I'll be across the hall if you need anything." Monty steps back, his gaze glued to her, shadowed and turbulent with longing.

Then he turns away.

I shut off the light, and the room settles into heavy, tranquil quiet. I lie there, listening to the rhythmic sound of her breathing, feeling the steady rise and fall of her chest.

The tension in my body slowly ebbs, replaced by a deep, bone-weary exhaustion.

"You all right?" Leo shifts, his hand brushing my ribs.

"Yeah. You?"

"I really want to fuck with him."

"No."

"Hear me out." He angles his face toward mine on the pillow above her head, whispering, "Let's pretend we're jerking off. I'll grunt and make slapping sounds loud enough for him to hear while you moan my name."

"What the fuck is wrong with you?"

"We need to test him. Expose his true nature."

"He won't come in here for Mississippi seconds, if that's what you're thinking. He's not Denver."

"Mississippi seconds?"

"Redneck family bonding."

"What filthy corner of the Internet have you been haunting?"

I sigh as the shadows of our past press me into the mattress. "Despite how we feel about Monty, he has no interest in fucking men or children or family members. That's not his kink."

Frankie's his kink. She's all he cares about, and it's not a healthy obsession.

The same could be said about our obsession with her.

"Go to sleep, dumbass." I shove his face away.

He tries to shove back, but I see better than him in the dark and dodge him easily.

She doesn't even stir.

We lie there, the three of us tangled in the warmth and intimacy of skin on skin. If heaven exists, this is it.

We made it through all the interviews without a hitch. I've been eating my weight in delicious food. There isn't a constant, soul-sucking chill in the air, and I don't have to leave the bed to throw a log on the fire.

Here, we don't even need a fire.

Closing my eyes, I let my gratitude and contentment sink into my limbs. My last conscious thought circles around Frankie and the psychiatrist she wholeheartedly trusts. Maybe he can help her.

If he doesn't, I'll make him wish he never met her.

Sleep doesn't come easily, but it comes.

Sometime later, in the quiet moments of the night, my eyes jolt open, adjusting to the absence of light.

The instinctual need to sit up hardens my muscles. Propping on an elbow, I find Leo already braced on his, rubbing his eyes.

Frankie lies on her stomach between us, one leg butterflied, her face scrunched in sleep.

A soft sound jerks my head to the door.

On the floor, Monty sits with his back to the doorframe and his head lolling to the side. Snoring.

We should've locked him out. Though he probably has a

key.

Leo catches my eyes in the gloom.

Should we wake him? Or let him sleep like a dog on the floor?

The latter is the more satisfying option and the one Leo decides on as he burrows in against her and goes back to sleep.

Guess I'm taking the first watch.

Two days later, I sit across from Dr. Doyle Whitaker, soaking in the sweet, apricot glow of the afternoon.

Oh, how I missed the warmth of sunshine on my face.

The private den makes an ideal spot for therapy, with its rich wood paneling and window views of the Sitka Sound.

Surprisingly, all three Strakh men decided to see Doyle as their therapist. I have suspicions about their easy cooperation, especially after Monty's tantrum, but whatever.

Since Leo and Monty are still in the gym, they suggested that I take the first session.

Kody waits in the hall, probably leaning against the door with his supernatural senses on high alert. If a salty tear so much as leaves my eye, he'll smell it and barge in.

I don't plan on crying.

"This is a safe space." Doyle reclines in the armchair, his posture inviting and open, his notepad resting on his thigh. "You can share anything with me."

"I know."

"If you're not ready to talk about what happened, that's okay, too. We can discuss anything you want."

He only knows what the news is reporting. It's up to me to talk about Denver's abuse, Wolf's death, the plane crash, Monty's betrayal, my polyamorous relationship with Leo and Kody...all of it. Or none of it.

Sharing those personal things with him would be different than discussing it with detectives and reporters. Outside of this room, the information would be twisted and used against me.

In here, it would be confidential and used to help me heal.

Doyle watches me patiently, his dark hair tousled across his forehead, his hazel eyes softening with professional concern.

I forgot how handsome he is close up. His chiseled jawline and firm lips give him a hard edge, but he has the eyes of an empath, sensitive and gentle, creating an impression of boyish innocence. I know better. He's a decade older than me.

"Frankie." The deep tenor of his voice swirls through me, calming my nerves. "What's on your mind?"

Slowly, I breathe in, then out, my thoughts flitting to the morning I was abducted. Monty needs to talk about that morning as much as I do. If I open the dialogue with Doyle, maybe Monty will do the same, and we can move on with our separate lives.

"I had a miscarriage." My gaze shifts to the window for a moment before settling back on Doyle. "I was pregnant with Monty's baby when I was abducted."

His expression remains neutral, encouraging me to continue.

I walk through the fight about the pregnancy, my decision to leave, the kidnapping, my attempt to escape on the snow machine, and the miscarriage. I include all the relevant details without mentioning Wolf. Making his existence known would open a conversation I'm not ready to have. Not in this first session.

"Have you forgiven Monty for the way he handled the pregnancy?"

"Yes. I think so. But I haven't forgiven him for the other thing."

"What other thing?"

"He fucked another woman while I was being held captive by his brother."

"Oh." Doyle straightens, his throat bobbing with a swallow. "I'm sorry."

"I don't want condolences. Monty thought I left him, and he tried to move on. He doesn't deserve all the blame."

"Why do you say that?"

I murdered his brother and fell in love with his only surviving relatives. All this animosity, guilt, and back-and-forth emotion is a reaction to the pain inflicted by both Denver and Monty.

Since I'm not ready to share any of that, I settle on, "I'm not perfect."

"Yet you're angry with him." He writes something in his notes.

"Of course, I'm fucking angry. Blinding, raving mad. But it goes beyond that. He's distrustful of everyone, making me distrust *him* even more. He questions everyone's motives, including yours."

"Mine?"

"Yeah."

Thanks to Monty's paranoia, I'm questioning Doyle's motives, too. It's maddening.

"He thinks everyone is out to get me," I say. "But what about him? Isn't *he* out to get me?"

"Is he?"

"I don't know. There's so much to unpack, and I'm losing the energy and will to make the effort."

"I understand your feelings, and your concerns are justified. Couples often struggle after traumatic events. It's not uncommon for one partner to become overprotective, thinking they're doing what's best. It can create tension and lead to misunderstanding and resentment."

"This is more than that."

I'm in love with two other men.

"Have you talked to him about how you're feeling?"

"Yeah. He listens. He seems more attentive and

compromising now than before...the trauma."

"It sounds like his actions come from a place of fear and insecurity. He's afraid of losing you, but his methods are pushing you away."

"He's already lost me."

Even as I say that, I know it's not true.

I'm trying so hard to remain angry with him because if I'm not angry, what am I? If he's not out to hurt me, what is he?

He's a threat to my relationship with Leo and Kody, that's what.

But he's not a threat to me. I can't believe the worst in him. I just can't.

"Okay." Doyle lifts his pen from the paper and meets my eyes without judgment. "Sometimes the best thing for a relationship is to step back. Give each other space to heal individually before you can heal together."

"We're not intimate. We don't share a bed. Not since my kidnapping. I've been sleeping in the guest house. Except the night of my panic attack, I slept across the hall from him in case I got triggered again."

"Do you want to talk about that? The PTSD episode?"

"I don't remember it. Is that normal?"

"Yes, dissociation is a common symptom of PTSD."

"When Monty called you, did he tell you what happened during the episode?"

"Yes." His expression softens.

"Did he tell you he triggered it?"

"He said he approached you from behind."

I nod. Leo and Kody come up behind me like that all the time, and I'm fine. But I keep that to myself.

"What if Monty is my trigger? I don't believe he would ever physically hurt me. But deep down, I wonder if I fear him."

"Can I be honest with you, Frankie?"

"I sure as hell hope so."

"I've known you for many years." He closes his notepad and sets it aside, bending forward. "I've always admired your inner strength. You're wildly independent and tenacious and—I hope you don't mind me saying—you are incredibly beautiful. You deserve someone who knows how to take care of a woman, how to touch you softly and fiercely at the same time, how to both claim you and set you free, and how to stand in the brilliant emerald glow of your soul without snuffing out your light."

"Um..." I stare at him, stunned. "Thank you. That's..."

"Monty isn't good for you. He's controlling, possessive, and selfish. The typical wealthy playboy with commitment issues and family secrets. I think you're right to fear him. You're better off without him."

"Wow. Okay..." The tips of my ears burn. "Have you always thought that?"

"Yes. I've seen how his behavior affects you." He gives me a reassuring smile. "You deserve someone who respects your independence, encourages your career, and supports your healing and reproductive rights."

Ouch. Yeah, Monty doesn't check most of those boxes.

Now would be a good time to tell him I have someone who does. Two someones. I don't need to get into my sex life, especially after that weirdly flattering and slightly unprofessional declaration.

Leo and Kody will probably make our dynamic perfectly clear to Doyle during their sessions with him. But right now, I just want to focus on my support system.

"There's something else." I rub my palms on my jeans. "It's about Leo and Kody."

"Go on." His eyes sharpen with interest.

"During our captivity, we became very close." I draw a breath, my thoughts gathering. "We helped one another through a lot of harrowing, painful things. We escaped together, survived a plane crash, and now we're facing a rough transition. They mean everything to me."

"You developed a trauma bond. It's a survival mechanism. A source of strength and support." He tips his head, rubbing his jaw. "It's normal to feel a deep connection with them after what you've been through."

"I understand that, and while we share that special

connection between the three of us, I feel it's important for them to build a relationship with Monty. He's the only family they have left, and they need stability. Monty can provide that. But it's...complicated. Monty's distrust and jealousy issues are getting in the way."

"He feels threatened by your relationship with them."

"For sure. But I don't want him blaming Leo and Kody for our broken marriage. If they weren't in the picture, Monty and I would still be separated. Leo and Kody have suffered their entire lives. They've never experienced the love and unconditional support of a tight-knit family. I want them to have that."

"Family and relationships are crucial, especially after traumatic experiences. But these bonds can't be forced. They must develop on their own."

"I know." Sighing, I look away. "I just want them to feel safe and loved."

"You care deeply about them, and your desire to see them happy is commendable. But you must be patient."

"Patience isn't exactly my thing."

He squints at me, staring too closely. The subtle shift in his posture suggests he's gearing up to say something important.

"Most of our conversation today has been about Monty, Leo, and Kody. Their needs. Their well-being." He dips forward, tilting into the space between us with elbows braced on his knees. "What about you? How are you feeling in all of this?"

I blink, suddenly aware of the tension in my shoulders and the tightness in my chest.

"I...I guess I haven't thought about it. I'm grateful to be free. Each day brings a sense of wonder that I am alive and no longer have to fight every waking second to stay that way. But I survived only a fraction of the hell that Leo and Kody endured. They've never lived outside of the Arctic. Their transition is so much harder than mine. And Monty..." I blow out a breath.

"*Your* recovery is just as important. You've been through significant trauma, too. Do you want to talk about what happened with Denver?"

I swallow hard, already shaking my head. "Not today. The details are...ugly and overwhelming. I need to work up to it."

"That's understandable. How about we just talk about what you're feeling?"

What am *I feeling?*

I sit back and pry open some of those doors. "I was held against my will for nine months. Six days ago, we did the impossible and escaped. We're free, but I don't feel free. Not like I did before the abduction. I'm constantly on edge, waiting for something else to go wrong. Like, at any minute, the devil will reach out of the shadows and drag me back to hell."

His eyes flash with a ghost of something darker, but it's gone so quickly I'm certain I imagined it.

"PTSD can manifest in many ways." He laces his hands together. "Feeling constantly on edge is a common symptom. But you're safe here. With me."

"Sometimes I feel like I'm losing my mind."

"That's a natural response to what you've been through. Just remember, the devil—*Denver*—is dead."

"The devil has many forms, many faces. Some might say he's immortal."

"Your nightmares, your demons, they're a reflection of your trauma and can be incredibly powerful and persistent. But they're part of your past."

Unless the stalker in Denver's riddle is real.

"The past and present try to blur together sometimes." I look down, my hands twisting on my lap. "Every time I close my eyes, I'm back there. I can't escape it."

"Escaping isn't about running from your fears. It's about facing them, understanding them, and finding ways to cope with them. It's a process, one that takes time. You need to take care of yourself, Frankie. Your heart is deeply scarred. Give yourself time and permission to heal."

"I'm trying. But I feel like I have to be strong for everyone else. If I fall apart, who will hold everything together?"

"You don't have to carry all of this on your own. Ask for help. Lean on others."

"Trust me. I lean plenty. Like this session? Monty's paying for it. He feeds me, clothes me, provides a roof over my head."

"He's your husband."

"Only on paper. I don't want to be dependent on him. I'm so used to being the one who takes care of everyone."

"That's the nurse in you." He reaches out, placing a comforting hand on my arm. "You've shown incredible strength, but even the strongest people need support."

"Yeah." I slide my arm away. "You're right."

"It's a process. Focus on mini-milestones. You've already started by meeting with me and opening up. It's a big step."

"Okay." I roll back my shoulders, absorbing his words.

"You matter, Frankie. Your feelings and needs are just as important as everyone else's. Through therapy and a solid support system, you'll get through this."

"My support system is incredible, but they're struggling, too. I'm pushing them into therapy, even though they don't want it and don't think they need it."

"Monty set up sessions for all four of you to meet with me. They may not like it but..." He grins. "This will only hurt a little."

"What did you say?" A chill trickles across my scalp.

"He set up sessions—"

"No. You said..."

Don't struggle. This will only hurt a little.

My breath quickens. My chest tightens, and my gaze darts to the exit, the first hints of panic creeping in.

I know what's coming. I've seen this before, in Kody, in myself.

Closing my eyes, I focus on breathing. Inhale for four, hold for seven, exhale for eight. Repeat.

"Frankie?" Doyle's voice fades into the background.

My hands grip the edge of the chair. I know this is my body's fight-or-flight response, my sympathetic nervous system in overdrive.

Breathe, Frankie. Fucking breathe.

Sweat beads on my forehead. A trickle runs down my back. But I keep counting, keep breathing, and slowly, my heart rate starts to slow.

I'm safe. I'm here. I'm now.

The rational part of my brain fights to regain control. I let it.

I keep my eyes closed for a few more minutes, giving my body time to settle. The wave of panic recedes, leaving me exhausted but functional.

I know I'll have to face this again, but for now, I've won.

Opening my eyes, I straighten in the chair and take a deep breath.

"You had a panic attack." He's closer than he was before, his hand gripping the armrest of my chair.

I glare at it until he removes it and sits back.

"I started to panic, and I pushed it back."

"Which part of what I said triggered it?"

"Something I heard from my captor's mouth."

"Do you want to talk about it?"

"No. I'm good."

"Frankie, I think—"

"I'm a nurse. I know what my body's doing, and I can handle it." I cross my legs. "Now where were we?"

His lips press into a line, and he pulls in a breath. "Monty set up sessions for all four of you."

"Monty. Right. What if it's a conflict of interest? How can you help him when you think so little of him?"

"My sessions with Monty will focus on his personal issues, mental health concerns, and goals rather than addressing your concerns as a couple. If I find that I'm inadvertently siding with you, and it compromises my ability to treat him, I'll have an open discussion with him about it and likely refer him to another psychiatrist."

"Okay." I nod slowly and continue counting in my head, measuring every breath. "Thank you."

"You're welcome, Remember, the devil may have many forms, but so do your strengths. We'll find them together."

His eyes burn with a genuine desire to help me. It doesn't erase my fears, but it makes the fight feel a little less intimidating.

With a warm, encouraging smile, he wraps up the session and assigns journaling as homework. If he only knew how comfortable I am with that task.

How will the guys take to it as part of their treatment?

The notion of us healing feels so far away. It's a daunting, ambitious goal but also a hopeful one.

As I walk Doyle to the door, his words echo in my mind, a reminder that I can't take care of everyone all the time. I can stitch their surface wounds, but I can't heal the ones inside. And they have so many.

"Kody should be right outside." I reach for the knob. "Do you want to see him next?"

"Sure. Monty scheduled me for the entire day."

I open the door and peer into the hallway.

Empty.

Alarm spikes through me, but I quickly shrug it off.

"Looks like he stepped away. Probably in the restroom." I turn back and gasp, shocked to find Doyle standing so close.

"Sorry. Didn't mean to scare you." He grips my bicep to steady me, his fingers sliding down my arm.

"It's fine." I step back, crossing the threshold into the hall.

"Are you sure?" He searches my eyes, his body following my retreat as if I'm pulling him in. "You look shaken. Are you still fighting a panic attack? Maybe you should sit."

"No." I put my hand up, accidentally brushing his chest. "Just need a minute."

"Yes, of course." Standing just inside the den, he lowers his chin and releases me from his penetrating stare. "Remember, you can always reach out if you need to talk, even if we're off the clock."

His fingers graze against mine, offering comfort.

But I don't feel comfortable. Not with him hovering close enough to taste the spearmint on his breath.

As his hand lifts toward my face, I catch movement from the corner of my eye.

A menacing shadow peels away from the darkness of an adjacent doorway, and those black eyes lock onto Doyle's hand as he touches my chin.

Kody, no!

His face contorts with rage. Before I can react, he lunges with a feral roar.

"Get your hands off her!" Kody slams into Doyle, sending my heart into overdrive.

"Stop! Stop!" I try to shove them apart, but it's like moving two brick walls.

With Kody's weight loss, Doyle outmatches him in bulk and strength. But he can't rival Kody's savage fury and predatory speed.

They crash into the wall, swinging their fists, wrestling, spitting, and knocking over an end table.

"Stop it! Both of you!" I leap into the fray, palming their faces and catching my skin on sharp teeth. "Fuck!"

At the sound of my yelp, they break apart.

Eyes locked, they heave through seething breaths, dousing the room in aggression and testosterone.

"He's been touching you, hasn't he?" Kody snarls. "He's trying to take you from me!"

"Frankie?" Doyle steps back, his features scrunched in confusion. "What's going on?"

"Calm down." I flatten my hands on Kody's pumped-up chest, trying to hold him back. "It's not what you think."

"I saw the way he looks at you." His body trembles with barely contained ire. "He had his hands all over you."

"Kody, please." My voice shatters. "You're scaring me."

His eyes fly to mine, softening for a split second. An agonized sound wrenches from him, and he spins away, pacing through the room with his hands in his hair.

Doyle clears his throat, regaining some of his composure. "It's clear there are some strong emotions at play here. Perhaps we should continue this another time."

"You think?" Kody thrusts a finger at the door. "Get the fuck out!"

"No! This isn't your call." I ball my hands at my sides. "Other people in this house want to get help." I give Doyle a quick scan, looking for injuries. No blood or bruises. Just a little ruffled. "If you want to leave, I understand."

"I'm here for the day. If you direct me to the restroom, I'll freshen up." He wipes a hand down his button-up shirt, checking his appearance. "Will you send for Leo and Monty?"

"Yes, of course. The bathroom is right across the hall. I'm sorry about—"

"Don't fucking apologize to him." Kody stalks toward me.

I shoot an apologetic look at Doyle and slip into the hall, knowing Kody will charge after me.

My cheeks heat with embarrassment as I march toward the gym. My head throbs. My insides knot, and if he says one wrong thing, I'm going to light his ass up in front of God and everyone.

"Woman." Kody chuffs and grunts down my neck like a pissed-off bear.

I hold up my middle finger and round the corner, colliding with a hard chest and the scent of woodsy body wash.

"What the—?" Leo catches me, softening our crash. "Hey." He lifts my chin, instantly sensing my distress. "What's wrong?"

"Your brother showed his ass."

Kody scowls, folding his arms.

Monty strides into view, fresh out of a shower like Leo. He takes in our stand-off and immediately goes still, his blue eyes icing over.

Great. More alpha energy. Just what I need.

"Dr. Whitaker is waiting for you both in the den." I gesture behind me.

Neither of them moves.

I glance at the bandage on Monty's neck and sigh. "Kody and I need to talk. Please go to your session, and we'll regroup afterward, okay?"

"Come on." Monty jerks his chin at Leo and strolls down the hall.

Leo exchanges a look with Kody. Whatever passes between them satisfies Leo enough to turn and follow Monty. I watch them go, my heart still pounding as I pivot back to Kody.

Words abandon me in the vicious fury of his glare. All I can muster is a guttural sound of frustration and disappointment.

Veins pulse in my throat, a drumbeat for the war song I'm going to unleash in his face.

But not here.

I storm off toward the nearest exit, stepping outside into the sunshine. Kody trails me, his footfalls relentless.

I can't believe him...attacking my therapist like that.

"Frankie, wait." He's close enough to stuff his drugging scent up my nose. Winter berries and wildfire with snarling nips of aggression.

He can shove that delicious, earthy aroma up his ass.

As I pass the rear of the main house, my scalp crawls. I feel something in my periphery, something that shouldn't be there.

My breath catches, and a jagged lump hardens in my throat. It takes me a second to register that this feeling along my skin is the sensation of being watched.

I halt abruptly, causing Kody to crash into me.

His hands grip my shoulders, steadying us both. "What the—?"

I'm not listening, my gaze sweeping over the sprawling, towering expanse of the estate. Balconies, alcoves, windows...

There. My eyes lock on an upstairs window. One of the guest bedrooms.

The sun outside glares against it, casting the interior in

shadows. But someone is there. I can't make out any features, just the unsettling outline of a man staring back at me, still as a ghost.

The birds' songs fade, replaced by an eerie silence and the pounding blood in my ears.

Who is that? My mind races. Oliver? A security guard? But why would they be upstairs? And why are they just standing there, staring at me?

"Look at me." Kody grabs my face, forcing my gaze to his. His eyes, dark and intense, search mine. "It's my job to protect you."

I yank free with a grunt, whipping my head back to the window.

The shadowed shape is gone.

A chill skitters through me.

Did I imagine it?

No, it was real. And it makes my anger burn hotter.

Turning on my heel, I charge toward the guest house. But I glance back a few times, unable to shake the feeling that something is watching and waiting.

By the time I reach the door, I'm so worked up that I have to punch the security code several times before it opens.

Three angry strides into the sitting room, I whirl on him.

"What were you thinking?" I throw my hands up, voice shaking. "You can't just attack people like that!"

"I can, and I will. No one touches you." He prowls toward me, flexing his hands.

I stumble back. "He's my therapist, you caveman. He's trying to help me."

"By helping himself into your pants?"

My airway catches fire, and I see red. "How dare you!"

"Oh, I dare." His whole body bends into me, swallowing the space between us with snarling intimacy. "Is he married?"

"Fuck you. You don't get to—"

He shuts me up with his mouth on mine and his hand collaring my throat.

I whimper into his possessive kiss, uselessly pushing against his chest.

The instant his hot tongue unfurls against mine, he wins. He steals the oxygen from the room, crashes over my anger, and shatters my knees into glass.

For a stupidly weak moment, I forget why I'm mad. There's only the pleasure of his lips, the warmth of his hands on my throat, and lower, below his belt, the hard, beastly stab of his need.

The man views every argument as an opportunity to fuck my brains out. He also has endless stamina and won't stop until I'm unstrung, soaked in come, and too exhausted to argue.

"No." I shove out of his hold and circle the couch. "I'm not rewarding you for being an absolute savage."

"Punish me then." Prowling after me, he unzips his jeans and frees his tree-trunk cock. "Sink those sharp little teeth into me."

Dear God in heaven, how do I say no to that? My gums tingle. My skin sizzles, and my pussy throbs like a clenching fist.

But I have to be strong.

If I don't stand up to him, to all of them, they'll walk all over me with their jealous tempers and raging dicks.

"I know you're trying to protect me, but this isn't the way." I scuttle backward, chased into the kitchen, while sidestepping his irresistible hands. "We need to find a better way to deal with this."

That doesn't deter him in the least. With his cock jutting like a goddamn weapon, he's hard and feral and wants to fuck me with all that possessive fury.

As he corners me against the counter, every ounce of me wants to surrender to his animalistic sex drive. Letting this gorgeous beast nail me when he's angry would be the greatest sex of my life.

Don't give in. Be strong.

"You can't fix this with orgasms." I duck my head, dodging his snapping jaws.

"Not fixing it, woman. Just getting us to a place where we can." His eyes are wild, his breathing heavy, but there's a tinge of something else beneath the jealous rage. Something fragile and haunting. "He's not just your therapist. I saw it in his eyes."

The desperate edge to his voice, the fear on his face, the lifetime of trauma and pain welted across his back, it's all there, choking him, tunneling his vision.

When he reaches for me again, I expect him to bend me over the counter. Instead, he wraps me up in a crushing hug, his muscles shaking and his grip so damn tight he squeezes the anger out of me.

"My beautiful, savage caveman." I cup his granite jaw and bring our foreheads together. "I'm yours. You and Leo and me, we're bonded. Mated for life. Denver couldn't divide us. Hoss couldn't break us. No one can take this from us."

I have to be strong for everyone else.

"I don't like the way he touches you."

"I'm yours." I kiss his angry lips.

"He intends to take you."

"I'm yours." I unbutton my jeans and push them down my hips.

"I can't let him hurt you." He yanks my arms behind my back and pins me against his chest.

"I'm *yours*." I hold his gaze, letting him scour my features until he sees my truth.

Releasing me, he lowers to the floor and pulls my clothes down with him. My jeans, underwear, shoes—everything comes off. While he undresses my lower half, I remove my shirt and bra.

His ascent back up my body is an unhurried climb as he drags his scorching tongue in one long lick from feet to breasts, making me shiver and squirm.

By the time he reaches my mouth, I'm drenched between my legs, out of breath, and aching to be impaled. His cock is so hard the veins strain beneath the skin.

Taking my face in his hands, he angles my head and crushes my mouth with his. His tongue doesn't ask. It demands, invading and claiming with brutal force.

I don't give it to him. I make him take it. And holy fuck, he does. It's primal. It's raw. It's the very nature of the untamed wilderness that lives in our veins.

He jams his fingers between my legs, driving them deep and working me into a moaning, writhing tangle of useless limbs.

"More." I gasp into his mouth.

But he's already doing it, replacing his hand with his massive cock. He's so unnaturally huge and stiff that I tense, knowing what's coming.

He lifts me, braces my rear against the counter, and drags me over the fat head of his dick.

Our eyes connect, and a strangled groan vibrates in his throat as he works me down his thick length.

The pressure, the heat, the beautiful, burning pleasure as he pushes harder, deeper, trembling, all-consuming—it's glorious. Even with his cock stuffed only midway in, I feel it twitching, swelling, throbbing root to tip.

The sensations slam into me, sharp and loud, thundering through my body with unholy desire.

Holding me still, he retreats a few inches. Then another hard push, a choked gasp between us, and sweet blessed hell, he's in, buried to the hilt.

"Why are you so big?" I sink my hands into his lush hair.

"Why are you so tight?" He adjusts his grip on my ass.

Then he moves, ramming that monster up between my legs like a piston, filling, shattering, shocking me like it's my first time. Every flex of his hips drives a punching fist inside me, a stinging blow of howling, clawing ecstasy.

Our bodies press tightly together, climbing closer, clinging harder, my inner thighs rubbing against his hips. He uses the strength of his legs to dig deeper, stroking all that hardness along every nerve and pleasure center inside me.

I cry out against his wet lips. His responding groan vibrates the walls. Shakes the whole damn island. He's pure sexual power, insatiable and tireless, maddening in his ability to go for hours, and exhausting to compete with. A competition I've never won.

My entire body shudders and ripples, twitching toward the

peak amid the flames of his pounding, primal virility. Hard to breathe while writhing in his intoxicating heat and ferocious kisses.

The man is a beast. A beast who kisses like he's staring down death. Who understands the value of each breath. Who earns every precious inhale and exhale. Who conquers demons and arctic blizzards with his woman at his side as we fight and fuck and reach for the future with forever in the palms of our entwined hands.

"I love you." His dark head lowers to mine, those black bear eyes peering into my soul, asserting his declaration, and sealing it with another blistering kiss.

I breathe the words back, into his mouth, down his throat, and over the scars that lie in the deep.

There's nothing sexier than a man who fucks with his whole heart. His heavy balls slap with his thrusts, dripping with my arousal, as his cock drives and swivels and batters into me with an urgency that shoves us both to the edge.

Bucking, kissing, panting, groaning, we set the air around us on fire. The fullness, the delicious grind, the sloppy fluids leaking everywhere, stretch me to the brink of unraveling.

Then I do.

I come undone, jolting, shouting, drowning in shimmering, body-shaking bliss. I spasm and clench, clamping down on the beast, milking him as he stares into my eyes, pumping, roaring, and spilling his hot come inside me.

Dizzying, gasping relief sinks us to the floor, tangled in a sweaty pile of wobbly arms and legs. Collapsing onto his chest, I can't lift my eyelids, let alone my head.

When he catches his breath, he spreads me out on the floor and licks the mess from my body. From ass to cunt and along my thighs, he glides his tongue, cleaning every last drop from my sensitive flesh.

He's a fucking animal, and I love it.

"What about you?" I gesture to his come-coated cock. "My turn."

"You put that mouth on me, and you won't leave this kitchen floor tonight." He stuffs himself away.

With a gentleness that contradicts the way he fucks, he dresses me, straightens my hair, and carries me to the couch.

Settling me on his lap, he reclines in a sighing, torpid, post-coital sprawl.

Then his eyes capture mine. “Now we’re at a place where we can fix this.”

Damn this man. He fucked all the anger out of me, and now I just want to curl up and cuddle.

He knew exactly what he was doing.

frankie

NINETEEN

Now we're at a place where we can fix this.

"So you don't like Doyle." I twist on his lap to see the broody expression I've grown to love. "Because he touched my hand."

"Your hand, your arm, your face. I saw it all."

"And you were what? Hiding in the shadows, trying to catch him in action?"

"Yes."

"That's not creepy or anything."

"It's my job to protect you."

"Protecting doesn't include stalking."

"I disagree."

"While you were stalking, did you see me move away from his touch? Did you see me handle it myself?"

"You don't need to handle it when you have me to protect you."

"Kody..." I blow out a breath. "You have to let me do shit on my own. What happens when I go back to work? My job is very hands-on. I touch people. *Patients*. They touch me, sometimes out of kindness, sometimes because they're in pain. You can't be there, interfering with my work. You need to let me do things on my own. You have to trust me to take care of myself."

"Doyle isn't one of your patients. He crossed the line."

"So what are you saying? Do you want me to find a new therapist?"

"Yes."

"Just like that? You won't even have a session with him and give him a chance?"

"I saw what I saw. It was in his eyes, in the way he looked at you. He wasn't touching you because he wants to help you."

"Monty put that shit in your head." I grind my teeth.

"Monty doesn't control my thoughts. I think for myself and trust my gut."

"And your gut says Doyle's harboring some depraved agenda?"

"What if he's the hunter? *The silent ache, the shadow that lingers, the present from your past?* You've known him for years. He is, in fact, from your past."

"What about Monty? Is he no longer on your list of suspects?"

"I didn't say that."

"Okay, so I'm not agreeing or disagreeing. But if Doyle intends to hurt me, wouldn't it be smarter to keep him close? Get to know him in your therapy sessions and let those tracker senses of yours smell him out?"

"It would be smarter to keep him the hell away from you."

"So here we are, circling back to my earlier point. You can't protect me every second, everywhere, all at once. Eventually, I *will* go in public without you. I'll go to work, see my gynecologist, hang out with my friends—"

"What friends?"

"I have friends. Point is if Doyle is the unknown shadow, he'll come after me. If we're no longer watching him, I won't see him coming. I'll be blindsided, caught unaware, just like the night Denver took me."

"If he comes after you, he's a fucking dead man."

"This is what I'm talking about. You can't go around attacking and killing people. It's illegal. You'll be charged and locked behind bars. Do you understand?"

He stares at me with so much emotion soaking the melty black depths of his eyes. "I just want to protect you."

"I know." I shift, straddling him and resting my chin on his chest. "But you have to trust me to protect myself, too."

"I do."

"Prove it." I coil a strand of hair around my finger, waiting.

"Who else does that work on? Leo? I bet he falls for it."

"What are you talking about?"

"The huge puppy dog eyes, hair twirling, fluttering lashes, and this sexy little pout..." He traces my bottom lip. "Woman, you are filthy sweet and charming as fuck, and when you bite your lip like that, you're lethal. Makes it impossible to deny you anything."

"I'm not trying to manipulate you." I crawl up his rippled torso and sink into his smoldering gaze. "I'm telling you very clearly that you cannot assault people. Not my colleagues. Not my doctors. Not the strangers I encounter in town. If you see something you don't like, you need to come to me, and we'll talk about it like adults. Can you handle that?"

"I'll try."

"Thank you.

"I'll do a session with Dr. Whitaker." He holds up a finger. "Just one. *Then* I'll go back to calling him a dead man."

I sigh. Because what else can I do?

As we stare at each other in the fading light, I know one thing is certain. I don't want to argue with him anymore.

The therapy session, the fight, the makeup sex, the unresolved emotions—it's enough for one day. I just hope I can find a way to navigate through it all without becoming a doormat in the process.

Being the only woman on an island of dominating, controlling men is exhausting.

But it's not Hoss.

This is a dream compared to what I escaped.

"We should go check on Leo and Monty." I start to rise.

"They'll find us when they're finished." He guides me back

to his chest.

He's so warm against my cheek. A bit hard and chiseled. But he's safe. One of my favorite places.

He pulls out his phone and browses the Internet. I watch him search on driver's license practice tests, effective muscle-building exercises, and industrial distillery equipment.

As he scrolls with one hand, the fingers of his other absently comb through my hair.

My eyes grow heavy. I fight the pull, but within minutes, I fall asleep.

When I wake, I'm alone.

Lying on the couch in the guest house, I squint through the mantle of nightfall.

A porch light glows beyond the window, illuminating Leo just outside the door, hands on his hips, expression pensive.

A deep voice muffles through the walls. I can't decipher words, but I know that tone belongs to Monty.

Is Kody with them?

Yawning, I rise to my feet and make my way to them.

The instant I open the door, their conversation cuts off, and three pairs of eyes turn to me.

"Hey." I lean against the doorframe and hug my waist, shivering in the cool night breeze. "Why are you out here?"

"Didn't want to wake you." Leo strides toward me. "You're cold. We can continue this inside."

Everyone shuffles into the cozy sitting room and open kitchen. I deliberately take the only armchair, hoping they'll all squeeze onto the couch.

They don't.

Leo and Kody sit on either end. Monty perches on the edge of the kitchen table, arms folded and legs crossed at the ankles.

"How did your therapy sessions go?" I ask Leo and Monty.

"No fighting or drama." Leo rubs his nape. "Pretty anticlimactic."

"And no touching." Kody gives him and Monty a pointed look.

"Not once." Monty narrows his eyes at me with condescension and superiority, the side of his mouth curling as if to emphasize he was right all along.

"So this is how it's going to be?" I sit back, head held high. "You're besties now, embracing your brotherhood through a shared hatred toward my therapist."

"Frankie," Kody gnarls under his breath.

"Part of me wants to call Doyle and tell him I've found someone else. A straight female psychiatrist who doesn't threaten the men in the Strakh family." I ignore the heavy glaring around me and shift to the edge of my chair. "But it's a slippery slope. I'll be working for Rhett again. One of my closest friends. He's an unmarried man. Very touchy-feely."

"He's gay," Monty says.

My nostrils flare. "A lot of my colleagues at the hospital are unmarried men. Sometimes we go out for drinks after our shifts."

"Cool." Leo nods. "We'll go with you."

"Sometimes, sure. But not always. What if you don't like them? What if one of them casually touches me? I won't eliminate people from my life who don't pass your approval. That's not healthy. Tell me you understand that."

"Remember when Wolf asked you about your red flag?" Kody asks. "You said you've always had someone. Boyfriends. Friends with benefits. A husband. None were platonic friendships."

Monty stiffens.

"I had schoolmates and colleagues." A flush burns my cheeks.

"Fuck buddies."

"What's your point?"

"You don't have female friends because they're jealous of you. And every guy you've befriended tries to turn it into something more. Tell me I'm wrong."

I look away, sifting through every friendship I've had since childhood.

He's not wrong.

The closest friendship I've made over the years is with Rhett. My gay boss.

"What will you do if Sirena propositions Leo or Kody?" Monty tilts his head. "She's a terrible flirt, but you already know that. That's why you demanded I fire her."

"You're right." I let out a stream of air. "I'm being hypocritical. Thank you for pointing that out." I fling him an annoyed look. "I don't like her for the same reasons you don't like Doyle."

"The difference is you're behind closed doors with Doyle." Kody works his jaw. "You have private sessions with him, and we don't know what's happening between you."

"There will be times when you're with Sirena alone. We need to trust one another."

"All right." Leo cracks his neck. "We'll do it your way, love. We'll continue to see your Dr. Whitaker, Kody included, and trust that you'll tell us if he touches you again."

That was easy.

Too easy.

I take in the blank expressions around the room. No objections. No snarly tempers.

"You already reached this decision together." I huff. "What did you do? Threaten Doyle in your sessions?"

Leo and Monty stare back, not a crack in their stony masks.

"Fucking great. You threaten your therapist—and mine—and when I fall asleep, you sneak outside and make decisions without me."

"We weren't sneaking." Monty pushes off the table and paces behind the couch. "We also talked about the ID situation."

"What about it?"

"You brought your license and passport back with you, which aren't expired. So you're good there. With Leo and Kody, I've been trying to expedite the process, but since they don't have birth certificates, it'll take several weeks, a lot of persistence, and some government connections. I know people who can pull some strings at the Vital Records office to speed it along. In the meantime, Leo and Kody need to learn to drive. Cars, boats, planes…"

"And motorcycles." Leo smirks.

"Of course." I roll my eyes and look at Monty. "And you're going to teach them?"

"You want me to give them a healthy family dynamic. This is what brothers do together."

He would know. He had a brother until he was eighteen. I know nothing about his relationship with Denver other than they lived in a private estate on Kodiak Island, learned Russian, got flying lessons, and had a crush on Kody's mother.

"Were you close to Denver?" I ask quietly. "Before you learned what he was?"

"No. I don't know how to do this. But I'm trying."

For you.

I hear the words he doesn't say but don't acknowledge it. "That's all I ask."

"So tomorrow..." He circles the couch and looks at his only family. "What do you say we take the yacht out? I'll show you how to operate it. You can see the ocean for the first time. Then we can dock in town and check out my car collection. Maybe take one or two out for some driving lessons."

"Sure." Leo tries to sound bored, but he can't hide the excitement that sets his gorgeous face aglow.

Kody doesn't react. Not outwardly. His eyes, though. They have smile lines and permanent stars burning into the dark depths. If I didn't know better, I'd say he couldn't be happier with this plan.

And if they're happy, I'm happy.

leonid

TWENTY

Daybreak unfurls in a whisper of golden light over the dock. The brisk air bites my skin and recharges my senses.

I left Frankie and Kody in bed to meet Monty before dawn and help him prepare the yacht for a day on the water.

By the time I arrive, Oliver already stocked the galley with drinks, snacks, and pre-made meals.

I trail Monty from aft to bow, checking the fuel and topping off the engine oil, as he answers my questions and explains all the nautical terminology.

No pretentious suit today. He wears jeans and a Henley, same as me. It makes him appear more approachable. Less intimidating. I don't have the constant urge to break his face.

The vibe between us flows effortlessly when we focus on machinery, technology, and weight-lifting.

Or maybe we just get along better when Frankie's not around.

I hit the gym with him every day, where we release our anger on the punching bag rather than on each other. Sometimes Kody and Frankie join us. Kody's leg isn't fully healed enough for heavy lifting, but when she runs the trails, he runs with her.

Monty and I haven't sorted out our differences since that first morning over breakfast. Every so often, I catch him glowering at me with murderous jealousy in his eyes. But outside those unguarded moments, we seem to have a temporary truce.

We're a lot alike. Same hot-headed tempers. Both natural leaders with a knack for learning how mechanical things work.

Doesn't mean I haven't checked every inch of this yacht for cameras, weapons, and recording devices.

I trust him about as much as I trust Doyle.

But she asked Monty to accept us, and he's making an effort to do that by teaching us the nuts and bolts of this new world.

"Hey, which one is for the bilge pump?" I scan the board of switches, attempting to test the electrical systems, but I need a diagram. "Monty?"

No response.

Stepping onto the deck, I find him standing on the starboard side, his hands clenched around the taffrail, his attention rapt on the path that leads to the estate. Something akin to eagerness etches his face.

I follow his gaze, squinting.

Then I see her.

Holy fuck.

As Frankie steps onto the path, the world slams to a stop.

A form-fitting sundress clings to the feminine shape of her body, leaving little to the imagination. The deep emerald green fabric complements her striking eyes and pale skin. Red hair falls in loose waves over her shoulders, catching the light and shimmering like fire.

I can't breathe. All the feeling in my body rushes to my cock as I drink in every detail. She's so beautiful it hurts. So fulfilling I'll never be thirsty again.

I've seen her in leggings, snow pants, threadbare jeans, designer trousers, skimpy little panties, and gloriously nude, but never in a dress.

She looks ethereal. A goddess come to life. Fucking radiant.

I want to pull her close and tell her how much I love her. I love her inner strength, her intelligence, her compassion. I want to shout it across the Sitka Sound and tattoo it on my skin. She would make fun of me for that, but I love that she calls me out on shit.

I love that she calls me *hers*.

But right now, it's her outer beauty that has me mesmerized. Every step she takes toward me is a promise, every glance a challenge. And I'm helplessly sucked in.

Beside her, Kody walks with a possessive hand on her back, his eyes darting between her and her surroundings. He knows exactly the effect she has on everyone, including the security team scattered around the perimeter.

I've met all the guards. They're blank-faced and professional. But they're also male.

Monty hasn't taken his damn eyes off her, his expression awestruck.

The flames of jealousy burn in my chest, pushing me forward. I hop off the yacht and meet her on the dock.

"Morning, handsome." She smiles up at me.

"Morning, love." I steal a kiss that leaves me wanting more. "You look fucking lush."

"Thank you." She rises on tiptoes and whispers in my ear, "I shaved my legs."

"Why?" I lean back, examining her bare skin beneath the dress. "What's the purpose?"

She sighs.

Monty clears his throat behind me, causing me to whip my head around.

His lips press together, and his throat jumps beneath the bandage, swallowing whatever he wants to tell her.

Instead, he says, "Shall we?"

We board the yacht, and she veers into the command deck, her hands deftly checking the controls and adjusting settings. Of course, she knows her way around this vessel. It's hers as much as it's his.

Because they're married.

The thought stirs a blizzard of emotions in me. There's jealousy. Always. But also admiration. She's too independent to be a passenger princess. She also has her own boat—the faded, rickety little cruiser in the adjacent slip—which she used to go to work every day. I love her even more for keeping that old thing.

"Frankie spent a lot of time on this yacht." Monty leans in the doorway, the low rumble of his voice hinting at intimacies that make my hackles bristle. "She knows it better than anyone."

Every surface, wall, couch, and bed.

I hear it in his tone, see it in his hooded eyes.

He not only fucked the only two women I've had sex with, but he also impregnated them. Not that I have any possessive feelings about Gretchen. I fucking hated that raping bitch. But my very complicated sexual history connects me to him in deeply disturbing ways that I try not to think about.

These are things I should be discussing with a therapist. Anyone but Dr. Whitaker. My session with him was a wasted hour of questions, which I refused to answer because I was too busy plotting his death with a growl in my throat.

And this was before Kody told me that the doctor put his hands on her.

"It's been a while." She looks over the displays and gauges with familiarity. "But I can still operate this fancy lady in my sleep."

"You want to steer her into the Sound?" Monty asks.

"Nope. I'd rather sit on the sun deck." She angles her neck, peering out the window. "Not a raindrop in the sky. You picked a great day for a cruise, Monty."

They share a private smile, and I'm back to wanting to gut him.

As I help Monty release the mooring lines to depart, two security guards board the yacht.

Monty catches my eye. "I'm not taking any chances."

I hadn't considered the need for security on this excursion. Kody and I are so used to protecting her by ourselves. That's our job. The thought of sharing that role grates even as I know it's the right decision.

Back at the bridge, Monty explains the yacht's controls to Kody and me. Frankie saunters off to the sun deck.

Then we're off.

Kody and I take turns at the wheel while Monty directs us. There's a lot to remember, but we learn quickly. Kody doesn't say much beyond his usual grunting, but I see the smile in his eyes. He's enjoying this as much as I am.

As we move farther from the shore, the vastness of the water spreads out before us. I saw the ocean from the plane when we flew in, but it was dark and distant. Down here, it looks bigger, breathtaking and deep, an endless ripple of blue beneath the cloudless sky.

Sometime later, she returns with a tray of champagne glasses filled with orange liquid.

"Mimosas." She passes them out and sets the tray aside. "Champagne and orange juice."

Monty raises his glass in a toast. "To family and new experiences."

We all clink our glasses together, and Kody and I exchange a look.

This is a celebration, a moment of unity and shared purpose, even if undercurrents of tension and distrust remain.

The bubbly drink fizzes on my tongue, the taste sharp and sweet. I prefer Kody's vodka.

She finishes her drink and looks at Monty. "When do you go back to the office?"

"I sold the Sitka office."

"What? Why?"

"You know why, Frankie."

Yeah, we all know. The night of her abduction, he stayed at that office instead of coming home and protecting her. I hope he chokes on his guilt for the rest of his miserable life.

"What about your company?" she asks. "You built it from the ground up. Please, tell me you're not selling it."

"I'm not. I hired more senior management, put strong executive officers in place, and delegated my responsibilities. I still own the entire enterprise and retain final approval on crucial decisions. When I'm needed, I'll work from my office at home. But I stepped away from the day-to-day involvement to focus on my personal affairs."

By personal affairs, he means *her.*

"I see." She wets her lips. "Meanwhile, I'll be doing the opposite."

"What does that mean?" I go still.

"I'm returning to the hospital, Leo."

"When? You've only had your freedom back for a week. Give yourself time to heal."

"The quicker she returns to work," Monty says, icy eyes fixed on her, "the sooner she doesn't have to depend on me. Isn't that right, darling?"

"I love my job." She holds his stare. "I miss it. And you guys need more bonding time without me in the way."

"Fuck that." I dip toward her. "You're not in the way."

Monty studies her, his fingers tapping on the instrument panel. "When you return to work, you'll have security shadowing you."

"I figured."

"We need to establish a safety plan, not just for reporters but for whoever else might be watching you."

"I know."

"That's it?" I screw up my face. "It didn't occur to you to discuss this with Kody and me?"

"Not everything needs to be a fight."

"Not a fight. But how about a conversation? No more lone ranger mentality, remember? Every decision is made collectively with everyone's agreement."

She's pushing this too soon. Kody and I can't get jobs until we have IDs. That will take weeks.

Given the scowl on Kody's face, he's thinking the same thing.

"We're not in the hills anymore where every decision is a matter of life or death." She squares her shoulders. "Things are different now."

I don't want things to be different, not where she's

concerned.

Why is Monty agreeing with this so easily? He doesn't strike me as the sort of man who gives into her every whim. Is it because he knows he has no leverage with her? Or does he know something that we don't?

"I'm going to call Rhett." She pulls her phone out of her bag and steps toward the door. "Maybe I can see him while we're in town."

With that, she breezes out of the bridge with her phone to her ear.

"That's a bad idea," I mutter.

"Which part?" Monty crosses his arms.

"All of it."

"You have a lot to learn, kid."

"Call me a kid one more time." I lean into his space, bridging the gap with a seething exhale. "Go on, *Uncle* Monty. I dare you."

"Enough." Kody shoves my shoulder, breaking us apart. "Save it for the punching bag."

I step back, letting the chill of the early April morning cool my temper.

"She's stubborn." Monty watches her through the window, tracking her movements across the bridge deck. "Her career has always been a point of contention. It's a battle I lost when we married and one I certainly won't win now."

We drift into silence as the yacht cuts through the glass-like water. The engines hum beneath my feet, a distant, powerful purr reverberating through my bloodstream.

Monty stands at the helm, a stoic thorn of power in my side. I want to hate him more than I do.

His calculating blue eyes, the same shade as Wolf's but older, scan the horizon with the intensity of a predator. It's a look I've grown accustomed to, the trait of a man who's always alert, always hunting.

The more time I spend with him, the more I notice our family resemblances. Like the exaggerated squareness of his jaw, especially when he's clenching it all to hell.

"Holy shit." His head jerks up, and he points. "Look."

I follow the line of his finger, searching the water. At first, I see nothing but calm, undulating waves.

Then something moves. A fin slices through the surface, sleek and dark against the shimmering sea. Another follows, then another, until a group of massive, sleek-bodied creatures emerges in slow, majestic succession.

"Whales?" I breathe, blinking, not believing what I'm seeing.

"A whole damn pod of them." Monty kills the engine and darts to the starboard deck for a better view.

A few feet away, Frankie leans over the railing, smiling with a hand on her chest.

I smile with her, gobsmacked.

Their giant bodies move with an elegance that defies their size, gliding through the water like titans of the deep. Low, rumbling moans vibrate through the hull, accompanied by melodic, otherworldly calls, each note rising and falling with lyrical grace.

Kody's wide eyes meet mine, and I feel it. The energy in the air. The music of life.

We're no longer surviving.

We're *living.*

He steps out to join her at the taffrail, his broody expression gone, revealing the boy I haven't seen for twenty years. The boy before the trauma and abuse, who was so easily captivated by the raw beauty of nature.

My chest swells with a swarm of feelings I can scarcely name.

I don't know how common a whale sighting is, but this feels like a gift, a glimpse into a world we were denied.

The beasts circle the yacht, exhaling with powerful whooshes that send plumes of mist into the air. The forceful sounds punctuate their softer melodies with primal power. It's the sound of life, of strength, of creatures perfectly adapted to their watery realm.

As they return to the depths, their tails rise into the air, each one unique in pattern and shape. They arch sinuously, dark and glistening, silhouetted against the sunlight. Water cascades off the edges, sparkling like diamonds and falling into the sea with a soft splash.

When the final one dives, its fluke lingers for a moment longer, a final flourish before slipping beneath the waves. The water closes over them, leaving ripples of serenity.

I steal another glance at Kody, noting the strange upturn of his lips, the softening of his hardened features. For once, the shadows in his eyes are chased away by the simple, unadulterated joy of witnessing something so pure, so untainted by the darkness we've known.

Monty returns to the bridge and starts the engine, his gaze still fixed on the horizon. The peacefulness on his face smooths his skin and relaxes his features, making him appear a decade younger.

Turns out not even Monty Novak is immune to idyllic moments.

I join him, a smile tugs at my lips. "That's something we never saw in the hills."

"No shit." He almost smiles back. "There's nothing quite like it. Makes you feel small and insignificant, doesn't it?"

"Right, because nothing says *small and insignificant* like standing on a billionaire's yacht."

He stares at me, blinks, then drops his head back and roars with laughter. He laughs so loudly that Frankie spins in our direction, her mouth hanging open.

It wasn't *that* funny. More on the edge of mockery, but maybe that's what he finds so amusing.

"You haven't even seen all the yacht's features." He flips on the auto-pilot and strides out the door, motioning at us to follow. "Come on."

leonid

TWENTY-ONE

Monty leads us into the heart of his floating palace, one hand resting casually in his pocket, the other gesturing fluidly as he points out the hot tub on the sun deck, bars on every level stocked with the finest liquors, and sleeping cabins that look more like luxury hotel suites.

Not that I've ever seen a hotel suite.

But I get the point he's making. He's filthy rich, lives large, and loves to show it off.

I follow with Kody close behind, both of us silently absorbing the opulence around us.

Frankie stayed on the bridge deck to take a call from her boss, which makes me twitchy as fuck. An unreasonable reaction. I've never met Dr. Rhett Howell.

That's a problem that needs to be rectified soon.

We step into the main lounge, and the air immediately changes. The space sprawls with polished wood and fine leather, dripping with wealth and impeccable taste. Soft, ambient lighting illuminates lavish sofas and armchairs. Large windows offer panoramic views of the ocean.

It's too fancy for my primitive, snow-cabin ass.

"Over here." Monty strolls to the main bar in the aft of the living room.

It isn't just a bar. It's a whole experience.

I run my hand along the smooth, curved teak wood. The shiny metal accents remind me of old-school ships. Plenty of comfy seats. Killer views of the ocean. And the bar top? Man, it's just one big slab of fancy marble with all these cool veins running through it.

Bottles of every shape and color line the shelves. I can practically taste the aged whiskey and fine champagne.

He pours himself a drink, the amber liquid catching the light, and offers us one, too. Kody declines, more interested in observing the setup.

"I'll have what you're having." I nod at his glass.

He hands it over and makes himself another. "Not your usual dive bar, huh?"

"We wouldn't know." Kody lowers onto the stool beside me.

"I worked hard for this." Monty takes a sip. "Every bit of it."

I respect that. He didn't inherit this life. He built it, piece by piece.

"It's not just about the money, you know." Monty tosses back another drink, his gaze distant. "It's about freedom. The ability to do what I want, when I want. To provide for those I care about. That's what drives me." Another gulp of whiskey. "It means fuck all if I have no one to share it with."

I understand that more than he knows. Freedom is something we've all fought for in our own ways. While our battles have been different, the end goal is the same.

None of it matters without Frankie.

"With hard work and compromise, you can have this, too." Monty looks at Kody, then me. "With freedom like this, you can have anything you want. You're the only one standing in your way."

"What are you saying?" My brows pull together. "What compromise?"

"Let me help you. If you want a pilot school, a distillery, whatever your dreams are, work with me. I can guide you through the logistics, be a silent partner, and help you make it successful. It's what I do."

"What do you get out of it?"

"A new challenge." His eyes glimmer. "And a percentage of the profits, of course."

A businessman, through and through.

I glance around, taking in the extravagance and comfort of it all. He has every material possession a man could want, but part of me remains unimpressed by the trappings of wealth.

The pod of whales stirred something in me that no amount of luxury could replicate. Their wild, unassuming nature calls to a deeper part of me, one that yearns for something more primal and authentic.

This yacht, this life, it's a world away from everything we've known.

But we're not in the hills anymore. We must adapt, evolve, and transcend from the feral, snarling animals raised in the wild into smarter, more refined, successful men.

Men who can properly care for Frankie in this strange, manufactured world.

A world where we can finally find the freedom and peace we've been searching for. A life we never imagined.

Kody sits beside me, silent as usual, but there's a light in his eyes I haven't seen before. He's curious, maybe even a little excited, though likely more by the sheer novelty of it all.

I give him a look, letting him take the lead.

"Put together a plan." He rolls his lips. "Give us an offer, and we'll consider it."

Monty smiles, a genuine, warm smile that transforms his stern features.

"Here's to freedom." He raises his glass.

For the second time today, I clink my tumbler with his and finish my whiskey.

He makes a third drink, this one with Kentucky bourbon, a splash of Amarena cherry juice, and two black cherries.

For Frankie.

My stomach hardens.

"Let's eat lunch then start on those driving lessons." Monty pushes off the bar, carrying her drink.

Kody and I rise, taking a second to find our footing against the gentle rocking of the yacht.

We follow the distant calls of seabirds through the narrow corridor with Monty in the lead.

"One more thing." He pauses at the doorway of the largest suite, turning to face us. "This one's mine."

I peer inside the main bedroom. It's bigger, more lavish than all the rest, a reflection of his status as the owner.

He steps closer, his expression stony. "No one fucks her in this bed but me."

"What the fuck did you just say?" Blood rushes past my ears.

"You heard me." He leans in, his breath fuming with whiskey. "Going forward, you get two versions of me. That's the only way this works."

I'm still stuck on the part where no one fucks her but him.

The walls close in. My chest pushes out. An animalistic sound rumbles in my throat, a warning of the bloodshed to come.

"Breathe." Kody stands behind me in the narrow hall and hooks an arm around my waist, holding me back.

"I know you're fucking her." Monty slams his hand against the wall beside my face, a loud cracking echo. "I can't stop you. I can't..." He sucks in a breath, his fingers clenching around the glass of bourbon. "But I do *not* want to see it, hear it, or have it flaunted in my face. Give me that much."

"Two versions?" Kody pushes me to the side, squeezing past me. "What does that mean?"

"When we're discussing business and planning your dreams, you get the brother. When we're working out, dealing with Frankie's therapist, or taking driving lessons, you get the brother. But right here, right now, I'm the husband. The husband in love with his wife. If I find you fucking her in my goddamn bed—" he stabs a finger at his suite "—you get the husband, not the brother. Understand?"

"Yeah." Kody pushes back against me, stopping me from

slipping around him. "We get you."

"I need to hear it from Leo."

He's not demanding his wife back. He's asking us not to be cruel.

"Yeah." I drag a hand down my face and rein in my temper. "I get you."

"Good." He straightens, cracks his neck, and continues down the corridor like nothing happened.

I trail behind, my mind swimming. "So Dr. Jekyll is the brother, and Mr. Hyde is the murderous husband?"

He pauses and pivots to face us. "Put yourself in my shoes. How would you deal with it? What would you do?"

If I was married to Frankie and she loved two other men? I would steal her back, force her to be with me, whatever it took. I guess that makes him a better man than me.

"That's what I thought." He clicks his tongue.

"Am I talking to the brother or the husband? Because I'm a little confused."

"The brother. Try to keep up." He turns away, striding across the deck toward her.

"*Good and evil are so close as to be chained together in the soul.*" I shudder.

Kody grunts. He knows the classic lore of Jekyll and Hyde too well. Denver used to read it to us during the long, monotonous months of darkness.

Monty delivers the bourbon to her and heads in the direction of the galley.

The midday sun hovers, casting a glow over everything, especially Frankie.

I prowl toward her.

She was my only source of light in the hills of shivers and shadows. In the halo of sunlight, she shines even brighter, glistening with warmth and luminescence, her expression serene, a rare and precious kind of peace.

As I press in behind her, she reaches back, her hand slipping into mine. The touch of her skin calms me, centers me. I squeeze her fingers, grateful for her presence.

"What happened?" She glances at Kody, who follows Monty to help him with the food.

"Ask Mr. Hyde."

"Uh oh. That sounds ominous."

I tell her about the conversation at the bar and his offer to help us. Then I recount the confrontation outside his suite and his warning about his dual personalities.

She loosens a breath. "Why can't he just move on?"

"Impossible." With my arms around her from behind, I drag my nose through her hair, inhaling her cherry scent. "No one can move on from you. You're the ultimate destination."

"Were you thinking about my vagina when you said that last part?"

"Always thinking about that pretty pink part of you, love."

"Knew it." She sips her drink, eyes on the shimmering horizon.

Monty and Kody return, and the four of us share a quiet meal on the sun deck.

As usual, Oliver went all out, preparing a spread of smoked salmon with capers and some kind of creamy white sauce drizzled over it. The salad looks like art with mixed greens, bright cherry tomatoes, and slivers of something purple, all topped with edible flowers. Yeah, flowers we can eat. Who knew?

Steak is the main course, seared perfectly with a crust that smells like heaven. It's sliced thin, juices pooling on the plate, and served with tiny roasted potatoes and asparagus.

We eat mostly in silence, the only sounds the clink of cutlery and the occasional call of a gull or puffin.

Throughout the meal, Monty tries to be the brother, commenting on the weather or some idle bullshit. But every time he looks at her, the husband burns in his eyes.

He's delusional if he thinks he can separate the two.

When we clear the dishes, he and Kody head down to the bridge to turn us back toward Sitka's harbor.

I follow her to the railing, wrapping around her back and running a hand along the bare skin of her thigh. I fucking love how easy it is to access her body in this dress.

She leans her head back on my chest. "I'm going to stay on the yacht while you guys do your driving lessons. Rhett is meeting me—"

"No."

"Leo." She huffs. "If I go with you, you won't be able to concentrate on driving. Learning involves hard braking, oversteering, near collisions...not the safest conditions for a passenger. But if I wait in the garage while you take turns driving, it'll only make it harder for you to concentrate. You won't be able to see me, and you'll be worrying about someone snatching me, even with the guards nearby."

"I'll worry no matter what."

"I know. But it's safer for me to stay on the yacht. I won't be out in public or wandering around in town. I won't step one foot off the yacht. Rhett is coming to me, and I'll have a security guard stay behind."

"Both guards."

"You need one with you. If you guys run into reporters—"

"You fucking serious? You think I need someone to protect me?"

"Don't sound so insulted. You obviously think I need two guards to protect *me*."

"Because..." I put my mouth at her ear and breathe, "Spaghetti arms."

"Fuck off." She jabs me in the gut with a pointy elbow, making me laugh.

That fires up both her elbows, which I quickly wrestle into submission.

"Shh. I'm just teasing you." I nuzzle her neck. "Tell me about your boss."

"He's the Chief of Surgery. Medical degree from Harvard. Highly intelligent. Early forties. He's a stand-up guy, Leo. Super nice."

"Let me guess, he also volunteers at the local orphanage and rescues kittens in his spare time?"

"Nope. That's his fatal flaw. No spare time. He's married to his job. Lives alone. No domestic partners or close friends."

"Yet he's making time to see you."

"Only because I'm in town, and the hospital is just over the bridge."

"Bet he's hoping for some details about your captivity."

"He won't get any. Maybe someday, but not right now."

The strange tone in her voice has me turning her in my arms.

"What did you talk about with Doyle?" I search her vibrant green eyes.

"The miscarriage." She looks away. "Monty and his relationship with you guys. I need to work up to the rest of it."

"He asked me if I was fucking you."

"What?"

"Not in those words, but the question was direct and accusatory as if I'm a home-wrecker or something."

"That's *not* okay." She mutters something under her breath, words lost to the breeze but rich with annoyance. "You need to see a different therapist. All of you. This isn't working out with Doyle."

"I don't trust him. None of us do. So we'll continue to see him until we figure out his angle."

"I can't stop you from doing your thing."

"My thing?"

"You know the thing. Pounding your chest. Peeing on your territory."

"I don't do that."

"Right. So while you're *not* doing that with Doyle, you also need to see another therapist for real. That includes all of you."

If a therapist is going to dig into my personal shit like all those reporters and detectives, I'll pass on that. But I won't have that argument with her right now.

"We're here." I turn her toward the cluster of buildings emerging on the horizon.

I saw Sitka when we landed last week. Kind of. It was dark when we drove from the airport to Monty's yacht. Seeing it in the daylight, crowded with people and traffic, will be a different experience.

"There's a cruise ship in port." She shields her eyes against the sun. "It's going to be busy today."

She already warned us about that. Sitka has around eight thousand residents. A cruise ship can swell the population by another four thousand.

"Ready to see the world? Or at least, a small remote part of it?" Infectious excitement radiates from her.

"Yeah, love." My heart races. "I wore my best beard for this."

leonid

TWENTY-TWO

Leaning against the railing with Frankie in the cage of my arms, I devour the picturesque view of Sitka, hypnotized.

Majestic mountains loom over the harbor, the peaks capped with snow even in the spring. A harp-shaped bridge spans between the islands. Quaint shops and restaurants line the waterfront, a long maritime history weathering their wooden facades.

Brightly colored buoys mark the channels as Monty steers the yacht into the marina, treating the chaotic harbor like another routine part of his day.

Frankie points out the hospital where she and her mother worked. I knew her mother passed a few years ago from cancer, but I didn't realize she was a nurse, too.

The hospital sits on a smaller island in the distance, dwarfed by the massive white hull of the cruise ship. Watercraft of all sizes bob in the water. The strange, potent scents of saltwater, fish, and diesel burn my nose with sensory overload, but in the best possible way.

"This is a working harbor, not just a tourist attraction." She gestures at the rows of wooden piers, each one busy with fishermen unloading their catch. "My father worked in the fishing industry, but I don't remember him. He died of heart disease when I was young."

She goes on to describe how she spent her youth kayaking, boating, and exploring the numerous islands. During the winter months, when other kids were sledding and cross-country skiing, she remained indoors and read cozy mysteries.

For a woman who despises the cold as much as she does, she survived the harshest Arctic conditions with barely a complaint.

She has no idea how fucking tough she is.

As the marina grows closer, so do the people. The crowds, the noise, the sheer vibrancy of it all—everything is an unfamiliar and new experience. I've only read about places like this, seen them in movies, but witnessing it firsthand is something else entirely.

Monty maneuvers the yacht into its berth with expert precision, and I feel a twinge of envy at how effortlessly he handles everything.

With freedom like this, you can have anything you want.

Once we're docked, she tells him her plan to stay behind.

Unlike me, he doesn't bat an eye. He simply paces off toward the security guards to work out the logistics.

Kody starts arguing with her, and I leave him to it, knowing he won't get anywhere.

When I reach Monty's side, he's midway through his instructions to the guards.

"She doesn't leave your sight. When she uses the lavatory, you wait outside the door. She doesn't step off the yacht. No one boards except Dr. Howell. If anyone is with him, deny entry and call me." He directs a finger at his chest. "If she tries to leave, stay with her and call me. If anything feels off or suspicious..."

"We'll call you, Mr. Novak."

She walks with us to the port side as Monty gives her the same instructions he gave the guards.

Leaving her behind feels like I'm ripping out a vital organ. It's not natural. But this short separation will be a good test for the three of us. Kody and I need to know we can handle this new world without her always by our sides.

"We won't be long." Monty steps off the yacht without another word.

"Have fun." She rests her hands on her hips and hardens her voice. "No fighting."

"No promises." I cast one last glance at her, my gut twisting.

Kody lingers, his dark eyes glued to her.

"Come on." I bump his shoulder with mine, propelling him into motion.

Monty leads the way through the maze of docks and onto the coastal road. The town buzzes with activity. People mill about, their chatter and laughter filling the air.

Every time a car zooms by, I flinch and reach for the rifle that's not there. Kody burrows into his hunched shoulders, trying and failing to block out the sudden bursts of noise.

I catch myself staring at everyone and everything, especially at the children and the dogs on leashes.

When a family with wailing kids hurries by, Monty pauses, his voice low. "Have you ever seen a child?"

"Wolf, I guess." I crane my neck, watching the adults wrestle their screaming toddlers. "Twenty years ago."

"What about a dog?"

"Only wolves." Kody stands stiffly, hands shoved in his jean pockets.

"Yeah, these pampered pets aren't wolves." Monty laughs.

It's disorienting and surreal. Kody feels it, too. His eyes dart around, taking in the chaos with cautious curiosity.

"I usually have Kai drive me." Monty studies us too closely. "But I thought it would be nice to walk since it's not raining. Do you want to keep going?"

Kody and I nod. It takes a helluva lot more than kids and dogs to spook us.

"It's just around the corner." Monty continues down the street.

"Do we need to worry about reporters?" I ask.

"No." He pauses, opening a door for a woman carrying an

armful of boxes.

"Thank you, Mr. Novak." She blushes and ducks her head, smiling shyly.

Once she's inside, he continues down the road. "I have Sirena watching for media activity. There's no press in town today."

Always one step ahead.

Even so, my senses remain on high alert.

Walking through the town feels like I'm walking in someone else's shoes. Each time I make eye contact with someone, they stare back with interest or surprise.

It's weird, being the focus of all these strangers' attention. Part of me wants to shrink away, to disappear into the background, but another part feels an electric thrill. It's like I'm on display, a rare specimen they've never seen before.

When they stare, I stare back hard. They always look away first.

"You two draw a lot of attention." Monty glances at us, wearing a remote expression. "Especially from the ladies. You'll get used to it."

"He claims it's a family thing," Kody mutters under his breath. "The way we look. Says being attractive is a blessing and a curse."

We're attractive? I snort. More like wild, filthy animals. Nothing like these people with their loud voices, fancy hairstyles, cloying perfumes, and brightly colored clothes.

Every face that turns my way glares like a spotlight, and I wonder if that's what they see. A rugged, uncivilized outsider from another world. Kody and I tower over every person we pass. We're more muscular, too, and we're not even at our normal weights.

I keep my head up, pretending like I belong here. Kody stalks beside me, doing the same.

As we push through the throngs of people, I absorb the colorful signs, the smell of food, and the snippets of conversations. It's all so vivid, so alive. Cars and buses clog the streets, their engines adding a constant hum to the cacophony of sounds.

Monty strides ahead, seemingly unfazed by the hustle and bustle. We follow closely, matching his confident pace. It's a rush, being immersed in this living, breathing mass of humanity. Part of something bigger.

On the next street, he leads us to a nondescript building.

Entering a code into a keypad by the door, he steps inside. "Welcome to my garage."

The overhead lights click on as we enter, illuminating a huge, windowless room.

Not just any garage.

The spotless floors shine with glossy gray paint, and holy fuck, this place is massive, stretching out at least ten cars deep. It reminds me of the Batcave, only brighter, shinier, and even more impressive.

Car lifts suspend hypercars in mid-air, giving the whole place a high-tech, futuristic vibe. And the cars...

Everywhere I look is a Ferrari, Lamborghini, Bugatti, Koenigsegg, the list goes on. I also spot luxury cars—a Bentley, Rolls-Royce, and Range Rover—each one polished to perfection, reflecting the lights like mirrors.

Kody and I exchange a glance, our eyes wide. He doesn't know the names of most of these rare, exotic beauties. He didn't devour the car and motorcycle magazines that Denver brought home like I did. But he understands finances and the value of the dollar.

Denver was passionate about economics and taught us everything he studied and researched. Kody's probably thinking about all the things he could do if he had even a fraction of this wealth.

Monty strolls among the cars, inspecting a fender, dusting off a headlight, clearly proud of his collection. Honestly, I can't blame him. Each car here probably costs more than I'll earn over the course of my entire life.

"This is some serious hardware." I whistle low, unable to wrap my head around the sheer amount of money sitting in this room. "You could buy a small country with what's in here."

"These cars are museum pieces. Rare works of art. I don't

drive them." Monty grins, enjoying our reactions.

I amble over to a Lamborghini Aventador, my fingers itching to touch it. The paint job is flawless, a deep, glossy black that swallows all the light around it.

Next to it is a Koenigsegg Jesko, one of the rarest cars in the world. The carbon fiber body resembles something out of a sci-fi movie, all sharp angles and aerodynamic curves. The red paint is too bright for my tastes, but the craftsmanship, the power...this machine is built for one thing. *Speed.*

"We're taking this one out for driving lessons, right?" I thrust my thumb at it.

"Sure." Monty lifts a shoulder. "Any one you want."

"You're kidding."

"I wouldn't have brought you here if I was."

"Which one is the easiest to handle?" Kody crosses his arms, glancing around. "And holds more than two passengers?"

"The Bentley." Monty nods toward the rear of the garage.

It's on the tip of my tongue to say *boring.* But no one would call a Bentley boring.

"This is wild." I shake my head. "When you find something you like, you don't fuck around."

"You could say that." Monty's voice drops, his expression darkening.

He's no longer thinking about his damn car collection.

Kody stiffens beside me.

"Enough gawking." Monty takes off toward the Bentley. "Let's get to work."

"Let it go." I clap Kody on the shoulder. "Focus on learning."

We follow Monty deeper into the garage. As much as his obsession with Frankie eats me up, I get it. He wants the best of the best, and she's worth more than his yacht, jet, private island, and car collection combined.

And she's the one thing he can't have.

We pile into the Bentley, Monty in the driver's seat. I sit beside him in the front with Kody in the back. The engine roars to life, and he takes us out of the garage.

As we drive through the town, people turn their heads to

watch us pass. Either the Bentley is an unusual sight in this remote town or they recognize the man driving it. Probably both.

We cross over a bridge, and I roll down the window, savoring the scent of saltwater and pine in the air.

"How did Frankie meet Rhett?" I ask. "Did he hire her?"

"They met in Anchorage during her residency. When he accepted the Chief of Surgery position and moved to Sitka, he brought her with him. She grew up here, so it was an easy decision for her. Especially since her mom had just been diagnosed with cancer."

Once we're out of the town, Monty hits the gas, and the car surges forward, taking us onto the rural Alaskan mountain roads. The scenery changes rapidly, giving way to vast stretches of untamed wilderness.

Towering pine trees flank the road, their dark green needles brushing against the cerulean sky. Snow-capped mountains tower around us, the jagged peaks piercing the horizon.

The road twists and turns, carving a path through the rugged terrain. Every now and then, we catch glimpses of wildlife. A deer darting across the pavement. An eagle soaring high above. The beauty of this place is raw and untouched. It feels more like home.

"You met her in the hospital?" I glance at his stony profile. "You were her patient?"

"Yeah. I was playing basketball with some of my colleagues and dislocated my kneecap. She was the trauma nurse who put me back together." He swallows. "I've replayed that day a million times in my head. It was a chance meeting. I don't know how Denver could've orchestrated it."

"He couldn't have known you would get injured," Kody says from the back seat. "But if he was connected with someone in that hospital..."

"They could've assigned her to me for some nefarious reason." Monty nods. "That's a lot of *could'ves* and *what ifs* with no supporting evidence. All we have is the ramblings of a psychopath."

"A psychopath who knew you met her in the hospital." I grit my teeth. "How did Denver know that?"

"She never told him?"

"No." I drum my fingers on my knee. "He said the first time he saw her was in that hospital, two years before he abducted her. Said he got a kidney stone while fishing in the Sitka Sound, and when he arrived at the hospital, he saw her in the hallway."

"He had a different story in his video." Kody shifts behind me. "He said he saw her during her residency in Anchorage, long before Monty knew her. So which is it?"

"Someone knows." My ribs tighten. "And that someone is the who in his riddle."

"You still think it's me?" Monty's hand twitches on the steering wheel.

"I haven't ruled anyone out."

Scowling, he pulls over on an empty stretch of road. "Take the wheel."

I slide into the driver's seat, heart pounding, as he gives me a few pointers.

Then we're off.

The pedal responds to my touch like an extension of my foot, jolting us forward. After a few hard brakes and jerky whiplashes, I'm driving, turning, speeding up, and grinning so hard my cheeks hurt.

The Bentley hugs the curves of the road, its engine purring like a contented beast. Much easier to drive than the snow machine.

The scenery blurs past in a rush of green forests, white snow, and blue sky. The freedom is intoxicating, a reminder of why we fought so hard to escape the hills.

"Not bad." Monty clears his throat and drags his gaze to mine. "I mean it. You're a quick learner. Fast reflexes. You have a natural skill for driving, piloting, and operating machines."

"Thanks." Refusing to read too much into his praise, I find Kody's eyes in the rearview. "Ready to take over?"

"Thought you'd never ask."

The salty sea breeze caresses my face, and the yacht sways rhythmically beneath me. With each deep breath, I drift a little further away from the horror and pain of the past nine months. If only for a moment.

Monty's security guards stand nearby, trying to blend into the background. I appreciate them more than they know. Without their watchful eyes, I wouldn't be able to relax.

Not without Leo and Kody at my side.

I'm too dependent on the constant, vigilant protection of my feral boys, and they need a break from me to enjoy their new freedom.

Leo will flip when he sees Monty's car collection. Even Kody will be reluctantly wowed. I smile at the thought of them hitting the gas and pushing Monty's precious toys to their limits. I saw how hard they drove the snow machine and dirt bike.

Monty won't care. His collection may be worth a fortune, but what matters more to him is having someone to share it with. I was never that person. He wanted me to take an interest, to share in his love for speed and performance. I tried, but I'm not a car enthusiast, plain and simple.

Doesn't matter. Leo and Kody will do car stuff with him.

I lean back in my chair and let the sun warm my skin. I miss my job. I miss the chaos of the emergency room, the adrenaline rush of saving lives, and the camaraderie of my colleagues. I miss feeling like I belong somewhere, like I'm making a difference.

Lost in my thoughts, I sense someone behind me. I glance over my shoulder, and my breath stumbles.

Standing there, looking as handsome as I remember, is Dr. Rhett Howell.

Dressed in green scrubs, his blond hair slightly longer than usual, he greets me with winter blue eyes and a smile that lights up his flawless face.

"Rhett." I rise from my seat.

"Frankie." He spreads his arms wide.

We meet in a warm embrace. The sterile, astringent scent of his skin brings back a flood of memories from the hospital.

"Look at you." He steps back, giving me a clinical once-over, his expression creasing with concern.

"Don't say it."

"You lost weight you didn't have to lose."

"Unlike you. Always the picture of perfection."

"Well, someone has to uphold the standards." He winks, charming as ever.

"Sit, please." I gesture to the chairs on the deck. "Can I get you something to drink? Water? Wine?"

"No." He waves a hand dismissively. "I'm still on the clock."

"Of course you are."

"How's Melanie Stokes working out for you?"

"She's been great. Thank you for referring her."

We settle into our seats, our knees brushing as we angle toward each other.

"So how have you been really?" He glances at the security guards, his tone shifting, deepening. "I heard what happened. The news was...well, it confirmed my worst fears. When you didn't show up for work or answer your phone, I knew." His jaw flexes. "Monty called me the day after you missed your shift. Said you left him. He...”

“He what...?” I lean toward him with my whole body, willing him to finish that sentence.

“It doesn’t matter. I don’t want to upset you.”

“It’s okay. *I’m* okay. I’d really like to know what he said.”

“Frankie, he was devastated. Completely destroyed. Could barely string together two words. He called me, hoping I’d heard from you or knew something. That beautiful, cold man was a fucking mess.” He shakes his head. “I don’t know what happened. From what the news is reporting, I can only deduce that it was terrible.”

“A lot happened, but I don’t want to talk about it right now. It’s too fresh. Let’s just say the media got some things right and some things wrong.”

“I assumed as much.” He smiles sadly. “Whenever you’re ready to talk, I’m here.”

“Thank you.” I straighten. “Actually, I wanted to talk about returning to work.”

“Your position is always there for you. Whenever you’re ready to start, it’s yours.”

“I want to start immediately.”

“I thought you needed a period of adjustment.” He curves a brow.

“I adjusted.”

“It’s only been a week.”

“A week too long. I’m ready.”

“Then consider yourself rehired.” He reclines in the chair, exuding contentment and control. “The team will be so excited to have you back.”

We chat about the hospital and the changes that happened while I was gone, and he catches me up on all the latest gossip.

“Dr. Simons finally decided to retire.” He smirks.

“No shit?”

“I think he’s more excited about his new wife than his retirement.”

“Another one? Is this his sixth wife?”

“She’s number seven and barely legal.”

"Sounds about right. What about Nurse Letty? Is she still terrorizing the interns?"

"It's her life's mission. Last week, she had one poor intern convinced that the ghost of old Dr. Jenkins still roams the halls at night."

I burst out laughing. "I miss her."

We continue talking, the conversation flowing effortlessly. Rhett always has a way of making me laugh, and today is no exception. He tells me about a prank he pulled on one of the surgeons, involving a rubber chicken, a condom, and a very confused patient.

I laugh so hard I'm in tears.

"There's a new intern who's already making waves." He strokes a thumb under his lip, watching me. "She's incredibly smart, hard-working, and has an obnoxious, rebellious streak. Reminds me of someone I know."

I roll my eyes. "I wasn't that bad."

"Frankie, you were a nightmare." He coughs. "But in the best way. You challenged everyone, and it made us all better."

"Flattery will get you everywhere, Dr. Howell."

"I'm counting on it. But seriously, we've missed you. The whole team has. It hasn't been the same without you."

"I've missed everyone, too." A lump forms in my throat. "It's been hard being away. But I'm ready to get back to doing what I love."

"And we'll be there to support you every step of the way. You've always been one of the best, Frankie. Strong, determined, and ready to take on the world."

"Thank you." My cheeks flush. "So what about you? How have you been?"

"Oh, you know me. Just the usual—saving lives, dazzling the masses, and maintaining my impeccable fashion sense." He gestures at his scrubs.

"Sounds exhausting."

"In all honesty, though, it's been good. Busy, but good. I've been focused on the new cardiac program we're implementing. It's going to be a game-changer for the hospital."

"That sounds amazing. You're always pushing boundaries."

"I try. But enough about work. Tell me about all the men in your life."

"I'm sorry?" My heart skips a beat.

"According to the photos in the news, that handsome devil you married has an equally handsome brother and nephew. They're living with you, right?"

Right. Our interviews haven't aired, but the media has been teasing them. Leo and Kody have recognizable faces now. Maybe not among the tourists coming off the cruise ship. But the locals will know who they are, especially if they're spotted with Monty—the most recognizable man in Alaska.

When I called Rhett earlier, I didn't mention the guys were with me. Rhett never stays away from work long, so I expect his visit to be short, hopefully avoiding any run-ins with the Strakh men.

Rhett is too damn perceptive. He used to comment on how Monty and I were always all over each other. He'll notice that we don't even touch now.

He'll also notice the way Kody and Leo look at me.

I'm not ready for those questions. Rhett is my friend, but he's also my boss. I need to keep my work and personal life separate.

"Yep." I keep my expression neutral. "They live on the island."

"Come on, you have to give me more than that."

No, I don't.

I don't have to give him anything.

Sitting back, I cross my legs and meet him stare for stare.

"Still rebellious, I see." He grins. "Glad you haven't lost that fire."

Oh, my fire burns much, much hotter these days.

What would he do if he knew I killed Monty's brother in cold blood?

Safe to say, that position at the hospital wouldn't be mine anymore.

As the afternoon wears on, Rhett and I talk about everything from hospital politics to the rise in missing person cases across Alaska. Each time he mentions a murder, boating accident, or tragic event he saw in the news, I know what he's doing. He's hoping it'll make me open up about my own experience.

Instead, I change the subject back to him.

As he tells me about his last surgery, my phone buzzes in my pocket. I pull it out, expecting a message from Leo or Kody.

Unknown Number: My love for you is an obsession. Your rejection of me is a compulsion. Somewhere between obsession and compulsion is impulse.

My smile falters as I read the words again. They don't make sense. It must be a wrong number. Or someone's playing a sick joke.

Then why am I breaking out in a cold sweat and shaking uncontrollably? I can't seem to draw enough air.

I look up at Rhett, trying to keep my face blank. He's still talking about his surgery, his eyes on the harbor, completely unaware of the terror unfolding inside me.

My phone buzzes again.

Unknown Number: Keep Dr. Howell out of this. If you want him to live, you'll put that cherry-red smile back on your face. This stays between you and me, little girl. Not a peep to anyone.

I freeze, every muscle locked in place, paralyzed by horror.

Little girl.

That's what Denver called me.

"Everything okay?" Rhett glances at my phone.

"Just Monty checking in." I swallow past my sandpaper throat. "You were saying?"

"Something's wrong." He eyes me too closely.

"I'm sorry. I have a lot on my mind."

"Talk to me, Frankie."

"I can't. I'd rather you distract me. Please. Tell me about the surgery. The massive aneurysm was in the ascending aorta?"

"Yeah." He scrutinizes me, those intelligent eyes seeing straight through me. "It was dangerously close to rupturing. We had to work fast. One wrong move..."

I tune him out, unable to focus.

Peeking at the security guards beneath the veil of my lashes, I keep my movements subtle. Too subtle. They don't make eye contact.

I don't know what to do. Whoever sent the message must be watching me.

My hands tremble as I type a quick message back, demanding the identity of the sender. But before I hit send, another text comes in.

Unknown Number: Who am I? I think you know. We share the same heart of frost and scars.

Panic surges. My mind races. Who the fuck could it be? An ex-boyfriend? Monty? Doyle? Sirena? One of Rurik's enemies? Someone who knew Denver?

Every creak and rustle amplify around me. Shadows twist and loom, transforming familiar corners of the yacht into menacing hiding spots.

An intruder couldn't be on the boat. Not without the guards knowing. But dozens of other ships bob around me. Boats with darkened windows and shaded alcoves. Perfect for concealment.

Across the dock, buildings border the shoreline, the sunlight reflecting off their glass panes, making it impossible to see inside. But with a pair of binoculars, someone could see *me*.

If it's Monty, he doesn't need to see. He already knows what I'm doing and who I'm with.

My chest gives a sharp pang.

"You're freaking out," Rhett says.

"Nope. I just need to deal with this text. Keep talking. I can listen while typing."

He continues the graphic recount of his surgery while I

quickly send a text to Leo and Kody.

Me: Is Monty on his phone?
Leo: Yes. Why? What's wrong?
My pulse pounds in my ears as I bite down on my tongue, trying to think of a plausible response without alarming him.
Me: I don't want him ignoring you.
Leo: We don't need a babysitter, love. You sure you're okay?
Me: All good. Just be careful, okay?
Leo: Always

Ice shivers down my spine, raising the hairs on my nape. Did Leo check the yacht for cameras this morning? Is Monty watching me on his phone? Or could someone else have planted cameras here?
A quick scan of the area tells me nothing.
Denver hid cameras in my house, and I never noticed them.
"I had to carefully clamp the aorta and make a precise incision to remove the damaged section." Rhett drops his head back, exhaling. "Talk about stressful."
"How did you stay calm through it?" My hands shake, slick with sweat, as I reply to the unknown number.

Me: Tell me who this is.

"It's all about focus," he says. "You tune out everything else. The room, the noise, even your own heartbeat. It's just you and the task at hand."
I hit send and receive an instant response.
Message Not Delivered. The phone number you are trying to reach has been disconnected or is no longer in service.
It takes me a second to process.
They cut communication. There's no way to contact them. Probably an untraceable number.
Would Leo have noticed Monty using a different phone?
Is someone still watching?

I feel eyes on me, making my skin crawl. My shoulders inch up around my ears, my mind in a state of hyperfocus. Glancing around as discreetly as possible, I try to spot anything or anyone unusual, but I see nothing.

Horror grips tighter, constricting my chest. I'm afraid to say anything to Rhett, terrified of what might happen to him. I can't risk his life.

Drawing a quiet gulp of air into my lungs, I force myself to stay calm and put my phone away. "Did everything go smoothly?"

"Yep. Everyone knew exactly what to do. It's moments like those when you really appreciate having such a skilled team around you."

Leo and Kody are my team, and I need them. But I won't call them back here and put them in the cross-hairs of this...this...I know exactly what it is.

Not all wounds bleed. Not all scars show. Some live beneath bones, cold and alone. In the chambers of frost, pain is my art.

Denver's riddle isn't an empty threat.

"Assembling the right people is one of your strengths." I force a smile onto my face. "Tell me more about this new cardiac program you're implementing."

"It's incredible." His eyes light up. "We have some of the best minds working on it. The goal is to reduce recovery times and improve overall patient outcomes. It's going to revolutionize how we handle cardiac care."

As he talks, I nod and maintain my smile, but my mind is elsewhere. Every fiber of my being crawls with dread, every shadow and sound taking on a sinister edge.

I keep glancing around, looking for any sign of the person who sent those texts. The security guards stand closer now, their eyes scanning the area.

Rhett doesn't notice my distraction, too caught up in his passionate explanation. I'm grateful for that. The last thing I want is to put him in danger.

I listen to his words, but they barely register. My thoughts race, trying to figure out who could be behind this.

"Frankie, are you sure you're okay?" He breaks through my spiraling thoughts.

"Yeah." I blink, realizing I've been staring blankly at him. "Yep. Sorry. Just a little tired." I hope my smile looks convincing.

"It's okay. I understand." He reaches over and gives my hand a reassuring squeeze. "You've been through so much."

He has no idea.

His touch is comforting, though. Different from Doyle's. I don't know why. Maybe because I've known Rhett longer.

Or maybe because I know he would put the moves on Monty before he would ever cross the line with me.

I squeeze his hand back, grateful he's here, but I know I have to be careful.

We continue talking, or rather, he continues talking while I do my best to stay engaged.

My phone remains silent, but the threat remains.

I'm being watched.

Someone is out there, waiting for me to make a mistake.

"I should get going." Rhett checks his watch and sighs. "Duty calls."

Going? And leave me here alone with two guards I don't know?

I can't bear it.

"Don't go yet." I lurch forward, clutching my throat, barely stopping a cry from shrieking free. "I mean...if you can stay, please stay."

Kodiak

TWENTY-FOUR

The wheel vibrates beneath my fingertips as the Bentley slices through the Alaskan wilderness, the tires gripping the road like claws. The sheer intensity of cornering at high speeds, rapid braking, and counteracting these forces makes my dick hard, matching the hungry rhythm of my heart.

Learning to drive checks off a box, a skill we need in this world.

But driving this sexy car? It's goddamn thrilling.

"Bet you couldn't take that turn as smoothly as I did." I meet Leo's eyes in the rearview.

"Pull over, rimjob," he shouts over the roar of the wind. "Watch and learn."

Beside me, Monty assesses every move we make, providing instruction, but only when we need it. His presence no longer chafes. Not right now. All I can think about is the road ahead and the rush of adrenaline as we switch drivers again.

Leo slides into the driver's seat with practiced ease, his gold and blue eyes glinting with challenge.

The rivalry between us lights a fire in me. But it's less about besting Leo and more about sharing this experience with him.

We all need something to ground us, something to remind us of who we are and what we've accomplished.

For Monty, it's his car collection, expensive suits, and fine liquors—the proof of his success.

For Leo and me, it's been survival, scraping by on guts and adrenaline.

But this...this is another level.

By the time we head back to the garage, my entire body buzzes with vitality. I replay the powerful thrusts of speed, the g-forces exerted on my muscles, the scent of burning rubber and exhaust, every twist and turn of the road—all of it etches into my memory.

"Well done, both of you." Monty steps out of the car, his expression indifferent. "A few more practice runs, and you'll be ready to take the test."

As we walk back to the yacht, the sun perches on the horizon, setting the harbor ablaze and wrapping a distant volcano in velvety robes of pink, orange, and purple.

Small boats come and go from the islands. Eagles and gulls worry the air above the fish processing plants. Yet, from the concrete path beneath my feet, this busy world seems at peace.

"Let's stop in here for a minute." Monty takes a detour, heading down a narrow alleyway.

I share a look with Leo, my muscles coiling. Is it a trap?

Monty reaches for a door, glancing over his shoulder with a dare in his eyes. Then he steps inside, swallowed by the blast of music and lively conversations within.

I stare at the faded wooden sign overhead.

Tipsy Sailor

"Have you heard from Frankie?" I remove my phone.

"Not since her last message."

I text her again.

Me: How are you doing?
Frankie: Still talking to Rhett.
Me: Want us to head back?
Frankie: Take your time.

"She's okay." I show Leo the messages. "I can't decide if we should rush back to her or see what this is about." I gesture at the door.

He shrugs. "You're dying to see what's in there."

"So are you."

Curiosity wins, and I follow him into the establishment.

The scent of wood smoke, grilled fish, and aged spirits bombard my senses. The clatter of dishes competes with the hum of dozens of conversations.

Nautical memorabilia adorn the walls—old ship wheels, fishing nets, and framed photos of past fishing hauls. Half of the tables are occupied. Some patrons laugh and talk. Others sit quietly and eat. With the cruise ship in the port, this place should be packed with an energy that thrums the air.

Maybe it will fill up later.

I weave through the small crowd to catch up with Monty, careful not to bump into the servers balancing trays of drinks and plates of steaming food. He leads us to the bar, a long counter lined with high stools.

Heads turn. Women stop and stare. These aren't the stares that people gave us on the streets. The gawking here is more intimate, direct, suggestive, climbing up and down my body, and lingering longer than polite. Unnerving.

Leo and I take the empty stools beside Monty at the bar. The bartender gives a friendly nod and continues mixing a cocktail. I watch, fascinated by the quick, expert movements, the clink of ice, and the splash of liquid in the glass.

"Three rounds of your handcrafted vodka." Monty flicks a finger at the bartender.

Handcrafted vodka?

That explains the scent of fermenting corn. It also hints at why he brought us here.

This is more than a restaurant and bar.

It's a distillery.

I shift uncomfortably, my gaze sweeping the room. Low lighting barely illuminates the space. Not in a cozy, intimate way. The mysterious nautical atmosphere comes off as forced and gimmicky.

The tables resemble barrels, making them awkward to sit around. Giant anchors, life preservers, and nets with plastic fish entangled plaster the walls.

The whole place feels like it's trying too hard to embrace local pride and tradition. It's a tourist trap that's more interested in people's money than their experience.

"If this was yours," Monty says, "what would you change?"

"Everything."

"Be specific."

"I don't know where to start."

"You start by knowing what you want." His blue eyes burn into mine. "Then you fight like hell to get it."

I give the bar another perusal, focusing on its patrons.

The women here don't look like Frankie. Skimpy dresses drape their ample curves. Floral perfumes overpower the earthy scent of spirits. None of them have skin like porcelain, girlish bodies, or hair the color of sunlit rust and twilight embers that tumbles everywhere in wild rebellion.

Feminine faces stare back at me beneath unnecessary layers of paint on their eyes, cheeks, and lips. They drink and smile and toss their glossy, tamed hair while pretending not to watch us with interest that borders on desperation.

Leo soaks in the attention with intimidating confidence, his snarly scowl only making them lean forward and stare harder.

Monty sits at the bar as if we're the only people in the building. I guess he's used to the silent propositions and bold glances.

"I want a distillery that embodies the flavor of its vodka and tells a story of survival in the Arctic. Not a tourist attraction that shoves its theme down people's throats with its overpriced alcohol."

"Good answer." Monty motions at the bartender. "Let Pilip know I'm here."

"Sure thing, Mr. Novak." The young, spindly man delivers our vodka and disappears through a side door.

Pilip? That sounds like an Inuit name.

I give Monty a questioning look.

"Pilip is the owner." He sips his drink. "It's easier to buy a distillery than start from scratch. Less red tape and legalities. Everything is already established."

"This place is for sale?" My pulse quickens.

"No."

I tilt my head, trying to understand. "How many distilleries are for sale around here?"

"This is the *only* distillery in Sitka. But anything can be bought for the right price."

I can't be bought.

Taking a sip of my drink, I find it as bland as the vodka on the plane.

As I push it away, a group of women approaches us, their eyes sparkling with the buzz of alcohol.

"Tourists," Monty mutters, glancing at his watch, his mind seemingly elsewhere.

One of them, a blonde with a sultry gaze, sidles up to Leo and trails her fingers down his arm. "Did it hurt when you fell from Valhalla?"

"Look at his eyes." Another woman sighs. "This one conquers kingdoms."

Leo hisses, brushing away the woman's touch.

"I'll let you conquer me." The blonde licks her red lips.

"Not interested in easy conquests," he barks.

She sucks in a breath.

Her friend angles toward me, a redhead with hair so bright it glows with a plastic-like sheen.

"I'll make you work for it, handsome." Her voice drips with insinuation as she teases my chest with fingernails so long and sharp that she would injure herself if she attempted to masturbate.

"No." I bare my teeth, pushing away those dangerous claws.

"Are you sure?" She pouts, her lower lip jutting in a way that's probably meant to be enticing. "I'm not easy. But for you, I can be."

Beside me, Monty turns his back on another woman. "Not interested." He flicks a hand at the crowd of females around us, hardening his voice. "Move along. Now."

The tension in my shoulders eases as they scatter, returning to their table.

"Is that normal?" I stare at my drink, my back twitching beneath the probe of dozens of eyes on me.

"When you're the most attractive man in the bar…" Monty rakes a hand through his hair, mussing the black strands. "Comes with the territory."

I steal a glance behind me. Several men now surround the women who propositioned us. The males press in too close, touching, smiling, and invading personal boundaries, but the females seem to welcome the attention.

"Did Frankie come here?" The thought stiffens my spine. "Is this where she drinks with her colleagues?"

"No." Monty follows my line of sight, glowering. "The locals avoid this tourist trap."

"Why are *we* here?" Leo asks.

"With Kody's vision and my financial backing, this place could be a hot spot for both tourists *and* locals."

His words resonate within me, igniting a fire that's been smoldering for years.

This isn't just about survival anymore. It's about building a future, about creating something that tells our story. And for the first time, I believe it's possible.

While we wait for the owner, Monty returns to his phone, a frown knitting his forehead as he types.

"What's wrong?" I crane my neck, unable to see his screen.

"Sirena's here." He pockets the device and twists toward the door.

She walks in, drawing every pair of eyes in the bar.

Tight denim molds to her long, shapely legs. That's as far as my perusal goes before Leo's hand smacks the back of my head.

"I wasn't checking her out." I grunt.

"Sure you weren't." He sweeps his gaze over the crowd. "You and every other hard dick in this place."

She might be the most beautiful female here, but my dick only responds to one woman.

Monty hasn't spared her a glance beyond his quick acknowledgment when she walked in.

Men whistle and leer as she passes, but she doesn't flinch. It's like they don't exist to her.

I track her in my periphery like I track everyone else in this place. She carries herself with the kind of confidence that makes everyone take notice, her head held high, and dark hair flowing down her back.

But she only has eyes for us.

As she approaches, the crowd parts, drawn to her but knowing better than to get too close.

"Hello, boys," she purrs.

I return to my drink, preferring the tasteless vodka over her sugary conversation.

Monty doesn't pay her attention, leaving us to deal with her as he buries his nose in his phone.

I focus on the bar, on all the ways I would change it if it were mine.

Sirena moves closer to me and rests a hand on my thigh.

I loosen a low, warning sound deep in my chest. "Remove your fucking hand."

She blinks, a look of surprise crossing her face before she chuckles and withdraws her hand. "Easy there, big guy."

"Why are you here?"

"I heard you were in town."

"How?" I glare at her, my patience wearing thin.

"It's my job to know." At my glance toward Monty, she shakes her head. "I have a lot of customers, baby. I need to know who's coming and going from this port." She pitches forward, tits first, and exhales hot breath in my ear. "You three are by far my sexiest clients."

"I'm not your client."

"Even better."

"I'm only going to say this once." Slowly, I rise from the stool, donning my scariest scowl.

One peek at my face, and she stumbles back.

"Don't touch me." I tower over her, forcing her back

another step while keeping a foot of space between us. "Don't look at me. Don't fucking talk to me unless it's important. And just to be clear, your opinions about our sexiness aren't important."

A sound draws my eyes to the bar. Monty and Leo have their backs to me, but given how their shoulders shake, they find my speech amusing.

Sirena, on the other hand, sucks in a breath as a flush rises from her low-cut shirt and blotches her heavy chest.

"Fuck you." Her words spit like venom.

Turning on her heel, she struts out the door amid more whistles and cat calls.

"Damn, bro." Leo tips an eyebrow at me. "Fucking harsh."

Before I can respond, the owner appears, a man in his late forties with a stout build and a face weathered by years of hard work.

"Mr. Novak, it's a pleasure to have you in my establishment." He extends a hand.

"Pilip." Monty shakes it, sliding him a polite smile.

"What brings you in tonight?" Pilip turns to Leo and me, recognition dawning in his eyes. "Oh! You're the brother and nephew I saw all over the news."

I press my lips together, my gaze hard.

"We'd like a tour of the distillery." Monty pockets his phone.

"Of course, of course. Right this way."

Would the man be so eager if he knew Monty was interested in buying it?

Monty makes formal introductions, giving him our names. Then we follow him into the back and through a network of gleaming stainless-steel stills, polished pipes, and rows of filtration tanks.

The scents of sweet corn, earthy wheat, and the faintest hint of rye envelop me in a sensory experience that transports me back to the cellar in Hoss.

Pilip talks animatedly, explaining the process and the history of the place, but my thoughts are elsewhere.

I see the future so clearly. A vision of transformation. I

would keep the state-of-the-art equipment. But everything else would go.

My vision comes together in my mind. With passion and hard work—and Monty's capital investment—my ideas can become a reality.

As we finish the tour, Pilip looks at us expectantly. "Do you have any questions?"

Monty glances at me, giving me the floor.

I take a deep breath, feeling the weight of the decision. "We'd like to discuss a potential purchase."

"Oh…uh…" Pilip smiles. "It's not for sale."

Monty throws out a number that sends the man into a choking fit.

If I hadn't seen Monty's car collection, I would've been choking, too.

"Let's sit down and go over the details." Monty gestures toward the private room in the back.

Leo catches my gaze, wordlessly asking if I'm sure about this.

Monty hasn't given me his offer as my investor. Right now, this is just a conversation. A potential purchase. Nothing is set in stone. I won't sign or agree to anything until I discuss it with Leo and Frankie.

Nodding, I let Leo see the hunger in my eyes. The hunger for a dream I never thought was possible.

As Monty follows Pilip toward the back, Leo steps into my space and wraps his arms around me.

"I'm happy for you." He shifts, resting his hands on my shoulders. "I'm going to leave you to it and go see our girl."

"Good." I straighten. "I won't make any decisions without you."

"This is your dream, fuckwit." He lightly slaps my cheek. "You already have my support."

With a feral grin, he turns and stalks away.

Pulse racing, I find Monty and Pilip sitting at a table in a nearby room.

Within minutes, Monty dives into negotiations and

financials, his expertise shining through. I focus on my vision, ensuring that every detail aligns with the story I want to tell.

I still don't trust that Monty has my best interests in mind. But there's one thing I know for sure.

With or without him, this is happening. Nothing will stand in my way.

leonid

TWENTY-FIVE

The cool night air kisses my skin as I stroll through the seaport, the stars emerging one by one, illuminating the dark Alaskan sky.

It's been a day of ups and downs, a rollercoaster of power struggles and transitions—clashing with Monty, operating a yacht, driving a car, fending off women, touring a distillery, and watching Kody pursue his dream.

But at the end of the day, it all circles back to Frankie. She's our binding force. The spark that freed us from Hoss. The reason we strive to be more than our scars.

I pick up my pace.

Monty's yacht looms ahead, bigger and grander than all the others in the quiet harbor. Its sleek lines and multiple decks glisten in the moonlight, guarded by two burly men in dark suits.

Their eyes track my approach. I give them a nod as I board, adjusting to the sway beneath my feet.

I find her on the bridge deck, sitting in the shadow of the overhang with a tall, attractive man.

Dr. Rhett Howell.

Good. I wanted to meet him. Hopefully, he won't give me a reason to smash his pretty face.

They can't see me in the unlit cabin as I draw near, allowing me a few seconds to observe them undetected.

Scrubs cling to his athletic frame, his hair meticulously styled. His forearms flex as he talks with his hands.

Her head tips to the side as she listens, her shoulders slightly hunched. Every so often, her eyes dart left to right, clouding with a strange wariness.

What the fuck is he telling her that's putting her on edge?

I step onto the deck.

Spotting me, she jumps up, and some of the tension lifts from her features. Until she cranes her neck and realizes I'm alone.

"I left Kody and Monty behind. Needed to check on you." I erase the space between us and nudge up her chin, examining her eyes. "What's wrong?"

"Nothing." She brushes me off. "This is Dr. Rhett Howell. Rhett, this is Leo."

"Nice to finally meet you." He stands, offering a hand. "Frankie speaks highly of you."

I squeeze his grip firmly, dissecting his body language, delving for artifice.

"I have to say, Frankie wasn't exaggerating." He chuckles, releasing my hand. "With your amazing hair and that death stare, you're a full-throttle version of a Viking god." He swallows. "Magnificent."

I release a vibrating, gravel-roughened sound that drains the color from his face.

"Thank you for staying, Rhett." She sidles between us, putting her back to me. "I'm sorry I kept you."

"Anything for a friend." He waves her off, his gaze creeping back to me. "Besides, it's not every day I get to meet a bona fide Tarzan of the Arctic."

What the fuck?

I grip her waist and tug her against me. Her spine stiffens against my abdomen as I hold her in place with a hand on her collarbone. Watching him closely, I note the way he tracks where I touch her.

She didn't tell him we're together.

I don't know whether to be pissed off or worried.

Something's wrong with her, something skittish and troubled, shivering the frenetic air around her. Her hands fidget at her sides, fingers clutching at invisible lifelines, and sweat beads along her hairline, glistening like dew.

Every twitch in her body sets my instincts on edge.

Rhett seems oblivious. "I should get going. Early shift tomorrow. It was a pleasure, Leo."

I don't acknowledge him, my attention locked onto Frankie.

He steps off the yacht, his departure as unremarkable as his presence.

"What happened?" I spin her in my arms and touch her trembling chin and bloodless lips. "What did he do?"

Her eyes widen, pupils as dark as the polar night, leaping from shadow to shadow.

"Nothing." She pulls away, her fingers twisting in the fabric of her dress. "I'm just tired."

"Look at me when you lie to me."

Those beautiful lashes lift, revealing a terrified expression that rips open my chest.

Backing away, she rubs her brow, her voice a broken whisper. "I need to lie down."

The sensation of wrongness burrows deeper, chilling my blood.

"You apologized to Rhett for keeping him here." I advance on her. "Why?"

"He's a busy man." She grabs her phone from the table and pads into the cabin. "I held him up, chatting about work."

"You're lying." I stay with her, my eyes narrowing. "I know something's wrong. Talk to me."

She hasn't asked about our driving lessons or why Kody isn't here. Her breath comes shallow and fast, each exhale a ghostly gust in the silent harbor.

The tightness in my chest increases, feeding on her fear.

Without another word, she strides away, her steps hurried and unsteady. I chase her through the main cabin, passing the security guards, who exchange glances.

"Frankie." I release a sharp exhale, the promise of confrontation escaping my lips. "Come back here."

She stops abruptly, her back to me, her shoulders quivering. "You don't understand. There are things...things you don't know."

"Then help me understand." I capture her arm. "Fucking tell me."

She turns, her eyes stark with alarm, pricking at my heart as she places her small hand over my mouth, silencing me.

I follow her line of sight to the ceilings, the windows, the doors.

Does she think someone's watching us? Listening?

I take a closer look around the cabin, my scrutiny growing sharper, wilder, cutting through the haze of panic.

She angles away, her walls snapping back into place. Her jaw sets firmly, muscles tensing as if to lock away words she refuses to free.

Then she's on the move again, rushing down the hall toward the sleeping cabins.

My pulse thunders as I prowl after her, unhurried, letting her think she's escaped me. I don't need to see her to know which turns she takes. Her intoxicating scent tugs on my every breath, pulling me with her.

Her trail leads to the first guest cabin. I sweep inside and lock the door.

The soft click magnifies the pressure in the air. She moves with urgency, her eyes scanning every corner of the tiny room, her feet barely touching the floor as she searches the walls, ceilings, and mattress.

"Frankie." Worry ravages me as I watch her. "It's clean. I already swept the entire yacht this morning. There are no cameras."

"Are you sure?" She freezes, clutching her phone to her chest, her features contorted with indecision.

"Without a doubt. What happened?"

Whoever frightened her will feel the full force of my goddamn wrath.

Hauling a gulp of air into her lungs, she unlocks her phone and hands it to me.

The screen opens to a conversation with an unknown number.

Cold dread pummels my insides as I read the messages.

The cryptic insinuations, the threats, every twisted text preys on her fears. And the last message...

Who am I? I think you know. We share the same heart of frost and scars.

It triggers an unwanted image of Denver's cruel smile in his video, resonating with the same dark undertones of his riddle.

Hell, some of those words—heart, frost, scars—were in the riddle.

My stomach drops like a block of ice as I lower to the bed, trying to tamp down my rising fury. "Why didn't you call me?"

"I was afraid this person would hurt you." Her voice breaks. "I didn't know what to do. I tried to ask you about Monty, about his phone."

"Monty was on his phone most of the afternoon." I rack my brain, trying to piece together the timing.

"Did he use different phones? A burner might look smaller or cheaper."

"I don't remember." All these gadgets look the same to me, and the day's events blur together.

"What if it's him? I didn't alert the guards because they work for him." She makes a keening sound, her face crumpling. "What if he's behind this?"

"Hey, hey." I toss her phone aside, hook an arm around her waist, and pull her onto my lap, positioning her to straddle me. "We don't know if it's him."

The possibility wrings my gut with sickening dread. Monty, the man who should protect her above all else, the man who has everything except the one thing he wants.

If he's terrorizing her...

My breath snarls and seethes, gathering strength, the

precursor to a raging storm about to break. Heat surges through my veins, my fists clenching against her lower back.

I can't lose control. She needs me to be calm, to be her anchor.

Closing my eyes, I mentally bottle the storm, each ragged breath pushing it down. With each slow exhale, I will my heartbeat to steady, each beat shoving me away from the precipice. The snarl fades. The seethe ebbs. I bury it deep where it won't consume me.

"Where's Kody?" She places a clammy palm on my cheek, shaking on my lap.

"He's with Monty at Tipsy Sailor." I draw a finger down her cheek, tracing the rigid line of her jaw. "They're negotiating with the owner. Monty is trying to buy it for Kody."

As I explain the tour of the distillery and conversation with Pilip, her eyes widen with fresh terror, the panic building.

"He's alone with Monty." A tremor runs through her, driving her fingernails into my shoulders. Her breathing quickens, short and shallow gasps chopping her words. "What if that was Monty's plan all along? To get Kody alone?"

"Frankie." I take her face in my hands, trying to catch her gaze. "Look at me."

"We have to call Kody. Warn him." Her eyes dart around the room, unfocused and frantic. "No, wait. We can't. Monty would know I told you. If Kody leaves, Monty will know. He might try to hurt him."

This woman. This brave, stunning, stubborn goddamn woman.

She held herself together for the past couple of hours, talking to Rhett while pretending she didn't have threatening messages on her phone. She maintained her composure throughout the evening, refusing to call and put us in danger.

She dealt with it without freaking out.

Until now.

Not because she fears for her own life but because she's worried about Kody.

I should redden her ass for choosing to protect us over herself.

"Listen to me." I hold her head, forcing her gaze on mine. "Kody is a mean son of a bitch. He smells danger coming from a mile away."

She's not listening, too panicked to process what I'm telling her, the hysteria coming in too strong.

Her chest heaves rapidly as she clenches her teeth, trying to keep it together, but the signs are there. Her fingers scrape against my skin, her body tensing like a coiled spring ready to snap.

"Eyes on me." I harden my tone, sounding harsher than I intend. "Breathe with me, love."

She finally obeys, the liquid depths of her gaze swimming with fear, pupils dilated, her face devoid of color.

"We'll figure this out." I wrap my arms around her trembling body, pulling her pelvis tightly against mine. "Right now, you need to breathe. Focus on me."

Her heart pounds against my chest, her breathing erratic, falling apart.

"Feel me." I press a gentle kiss to her forehead, then her mouth, trying to calm her.

Her lips open against mine, soft and pliant, but the tension in her posture remains.

"Breathe in. And out." With my mouth against hers, I breathe with her, for her, ordering her lungs over and over again until she matches my rhythm.

"It's going to be okay," I whisper between kisses and breaths.

"How? How will it be okay?"

"Don't know yet, but I'm working on it. Need you to trust me."

She clings to my neck, her fingers stabbing my back, her nerves fraying and breaking. Tears swell in her eyes, the bitter tang of her fear piercing the air.

My heart panics at the sight of her in pain. The chance this might escalate into a full-blown panic attack tears at me.

Emotions bubble up in her chest, pushing against the back of her throat, choking her. She wheezes, clawing at my neck.

"No, no, stay with me." I kiss her again, deeper this time, hungrier, more demanding.

Her inhale untangles. Her exhale detaches from her airway, and slowly, she begins to breathe, to respond, her lips moving against mine.

A moment later, she melts into me, parting her mouth with a sigh that I consume and conquer.

I'm no longer kissing her to console her. My tongue thrusts in a rhythm that heats and seduces. But I don't know who's seducing whom.

Straddling my hips, she gently rocks on my lap. Her hands grip my face. And her mouth. Her gorgeous fucking mouth eats at mine.

My cock stiffens, pushing at my zipper, and her nipple pearls under the heat of my palm.

No bra.

As she thaws beneath my caresses and moans against my lips, a thousand dirty fantasies flash through my mind. A lifetime of sinful things I want to do to her. But we have more than just one night.

We have forever, and even that won't be enough time with her.

"Arms up." I lift her dress, pulling it over her head and off.

The sight of her naked form, all that snowy white flesh, wrenches a groan from my throat. I reach for her, desperate to map every flawless inch with my mouth and hands.

She reaches for me at the same time, stripping my shirt and opening my jeans. I shift, rolling us to the bed in a tangle of tongues and limbs.

Lying beneath me, she trails a fingernail down the center of my chest to the scar on my abs. I take her hand and kiss the pads of her fingers. No plastic claws or razor-sharp tips on my girl. Instead, she wears callouses, tiny scars, and patches of healed frostbite like badges of her survival in the harshest winter.

She isn't shaped like the women in the bar. My redhead vixen is smaller than every person here with tits that barely fill my mouth. But where she lacks in size, she more than makes up for in grit and ferocity.

I love her madly, immeasurably, incomprehensibly, beyond the point of pain.

Setting my mouth in the dip of her quivering tummy, I cage her in, one hand beside her head and the other next to her waist. Then I lick the succulent pathways of her beautiful body.

No words pass between us. No dirty talk. No soulful declarations. Just eye contact. That's all we need as I wander in the gentle hollows and shadowy valleys of her soft skin, my teeth nipping, my lips worshiping.

When I reach the white lace between her legs, I yank it up like a string through her folds, exposing flesh that feels like lips against my tongue.

The fabric grows wet, from my mouth, from her cunt. With one hard yank, I rip away her underwear, tossing the ruined scraps.

Settling in, I don't just lick her. I feast on her, messy and loud, releasing a vibration of groans that tells her she has the most delicious pussy in existence.

"I'm so close." She shudders and writhes against my face. "Don't stop."

That's exactly what I do. I pull back and climb up her body, pushing down my jeans as I go.

"Wha—?" She pants, eyes wild. "What are you doing?"

"You're coming with me." My cock jerks against her inner thigh, dripping with anticipation. "Together."

I want to fuck her into oblivion, mark her with my bites on her neck for all the world to see.

But not tonight.

Tonight, she needs solace, succor, and languorous love-making.

"Okay." She palms my ass and squeezes my hips with her thighs. "Together."

"Open for me." I position myself at her entrance, my legs shaking with restraint. "Take as much as you can."

I push in, just the tip, and she clenches so hard I'm locked in purgatory.

"Fuck." I grunt, trying to go deeper. "Let me slide it in, Frankie. Let me in."

She whimpers and widens her legs. "You guys and your oversized dicks."

I ease out and slowly, gently work myself in, stroking with short, shallow thrusts until I bottom out with a guttural grunt.

She liquefies around my cock as if the feel of me inside her brings the deepest relief.

Softly, languidly, I stroke in and out. At this pace, I feel her everywhere, every pulse, every precious inch. She moans into my mouth, yielding to the heavy friction and bending beneath my weight.

"Feels so fucking good. Come here." I sit back on my heels and tug her toward me. "You're so fucking hot."

Pressing a hand to her belly, I feel my hardness moving inside her, against my hand, slow, slower, achingly perfect. A gentle glide, so wet and effortless despite the squeezing tight fit.

"You were made for this cock." I push deeper, swelling harder, hissing past my teeth. "Your pussy's so warm. So wet. Yeah, pulse around me. Just like that. Fuuuuck."

With each long, luxurious thrust, I revel in the warm, swarming power of it. I don't need to ram my way in. Her body knows me, opens for me, and allows me to make space without causing her pain or discomfort.

"I'm so happy when I'm inside you." Moaning, slow and lazy, I ride, the world outside forgotten, all fears put on hold, dominated by slick, drugging pleasure. "I feel alive when I fuck you. Ahhhh, God. Fuck, yes."

Finding her hands, I restrain them against the bed above her head, wrist to wrist, making her feel every tunneling plunge as I grind against her clit.

She plants a foot on the mattress and hooks her other leg around my hip, lifting into me, meeting my painstakingly slow rhythm, and spiking my pleasure into the cosmos.

"Leo." Gasping, she pins me with those soulful green eyes. "I'm close."

I cup her face, fingers stroking her temple, and finish her off.

Our love, our connection, our divine sexual chemistry—all of it culminates in a synchronized eruption of spasms, goosebumps, and glittery, groaning relief.

"I'm going to fuck my come into you." My mind fractures as lightning races through my body, shooting shockwaves to every limb. "Fuck, Frankie. Fuck!"

I groan, long and loud, collapsing on her, reeling, twitching, shattered to my soul.

Aftershocks ripple through her cunt, squeezing my cock, compelling me to thrust a few more times. I devour her mouth in sloppy, breathless kisses until we're empty and listless. Then I roll off her.

"Thank you." Panting, she stares at the ceiling and blindly reaches for my hand. "Thank you for coming back for me, for being here."

"I'll always come for you." I lift her fingers to my mouth, kissing them and grinning. "My filthy, sloppy wet, come-filled girl."

Her laughter fades into a sigh. "The thing is you're not just here when life is beautiful. You show up when it's completely falling apart and make it beautiful again."

She is life, and she's always beautiful, even when she's falling apart. Anything less than this inspiring, heart-shaped, purely sacred woman isn't a life at all.

But as I put us both back into our clothes and pocket her shredded underwear, the shadows of reality creep back in.

The threat is still out there, and our struggles are far from over.

leonid

TWENTY-SIX

Frankie and I lie on the bed in the guest cabin, our bodies facing each other, noses almost touching. Our hands lace together, fingers intertwined with an intimacy that stokes my protective fire.

Those fucking texts weigh heavily on my mind. I wish I had a better grasp of phone technology. The urgent need to talk through it with Kody has my heart rate pinned in the red zone.

The situation is dire, but we've faced worse. The key now is to remain vigilant, to out-think and outmaneuver whoever this nutjob is.

As I lie there, staring into her burdened eyes, determination charges me. We'll uncover the truth, and we'll protect what is ours. No matter the cost.

"What are we going to do?" she whispers, her breath warm against my lips.

"We'll start by figuring out who sent those messages. I'll learn what I can about the technology, see if it's traceable. In the meantime, we'll be careful, watchful. We won't let them scare us into hiding."

"I told Rhett I was ready to return to work."

"Not until we know who's threatening you."

"But you just said—"

"We're not hiding. Being careful means staying together. So unless I can shadow you at the hospital..."

"You can't." She looks like she might argue but instead asks, "What if it's Monty?"

"I'll go through his phone when he returns."

"If he used a burner, he would've tossed it."

I need a damn manual to explain burners, unknown numbers, and the inner workings of electronic communication.

"What did you tell Rhett?" I ask.

"He only knows what the media knows. When he started to leave, I panicked." She sighs, a jagged, weary sound. "So I told him the truth. I'm afraid to be alone right now because of things that happened to me in the Arctic. I kept it vague, and he stayed without prying for details."

"You should've called me."

"I couldn't."

Because a cowardly cunt-rag with a phone threatened our lives. Someone should tell that cunt that I'm the one to watch out for, the fangs in the shadows, the knife in the heart.

I'm coming for you, you dead motherfucking cunt.

"I hate feeling so helpless," she murmurs. "I hate that someone out there has the power to send me into a panic attack. I used to be stronger than this."

"There's a limit to how many punches a person can withstand before they collapse. You've endured more hits than most people, and you're still standing."

"I'm quite horizontal at the moment." She trails her toe along my calf. "Don't think I can stand if I tried."

"You're not helpless. You're one of the strongest people I know."

"Tell me about your afternoon." She rests a hand on my jaw, caressing my short beard. "The driving lessons and Tipsy Sailor. I want to hear everything."

I give her the highlights from beginning to end, including all the ways I'm a better driver than Kody.

As I talk, her stress melts away under a tired smile. That

smile lingers throughout my narration of the fawning women at the bar. She even laughs when I describe how Kody shut down Sirena.

But as I describe my favorite cars in Monty's collection, exhaustion sets into her features, the fight in her eyes slowly losing to the pull of sleep.

Her eyelids flutter. Her breathing deepens. Despite her efforts, she succumbs to the rest her body desperately needs.

I want to step out and watch for Kody, but I won't leave her alone.

"Sorry, love." Carefully, I lift her in my arms, grab her phone, and carry her into the sitting room in the main cabin.

She startles awake for an evanescent moment before passing out again.

Her head rests against my chest as I settle onto the couch, holding her tightly, my heart clenching with vicious protectiveness.

Beyond the lapping of waves and occasional splash of jumping fish, the harbor is eerily quiet. Shadows play in the periphery, shifting with the yacht's movement, keeping me on edge.

The silhouettes of the guards bleed into the dark backdrop. One stands at the bow, scanning the water. Another patrols the decks, his steps methodical and silent.

Even though I know they won't protect us from Monty, I'm glad they're here so I can focus on Frankie.

As I watch her sleep, my resolve hardens. Whoever is behind this, whatever their motives, they will not win.

They will not break us.

I brush her hair from her face, exposing her serene expression, soft in sleep. The turmoil she endured while I was in town makes me fuming mad. I'll do anything to keep her safe, to shield her from the horrors that haunt her.

At last, the sound of advancing footsteps breaks the quiet. I recognize Kody's gait, deliberately heavy so that I hear him.

She shifts in my arms but doesn't wake as he enters the cabin. He stalks directly to her and drags his nose along her scalp, inhaling deeply, smelling her. Then those black eyes ensnare mine, probing, questioning, sensing something's wrong.

Standing behind him, Monty watches our interaction, his expression unreadable.

I hold the air in my lungs as I carefully set her on the couch, trying not to wake her. But she stirs anyway, lifting her head.

"Kody." Her cheeks rise with an unguarded smile of relief.

As I hand him her phone, I keep my attention on Monty's reaction. His brow furrows deeply, confusion carving across his face.

We wait while Kody reads the messages, his features darkening. He returns the phone to her, his eyes churning with primal dominance.

The sight of his quiet rage calms me.

"What's wrong?" Monty asks, his voice flat.

"She received threatening messages from an unknown number." I hold Monty's assertive gaze. "Let me see your phone."

"No." He gestures for her device. "Show me."

I hold out a hand. "Your phone first."

His eyes flash dangerously. No brotherly love there. Only shivery, insulted, self-righteous outrage. Then he blinks, and it clears away, replaced by rankled exhaustion.

"Monty." She sits up, her voice husky. "When I asked you if you were hiding anything from me, do you remember what you said?"

"Yes." He grits his teeth.

"What did you say?"

"If you ask, I'll give it to you. I'll give you anything you want."

"I'm asking." She nods at his pocket, where he keeps his phone. "This is how you earn my trust."

After a tense moment, he sighs. "If I wanted to send you threatening messages, I would use an online service that allows texting with a fake sender ID. The same way cybercriminals change the sender ID to impersonate friends, family, and legitimate companies. If I were your unknown number, it wouldn't show in my sent or deleted texts. The evidence wouldn't appear on my phone at all because I'm not a fucking idiot."

"Then you won't mind me poking around," I say.

Oh, he definitely minds.

His lips flatten in a seething line, holding back all the ways he wants to tell me off. Then he looks at her. His face softens, and he reluctantly hands over his phone.

I scroll through his most recent messages. Texts from Sirena about media sightings in town—or lack thereof. Another text states she heard we were at Tipsy Sailor, and she's on her way inside. Other messages go back and forth with various colleagues and assistants, nagging him to sign off on documents and reschedule meetings that he missed. Then there's a conversation with a guy about flight school.

I hold that one to his face, lifting my brow in question.

"It was just an inquiry." His nostrils flare. "If you're not interested..."

"We can discuss it later." I continue searching for the messages I don't see—the cryptic ones to Frankie.

"There's nothing here." I pass it back to him. "Empty your pockets."

"No." He scowls.

"Then I'll search you myself." I step closer.

"The hell you will."

"I'll do it." She stands, drawing his furious gaze. "Please."

He works his jaw then gives her a curt nod.

I stiffen, hating the idea of her going near him. I already know she won't find anything.

"Forget it." I reach out to halt her.

She slips away from me and circles Monty's rigid frame.

He turns to stone as she pauses behind him and sweeps her hands down his hips. My blood simmers as she frisks the front and back pockets of his jeans, stroking his goddamn ass.

He closes his eyes, throat bobbing, clearly savoring her pat down.

"Wallet." She shifts to his front. "Keys...and..."

Her fingers go still.

Right beside his dick.

His eyes slowly open.

As I lunge forward, she holds up a finger, demanding me to stay back, to trust her.

Goddammit.

She presses on his pocket, and a wrapper crinkles.

"Condom." She clears her throat.

"Tell me, *wife*," he says through his teeth, grinding each syllable, "why would I have a condom?"

"Not my business."

"Everything I do is your business. Remove it from my pocket."

"No."

"You started this." He stands taller, his posture challenging. "Finish it."

Fuck me. She never backs down from a dare.

Stabbing her hand into his pocket, she yanks out...

A Band-Aid?

One of those large square pads in a wrapper.

"Oh." Slowly, her eyes lift to the one on his neck.

He holds out his palm, and she sets the bandage on it.

"No." He pockets the Band-Aid and extends his hand again with a firm, drawn-out command. "Your phone."

She gives it over and slumps onto the couch.

He doesn't waste time reading the texts, his face contorting with rage.

"You thought this was me?" he roars, his temper boiling over. "These messages are fucking disturbing. Threatening. They're from someone who knows her, who knows us."

"They knew she was with Rhett." Kody hardens his eyes. "That narrows it down to the four of us and the security guards."

"And anyone Rhett might've told." She rubs her head. "I was missing for nine months. For all I know, he told the entire hospital he was coming to see me."

"Text him. Ask him who he told." Monty sets her phone in

her hand and stalks to the port side, staring out the windows at the waterfront. "Anyone with a camera phone could've zoomed in and watched Rhett board the yacht."

A sharp intake of air burns my throat.

"If I had to guess," he says, "the sender used SMS spoofing. The number was probably a temporary number used by the spoofer for a short period and deactivated after the spoofing attempt."

"That would explain why I couldn't respond." She purses her lips.

"*Somewhere between obsession and compulsion is impulse.*" Monty paces the cabin, cursing under his breath. "That's a Pushkin quote."

"How do you know?"

"When I found the book of poems in my father's office, I acquainted myself with the poet's work."

He freezes and turns toward a side table. With a guttural bellow, he swings his arms and sends a lamp crashing into the wall.

She flinches, and Kody shifts, putting himself between her and Monty.

Gripping the back of an armchair, Monty straightens, rolls his neck, and with a startling switch in his demeanor, he takes control of the situation. "We're returning to the safety of the island. Right fucking now."

My raw nerves fray as he storms off toward the helm, his gait decisive and controlled.

"It could still be him," Kody mutters.

"Do you think his reaction was an act?" I look at her.

"No." She chews on her lip. "He can pull off stoic and distant. But when he's upset, his temper flies just like yours. That—" she points in the direction he went "—was Monty under duress."

With resistance, my gut agrees.

If the unknown number isn't him, who is it? And what do they want?

The tension heightens as we prepare to depart. The yacht's

engine roars to life, and Monty navigates us out of the harbor.

As we gather at the helm, Kody takes over the controls for the short ride back. I imagine he'll be operating his own boat soon, maybe a little cruiser like Frankie's.

The engine hums as we carve a path through the black velvet water. Emotions simmer, each of us adrift in our private thoughts, the gravity of those texts dragging at our souls.

"How did the negotiations with Pilip go?" I ask, breaking the silence.

"Monty made an offer Pilip couldn't refuse." Kody's grip tightens on the wheel, his voice steady yet tinged with something deeper. "Now it's up to us to work out the details."

"That's awesome, Kody." She sits beside me, her hand resting on my knee. "What kind of details?"

"There are a lot of decisions to make." He shifts his midnight eyes to Monty. "The biggest one is whether to trust Monty as my brother, let alone my investor."

Spoken and unspoken accusations twist the air around us.

"I'm standing right here." Monty crosses his arms. "Whatever's on your mind, say it."

"This distillery is my dream, but it's also a huge risk." Kody stares at the dark water ahead. "If you're behind those messages, everything changes."

"I'm the one taking the risk."

"The financial risk," I interject. "That's not the only risk. If Kody goes down this road with you and you betray him, he can't stay in business with you. All that hope you've given him..."

"It crushes, darling," she whispers.

Damn you, Wolf.

My chest constricts.

Monty remains silent, his expression cryptic, but I see objections swirling in his eyes.

"It's not just about the distillery." Kody's knuckles blanch on the wheel, his gaze never leaving the water. "The messages, the threats, the uncertainty. I need to know that you're on our side."

"I've done everything I can to protect this family." Monty

softens his tone. "But trust is earned, not given. I understand your doubts."

"We have to give you a chance to prove yourself," she says. "If you help us figure this out..."

"You have my word. I'll do whatever it takes to prove I'm not the one behind this." He turns to Kody. "I want to help you make your dream a reality. But I can't do that if you don't trust me."

"All right." Kody's grip on the wheel loosens. "We'll work on this together—negotiating the terms for the distillery and hunting down the unknown number. But know this." He levels his predatory eyes on Monty. "If I find out you had anything to do with those messages, I'll rip your fucking spine out and clean my teeth with your bones."

"Jesus." She pinches his waist, making him grunt. "We're not cannibals."

"I'm killing him the way I want." He faces forward again, grumbling, "And I'll die on that hill."

She sighs. "How about we all focus on...I don't know...*not* dying?"

Monty presses a curled finger against his mouth, and I realize he's holding back a smile. When he meets my eyes, I can't help it. I laugh.

It's the stress relief we need because, within seconds, we're all grinning, including my sulky, caveman brother.

"Frankie, you should've seen Monty trying to teach us how to parallel park," I say. "He couldn't even do it himself."

"It was a tight spot." Monty exhales wearily.

I run my knuckle down her lower back. "What I'm hearing is you can't handle tight spots."

She chokes on her spit.

Wolf would've loved this. He had a knack for finding humor in the darkest moments.

"Rhett responded." She squints at her phone. "He told a few of the nurses he was going to see me." She groans. "They gossip. It's kind of their thing. The entire hospital probably knew before he even left."

Fuck. That means any person she worked with, all people from her past, could be a threat to her.

I know how badly she wants to reclaim her role as a trauma nurse and rebuild the pieces of her life that were fractured. But she can't return to work yet. It's not safe, and I fucking hate that for her.

As the conversation shifts back to our driving lessons, Kody recounts how I nearly smashed the Bentley into a tree. Monty merely shrugs, and Frankie listens intently, throwing in jabs about our recklessness.

As if she's one to talk.

"Were you patient with them?" she asks Monty.

When he doesn't answer, I nod. "Yeah. He's a good teacher."

That's not saying much. Denver was patient and helpful throughout our upbringing. Until he wasn't.

"Tell me about the flight school." I meet Monty's gaze.

He delves into the basics, explaining the types of pilot licenses, categories of aircraft, education, flight hours required, and advanced training. What he doesn't mention is the cost.

"How much?" I ask.

"I'll cover it."

"How. Much?"

He rattles off the obscene price for basic flight school.

"No." I suck in a breath. "I'm not a fucking leech. I already owe you—"

"You owe me nothing. The way I see it, I'm indebted to you."

"How so?"

"You kept her alive in the Arctic Circle for nine months."

"She did a damn fine job keeping herself alive."

"No, I didn't." She dips her head. "A bear nearly ate me. I drowned in a lake. I sure as hell didn't fly the plane that got us out of there."

"I'm not taking his money, Frankie."

"Here's an option..." She taps her chin. "You and Kody can make some videos of you chopping wood with your shirts off. Think about it. A Viking and an Alaskan lumberjack. It would go viral and make a shitload of money."

"I don't know what that means," Kody mutters.

"Liar. I've seen you scrolling for hours through videos." I shake my head. "And the answer is no. We have more fucking pride than that."

"Then accept Monty's offer." She crosses her arms.

"What if I told you it was your inheritance?" Monty lifts a brow. "Denver had money. Nearly as much as I have. It'll be hung up in probate for a while, but not forever. You're his only heir. It's yours." His eyes shift to Kody. "And Rurik's fortune will go to you."

Silence. Thick, poignant silence.

We hadn't considered that.

"Where is Rurik's money now?" Frankie asks.

"Tied up in offshore accounts." Monty rubs his temple, looking exhausted. "I never touched it. Never tried. I want nothing to do with it."

"It's dirty money." Kody frowns. "We don't want it, either."

"Don't be an idiot." She sits taller. "Monty didn't touch it because he didn't need it. You *do*."

"She's right." I find her hand, my thumb gliding across her knuckles. "We're in this position because of choices made by Denver and Rurik. The money may be dirty, but we earned it through every scar they inflicted on us. I see it as blood money."

Kody exhales in reluctant agreement.

The rest of the ride passes in quiet introspection. As we approach the island, something akin to resolution circulates in my veins.

We have a plan—the distillery, flight school, protect Frankie, and depend on Monty until the inheritance comes in.

Is he the threat? I'm not so sure. But I can't let that possibility linger without taking action.

If this is a trap, we'll set a trap right back and use him in the process.

We need to create a situation where Monty thinks he has the upper hand, where he believes he can terrorize her without us knowing. If he takes the bait, we'll have our answer.

I know exactly how we'll do it.

"Threatening messages aside..." She leans her head on my shoulder, her eyes half-closed. "Today was a really good day."

"Yeah." As I rest my lips on her brow, my eyes connect with Monty's. "It was."

monty
TWENTY-SEVEN

The grandfather clock chimes with a solemn cadence, marking the passage of time in the den. It's been two months since Kody became the owner of Tipsy Sailor, with my backing as a silent partner.

Two months of progress on so many things. Except the one thing I want.

My wife.

I sit in a leather armchair, its creases worn from years of use. The room smells of wood polish, expensive bourbon, and testosterone-fueled distrust.

Across from me, Dr. Doyle Whitaker lounges with pedantic confidence, his pen poised over a notebook, his eyes scanning me with a practiced clinical detachment.

Ten minutes into our session and my head pounds like a motherfucking bitch.

"If you're not going to talk," he says, "why am I here?"

Therapy is a charade, a waste of time. Frankie thinks it will help, but I know better. This man, with his calculated concern, cannot be trusted.

I meet his gaze with steely silence, refusing to give him the satisfaction of a response.

He shifts in his seat, undeterred by my hostility. "It's been over two months since Kody and Leo moved to the island. That's a significant change. How are you adjusting to their presence?"

Adjusting. The word feels grossly inadequate. My life has been in raging, sucking turmoil since their arrival.

Every day, my beautiful wife slips further from my grasp. Kody and Leo, with their feral energy and constant hovering, complicate everything.

She's never alone. Never without one or both of them breathing down her neck.

They leave no room for me, no angle to make a move.

"I don't need to adjust." I interlock my fingers in the space between my knees. "This is my island. They adjust to me."

He nods, jotting down notes. "You mentioned before that you don't trust easily. Let's explore that. Why do you find it difficult to trust those around you, including Frankie?"

A snarl rises in my throat, but I swallow it down.

She's the only one I trust. She needs someone strong, someone who can protect her from the world. That someone is me.

"Trust is earned," I say flatly. "Most people haven't earned it."

"What about your parents?" His pen scratches across the paper, an irritating sound that grates on my nerves. "Losing them must've been difficult. Do you think their death affected your ability to trust?"

"Digging up the past won't change anything. They're dead, and I have no interest in bringing them back."

"It's not about bringing them back. It's about understanding how their loss shaped you. Sometimes acknowledging our pain is the first step toward healing."

"You think I need to heal?" I laugh, and it sounds bitter and harsh. "What I need is for you to stop lusting after my wife."

He loosens a steady breath, unfazed. "You seem very protective of Frankie. Can you tell me why?"

My fists clench, nails digging into my palms. Protective

doesn't even begin to cover it.

She's mine. My wife, my soul, my reason for existing. The thought of her with anyone else, of her being harmed, ignites an inferno in my veins.

Leo and Kody are a whole other complication. They have their driver's licenses now and are free to use my boats and cars. A freedom that both pleases and infuriates me.

It means they can take her places and give her experiences outside the confines of this island. It also means I can't keep her under constant surveillance. The thought alone drives me to the brink of madness.

Worse, they prefer to take her crappy little cruiser which could break down at any moment and leave them stranded in the Sitka Sound.

They're in Sitka now. She goes there every day. Not to work at the hospital—we can't leave her unguarded. When Leo attends flight school in town, she accompanies Kody to the distillery.

Tipsy Sailor is temporarily closed for renovations. When it reopens, it will be under a new name and ownership.

I picture her standing among the scattered tools, dust-covered floors, and half-finished walls, her eyes sparkling with pride as she watches Kody work tirelessly toward realizing his dream.

After everything he and Leo have been through, they deserve happiness, but I can't shake the fear that it will come at the cost of her safety.

With Leo in school and Kody focused on renovations, I have two guards trailing her at all times.

I can't be there every day. I have a goddamn company to oversee despite being woefully absent from it lately. She won't stay on the island with me alone, and in their need for independence, they don't want me tagging along.

Sometimes I go anyway.

But not today.

Today I'm stuck with Dr. Dipshit.

"She's my wife," I finally say. "It's my job to protect her."

"Protect her from what?" His eyes bore into mine. "From the world? Or from yourself?"

The question sours the air, a challenge I refuse to entertain. He thinks he can unravel me, dissect my mind, and lay bare my weaknesses.

He knows nothing.

"Did she tell you she has a stalker?" I tap my fingers on the armrest, steady and controlled.

"She mentioned that."

"Did she mention that you're a suspect?"

He tilts his head, considering the question. "No. She believes *you* are a suspect."

"Sharing that with me is a breach of doctor-patient privilege."

"Sharing something you already know? I don't think so. Look, I understand you're trying to keep her safe." His gaze softens, a methodical move to appear empathetic. "But sometimes, our efforts to protect can become suffocating."

His words strike a chord, but I bury the discomfort.

She needs me. Without my protection, she would be lost, vulnerable to the dangers that lurk around every corner.

He switches topics. "Let's talk about your relationship with Leo and Kody. How are things between the three of you?"

The man is fucking relentless. It makes him good at his job, like a double-edged sword, cutting through problems and leaving wounds in his wake.

I might as well engage to see if there's any merit to his methods. *For Frankie.*

"We're trying to find a balance." I glance out the window, the ocean a calming presence. "Between their independence and my need to mend my marriage."

He knows better than to ask me outright if they're fucking her. We've all been seeing him for two months. Well, all of us except Kody. But if Doyle has any intelligence in his pea-sized brain, he's figured out who is fucking whom.

Leaning back, he taps his pen against the notebook. "Why are you fighting so hard for your marriage?"

"I love her," I say simply.

"Love is a powerful motivator, but sometimes our jealousy can overshadow our love."

The accusation is a spark in dry tinder, setting me ablaze.

He thinks he understands me, but he hasn't even scratched the surface. My brother kidnapped and raped my wife. He raped Kaya, Kody, Leo, and my only son. He raped children, his own flesh and blood.

Fire crackles and roars beneath my skin, and adrenaline floods my circulation. I'm her protector, the alpha of this family, and I failed to defend what is mine.

My blood pounds in my ears. The thought of harm coming to her again fills me with feral rage, a burning need to destroy any threat, to rend flesh and break bone.

This is more than instinct. It's in my brutal, sinister Strakh blood. The drive to protect her is as vital as the air I breathe. It courses through my veins, breeding a thirst that can never be quenched.

She may not trust me, but she relies on me. While I still draw breath, I will not fail her again.

"My love for her is not some petty jealousy." I lean into the space between us. "It's primal, clawing, and fucking ruthless. You get me?"

"It's possessive and overbearing. That's not good for either of you. Have you considered that your jealousy is rooted in fear? Fear of losing her?"

"That's *your* fear, not mine."

"What are you talking about?" His eyes widen, caught off guard.

"Don't play dumb. I see the way you look at her. The way you *touch* her. How often do you jerk off to thoughts of my wife in your cold, empty bed at night?"

"My relationship with Frankie is strictly professional."

"What's your angle? To sow insidious seeds of doubt about our marriage, slowly tear us apart, then swoop in and fuck her?"

"This is not about me, and you're already separated. I'm here to counsel you individually."

"Stay away from her, Doyle." My heart pounds. "Or you'll find out just how far I'm willing to go to protect what's mine."

"Threats won't solve anything." He straightens, holding his ground. "You need to work through this, for your sake and Frankie's."

"We're done here." I rise to my feet. "I have better things to do than listen to your bullshit."

"All right." He stands as well, his expression resigned. "But remember, these sessions are for your benefit. I'll be here if you need me. If you don't want to talk to me, I can refer you to someone else."

I turn away, facing the window, not bothering with a response or a farewell.

As his footsteps retreat down the hall, I listen for the security guard to escort him off the island. A moment later, Doyle steps onto the path outside, trailed by one of the guards toward the dock.

My thoughts turn to Frankie, Kody, and Leo. They've been in town for hours now. Sometimes they share dinner in a restaurant or stroll along the coast and don't return until after dark.

Frankie has money saved, not enough to live on, but enough to eat out and fuel her cruiser. Her savings will run out before she returns to work. Will she come to me then? Let me support her in every way?

I can only hope.

The house feels empty without her. The echo of voices, the warmth of Frankie's nearness, all missing. I find myself in the kitchen, staring at the untouched dinner that Oliver prepared for her. She should be here, not gallivanting around Sitka with Leo and Kody.

My phone buzzes, a call from Sirena.

"Yes?" I answer.

"Frankie and Kody are leaving the distillery, returning to the flight school to get Leo."

"Reporters?"

"None."

Our interviews aired last week, causing a commotion, but it

has since died down. The vultures have moved on to more scandalizing stories.

"Dr. Whitaker is headed back to Sitka." I stare out the kitchen window. "Keep an eye on him."

"On it."

"Any update on locating the cabin?"

"No." Her soft sigh drifts through the connection. "My team has swept nearly twenty percent of those hills. There's a lot of ground to cover. This would go faster if Leo or Kody joined them."

I agree. They might recognize landmarks or something familiar. But they won't leave Frankie, especially not to return to that cabin. I can't blame them, but every day, our chances of recovering Wolfson's body diminish.

"Keep searching." I disconnect the call, my thoughts returning to Frankie.

The stalker remains unidentified. No messages or threats since the first one. I'm keeping Sirena out of that investigation. The only thing she knows beyond what we told the press is that I had a son in those hills. Everything else is on a need-to-know basis, and she doesn't need to know about the depravity in my family.

Doyle's words echo in my mind.

Our efforts to protect can become suffocating.

He doesn't understand. No one does. Frankie is my world. I need to find a way to keep her safe without losing her.

And for that, I need to confront the darkness inside me.

Leo and Kody sit with me at a corner table in a cozy restaurant with a clear view of the bustling dining area.

Kody's fingers curl around mine on the table, his scarred hand rough but gentle like his eyes. Leo's palm rests on my thigh, his thumb stroking, always restless. His rugged features soften as he looks at me, and Kody's brooding intensity gives way to a tenderness that swells my chest.

We're a tangle of broken souls, stitched together by shared pain and longing. Longing for one another. Longing for a future full of affection.

We already know what hell looks like. No more punishments are necessary.

Give us more of this—soft evenings, good food, and stolen kisses, sweet as dark cherries.

Leo and Kody are happy here. In Sitka. In this new life. Happier than I've ever seen them.

Despite the unsolved threat that's been haunting us for two months.

Our security guards—Carl and Jasper—stand outside, watching us through the front windows while scrutinizing the locals and tourists inside and on the street. While I appreciate their constant vigilance, they make me anxious. We have no real privacy, no peace from the fear that seems to follow us everywhere.

Soft amber lighting casts a glow over the wooden tables, the atmosphere heavy with the mouthwatering aroma of grilled seafood and hearty stews. Vintage photographs of Sitka's history, fishing boats, and native Alaskan art adorn the walls, giving the place a timeless charm.

Monty and I used to eat here often. Part of me wishes he was here now.

Over the past two months, the tension between him and the guys has relented. The three of them get along remarkably well when I'm not around. They actually seem to enjoy one another's company.

Sometimes, I wonder if my presence holds them back from a deeper bond.

Monty will never have the connection Leo and Kody share, but he's trying. When they're in the gym or discussing business, he interacts with them like an older brother.

But when I'm there, he's the husband.

Except he's not the husband I knew before my abduction.

I can't put my finger on exactly what it is. It's so many things. He's more humble and less guarded. More self-reliant and less pampered. He's still a controlling, overbearing, hot-tempered alphahole, but he no longer storms off during an argument. He concedes and compromises. He drives his own vehicles, spends less time in his office, and sees a therapist. A therapist he hates, but he's doing it. He's getting help.

Bottom line, the man he is today wouldn't crush a pregnancy stick beneath his shoe. He's matured since that morning.

In a good way.

In a great way.

In a terrifyingly attractive, sexy, he's-no-longer-mine, and dammit-I-can't-think-about-him-like-that way.

A server places our dishes before us. She gives me a friendly smile and turns to Leo and Kody, tucking that smile between nibbling teeth while batting sultry eyes.

I can't even be mad about it. They have that effect on every woman they encounter. Just like Monty.

We ordered a feast to share. Freshly caught salmon, seared to perfection and drizzled with a tangy lemon-butter sauce. A bowl of Alaskan king crab bisque, its rich fragrance bursting with a promise of flavor. And a platter of roasted vegetables, their vibrant colors bubbling through the butter.

Kody pours us each a glass of imported blueberry vodka and raises his drink, his obsidian eyes meeting ours.

"To Frankie's garden that will never grow." He smiles an actual smile that crooks up both sides of his mouth. "Now we can laugh about it over a real meal far away from Hoss."

"Whatever, you ass." I laugh.

"And to the pemmican that saved us." Leo's eyes glint. "May we never eat it again."

"Here, here," we say in unison, clinking our glasses together.

The vodka tastes smooth, with a hint of sweetness and a harsh afterburn. It doesn't come close to Kody's recipes.

We've been sampling all the vodka around town, checking out the competition.

There is no competition.

When his distillery opens, it will blow minds and taste buds. Vodka connoisseurs and critics will come from all over the world to sample his product. Locals and tourists will show up in droves to be part of the scene. His vision for the ambiance is classy and sophisticated and wildly surprising for my snow cabin boy.

I should've known better.

We've come a long way from counting beans and rationing pemmican. After two months of good nutrition and exercise, I feel more like myself, stronger, curvier. Curvy for me, anyway.

But Leo and Kody? Yeah. They've filled out, their bodies more sculpted and powerful than ever.

Leo's once lanky frame is now stacked with lean muscle, his shoulders broad and strong. He keeps his beard trimmed and shoulder-length hair neatly braided into a knot, looking like a cleaned-up Norse warrior with pectorals sculpted from marble.

Every woman in the restaurant is hot under the table and squirming in her seat as every gaze openly stares at the hot Viking. Hard to look away from his chiseled jawline and those battle-honed blue and gold eyes. And his body. His shirt molds so tightly to his well-defined chest that it shows off every carved ridge.

Kody, too, has transformed. His already impressive physique has become even more imposing, each muscle perfectly defined under his tanned skin. His dark hair, short and tousled, accentuates his brooding, intense gaze. The scars crisscrossing his arms and back add to the aura of danger and allure that draws every eye in the room. But it's his unwavering focus on me that sets my heart racing.

I don't care how many women ogle them. I'm the only one who gets to see them in the gym, brawling and pumping iron, shirtless and sweaty.

I'm the only one who gets to feel them when they're fucking, thrusting and grunting, deliciously naked and rock-hard.

My guys never disappoint.

Watching them navigate their new world is both bittersweet and rewarding. They've adapted quickly in such a short amount of time. They've always been hardworking. In Hoss, it was physical labor, relying on their powerful physiques to hunt, gather, and survive.

But here, they're working smarter, utilizing their sharp minds to master technology, learn the rules of society, and become self-sufficient. They're not just following their dreams. They're laying the foundation for our future.

That also means they spend a lot of time on their phones.

"Leo." I glare at the device in his hand. "Eat."

"Monty's working out." He continues to stare at the screen. "Second time today."

"I wish you wouldn't monitor him." I sip my vodka. "That's not the point of the cameras."

Installing cameras throughout Monty's estate was Leo's idea. The night I received those threatening messages, he suggested we set a trap for Monty.

At the time, I was willing to do anything to prove or disprove Monty's guilt. So I withdrew money from my savings, invested in high-end surveillance equipment, and helped Leo discreetly hide cameras in every room Monty uses, including his bedroom and bathroom.

If and when I receive another threat, the recording devices will catch Monty in the act. But only if he's home.

For two months, we've spent every day in town, away from Monty, all the while expecting something, anything to set off the trap.

Monitoring him without his knowledge doesn't sit right with me. I can access the video footage on my phone, but I don't. It's a violation of privacy, and I want to remove it.

"It's driving me crazy." Leo pockets his phone. "It's been two months and nothing. No threats. No strange behavior. Just...nothing."

"It's like he's too careful." Kody takes a bite of salmon, chewing thoughtfully. "Or worse, he's playing us."

"Well, I, for one, am glad I haven't been terrorized." I swallow a spoonful of soup.

"That's not what we're saying, love." Leo frowns. "I'm relieved no one has fucked with you again. But we can't let our guard down. Not until we're sure."

Kody nods. "We're doing everything we can to protect you. Even if it means watching Monty's every move."

They're not the only ones protecting me. Monty keeps guards on us at all times.

He also hired a self-defense instructor who came to the island to teach me the basics. The woman had a lot of energy and whipped me into shape. After finishing the eight-week course, I feel more confident in fending off an attacker.

"I had my first solo landing today." Leo's grin lights up his gorgeous face. "It was incredible. Being up there, completely in control, and actually knowing what I'm doing...it's like nothing else."

"I'm so happy for you." My insides flutter with excitement. "I knew you'd do great."

"That completes your recreational pilot certificate, right?" Kody asks.

"I still need to pass the exam, but yeah, I'm close."

"Then on to the next certificate." I squeeze his hard thigh.

"Yep. Bigger aircraft, farther distance, night flying, all the fun stuff." He tilts his head, looking at Kody. "How's the distillery coming along?"

"The renovations are almost done. We're on track to start production in a few months. I've been experimenting with some new flavors."

"Like what?" I ask.

"A North Star Cherry vodka with a hint of Alaskan wildflowers." Kody winks at me. "And there's a lemon one with spruce tips. It's different, but I think it'll be a hit."

"I can't wait to try them." My heart soars for both of them.

They've come so far, each pursuing their dreams despite the shadows that haunt us.

We talk and laugh, the alcohol loosening our tongues long after we finish eating and pay the check. Kody tells more stories about the distillery renovations, his passion shining through. Leo teases him, his smile contagious.

I lean into Kody, tracing the scar on his palm. He closes his fingers, catching my hand and bringing it to his lips. "I love you, woman."

"We both do." Leo reaches across the table, his hand covering ours.

I close my eyes, savoring the warmth and intimacy of our bond.

As dusk darkens the window and rain spits against the glass, I excuse myself to use the restroom.

"I'll be right there." Standing, I point at the door five tables away and smooth down my dress. "You can watch me from here."

They nod, their eyes following me as I walk away. I can feel their protective gazes even with my back turned, reminding me how deeply they care.

It's a private restroom with a single toilet. I lock the door and do my business. Then I take a moment to gather myself, splashing cool water on my face and looking at my reflection in the mirror.

My mind drifts to the future, the dreams we share, and the life we're building. Monty's a vital part of that.

He can't be behind those messages.

I'm starting to believe there's no threat at all. Someone was just fucking with me, and they've moved on.

We need to remove the cameras before they cause actual harm to our family.

As I leave the restroom, a man steps into my path. His smile is crooked, his demeanor non-threatening, but his sudden approach raises my hackles.

"Hey." Eyes unfocused, he slurs in my face, "God, you're beautiful."

Wobbling, he reaches for the high-top table beside me. I don't know if he needs it for balance or if he's deliberately stumbling against me, but in a blink, his ribs knock into mine, and his hot breath coats my neck.

Oh, God, no. The dumbfuck has no idea he just started World War III.

Pushing him off me, I angle my head toward our table to stop what's coming.

But it's already empty.

frankie
TWENTY-NINE

An inhuman bellow of rage singes the air, sending a chill across my scalp.

"No!" I spin, slamming into Kody's chest.

His arms come around me. Behind him, Leo stalks toward the drunk man with a calmness that lifts the hairs on my nape.

"Whoa!" The man's hands fly up in surrender. "I didn't mean to—"

A fist cracks across his face, whipping his head to the side in a spray of blood. His body follows the momentum, crashing onto a table and breaking it.

"Leo, no!" Pulse spiking, I shove against Kody's grip. "Stop!"

Leo tackles the man to the floor, letting his fists fly in a haze of homicidal fury. Over and over, his knuckles connect with sickening thuds, a Viking waging all-out war.

Kody breaks away in a blur, joining in the assault, his strikes precise and relentless.

The man sprawls beneath them, his cries drowned by the sounds of smacking flesh and cracking bones.

"Stop it! Both of you!" I shriek, my voice lost in the chaos as I try to wrestle them away. "Please, stop!"

They don't hear me. Don't feel me pulling on them. I'm not strong enough, and they're lost in their rage, their need to protect me overshadowing all reason.

Blood splatters, and sweat and tears permeate the dining room, painting a grotesque picture of their wrath.

"You're going to kill him!" I scream louder, my vocal cords burning.

The crowd recoils in horror, their whispers of alarm jangling in my chest.

When I hear someone mention the cops, I know this will only get messier. And soon. The police station is a block away.

The urge to vomit the nerves in my stomach overwhelms me. I whirl toward the entrance to alert Carl and Jasper. But they're already inside, shoving through the crush of bodies.

They grab at Kody and Leo, trying to pull them off the man, but it's like separating wolves from their prey.

My mind wails.

Kody whirls on Carl, his fist connecting with the man's jaw with a crunch. Carl stumbles back, clutching his face, blood seeping through his fingers.

Every nerve ending fires with fear as I search for a safe way to end this. I'm at a loss.

Jasper lunges at Leo, who twists and lands a vicious kick to the man's midsection, skidding him across the floor.

The guards fight back, their efforts becoming more desperate. Carl locks down Kody's arm, twisting it behind his back.

"Kody!" I rush in, attempting to capture his eyes. "Look at me! Calm down!"

He roars in fury, his free hand swinging back to strike Carl's temple, and the impact crashes the guard into a nearby table.

Leo snarls, eyes wild, as he takes down Jasper with a swift, brutal punch to the gut.

The sound of sirens just outside the door sends a ripple through the crowd.

A man shouts, "The cops are here!"

Tears sting my eyes, and my throat closes.

They're going to jail. They'll be handcuffed and separated from me. That won't go well.

The guards redouble their efforts, finally managing to subdue Kody and Leo with the help of reinforcements from the crowd.

In the end, it takes eight men to wrestle them to the ground, their bodies still thrashing, breaking my heart.

Blood and sweat slick their skin, their breaths coming in harsh, ragged gasps. Pinned to the floor on their stomachs with several men kneeling on their backs, they look battered and bruised and absolutely terrifying, like avenging gods in the aftermath of battle.

A flurry erupts outside the front door.

The cops.

I have less than five seconds to prepare them for what's about to happen.

Dropping to my knees beside their prone positions, I rest my hands on them and talk fast. "Listen carefully. You're going to be arrested, handcuffed, and taken to jail. Remain silent and ask for your lawyer. You'll turn over your IDs and give your name and address, but do *not* say anything else. Don't talk to the officers. Don't talk to your cellmates. Assume every conversation will be recorded and used against you." Spotting the approaching police, I rush through the rest. "Don't unlock your phone for them. They need a warrant for that. You'll be searched, photographed, and fingerprinted. Don't resist."

"Step back, ma'am." An officer nudges me away as four others climb over Leo and Kody.

Handcuffs click into place, the sound of cold metal shattering through me with harsh reality.

Their possessive glares stay with me, and slowly, their bloodlust fades, replaced with a startling realization.

They're going to be taken away from me.

I edge closer, squeezing through the mob as they're hauled to their feet.

"I won't be able to see you until Monty arrives, and maybe not even then." A sob rises, and I choke it down. "You'll probably spend the night in jail."

Maybe longer.

"What about you?" Leo clenches his jaw, teeth grinding to hold back a roar.

"I'll stay with the guards until Monty arrives. I'm fine."

I'm not fine.

I'm barely holding it together.

"I love you." Lunging past the nearest cop, I crash into Leo and take his blood-soaked face in my hands. "Remember what I said. The lawyer will fix this."

As they rip him from my grip, I reach for Kody, capturing his elbow for a brief moment before they take him, too.

I watch, helpless and trembling, as they're dragged away, their eyes burning into mine until they're forced out the door and into the back of a police car.

The man they attacked lies on the floor, a mauled mess of blood and bruises, as paramedics treat him.

One drunken mistake nearly cost him his life.

The consequences of their actions compress my chest, making it hard to breathe. I brought them to this. It's me. I'm at the center of every brawl, my presence the catalyst for their rage. They have aggression issues, and I make it worse.

I want to cry, to beg for forgiveness, but the sounds die in my throat. This is my curse, my never-ending cycle of pain and retribution.

The chaos in the restaurant closes in around me, diners murmuring in shock, employees cleaning broken furniture, and officers taking statements.

"We need to call Monty." Carl sits on a stool, his face bloody from Kody's fist, as a paramedic tends to him.

"I'll do it." I glance around for a quiet corner.

It's too loud in here. The noise, the panic...I can't hear myself think.

"I'm stepping outside to make the call," I say to Jasper, my voice trembling.

He nods and gestures for me to lead the way.

"Are you okay?" I give him a clinical once-over.

"Yeah." He smirks. "Just another day in the office."

frankie

Outside, the drizzling summer rain pricks my skin like needles.

I step beneath an overhang and pull out my phone, my hands shaking. As I scroll to Monty's number, my phone buzzes with an incoming call from an unknown number.

My lungs seize. My heart stops, and sinking dread buckles my stomach.

Jasper notices my hesitation and glances at the screen. "Answer it on speaker."

The security team knows about the threats. Monty made sure of it after the text messages.

I nod, swallowing hard as I accept the call and switch it to speaker. "Hello?"

"You're not alone, little girl." Cold and mechanical, a computerized female voice trickles down my spine. "I'm here, always watching. You can try to stay out of my way, but I'll get you, my pretty. I'll come for you and your guard dogs, too."

"Who is this?" My stomach wrenches.

"When you call Daddy Strakh to bail out your dogs, ask him who hid those flight logs in Rurik's wine cellar."

The call ends abruptly, leaving me in stunned silence.

Jasper's eyes harden, and he looks around, expecting danger to materialize from the shadows.

My breath bursts in shredded gasps, panic rising in my chest.

Someone is watching. How else would they know I was alone?

If I can monitor Monty, maybe he's doing the same thing to me.

"Can you give me privacy while I call my husband?" I angle my screen away from Jasper.

"I'll be right over there." He strides a few feet away to stand beneath another overhang.

My insides turn inside out as I launch the home monitoring app and open the most recent motion-activated recordings.

Instantly, I locate him in his bathroom, in the shower, and *oh, damn, Monty.*

He stands with his feet braced apart and a hand planted on the wall while his other works his cock, stroking himself aggressively, brutally to completion.

His head drops back, his jaw clenched tight, and although I have the live video muted, I know exactly what those gravelly, orgasmic groans sound like as they scrape past his lips.

Fuck.

He's not the stalker. I have the proof right here.

He couldn't have called me while he's in the shower, jerking off. I don't care how horny he is, he can't come that fast. Unless the phone was in his hand when he started.

I don't see it in the bathroom. The camera angle encompasses the entire space.

Only one way to know for sure.

With a shiver, I keep the video open and call his phone.

His head snaps toward the doorway, and he slams off the water. He doesn't bother with a towel as he charges toward the camera, bringing those rippled washboard abs closer, and closer, filling my entire phone screen.

My breath hangs in my throat. All I see is the thin, dark trail that leads to the semi-hard cock that I worshiped for three years.

Montgomery Loshad Strakh, you wicked, gorgeous man. What am I going to do with you?

His real name still sounds foreign to me, but it fits.

He's built like a sculpted Russian god of seduction and fucks with all the stamina and endurance of a stallion.

Damn him.

I hate how violently he can still make my body react. It feels like cheating.

Cheating on my lovers with my husband.

He steps out of the bathroom, out of view, breaking the spell.

Shit!

I quickly close the app and hold the phone to my ear.

"Frankie," he answers, out of breath. "What's wrong?"

"Leo and Kody were arrested."

frankie

THIRTY

Clutching the phone to my ear, I explain to Monty what happened in the restaurant.

As I finish answering his questions, the paramedics carry the injured drunk out on a stretcher.

"The victim will live." Dullness fills my chest, a heaviness I can't escape. "But he probably has a concussion, head wounds, and broken bones. He'll sue."

"He assaulted you," Monty says. "We'll get him on that."

"He was drunk."

"Doesn't matter. I'll call my legal team. They'll take care of it."

"Not Melanie?"

"My local attorneys will handle it faster. You said the guards are injured? Are they with you?"

"Jasper's here." I glance at the older man hovering a few feet away.

"Put him on the phone."

Monty's hurried movements rustle through the connection, the shuffle of clothes, footsteps, and quickening breaths. I assume he's coming, but I need to know for sure.

"Monty..." I tap my chest, trying to loosen the tightness as I say the words that feel so right and so wrong at the same time. "I need you."

Silence.

It lasts so long I wonder if he disconnected.

Then his deep baritone whispers in my ear, "You have me."

He's gorgeous, rich, and offering himself in no uncertain terms. What more could a girl want?

She wants his brother and nephew, that's what.

He clears his throat. "Just got out of the shower. Almost dressed. I'll be there in twenty minutes." Another pause of silence. "I'm sorry, darling. I should've been there."

"No. That's not..." Lowering my voice, I tighten my grip on the phone. "Something else happened. I received a call after the assault."

I repeat what the caller said and describe the synthesized voice.

"Goddammit! Fuck!" He makes a dangerous sound in his throat. "Put Jasper on the phone. Now."

I hand off the phone and stand there, shivering in the wet breeze and scanning the darkness for an unknown enemy.

Who is it? What do they want? Why do I attract psychos? What is it about me that draws them in? Is it because I married Monty and got entangled with the Strakh family?

If Denver is to be believed, it started long before that, when I was in Anchorage.

I met so many people during my residency, befriended dozens of members of the hospital staff, had one-night stands and ongoing sexual relationships with some of them. If the stalker is connected to my past in Anchorage, they could be anyone.

"Yes, sir." Jasper nods. "I understand."

Ending the call, he returns my phone and gestures through the window at Carl.

"What did Monty say?" I ask.

"We'll escort you to the station and wait there until he arrives." He nods at Carl as he steps outside, relaying the same information.

frankie

Carl opens an umbrella, holding it over me as we walk along the dark street in the rain.

One block later, we enter the police station, the stagnant air leaden with empty sadness. A holding ground for lost souls.

Leo and Kody don't belong here.

Since I don't see them, I assume they're getting processed in a back room.

The thought of them being handled roughly, possibly still in a state of feral rage, makes me stabby. I can't stomach the idea of them in a cold, impersonal cell, trapped behind bars.

They've been imprisoned their entire lives.

A lone officer sits behind a worn wooden desk, his eyes glazed with the monotony of paperwork.

The space reeks of disinfectant and stale coffee. Bleak fluorescent lights throw an unwelcoming glow over the linoleum floors and metal benches, the room largely empty, save for a few people in the waiting area, their expressions vacant and tired.

A clock on the wall ticks loudly, each second stretching into an eternity.

Nothing here is meant to be comforting.

The officer behind the desk looks up as I approach, scrutinizing the guards behind me. "Can I help you?"

"I'm here for Leonid and Kodiak Strakh. They were just brought in."

"They're being processed." He returns to his stack of papers, dismissing me with a bored flick of a hand at the metal chairs along the wall.

I take a seat with Carl and Jasper standing on either side of me, drawing every gaze in the room.

The minutes slowly pulse by like the ache in my chest. Stress pummels every organ, nerve ending, and brain cell. The quiet hum of ceiling fans, the rustle of paper, the static of florescent lights—all of it grates, adding to the coil of fear, guilt, and worry in my stomach.

Just as the anxiety becomes unbearable, the door to the station swings open. Monty strides in, his dominance commanding immediate attention.

His wintry blue eyes instantly home in on me, flooding me with relief.

As the most powerful man in Alaska, he dresses the part. A crisp white shirt clings to his muscular body, his suit pants molding to his sculpted ass as if tailored by Satan himself.

Dressed to kill, he looks fucking sinful.

I really need to stop admiring him. My desperation to see Leo and Kody is much more pinching.

He crosses the room with purposeful strides, his powerful gait exuding control and unshakable confidence.

"Frankie." He lowers to his haunches before me, inspecting me for signs of a panic attack or physical injury.

His hand gently cups my face, shooting electricity through my body as his thumb brushes my cheekbone.

For a moment, I allow the touch, needing it.

"Thank you for coming." I lean back, breaking the connection.

"Always." Concern and love radiate from him, twisting me up and introducing more problems. "Stay here."

With a pointed look at my guards, he strides to the officer behind the desk.

"Mr. Novak." The cop recognizes him immediately, sitting straighter in a show of respect.

It always amazes me how easily he can have everyone jumping and doing his bidding. He doesn't even need to open his mouth. His authority and notoriety precede him.

Within seconds, he has the chief of police on the line and bending over backward to meet his demands.

"Yes, I understand the situation is complex," Monty says into the phone, quietly yet intensely. "But I need to speak with my family immediately." He listens, head cocked. "Very good. Thank you."

Monty disconnects and relays the chief's orders.

"Of course, Mr. Novak." The officer behind the desk nods. "Right away."

Monty turns back to me, his hand extended in a wordless command.

I rise, closing the distance and placing my palm in his. My entire body tingles as he curls those strong fingers around mine.

The officer leads us toward the holding cells, and I'm grateful for Monty's strength and his ability to take control of the situation. But I don't need hand-holding through this.

Even as the thought of seeing Leo and Kody behind bars wrings my chest with pain, it's not like I'm going to pass out or hyperventilate.

I won't break.

Twisting my arm, I free myself from Monty's grip.

He shoots me a dark glare but says nothing.

We reach the jail, and another officer opens the door to the cell block, leading us down a dimly lit corridor. My breath catches in my throat when I see Leo and Kody in a private cell together.

Leo paces like a caged animal, his bicolored eyes flashing with helpless rage. Kody sits on the edge of the cot, an intense brooding shadow. They both look up as we approach, their expressions shifting from anger to relief.

"Frankie." Leo reaches through the bars, his hand grasping mine tightly.

"Are you okay?" Kody rises, his gaze roaming over me.

Then he peers into my eyes.

My God, I feel raw under the pressure of his glare. Seen inside and out. No one looks at me the way he does. This closely. This deeply. Like he knows my feelings for Monty have changed.

Everything has changed.

"I'm fine." I swallow. "We're fine. Monty is handling it."

Monty grips one of the bars, his fingers tapping in a methodical, controlled rhythm. Everything he does oozes dominance. It's who he is. A personality trait that runs in the family.

His drumming fingers halt, his scowl leveled on Leo. "Fix your hair. You look like a smacked ass."

"Blow it out your dickhole, you uptight cunt," Leo snarls.

"Did you eat a bowl of dumbass for breakfast?" Monty unbuttons the cuffs of his shirt like he'll fight him through the bars.

"Stop it." I push at his chest. "Both of you."

"We'll get you out of here." Exhaling slowly through his nose, Monty rolls up his sleeves. "My lawyers are working on it right now. But you need to keep your mouths shut and cooperate until we get this sorted. No more violence."

He speaks to them like a scolding brother, but it's the husband who turns to me with frightening slowness. His eyes take me in, narrowing with an icy warning.

"I'll give you a few minutes." He ambles away, lifting his phone to his ear.

A few minutes to what? *Not* make out with them through the bars? Is that what the warning was for?

Since he didn't tell them about the threatening call, I guess he's leaving that up to me.

Rubbing my lips together, I know I'll tell them, even if it makes their jail time more excruciating. It's what I would expect from them if our positions were reversed.

At least I can assure them I won't be alone on the island with my stalker. The cameras proved Monty's innocence.

I shift back to two pairs of livid eyes.

"What the fuck happened?" Leo clutches the bars. "There's something you're not telling us."

How the hell do they read me so easily?

"Everything will be okay," I whisper.

"Doesn't answer my question." His face moves closer.

So close I can count the specks of blood on his cheeks and smell the vodka on his breath.

He's blood-soaked and brutal, ready to kill anyone who touches me. But as I stand in the laser focus of that vicious, otherworldly gaze, I'm wildly, inappropriately turned on.

Inappropriate, considering what I'm about to tell them.

"The stalker called me." My tongue thickens in my mouth as I describe the call, the threats, and the computerized voice.

Shadows unfurl and seethe around them, their gazes flying to Monty.

"It's not him." I lean in until our mouths hover a hairsbreadth apart between the bars. "I checked the cameras seconds after the call ended. Monty was in the shower. When I called him, he left the bathroom to answer the phone."

"So you trust him?" Leo asks through gritted teeth.

"I didn't say that."

"You forgive him," Kody states. It's not a question.

My emotions have been through the wringer so many times tonight that I'm surprised my heart hasn't called it quits.

"The man you assaulted is in the hospital," I say. "There are too many details to work out tonight. But Monty's lawyers should have you out by tomorrow." My voice fractures. "I love you both so much."

"We love you, too." Kody's eyes soften, and he reaches out to touch my other hand. "Don't worry about us. We'll be okay."

"We've survived worse." Leo sighs. "At least this prison has heat and indoor plumbing."

"Let me see your hands," I say.

They extend their busted fists through the bars, and the sight makes my chest ache.

Their knuckles swell beneath bruises and broken skin. Patches of dried blood surround the cuts, and their hands tremble from the pain and adrenaline still coursing through them.

The damage could be worse, but all this could've been avoided.

"You need to wash your hands and keep them clean from infection." I nod at the sink behind them.

"You're going to stay on the island alone with him." Kody glowers at Monty, who stands out of earshot, talking to someone on his phone.

"Where else would I go?"

"You need to stay in the main house." Leo bites out the words as if they pain him. "Don't stay in the guest house by yourself."

"There are guards."

"Don't risk it, woman." Kody flexes his jaw. "If Monty's not the stalker, he's the only one who will protect you as fiercely as we do."

"Okay." I shiver, goosebumps erupting across my skin. "I'll stay in the main house."

"Not saying we trust him." Leo scowls at the man in question.

"We trust he won't hurt you," Kody says quietly.

"We just don't trust his dick." Leo makes a menacing sound.

"Do you trust *me*?" I curl my hands around the bars.

They both nod and wrap their fingers around mine, dwarfing my hands.

"Time's up." The officer signals from the doorway.

Monty ends his call and strides back to us, giving Leo and Kody a stern glare. "Behave."

"We're not children," Leo grumbles.

At twenty-five and thirty, Kody and Leo are definitely not boys. They're more manly than most men. They've lived harder lives. Their bodies endured the harshest conditions. Because of that, they're stronger, braver, more chiseled, more aggressive, and more ruthless than anyone I've ever met.

Except maybe Monty.

The three Strakh men together? They're masculinity on steroids.

"Let's go." Monty takes my hand, his grip firm.

It doesn't feel right to leave without kissing them.

It doesn't feel right to leave them here at all.

A riptide of anxiety crashes through me, quickening my pulse as Monty guides me away.

At the door, I glance over my shoulder. "I'll see you tomorrow. I promise."

Leo's hand tightens around the bars. Then he lets go and turns away.

"Be safe." Kody's gaze remains steady.

Monty gently tugs on my hand, pulling me around the corner, taking me from them.

The separation feels like a physical wound, each step away a sharp blow to my chest. My breaths come faster, louder as the panic rises, the fear of leaving them clawing at my composure.

"Hey." Monty pauses, scanning my face. He peers so closely that his breath fans my lips, coaxing me to look at him. "They're okay. They're safe. Do you need to sit?"

I shake my head and resume walking.

"Let me carry you." He grips my elbow.

"My legs work just fine."

With a sigh, he hooks his fingers around mine and leads me back to the dock with the guards on our trail.

Sitka's harbor stretches before us, the streets empty, devoid of the usual bustle. No footsteps, no voices, just the distant sound of waves bouncing against the dock.

The silence feels eerie, pressing against my skin like an unseen hand. I glance around, every shadow a potential threat, every alley harboring danger. My heart beats faster.

Monty walks beside me, his black hair gleaming in the streetlights. I cling to his strength, giving him more trust than I've given him in a long time.

Do I believe he'll physically hurt me? Will he climb into my bed and stab me while I sleep?

It's unthinkable.

But will he betray me again? Lie to me? Smash my heart beneath his shoe?

Not if I keep it locked far away from him.

We continue walking, the dock now in sight. Buildings loom on the waterfront, their windows like dark, empty eyes watching us pass. I can't shake the feeling that we're being followed, that someone lurks just out of sight, waiting for the perfect moment to strike.

My gaze darts left and right. Every movement in the corner of my eye makes me flinch. I see shadows where there are none and hear footsteps that aren't there. The night plays tricks on me, twisting my memories of captivity with the present terror of that phone call.

Monty's grip tightens, his thumb stroking the back of my hand in a rhythmic, calming motion.

"Look at me." He stops in his tracks.

I turn to face him, my eyes meeting his frosty blue ones. Wolf's eyes, but older, wiser, filled with a depth of emotion that anchors me.

"I won't let anything happen to you," he promises.

Monty Novak, my husband, my guardian. Despite the betrayal, despite the separation, he's still the man I once loved deeply.

We resume walking until a sudden scraping from a nearby alley makes me jump. My heart leaps into my throat, my grip on Monty's hand turning vise-like.

He doesn't flinch, his gaze fixed on the source of the noise.

It's just a cat scurrying away from us. The appearance and disappearance cut the tension, and I let out a shaky breath, feeling foolish for my fear.

Monty squeezes my hand and pulls me along.

We reach the dock, the wooden planks groaning under our feet. Boats bob in the water, their ropes creaking softly. I try to focus on the pace of our steps, matching mine to his.

One step at a time, Frankie. One step at a time.

As we board the yacht and prepare to depart without Leo and Kody, my body trembles with the effort to hold myself together.

It's just one night. I'll see them tomorrow. There's no reason to freak out.

I measure my breath, chasing away the burn in my sinuses as I sit beside Monty at the helm.

"Nothing will happen to them." He drapes an arm around my shoulders, pulling me close as he navigates the yacht into open water. "I promise. We'll get them out and hunt down the sick fuck who's stalking you."

He senses that something's changed, something's shifted between us, because he's touching me, invading my space, inching his hands down my body.

The one caressing my exposed knee grows bolder, teasing the hem of my dress and the valley between my thighs.

"Monty." I stiffen, squeezing my legs together and halting his fingers. "I love them."

He yanks his hand away with a hiss.

"I will never leave them," I say.

"Yes, you will."

"Really?" I sneer. "How do you know? Because you know everything?"

"Watch that fucking tone."

"Fuck you."

"Fucking you is a start." Low and velvety, his voice rubs against my overheated skin. "Bruising, claiming, ramming, burning, breaking, insides spilling, guts melting, spread open, ass up, crying out in the dark while you come on me, and I come in you. That's where we're headed."

By the time he finishes, he has my feet off the floor, my thighs around his hips, and my back against the bulkhead. He grips my hair, yanking my head back and forcing me to look at him.

As he stares into my furious eyes, he realizes what he's done.

"Fuck." He drops me to the floor and staggers back.

The panic on his face conveys more regret than words could. Though it's hard to forgive him with that raging boner tenting his pants.

I aim my glare at it.

"I didn't mean to upset you." He runs a hand through his dark strands, flexing the veiny muscles in his forearm. "I'm sorry. I've been celibate for so fucking long. My endless goddamn need for you is wearing me down."

He turns, bending to grab a water bottle from the mini-fridge, drawing my focus to places I shouldn't be looking.

The man knows how to wear a suit. Especially those pants. Tailored to his exact measurements, the expensive fabric makes his ass look delectable. I mean, he's always had an incredible ass. It should be illegal.

He offers the water, and I take a greedy drink. As he guzzles down the rest of it, his free hand swiftly opens the buttons on his shirt, exposing the results of two months in the gym.

All *V*-cut abs, bulging pecs, and narrow hips. Shiny shoes. Five o'clock shadow. Beautifully chiseled face, crafted by God.

Six foot-five inches of psychological warfare in a designer suit.

Heat burns my cheeks, and I avert my eyes, cursing my thoughts.

I don't need reminders of why I fell in love with this man.

"Remember what we were like together?" He grips my chin, forcing me to look at him. "We couldn't keep our hands off each other. Like hormonal teenagers in a constant state of hunger. I was hard for three years, living with you, living *inside* you, fucking you every day, on every surface, in every hole and position. Best three years of my life."

"It doesn't matter how happy we were." Releasing a breath, I hide beneath the veil of my lashes. "That was then. We're different people now."

"You still love me." His thumb slides over my bottom lip. "If you ignore that feeling, it will only end badly."

"Badly for whom?" I lean away from his touch. "You, them, or me?"

"Yes." His frosty eyes glint with danger, whispering warnings from his scarred soul.

He's suffered loss—the pregnancy, our marriage, the son he never met, his evil brother—and he's still fighting. Ambitious and fiercely passionate, he will raise hell and shatter heaven in pursuit of his ultimate desire.

And that desire is me.

"I can't get you out of my head. I wish I could. But I can't." He edges closer, lifting his arms to grip the overhead above us as he leans in.

Level with my face, his waistband slips dangerously low on his lean hips, revealing every inch of his rippled abdomen.

It's impossible to look at him and *not* feel like I'm cheating.

"Christ, I want you. Your mind. Your body." He lowers a hand from the overhead to stroke my cheek before sliding down to caress my throat. "You're so goddamn pretty. Let me play with you."

"Nope." My ears inflame as I jump up, backing toward the door. "You got your dirty talk in. Now we're done."

"We'll never be done." He prowls toward me, caging me

against the door. "You used to love dirty talk."

I still love it. With Leo and Kody. I can't love it with Monty.

"I won't let you go." He dips his head, his deep voice caressing my ear, conjuring erotic memories of his flesh against my flesh.

"If you don't step back..." I lift on my toes and meet his molten, sapphire eyes. "I'll show you what you paid for in my self-defense course."

The corner of his mouth twitches, just barely, and his brows knit together before smoothing into a blank slate, erasing any readable signs.

Sliding his hands into his pockets, he returns to the helm as if the interaction never happened.

Immediately, I miss his body heat, and I hate myself for that.

kodiak

THIRTY-ONE

Cold, hard, suffocating—every metallic clang in this stark, soulless box reverberates through my bones. I press my forehead against the steel bars, tracking the sound of Leo pacing behind me, the floor trembling beneath his fury.

Frankie's gone. Vanished around the corner with her hand locked in Monty's grip. The image burns behind my eyelids every time I blink.

I saw the way Monty looked at her, the possessiveness in his eyes, the triumphant curl of his lips. It was the look of a man reclaiming what he believes is his, a tsar asserting his dominance over his territory.

The cameras prove she's safe to be with him. She's forgiven him for the rest.

She no longer has a reason to hate him.

Where does that leave Leo and me?

I can't stop replaying her walking away, the way she glanced back at us, her features ashen with anxiety and confusion and the faintest shade of something else.

Something softer.

Her feelings for Monty are changing, deepening, and she

went home with him. Alone.

I sink my hands into my hair, fists clenching, tugging at the strands.

The memory of our day together—the progress with the renovations, the amazing dinner, delicious food, stolen moments of solace and passion—it's all tainted with pain.

Leo removes his shirt and flings the blood-soaked thing into the sink.

The welted skin on his stomach twists as he leans against the wall opposite me, his eyes twin orbs of storm and fire.

Our scars run deep. Violence is our lifeblood. The eternal night will follow us forever.

"We fucked up." A vein pulses ominously at his temple, a dark river of vehemence.

"Yeah." I swallow, my throat raw. "But she's safe now. That's all that matters."

"Safe with him. The man who betrayed her, who drove her into our arms." Venom italicizes his words, but it's pain and fear that turns them red.

He's as scared as I am of what this means for us.

Monty loves her beyond the point of obsession. Just because he's not the one threatening her doesn't mean he's not a threat to our relationship with her. He's as protective and possessive as we are, if not more.

"He's clean, and we're not." He presses the heels of his hands to his eyelids. "We ruined her night, made a whole goddamn mess of it, and the worst part is that we weren't with her when she received that call. The stalker probably waited two months for us to make that mistake and leave her by herself. And we just handed her over to the man who's been desperate to fuck her since the day he lost her."

Every word hammers a nail into my heart. I slide down the bars to the cold floor, burying my face in my hands.

"She'll forgive us." My throat closes with regret.

He doesn't respond immediately. Lowering to the floor beside me, he taps his foot against mine. "She loves us. *Love means you'll always have my forgiveness.* Remember when she said that?"

We were in the sauna. She said it to Wolf after he scared her in the kitchen with Denver.

My mind drifts back to the hills, to the nights when she lay between us like a whisper of moonlight, lifting the darkness from our tortured lives. Those nights feel like a lifetime ago, a dream we can never return to.

Not that I *ever* want to go back there. But sometimes, I miss the simplicity of living off the land and ending each day between her legs.

"She's already forgiven us," he says. "Doesn't change the fact that we're behind bars, and she's with him."

I close my eyes.

The future feels like a vast, dark ocean filled with unseen dangers and uncertain shores. I don't know what lies ahead for us. The only thing I know is the pain in my chest.

The hours pass slowly. I can't sleep, can't find peace in this cold place without her.

Is she thinking of us? Missing us? Or has Monty weaved his way back into her heart?

Leo shifts beside me, his back against the wall, the fire in his eyes dimming to a smolder. We sit in silence, two broken men in a cage, each lost in our torment.

My fear is crippling. Fear of losing her, fear of her choosing Monty over us, fear of being left behind in this desolate, cold cell.

"He took her," Leo growls, more to himself than to me. "He fucking took her, and we're stuck here like goddamn animals."

"We did this to ourselves." I slump against the bars, my voice hollow. "We have to believe in her. Trust in her love for us."

He lets out a bitter laugh. "Belief isn't going to get us out of here."

We're trapped, both physically and emotionally, bound by our mistakes and the chains of our past.

I want to scream, to fight, to tear down these bars with my bare hands. But I'm powerless.

Leo's voice cuts through the silence, rough and raw. "Do

you remember the first time we saw her?"

I remember my anger. Denver had done it again, taken another innocent and thrown her into our hell. But this time, it felt different. There was something about her that made my blood run cold.

I remember the icy air biting at my skin, the sky a dull gray blanket overhead, and Wolf's excitement as he unloaded markers and cigarettes from the plane.

I watched from the front porch, hidden in the shadows, as she slipped an ax inside her coat.

That was the moment I knew she was different. Different from all the others. She wasn't another victim. She was made of fire and fight. The kind that fucked shit up.

Then she emerged from the plane.

Even from a distance, her beauty shocked the breath from my lungs. Long wavy red hair around a flawless porcelain face. And small. So fucking small and breakable. But her size diminished none of the steel in her emerald gaze.

It's a memory I've replayed countless times—her legs swinging out of the plane, boots hitting the ground with a resolute thud, her heartbeat nearly audible in the frigid silence. She walked with her head held high despite the terror I knew she felt. The odds were stacked against her, yet she refused to let fear dictate her actions.

"I remember everything." I shut my eyes, reliving it. "My anger at Denver for bringing her there. Fear for what she might do. Shock at her stunning, impossible beauty. And something else—a strange, unbidden respect for her will to survive. She was different, and I knew that difference would change everything."

She altered the course of our lives. I don't know how it will all unfold, but one thing is certain. Frankie is not a victim. She wasn't then, and she isn't now. She's a force to be reckoned with, and I can't deny the impact she's had on me since that first unforgettable encounter.

"We don't deserve her," Leo says. "After everything we've done, everything we've put her through."

"Doesn't mean we stop fighting for her."

"And if she chooses him?"

The question hovers, a torment unanswered.

The thought of losing her, of her choosing Monty, is a pain too deep to fathom.

monty

THIRTY-TWO

The yacht knifes through the ink-black water, returning us to the island's safety. Standing at the helm, I endure Frankie's scalding silence, a penance for my behavior.

I came on too strong, unable to stop myself. I usually have better control. But it's been 314 days since I've had her alone.

314 days of hell.

Putting my hands all over her, however, isn't how I earn back her trust.

I glance at her, and she glares back with eyes that peel away my clothes and rip open my throat. A paradox of seduction and hostility.

Christ, it turns me on.

It reminds me of our courtship.

I went without sex for a year while I chased her. A year of suffering her rejections, her repulsion, her stubbornness, and the worst case of blue balls.

But when she finally gave in?

It was ebon nirvana. I took her to bed, and she showed me where the shadows of forgotten stars whisper secrets of eternity, where light and dark coalesce, and the divine and the damned fuse in perfect harmony.

As I entered her body, the pink velvet of her soul wrapped around mine, pulling me into an embrace that altered me on a molecular level.

Whenever I'm with her, the sun never fully sets, and the air shimmers with the soft sighs of the universe.

I didn't settle down with Frankie Novak. I settled up.

Being her husband is as intoxicating as it is humbling.

She's given me a luscious, technicolor life, and all I want is to bend her over the dashboard and fuck her ass until she passes out.

I also know that's not what she needs. She's too much in her head, and she doesn't feel safe around me.

Except something changed tonight.

Before I pinned her against the bulkhead, she looked at me differently. She looked at me like she didn't want to drive a stake through my heart.

She looked at me like the woman I married once looked at me.

On the phone, she said she needed me.

She has me. Always.

But I need to be cautious, extra tender, and patient. I need to remember that the pain of being forced, blackmailed, and abused for the sole pleasure of my sick brother creeps into her thoughts and lingers in her bloodstream.

I need to remember that her livid gaze and mutinous jawline are a result of everything I've failed to protect. They also represent the resilience that's kept her standing.

My throat tightens with regret and resolve. "First thing tomorrow, I'll launch a full investigation into finding your stalker. I want Sirena on it."

I expect an argument, but she merely nods.

She knows as well as I do that something needs to be done. The texts, the call, the threats, the implication they know where she is and who she's with—they've gone too far.

My hands flex on the wheel as I agonize over her abduction and the months of horrors she endured. She's been through enough.

"I have nightmares." Her fragile whisper shatters through my thoughts. "About killing Denver. No matter what he did to us, to Leo, Wolf, Kody, and all the others, I can't wash that blood off my hands."

Her confession pierces me. My brother was a monster. His death was inevitable, yet the burden of it falls on her.

She shouldn't have been the one to end his life. That bane should've been mine.

"I wish it had been me." My voice roughens with regret. "I should have killed him when we were young. It should've been my hands that removed him from this world, not yours."

"I did what I had to do." Her eyes meet mine. "But it doesn't make it easier."

"I'm sorry, Frankie. So fucking sorry."

"I know."

We dock at the island, the familiar silhouette of the estate rising against the night sky. I guide her off the yacht, our steps silent on the pier's wooden planks. This place is a fortress, guarded by a highly-skilled security team, their figures visible in every direction.

But even here, shadows lurk.

Inside the house, I lead her to the living room with the new couch I bought two months ago.

But she stops me with a hand on my arm. "There's something I need to show you."

Curiosity piqued, I follow her upstairs, through my bedroom, and into the bathroom.

None of her belongings remain in this space. It took me a few weeks, but I did what she asked. I removed her presence from my private rooms.

That seemed to satisfy her, but it's done nothing to soothe my heartache.

"Look." She points to a wall sconce next to the bathroom door, her expression tense.

I lean closer, examining the hardware. There, hidden in the ornate design, is a tiny camera.

"What the fuck?" Rage and violation surge through me.

Someone has been watching us. Watching her. "How long has this been here?"

"Two months." She pulls out her phone and opens an app. "We set a trap."

My anger thaws into relief. No one trespassed on the island. They did this. Her, Leo, and Kody. They spied on me. I can live with that.

I did the same thing to them.

I turn, following the angle of the camera. It points directly at the shower.

The recordings on her screen confirm it.

"We put cameras throughout the estate." Her voice wavers. "You have every right to be mad. We thought..."

"If the stalker contacted you again, you could catch me in action." I sigh. "Smart."

"I'm sorry."

"I don't blame you." I hold out my hand for the phone. "May I?" When she offers it, I ask, "You checked the cameras after you received the threatening call?"

"Yes." She points to one of the recent recordings. "You were in the shower."

I press play, watching a video of me jerking off. Unmuting it, I let my groans vibrate from the speaker. The sounds of me moaning her name, over and over, fill the air around us.

She crosses her arms over her chest, a barrier between herself and my obvious feelings for her.

Now she knows.

She knows I'm thinking of her when I pleasure myself.

She knows I'm not the one terrorizing her.

But I'm a threat to her nonetheless.

"I'm not mad." I disarm all the cameras in the app and hand back her phone. Then I pluck the small recording device from its hiding place.

This explains the changes I noticed in her tonight, why she's been looking at me so differently.

But it doesn't solve the stalker problem.

"I'll increase security." My fists crack the bones in my fingers. "No one will get to you on the island. You're safe with me."

"Thank you. For everything. For helping Leo and Kody, for showing up tonight. It means more than you know." She squares her shoulders. "I'm sorry for invading your privacy. I'll remove the cameras immediately."

"Leave them."

"What? Why?"

"Even though you can prove to Leo and Kody that I'm not your stalker, they still won't trust me."

"I already told them about the call and the video proof that it's not you."

"Even so, they'll continue to follow you everywhere and never take their eyes off you. Maybe the cameras will help them relax and give you space while you're home."

"I don't know if that's possible." She laughs. "Giving them access to your privacy isn't healthy for them. They need to learn to trust you."

"This will help them do that."

"At least remove the one in your bedroom."

"I have nothing to hide, Frankie. But I do fuck my hand in the shower." I give her the tiny camera. "If you want to watch that, you'll have to join me."

"Monty..." She makes a growly kitten sound.

"In the spirit of honesty, it's my turn to show you something." I motion for her to follow. At her frown, I soften my voice. "It's safe. I promise. I won't proposition you."

In the walk-in closet, I remove the night-vision goggles from a shoebox at the rear of a shelf and hand them to her.

"What's this?" Her face pales.

"I'll show you."

I lead her to the guest bedroom, through the closet, and into the unlit attic space.

"Power the goggles on." I show her the button, my insides coiling. "Good. Now put them on."

"I don't know about this." She squints at me in the dark.

"I know you don't trust me, but—"

"I'm trying."

She won't trust me after this, but I want full transparency. No more secrets.

Slowly, she puts on the goggles. After some adjusting, I guide her to the half-moon window. When she peers through it, directly into the bedroom she shares with Leo and Kody, she gasps.

"What is this?" She clutches the windowsill. "Why are you showing me this?"

"The first night you returned, I controlled the thermostat, forced you to open the French doors, and watched you with them."

Her knees buckle, and she stumbles back, retreating from the horror and shock before her. She rips off the goggles and whirls on me.

I confront the ire in her glare.

I deserve it.

Lowering to my knees, I tilt my head back and let her see every emotion written across my face in the moonlight. Guilt, remorse, love.

She studies my features, looking for deception, and her arms lower to her sides, the goggles dangling from her fingers.

"I'm sorry." I hold her gaze and wait for the backlash.

"How many times did you watch us?" A blush colors her cheeks, but she pairs it with hot rage.

"Only that night. It was too devastating to repeat."

"Your knuckles." She anchors her fists on her hips. "The next morning at breakfast, your hand was busted."

"I broke the window." I nod at the glass behind her, which was repaired by Greyson the next day.

"I watched you masturbate in the shower, and you watched me have sex with Leo and Kody." She blows out a breath, releasing her anger. "God, Monty. We've really made a mess of this. Please, stand up."

"I'm sorry." I remain on my knees, heart thundering. "It was wrong. I had no right to invade your privacy, especially after everything you've been through. I brought you here with the promise of security and safety, and I violated that."

Her hand moves, but not away. Instead, she rests her

fingertips against my stubble and traces the hard lines of my face, her gaze following the movement to the back of my jaw, around the shell of my ear, and down, along my neck, her thumb stroking my bobbing Adam's apple.

She touches me with gentle devotion, and I cherish it openly, hungrily. Goosebumps rise in reverence. My heart thrashes in its cage, desperate for her. She confounds and captivates me entirely.

"Leo must've suspected something." Hooded green eyes meet mine, provoking all manner of lustful thoughts. "He was adamant about putting a camera in here." She points at a shelf in the corner of the attic.

"He noticed the broken window the morning after it happened and asked me about it."

"What did you tell him?"

"I omitted the truth and simply said I'd have it fixed."

"Will you spy on us again?"

"No." My ribs expand with the pressure in my chest. "Keep the goggles."

"Oh, I am. Come on. We have more to discuss." She pads out of the attic and heads toward my bedroom. "If you want to change, I'll wait here."

She leans against the wall in the hallway as I slip into the bedroom and change into sweatpants and a T-shirt.

When I emerge a minute later, she makes a beeline down the stairs, through the main hall, and outside, taking the path to the guest house.

"You're sleeping in the main house tonight," I say.

What I want to say is *you're sleeping with me tonight and every night after.*

"I know. I want to put on my pajamas." She touches her chin to her shoulder, peering at me through her lashes. "Will you walk with me?"

Fucking spellbinding.

"Lead the way." I motion her forward, my eyes automatically falling to her heart-shaped ass, the delicate sway of her hips, and the nip of her tiny waist in that curve-hugging dress.

I would give anything to put my hands on her gorgeous body again.

She moves like a moonbeam on water, gliding with natural, effortless grace. There's something magical about her. Her poise, her determination, the fluidity of her movements. She's not just insanely sexy. She's alluring in a way I can neither describe nor ignore.

We walk in silence, the crunch of gravel under our feet. The island, dewy from the earlier rain, seems to hold its breath, waiting for something.

"I can't believe Leo and Kody are in jail," she says, breaking the quiet. "After fighting so hard for their freedom. I was afraid this would happen. Their tempers...They're too feral for this world."

"They'll adjust. They need time."

"I just..." Her shoulders sag. "I don't want to lose anyone else."

Entering her passcode, she breezes into the guest house and up the stairs. I follow, growing uncomfortable with each step. This may be my house, but it's her space. The space she shares with them.

In the upstairs bedroom, she tosses the goggles and the tiny camera on the bed.

"I'll just be a second." She slips into the closet and shuts the door.

One of her discarded shirts drapes over the chair. I grab it, pressing it against my face and inhaling. Christ, her scent. Cherry, vanilla, and something uniquely Frankie consume my senses, grounding me.

The closet door opens. "Do you care about them?"

"What?" I drop the garment.

"Leo and Kody." She steps out, wearing sleep shorts and a tight little tank top, looking absolutely edible.

Do I care about Leo and Kody?

I consider the question, really think about it. To do that, I separate them from her, imagine them single and navigating the world after a lifetime of isolation and abuse.

Their struggles aren't why I'm rooting for them.

It's their fight, their snarling, brawling, driven natures to get back on their feet every time they're knocked to their knees. That warrior spirit is something I can get behind. I want to see them succeed and will do everything in my power to help them.

"Yeah." I delve into the haunting depths of her eyes. "I don't want anything to happen to them. They matter to me."

"Why?"

"Because they're mine. My family."

Her eyes soften, glowing with unguarded warmth. If I were an optimistic man, I would interpret that as a look of a woman falling back in love with her husband. But I know we have a long way to go.

"Let's go sit on the oceanside balcony," I say, "and drink under the stars."

"Okay."

Back at the main house, we step out onto the grand balcony with our drinks in hand. The summer rain washed the air clean, leaving a balminess that clings to the skin.

The diamond glimmer of countless stars punctures the sky, the ocean a dark, undulating mass beneath us. The pounding waves resonate with the turbulence in my chest.

She sits beside me, all that red hair tangling around her in the warm breeze. The gap between us feels like an ocean, though she's only an arm's reach away.

"Monty." She draws in a breath. "I need to talk about the call I got tonight."

"Go on." Dread churns, always there.

"Some of the things that electronic voice said, calling you Daddy Strakh..."

My heart pounds, a primal urge to protect her roaring to life. But her next words cut the deepest.

"I can't stop thinking about it. I know it sounds crazy, but it sounded like something Wolf would say." A pained look crosses her face, and she takes a long pull from her bourbon. "He used to reference movies, especially Disney movies. The way the threat was worded reminded me of *The Wizard of Oz. I'll get you, my pretty. I'll come for you and your guard dogs, too."*

The mention of Wolf is a fist in my chest. My son, my tortured boy who I never had the chance to know, to save. He's a bleeding wound inside me, reminding me of my failures as a father. My grief over him festers every day, ready to consume me at a moment's notice.

"I promise you." I grip her hand, holding it tightly as if she might slip away. "I'll find whoever is threatening you. They won't get near you. Sirena has a team searching for Wolf's body, and we'll pull more resources to track this person down."

"Who knows about those flight logs and where you found them?"

"Melanie Stokes, Alvis Duncan..." My shoulders go rigid, bracing for her reaction. "And Sirena and her team."

"It could be her." She pulls her hand from mine, sitting stiffly on the lounge chair.

"It could be anyone. The riddle said this is someone from your past." I throw back my whiskey, swallowing half of it. "Could be an ex-boyfriend or someone you knew in Anchorage."

"How would an ex-boyfriend know about those flight logs?"

"Why would Sirena be stalking you?"

"She wants *you.* And maybe Leo and Kody, too. I don't trust her."

"Then I'll hire someone else to investigate this."

"I think that's best."

"Whatever you wish." Resigned, I finish my drink.

She nods, but the fear in her eyes remains. "Kody's made a lot of progress with the distillery renovations." She sips her drink. "He's building a small apartment in the back and wants Leo and me to move in with him."

Her words cleave me in half, a cold blade of jealousy and horror. The idea of her living with them, unprotected, with a stalker on the loose...no fucking way. I'll do everything in my power to prevent it.

"What about us?" I fight to keep my composure. "The family you wanted me to nurture?"

"My relationship with Leo and Kody causes you pain." She swallows, looking away. "I don't want to stand in the way of the bond you're building with them."

"You're not in the way." My voice rises. "You're the center of it. The one holding us together."

"I think you're doing great with them, Monty. I mean it."

"I'm trying. But I can't do it without you. I won't."

"I can't stay here. I can't stay on this island and pretend we're married and everything is fine."

"I'll ignore the comment about our marriage, *for now,* and focus on the glaring hole in your plan. You're *not* safe out there. The only place you're safe is here, with me. This island is fortified, guarded. I can protect you."

"I know you can. But I can't keep doing this to you. I can't be with Leo and Kody under your roof. It's not fair to you. Not now that I know your intentions are pure."

I wouldn't call my intentions pure. Not by a long shot.

"Frankie." I pull in a calming breath. "I appreciate that you're trying to protect my feelings, but I need you to stop. I can handle it. I've been handling it. What I can't handle is you living elsewhere, knowing you're in danger." I tilt my head and try a different tactic. "How will Leo and Kody pursue their careers while trying to watch over and protect you every second of every day?"

"You're right." She lowers her face to her hands and groans. "Fuck!"

"I want you to be safe." I shift, desperate to erase the distance and pull her onto my lap.

"I know. Dammit, I just want to go back to work. Every threat, every violation, makes it harder for me to do that."

"I understand." My heart aches for her. I know how much she loves her job, how much she needs it to feel whole. "But your safety comes first."

She straightens, looking up at me with those intelligent eyes. "Okay, I'll stay here. But they're staying with me."

"Okay." I smile, brushing a strand of hair from her face. "You need sleep. Come on."

I lead her to the guest bedroom across the hall from mine, tucking her into bed. She looks so small, so vulnerable. I lean down, pressing a kiss to her forehead.

"I'll watch over you," I whisper. "I love you, Frankie."

"I know. That's part of the problem." Her eyes grow heavy, closing as sleep tries to claim her.

Perched on the bed beside her, I watch her breathe. This woman, my wife, my world. I will do whatever it takes to protect her, to keep her safe. No matter the cost.

The night is still, but my mind is anything but. Somewhere out there, someone wants to hurt her. I won't sleep until I remove that fucker from the planet. When the time comes, I won't hesitate to take the killing blow.

"Monty," she mumbles, opening her eyes. "You should get some rest."

"I'll rest when there are no more threats against you."

"You can't protect me if you're exhausted."

"I'm not leaving."

"So fucking hardheaded." She shifts, inching away, making room for me. "Sleep here." She pats the empty spot. "Above the blankets. No touching. Promise me."

"I promise." I lie on my side, facing her with a fuzzy glow of warmth in my chest.

"I hurt you." She meets my gaze, her eyes fierce. "I regret it, Monty. So much. The pain I've caused you, the torment of knowing I'm with them. God, I can't believe you watched us."

"Frankie..."

"Having sex with them under your roof was disrespectful and cruel. The justification I gave myself, my resentment, my distrust...I was so angry with you. But that ends now. As long as I live here, I won't have sex with them. Not in your home." She pulls in a breath. "I'll still sleep with them at night. But that's all we'll do."

The relief that washes over me is immediate, overwhelming. But with it comes a stab of doubt. Leo and Kody will never sleep beside her without fucking her.

I wouldn't.

Except that's precisely what I'm doing tonight.

Before I can formulate a response, the rhythm of her breathing slows, the grip of sleep finally taking hold.

I watch her, my heart aching with love and regret. So much has been lost, but so much still remains.

monty

THIRTY-THREE

Amid the silken folds of the night, in the guest bedroom of my island mansion, I find a rare solace.

Breath by breath, Frankie inches closer to me in sleep, reaching, rolling, stripping away the separation between us, until finally, she settles into the heart space between my arms.

Her small, warm body seeks refuge on my chest, her hair spilling like molten copper around my ribs.

I lie perfectly still, every muscle held in a delicate balance of tension and reverence. The slightest movement could wake her, and the fragile connection we've rekindled would shatter.

The soft rhythm of her breath sings to my loneliness, soothing me in a way no one else can. For the first time in almost a year, I'm happy. Truly, deeply happy.

The love we once shared, a love I desperately hope to revive, feels close enough to touch. I refuse to sleep through a single second of it.

As dawn approaches, the room brightens, the Alaskan sunrise filtering through the heavy drapes. I need to rise. There's much to be done. But for a few more stingy minutes, I remain still, reluctant to separate us.

If she wakes and finds herself in my arms, she'll blame me for touching her, for breaking the boundaries of our relationship.

Holding my breath, I carefully extricate myself from beneath her featherlight frame. She stirs but doesn't wake, her body curling into the space I vacate. I watch her for a moment longer, committing the sight of her to memory, then slip quietly from the room.

I dress quickly, my mind racing with the tasks of the day as I make my way to my office, where I feel most in control. Papers and reports from my consulting firm clutter the desk, including a proposal I've been sitting on for Leo. All of that will wait.

The first call is to my legal team, inquiring about Leo and Kody. As anticipated, the attorneys secured a deal for them, resulting in the charges being dropped. The victim, who will recover without permanent injury, decided against pursuing legal action after being threatened for assaulting Frankie.

Leo and Kody will be released this morning and can return to the island using Frankie's cruiser.

I recline in the desk chair, a sigh escaping me as I imagine her joy at seeing them.

As long as I live here, I won't have sex with them.

Her promise makes me that much happier to bring them home.

Turning my attention to her stalker, I call Wilson next. I insist that he handles the investigation personally, without the involvement of Sirena or anyone else from his firm.

He's meticulous and trustworthy, a bulldog in his profession. And, unlike Sirena, he's never tried to fuck me.

At first, he's reluctant to take the case. The old bastard wants to retire and has started stepping away from day-to-day tasks. Same as me. But everyone has a price, and I eventually find his.

No one would turn down the money I'm offering.

Over a very lengthy phone call, I tell him everything—the details surrounding her abduction, Denver's crimes, his death, a list of his known victims, including Wolfson, my father's known enemies, the flight logs, and everyone on my household payroll and security team.

I answer every question he asks and leave no skeletons buried.

My father kept an accounting ledger throughout his life to keep track of his extensive criminal transactions. It includes bribes paid to law enforcement and politicians. Salaries paid to hitmen, enforcers, and accountants. And hush money paid to the families of Denver's victims.

The entries were meticulously maintained, some of them in a coded format. I've tried to make sense of it, but the ledger is thick, and I'm not a forensics expert.

I want to create a list of suspects from this ledger, but it will take too long to sort through decades of entries.

Wilson assures me that he has a team that can scrub it. So I remove it from the safe behind the painting in my office and ship it off to him.

He also wants Frankie to compile a list of every colleague, friend, ex-boyfriend, and acquaintance she's made through the years.

Everyone is a suspect.

By the time we hang up, he knows every dirty secret in my family.

It's unnerving to trust someone with so much incriminating information, but I'll tell him anything he wants to know if it will keep her safe.

The morning passes in a flurry of calls and emails, each a step toward restoring order and protecting my family. As I work, my thoughts drift back to her, to the warmth of her body against mine, to the hope that still burns in my chest.

When the legal team calls back, confirming that Leo and Kody have been released, I rise to my feet, stretching, muscles loosening with relief. Then I slip out of the office to deliver the news.

She's still asleep when I return to the bedroom, her form a gentle rise beneath the covers. I stand in the doorway, watching her, my chest heavy with emotion.

I long to reach out, to hold her close and tell her that everything will be all right, that we'll find our way back to each other. But I know that will take time.

And more groveling on my part.

As I turn away, her husky voice tiptoes over my shoulder. "Good morning."

"Good morning." I shift back, eager to rest my eyes on her again.

"Any news on Leo and Kody?"

"They're on their way home."

She closes her eyes, releasing a long, deep breath as if she was holding it all night. "Thank you."

"No need to thank me."

Thirty minutes later, I find myself standing on the dock beside her, the cool breeze off the water a welcome respite from the heat of the day.

When they arrive, I'll lose her attention. All her energy will narrow on them. At least, that's how it usually goes.

Except today feels different. Today, a sense of anticipation charges the air, a feeling that something is about to change.

When the boat finally arrives, I watch Leo and Kody disembark, their expressions weary but determined to move past their mistake.

Leo hugs her first. When he releases her into Kody's arms, he approaches me.

"Thank you." He maintains eye contact, a silent assertion of his sincerity. "I know you pulled strings and got us released early."

"My attorneys—"

"You pay their wages. We fucked up, and you paid for it."

"I helped you when you needed it. That's what family does. But you already know that." My eyes flit between him and Kody. "You do that for each other."

"We would do it for you, too." Kody paces toward me and claps me on the neck. "Thank you."

His touch is a brand, a symbol of acceptance. I don't hate it.

We make our way back to the estate. Oliver has prepared lunch, and we sit together, the conversation flowing easily despite the subject matter.

I update them on my decision to hire Wilson and tell them everything I discussed with him.

"You trust him?" She looks at me with those huge green eyes, making my pulse thrum.

"Yeah. I do."

"Okay." She pushes her empty plate away and stares at each of us. "We need to talk."

"What is it?" I lean back in the chair, steeling myself.

"I know that all of you don't like therapy, but you need it." She holds up a finger. "Doyle doesn't count. You're not opening up to him. You're threatening him. He gave me some referrals. For us to move forward, I want all three of you to see someone else. Someone you trust and respect."

"We can work on our anger without confiding in a stranger." Leo runs a hand through his hair.

"That's not true." She sets her jaw. "It's not just your anger. It's everything you've been through. Please. I want you to get help."

"No." Kody stands abruptly. "Instead of focusing on taming us into polished, trained men that you can take into public, how about we hunt down the motherfucker who's stalking you?"

"I don't want to tame you." Her eyes flash. "I want to keep you out of jail."

"Where did you sleep last night?"

"Upstairs." She sits taller, holding his glare.

"Alone?"

"Monty slept beside me." Her neck stiffens. "He didn't touch me."

He doesn't spare me a glance. Turning on his heel, he storms out of the dining room, his gait silent through the house. The front door slams behind him, making her jump. His attitude pisses me off.

"I'm with Kody on this." Leo's two different colored eyes bore into her, then me. "When we need therapy, we'll let you know."

"Don't pull away from me." She reaches for his fist on the table.

He doesn't move his hand. But he doesn't unclench it, either. "Are you with us? Or him?" He tilts his head toward me.

"I'm in a relationship with you." She grits her teeth. "But we're all in this together."

If she keeps her promise, she won't be having sex with them.

"What about you?" she asks me. "Are you going to get help?"

I could lie and win some points with her. But she deserves the truth. "I'll try."

She sighs. "I guess that's better than an outright *no.*"

"I'm going to check on Kody." Leo starts to stand.

"I'll do it." I push away from the table and leave the room without waiting for a response.

Making a detour to my office, I grab a photo from my desk. Then I head outside in search of my sulky brother.

Brother.

He doesn't trust me. Why should he? Our family history is a toxic bloodbath of pain and deceit.

But he's still my brother, and I owe it to him to try.

"Stanley." I approach one of the security guards. "Can you locate Kody?"

With a nod, he speaks to his team through his earpiece. Then he meets my eyes. "North shore, sir. The quiet side, by the rocks."

"Thank you."

Quiet side. We all need one of those, don't we?

A few minutes later, I spot him at the water's edge, a brooding silhouette against the endless expanse of gray-blue ocean.

He's a dark figure, dangerous and unapproachable, much like our father. But there's something different about Kody, a rawness, a depth of emotion that he hides beneath his hardened exterior.

It's easier, somehow, to think of him as my brother, despite the fact that he's tangled up with Frankie. Maybe because I see in him a reflection of my younger self, struggling to find a place in a world that's been nothing but cruel.

His stance is as unyielding as the rocks around him, his eyes fixed on the horizon, lost in an internal battle.

He doesn't turn as I approach, though I know he's aware of my presence. For a while, we stand in silence, the only sounds the rhythmic lapping of waves and the distant cries of gulls.

I'm about to speak, but words seem inadequate. Instead, I reach into my pocket and pull out the photograph.

The edges are worn, the image faded, but the girl in it is vivid.

"This is for you." I hold the photo out to him. "It's the only picture I have of your mother. I thought you should have it."

Kaya was sixteen in the photo, beautiful, with a wild, untamed look in her gaze. Just like Kody.

He takes the photo, his fingers brushing against mine. As he studies it, his expression empties, but I see the quick light of emotion in his eyes. Sadness, anger, a longing for a past he never got to experience.

"I never knew her." His finger traces the lines of her face, the only connection he has left of her. "Denver took that from me."

"I know. I'm sorry for that. I'm sorry for everything."

He remains silent, his gaze fixed on the photo. I see the tension in his shoulders, the unspoken distrust. It's not just about Frankie. It's everything—our fractured family, the years of captivity, the scars both seen and unseen.

"I never knew how to be a brother." I slide my hands in my pockets and stare out at the waves. "Denver and I...it was always a battle. He thrived on hurting people, and I ran away instead of facing it. We were never really brothers. But with you...I want it to be different."

"Why?" Kody finally turns his head, his black eyes locking onto mine.

"Because we've been through some shit, and maybe together, we can find a way out. We're both stubborn bastards. We both have walls. Maybe it's time to start tearing them down. I don't have all the answers, but I'm willing to try if you are."

"You think a few words can earn my trust?" He grunts, a harsh sound.

"No. Words alone can't. But actions can." I pick up a smooth rock and send it skipping across the surface of the water. "We want the same thing. Let's hunt down the piece of shit who's terrorizing her."

He looks at me, really looks at me, for the first time. There's a glimmer in his gaze, a crack in the armor he's built around himself. "You hired an investigator."

"Yes. I hired one when Frankie went missing, too. Didn't stop me from doing my own hunting."

"And when we find this stalker?"

"No cops. No laws." I edge closer, pushing against the intensity of his surly expression. "We'll kill them."

We stand in silence again, the photograph a fragile bridge between us. Kody's eyes soften, just a fraction, but it's enough. It's a beginning.

A sharp ring breaks the moment. I pull my phone from my pocket, the name on the screen sending a chill down my spine.

I answer on speaker. "Carl?"

"Mr. Novak," the security guard says. "We have a situation at the house. A package was delivered with the groceries. You need to see this."

Kody and I exchange a glance as a jolt of adrenaline hits me. We lurch into motion, the dread between us growing as our footsteps pound against the gravel path.

In the kitchen, Carl stands next to a plain, brown box on the stainless-steel counter, the top already opened.

"I didn't order that." Oliver stands off to the side, his hand clutched to his throat and eyes wide with shock. "I found it with the delivery."

Panic surges.

"Where's Frankie?" I spin, searching for her.

"Here." She steps in behind me with Leo at her back. Her forehead knits as she takes in the scene. "What's wrong?"

"Sir." Carl steps forward, concern etched on his face. "This is...delicate." He glances at Frankie.

Too delicate for Frankie? That's almost laughable. The horror she experienced in the past year would bring Carl to his knees. If anyone can handle it, she can.

"What's in it?" My insides knot as I reach for the box.

"Don't touch it without gloves." Carl offers me a pair. "Fingerprints."

Alarm bells ring in my head as I slide on the latex and glance at Kody. His gaze narrows, studying the package. It's unmarked, with no labels or identifiers. Just an ordinary box.

"All right." My heart thunders in my ears. "Let's see what we're dealing with."

I open the box carefully, peeling back the flaps. Inside, packed in dry ice, is a plastic bag. I wave my hand, the cold vapor swirling around my fingers as I reach in and lift the bag covered in frost.

"What is it?" Leo asks, his voice tense.

I squint, trying to make sense of the shape within the bag. It's not immediately clear, just an ominous, unidentifiable object. Cold seeps through the plastic, chilling my fingertips, coming from something.

Something that turns my stomach.

I set the bag on the counter and use a knife to carefully slit the plastic, the icy vapor hissing as it escapes. The contents shift, revealing a glistening, dark red mass.

My lungs collapse as I realize what I'm looking at.

"It's a heart." Frankie steps forward, her face pale as her medical training takes over. "A human heart."

A shudder runs through me, and my throat works, swallowing repeatedly against the rising bile.

I reach back into the box, my fingers brushing against something else. Another plastic bag, but this one contains a photo.

Pulling it out, I stare at the haunting picture, my blood running cold.

A man lies on the icy shore of a river, the rugged, frozen landscape around him stark and unforgiving. His hair is dark and tousled, his body, though pallid and lifeless, retains the tall, lean build of the Strakh family line.

What seals the identity beyond doubt is the blood-stained coat he's wearing. A coat I gifted to Frankie years ago. The one he borrowed from her the day he jumped off the cliff.

"No." She chokes, covering her mouth and shaking her head. "No, no, no!"

The image is clear enough to see the tear in the fabric where the rocks must have shredded it during his fall. But with the coat zipped closed, it's impossible to know the condition of his body beneath and whether it still contains a heart.

His face, though partially obscured by snow and ice, is undeniably Wolfson's, his shockingly familiar features passed down from me.

"Someone took this picture," I rasp. "Someone who wasn't Wolf."

"Someone cut out his heart," she whispers.

I go numb, the world around me fading to a dull hum.

My son.

The pain is too much, threatening to consume me, but I force myself to stay present, to be the anchor for my family.

Frankie staggers back, her face contorted in agony as she lets out a guttural cry.

"What the fuck?" Leo's furious roar crashes against me, his body curving into attack mode.

Kody stands frozen, the photo of his mother still clutched in his hand, forgotten.

"It can't be him. It can't be." She crumples against Leo, tears streaming down her face, her anguish more than I can bear.

I want to comfort them, to tell them it's a joke, a misunderstanding, but the evidence is undeniable. I remain frozen, unable to process the horror before me. My heart feels like it's being crushed in a vise.

"This...this isn't real." Leo wraps his arms around her, his voice breaking. "Maybe it's a fake. Someone could've created it to fuck with us."

"I'll have the photo analyzed," I say, monotone. "We'll

confirm its authenticity."

"Who would do this?" Her breath comes in ragged gasps, the sight of her tears a knife to my soul. "Who would be so cruel?"

Kody's reaction is the most heartbreaking. He stares at the photo of Wolf, his face contorted in pain, yet no tears come. His sadness is too deep, too profound to channel outward.

"You killed Denver wearing that coat." I point to the blood stains that cover the chest area. "Do you remember where the splatter concentrated?"

"No. I..." She studies the image. "I shot him and beat him with a pipe. The coat was ruined. That's why Wolf made me take his." Her voice breaks. "We argued about it."

"We'll figure it out. A DNA test will confirm it." I lift the photo closer to my face.

"Monty..." Her body shakes with sobs, her green eyes flooded with tears. "There's writing on the back."

A fist closes around my airway as I flip over the photo and read aloud. "To Frankie. *I have outlasted all desire. My dreams and I have grown apart. My grief alone is left entire. The gleanings of an empty heart."* My breath stumbles. "Another Pushkin quote."

"Why?" Leo snarls. "What the fuck does it mean?"

I don't have an answer. All I know is that the fragile threads holding us together are unraveling, and it's up to me to stop us from falling apart.

But how do I protect my family from a ghost? From a past that refuses to stay buried?

"Carl." I take a deep breath, forcing myself to stay composed as I look at the security guard. "Find out where this package came from. Check the delivery records. I want to know every detail. Oliver, go with him. Give him a list of your suppliers and contacts."

As they spring into action, I turn to Kody.

The bond we began to forge by the shore is now tempered in fire, our shared grief a new kind of brotherhood. We'll find the answers. We'll face this darkness together.

"No cops." Kody's eyes meet mine, and the wall between us cracks. "It's time to hunt."

monty
THIRTY-FOUR

"Everything circles back to Hoss." I pace back and forth in the sitting room, my fingers curling into fists, my insides a mayhem of sorrow, impatience, and cold, seething rage.

It's been two days since the gruesome package arrived. Two days without answers.

Leo and Kody stand nearby, their expressions mirroring my turmoil. Frankie sits on the edge of the couch, her face lined with fatigue.

We're all haunted by the contents of that box. Too haunted to sleep.

Locating the cabin has become our priority. If we find the cabin, we'll be closer to finding Wolf's body or the location where he was pulled from the river. There would be clues there. Footprints. Something.

But first, we need to know whose heart that is.

Without involving the authorities, I sent the box with the organ and photo to New York to be analyzed by a forensics team. I pulled strings, called on some discreet connections, and cut through red tape, with Wilson managing the investigation.

The results should arrive any day now.

From the moment the package arrived, we've done nothing but brainstorm, plot, and strategize, our collective minds focused on finding the stalker. We've gathered every resource, analyzed every clue, and formed theories that twist and turn with no end in sight.

The four of us have thrown ourselves into the task with a relentless hunger, driven by the urgent need to bring Wolf home.

Dead or alive.

Kody, his brooding eyes darker than usual, leans over a map spread out on the table. "If this stalker has been following Frankie, they must have access to surveillance equipment or resources. They know our movements, our vulnerabilities."

"We need to think about who benefits from this chaos." Leo runs a hand through his shoulder-length hair, the Viking braids tangling around his fingers. "Who gains from our suffering?"

Frankie sent her list of suspects to Wilson. People from her past, friends, associates, fuck buddies—it wasn't a long list. Still, I wanted to memorize every name and hunt them down myself just for touching her.

Wilson has the daunting task of cross-referencing our suspects with flights and passenger lists. Someone was near Hoss when Wolf jumped off that cliff. His body must've drifted miles downriver, but eventually someone found him and took that photo.

Someone was in those fucking hills, lurking in an unsurvivable place where no human would venture.

That same someone knows about the flight logs I found in my father's cellar. Wilson is circling back to Alvis Duncan in Whittier to gather more information on the men who collected those logs over the years.

"What are your thoughts on Pushkin?" She bends over a notepad on the oak coffee table, reading the riddles and poetry quotes for the hundredth time.

Beside her elbow sits the leather-bound copy of Pushkin's poems that I unearthed from the wall in my father's office. Months ago, I had the book analyzed for codes and cryptic messages. Another dead end.

"Alexander Pushkin." I take a deep breath. "To understand the quotes, you must understand the man. He was a Russian poet and literary genius, who suffered from morbid, delusional jealousy and fucked anything that walked. Like a paranoid, pathological Don Juan of his time. Ironically, he loved his wife and constantly accused her of infidelity. He was also known for his rages and would fight a duel at the drop of a hat. As it turns out, it was a duel that took his life."

"So he was unhinged?" Leo lifts the leather book, thumbing through the pages.

"Pretty much." My forehead twitches. "Whoever sent those quotes to Frankie knows I found the book of poems."

"Or they put the book in that wall, hoping you would find it." Leo inspects the spine and inner book flaps. "Along with those flight logs."

"Since the stalker enjoys referencing Pushkin..." She turns back to the notepad on the table. "It's safe to assume this person is unhinged, too."

"That's a given," Leo says.

Carl's investigation into how a human heart arrived with the groceries is another dead end. Someone must've slipped the box onto the pallet of food before it was loaded onto the boat in Sitka harbor. There were no cameras or eyewitnesses in the loading area.

Leo returns the book and crouches beside a different box on the floor. This one contains all the things they brought from Hoss. The flight manual, survival gear, Wolf's keepsakes and drawings, and the slippers Denver stole from me. Melanie also returned the journal, thumb drive, and bag of bones.

The kidnapping cases are still open and will probably remain so forever. But as expected, the detectives moved on to more pressing investigations.

Over the past two days, we've watched Denver's video multiple times.

The solution isn't here. I'm certain of it.

"We need sleep." I rub my pounding head.

"We need answers." Kody grabs his crossbow from the box, checking the strings.

"I just..." She bites her lower lip as if trying to hold back the words. "I don't know if I can handle it if it's him."

She means Wolf. But I don't know if she's referring to him being the stalker or the owner of the heart.

The photo could've been staged. Leo confirmed that Wolf had access to a digital camera. But none of them know if it was missing after his disappearance. They never thought to look for it.

We need to find that goddamn cabin.

"We won't jump to conclusions." I move to her side, taking her chin in my hand. "We'll wait for the analysis."

Her eyes are red-rimmed and swollen, a reservoir of unwept tears. She looks physically drained, with a noticeable lack of energy in her movements.

I step back and find Leo's gaze, giving him a silent demand to call it a day.

"We'll find him, love. But right now..." He moves in and lifts her into his arms, ignoring her protests. "It's time for bed."

He carries her upstairs to the guest bedroom where they sleep now. They moved into the main house after the package was delivered. When I ordered that move, they didn't argue.

Someone sent a human heart to my heavily guarded island. We're not taking any risks.

Two days later, the call comes.

Sitting in the gazebo beside the pool, we pore over the map Sirena sent, discussing the sections of the Brooks Range that her team has already scoured.

Pulse racing, I answer the call on speaker.

"Monty," Wilson says, "I received the results from the forensic investigator." Papers rustle in the background. "The heart matches Denver Strakh's DNA."

Shock slices through me. Frankie's mouth drops open, and Leo and Kody exchange puzzled glances.

"Denver's?" Relief floods in as I shake off the surprise. "How is that possible?"

"You said Denver's body was dumped in the tundra around

the same time that Wolf jumped off the cliff." Wilson coughs, his voice hoarse with age. "It's plausible that your perpetrator was waiting nearby and collected both bodies."

"The plane in the hills wasn't trophy hunters." Kody's jaw tightens. "We saw it a week after Denver died. It's connected."

"Maybe," Wilson says. "It doesn't show up on any flight logs in Alaska or Canada, so that alone makes it suspicious."

"Fingerprints?" I ask.

"None. Everything you sent was clean. Too clean."

"Whoever it is, they're fucking with us." Leo's unique eyes flash with anger. "And they have Wolf's body."

"The photograph was analyzed." Wilson sighs. "I'm sorry, but it's not a fake. The image is Wolfson, based on your identification. But it doesn't confirm whether he was dead or alive at the time of the photo." He explains the technical details about the camera that was used, the time of day, and the angle of the shot. "Wolfson could've set the camera on a timer, propped it against a boulder, and taken the picture. But that's inconclusive. Would a camera survive that fall? Would a human survive it? Right now, the only evidence we have is the heart belongs to Denver and Wolfson's body made it out of that river."

Wilson ends the call with the promise to continue digging through the long list of potential suspects. The writing on the back of the photo may help us identify the culprit once we have a shorter list of perpetrators.

"I killed Denver," Frankie whispers. "We received his heart. How is that possible?"

Kody scoots toward her, snaking an arm around her back.

"Wolf is still out there." Her eyes water. "He could still be alive."

The uncertainty gnaws at us, an ever-present agony made worse by a false sense of hope.

We all know Wolf didn't survive that jump.

"We need to find that cabin," I say, determination in my voice. "I'm calling Sirena."

leonid

THIRTY-FIVE

Sirena arrives on the island two days later, her presence immediately noticeable. She strides through the front door with an air of confidence that turns heads and an elegance that makes the air around her crackle.

With her long, dark hair in a single braid over her shoulder, she sweeps those cunning blue eyes over our little group as if already figuring out how to use each of us to her advantage.

Professionalism may be her armor, but flirtation is her weapon, and she wields both with deadly precision.

I watch as she engages with Monty first, her demeanor respectful and her body language all business. She holds out maps and documentation, detailing her two months of searching for Wolf's body.

She's good, really good, answering questions before they're asked and backing up her points with documentation and evidence. She's done her research and seems to know the hills better than Kody and me.

But it's the way she looks at us that stirs tension. There's a playful glint in her eyes, a subtle curve of her lips that suggests she's enjoying this a little too much.

Frankie stands off to the side, her narrowed gaze pinging from Sirena to me and back again.

My girl is wound tight, and who can blame her? The photo of Wolf's body has devastated us, but Frankie has taken it the hardest.

Her fire-red hair falls over her face as she looks down, lost in her thoughts, in her grief.

I want to hug her, kiss her, and make her come. But she's been standoffish and unreachable since the night Kody and I got arrested. Every attempt we've made to touch her has been shut down.

We're giving her space. For now.

"We'll fly over the Brooks Range here." Sirena taps a circled grid on the map. "We'll look for landmarks familiar to Leo and Kody and try to narrow down this two-hundred-thousand square mile haystack."

Monty nods, his stoic expression betraying nothing. He's a master of control, both in business and personal affairs. But even he can't hide the worry in his icy blue eyes when he looks at Frankie.

He wants to go with us, but someone needs to stay on the island with her. It's not just her panic about flying. The mere mention of returning to Hoss causes her to break out in a cold sweat.

As long as I live, I'll ensure that she never returns to that place.

Kody and I don't want to go back, either. But our relationship with the hills is different. It's the only home we've ever known, and right now, it may be the key to finding Wolf's body.

"When do we leave?" I ask Sirena.

"I'm watching the weather reports. Looks like we'll be clear to fly by the end of the week." She winks.

I glance at Kody, and his black eyes meet mine, a silent understanding passing between us.

We're both worried about what we'll find. Is Wolf dead, alive, or did he somehow escape the Arctic and is now stalking

Frankie? The last time I saw him, he tried to shoot her.

His intentions are as murky as the Alaskan waters, creating relentless, nibbling doubt.

That night, tense silence cloaks the estate. Frankie's distance has become a chasm that none of us know how to bridge.

I find myself sitting alone beside the pool, my feet dangling in the cool water. The stars offer little comfort as my thoughts churn with frustration and sadness.

The memories of Wolf, the haunting photo, and the uncertainty of his fate keep me from sleep.

The search for him feels like chasing shadows, and the hope of finding him alive only deepens my worry. If he is alive, where has he been for the past six months? Worse is the thought of him out there, possibly stalking Frankie.

Wolf wasn't stable on a good day. Even if his body survived, what has become of his mind?

The light tread of footsteps interrupts my solitude. I look up to see Monty approaching, his default stern expression softened by concern.

He rolls up his sweatpants and sits beside me, lowering his feet into the water.

Silence weaves between us before he finally speaks. "I have a proposal for you."

I raise an eyebrow. Monty is a man of many surprises, and his timing is never accidental.

"There's a seaplane base in Sitka I'm looking to buy." He tilts his head back, gazing up at the stars. "You could run seaplane tours out of it for tourists, use it as an instructor school, or maybe even a plane mechanic shop. Whatever you want. I'll give you the same offer I gave Kody. As a silent partner, I would take a small percentage of the profits. All negotiable, of course."

That's fair. And tempting. A shimmer of hope in an otherwise bleak situation. But the timing...

"Why now?" I shake my head. "With a stalker on the loose and the search for Wolf's body about to consume all my attention..."

"Because you need something to hold on to. Something to look forward to. We all do."

His words hit home. I want the dream he's dangling before me. Do I trust him? Not completely. But with every passing day, I find fewer and fewer reasons to hate him.

If I'm being honest, I'm rather fond of the arrogant asshole. Especially when he's the *brother* version of himself. I can't remember the last time I saw the husband come out.

"I'll think about it."

"Do that." He unfolds his muscled physique off the ground and stands over me. "Opportunities like this don't come often. And sometimes, they come when you least expect them."

As he leaves, the silence returns, but the weight on my shoulders feels lighter.

The offer is a distraction but also a promise of a future that doesn't revolve around the hills of shivers and shadows.

leonid

THIRTY-SIX

Days pass, and Frankie remains distant, holding our relationship hostage.

Kody and I have given her space, and we've all had a lot on our minds. But we're leaving tomorrow, and we'll be gone for a week. With so much up in the air, I won't let this wait until we return.

Communication is vital to our relationship. It got us through the darkest hours in the hills. She refused to let us hide from our feelings then, and I'll be damned if she tries to hide from us now.

"What's going on with her?" I haul myself out of the pool and shake the water from my hair. "She's putting up walls. That's not like her."

"She hasn't forgiven us for getting arrested." Kody tosses me a towel and wraps another one around his hips.

"Yeah, but there's more to it."

"Like our refusal to go to therapy? The prospect of us spending the next few days with Sirena? The bloody goddamn heart that was delivered? Or how about the fact that she's trapped on this island until we find the threat against her?"

Every one of those things seeps into the back of my throat and burns there.

Our gazes collide, sparking an unspoken understanding.

She chose us, and we need to remind her why.

After we dry off and put on workout clothes, we find her in the gym, running on the treadmill. She hates that machine, but the summer heat has kept her off the outdoor tracks.

The sound of her feet hitting the belt doesn't slow as we stride in and strip off our shirts.

We've worked hard on our bodies over the past ten weeks, our muscles more honed than ever thanks to Monty's top-of-the-line equipment.

I catch her eye in the mirror, offering a wink. Her lips twitch, but her expression remains focused on the run.

Kody heads to the weight rack, and I join him, picking up a heavy set of dumbbells.

We stand in front of the mirror, muscles coiled and tense, and put our heads in the zone.

For me, I only need to think of her. My woman. My forever. The one I fight for and protect. She deserves my strength. My dedication. She deserves the best of me.

Here we go.

Tightening my grip, I lift. Veins bulge. Muscle fibers ripple. Sinews and tendons work together. My breath comes in short, sharp bursts, the sound of primitive aggression.

Meeting her eyes in the mirror, I curl the next rep.

She stumbles on the treadmill, nearly flying off.

Before I can turn, she rights herself, glaring in my direction.

She can glare all she wants. I'm her predator. Her warrior.

I hunt for her. Not for food, not anymore. I hunt for danger. I fight for dominance. Every rep, every set is a battle, and my body is a knife, honed and sharpened.

I lift for her. Each drop of sweat and groan of pain is for her.

My reflection stares back at me, eyes on fire, teeth bared, expression unyielding.

Kody stands beside me, grunting through his mental zone, his physique impressive, stacked muscles bouncing with every movement. Weights clank, a savage symphony that echoes our raw, untamed power.

The dumbbell slams back onto the rack with a triumphant roar. I stand tall, chest heaving, heart pounding. My muscles ache. My body burns. But it's a good pain. I'm fucking strong. Capable.

Wiping the sweat from my brow, I grab the weights again, ready for the next set. Ready to prove, over and over, that I'm worthy, that I'm the savage warrior she needs.

She smacks the power button on the treadmill and jumps off, her face flushed with exertion, frustration, and longing.

Kody and I set down the weights and turn toward her.

"What are you two doing?" She rests a fist on her cocked hip.

I bristle defensively, my pride not far behind. "Reminding you."

"Reminding me of what?"

"Why you chose us."

A startled, shivering breath blows from her lips. "Shit." She drops her head to her hands. "Fuck."

I love surprising her, especially when it evokes a string of curses, but I'm confused by her reaction.

Kody looks just as dumbfounded.

"We miss you, woman." In two long strides, he lowers her hands and presses against her body.

I wrap around her back, trapping her in a sweaty cage of muscle. She's so small between us, so firm and solid. We haven't been the only ones working out every day. Her tight little ass flexes against my cock, surging an insistent, burning need through me, its intensity unbearable.

"Give me your mouth." He cups her face, lifting it, and his head jerks back. "You're crying."

"No, I'm not." She wriggles out from between us, wiping at her cheeks. "I'm sorry. Goddammit. I'm fucking this up."

She stands there, looking so damn vulnerable in her tiny running shorts and barely-there sports bra. This beautiful, maddening woman has the power to level us, and she has no idea.

"What's wrong?" My chest constricts.

"Why do you have to look so..." She gestures at our shirtless, sweaty bodies and whimpers as if she's in pain.

I know the feeling. "We could ask you the same thing."

"I love you." She sets her shoulders and looks at each of us in turn. "I love you so much."

"Is this about Sirena?" Kody's brows furrow.

"Or the arrest?" I ask.

"No." She glances around the gym as if she doesn't want to have this discussion here. "Where's Monty?"

"In his office." Kody narrows his eyes. "Why?"

"Finally." She heaves a breath. "I've been needing to tell you something since the night you were arrested. But the heart arrived, and Wolf's photo, and Monty is *always* with us. God, this is so hard."

"Out with it," I growl.

"I'm trying. But I need to say it all before you respond. Can you do that?"

"Is this about the night-vision goggles?" I ask.

"You know about that?"

"Yeah. We told him about the cameras. He told us about the cracked window. Then the three of us worked out our anger on the bag." I gesture at the punching bag behind her.

"Oh." A small smile cracks her face, the first one I've seen in a week.

"I removed all our recording equipment. We talked about it and decided that with the escalating threats, the cameras posed a risk. We don't know how tech savvy this stalker is or if they know how to hack a surveillance system, but the one I installed wasn't as secure as Monty's."

"Makes sense." She purses her lips. "Did he tell you about the promise I made?"

"No." Kody folds his arms over his chest.

"I don't want to hurt him. When he watched us together that night, we caused him deep, irreparable pain."

"Then he shouldn't fucking watch," I say, pointing out the obvious.

"Leo."

"Frankie."

"I told him we're not going to do that to him again."

A growl hangs in my throat.

"He's not the bad guy," she says. "He loves us and—"

"Do you love him?"

"I did. I loved the man I married. But he's not that man anymore. He's..."

"He's what?"

"Better."

"Do you love him?" I ask again.

She releases a trembling breath. "I love him the way I loved Wolf. But that's not exactly right. We..."

"You have history," Kody says. "Romantic history, sexual history, complicated history."

"Yes. All that and more. But I need you to listen. Are you listening?"

We both nod.

"I will never choose him over you. I love you. Not because you're gorgeous and built and sexy as fuck. I mean, you're all those things, but the real reason is because of the kind of men you are. Caring. Protective. Reliable. You don't seek power by trying to control me but by supporting and uplifting me. Before I met you, I didn't believe in soul mates. But I always hoped that if they were real, mine would be someone like you. Your imperfect love fits perfectly with mine, and now that we're no longer trapped in hell and free to pursue wistful things like love, you're the ones for me. So as much as I loved watching you pump iron with your shirts off, you don't ever need to prove your worth to me. You survived Hoss. That makes you more worthy than any man alive. You're mine."

Every word hits my veins like warm honey. "And Monty? Where does he fit in?"

"I don't know." She sighs. "What I do know is that it's not fair to him if we continue having sex under his roof."

"Did he put you up to this?" Anger flares inside me.

"No. This is my decision. I want to move past all this fear

and pain. I want to return to work, stop being dependent on him, and begin my life with you and Kody. Until then, we're going to be respectful."

Her resolution cuts deep, but I know she's right.

He's been supportive and kind to us despite his obsessive love for her. He'll never stop pursuing her, and if he knows we're not fucking her, he'll use that opportunity to wriggle his way back in.

"I'd rather die first." Lips curling back in a snarl, I bare my teeth.

"What are you going to do? Force me?"

"I don't have to force you, love. I only need to touch you, and wetness seeps from your body and down your legs, covering both of us with your scent." I advance on her. "Shall I demonstrate?"

"No." She retreats, her pupils dilating as she drinks in my shirtless torso. "Please, don't."

"All right." I plant my feet. "Go ahead. Draw a line between us." Lowering my chin, I glare at her through my lashes. "It'll be fun watching you cross it."

"You won't even be here. You're going out of town for God knows how long."

She's right. *Fuck.*

Arching a brow, she looks at Kody.

"I went twenty-five years without sex. You're worth the wait, woman." His nostrils widen with a deep inhale, and he releases his breath. "If your restraint can hold out, mine can, too."

Releasing a slow breath, she walks to us, directly into our arms.

If she thinks we'll sleep beside her every night without being *inside* her, she's crazy. I would never force her, but she loves sex as much as we do. Our chemistry is volcanic. Eventually, it will explode.

"I'm so worried." She buries her face in my chest. "What if you get lost in the Arctic and never come back to me?"

"Hey." I take her face in my hands. "We won't get lost. Monty equipped the plane with high-tech GPS tracking. He'll be watching our path, and we'll remain in constant communication with him through state-of-the-art equipment."

"We're practically invincible." Kody presses his nose in her hair. "We've survived worse things than Leo's flying."

"We'll have a more experienced pilot with us." I shoot him a glare and kiss her head. "We'll be fine. I promise."

After showering—*separately*—we crawl into bed, holding her between us.

She's the center of my world, and I'm determined to protect her, even if it means falling asleep with a raging hard-on.

"Leo." She shifts, rubbing her gorgeous ass against my cock. "You're making this hard."

"No, *you* are making it hard, love." I swat her rear. "Stop wriggling."

"I'm sorry."

"No, you're not, you wicked creature." I bite the delicate shell of her ear. "How about the tip? Just an inch? Two inches?"

"How about a twelve-inch tip?" Kody mumbles.

"You're both the worst." She groans.

I grin at her discomfort. "What gives us blue balls makes us stronger."

Kodiak

THIRTY-SEVEN

The next morning, Leo and I prepare to leave with Sirena.

The overcast sky slants a gray hue over the island, killing the mood. But rising to meet the dread is an urgent hunger for the hunt.

The instant I don my crossbow, it feels like an extension of my spine. Leo stands beside me, his rifle held with the ease of a man accustomed to its weight.

This is merely a scouting mission. We don't expect to run into trouble, but if we do, the pilot, James, is retired military and combat-trained.

With our gear strapped to our backs, Leo and I are ready to plunge back into the heart of our past. This time, we're stronger, sharper, and better equipped with technology to make it out of there alive.

And we won't be alone.

Frankie stands on the dock, her red hair catching in the warm breeze. She's brave, braver than most, and hides her fear well. But I hear it in her hoarse rasp, her words frayed at the edges, as she talks to Leo.

"Take care of yourself." He kisses her mouth, his tongue

delving deeply and aggressively, making Monty's face turn lava red. "I love you."

"I love you, too." She steps back, swallowing hard. "Both of you. Just...come back to me."

"Forever."

I press my way in, cupping her face. "Love you, too."

"We've done this too many times." She smiles up at me, the corners of her mouth quivering. "Saying goodbye to you never gets easier."

"It isn't easy because we have something worth holding onto. I'll carry it with me until we're together again."

My hand, rough and calloused, traces a path along her jaw. I tilt her chin up, forcing her to look into my eyes. There's a moment, a heartbeat of hesitation, where the world tilts, holding its breath. Then, like a tempest breaking free, our mouths collide.

My tongue follows the seam of her lips, coaxing them open and diving into the sweet, intoxicating warmth within. She tangles her hands in my hair, pulling me closer, fearing the moment I'll slip away.

The kiss deepens, turning from a feverish exchange to a slow, agonizing goodbye.

When we finally break apart, gasping for air, the world rights itself. I rest my forehead against hers, and the shadows recede, leaving only the raw, undeniable truth of our connection.

Every kiss with her is the greatest of all time, not because it's perfect, but because it's ours. We defy fate, laugh in the face of destiny, and bind our souls in a way that nothing and no one can ever sever.

And now, I must leave her in the hands of Monty.

I trust her, and I trust the bond we share, but her history with him looms large.

"Monty will take care of you," I force myself to say.

She juts her chin, her green eyes locking onto mine. "I can take care of myself, thank you very much."

"That's my girl."

Moments later, the boat pulls away from the dock. I lean

against the taffrail, watching her, a solitary figure standing resolute against the encroaching fog.

Slowly, the island fades into the distance, a sanctuary and a prison all at once.

She's trapped there, unable to go anywhere until the stalker is caught. While I never hear her complain, I know she's miserable. The thought of her suffering while we're out searching claws at my heart.

Forcing myself to turn away, I focus on the journey ahead.

We dock in Sitka, take a car to the small airport, and soon enough, we're airborne, the bush plane vibrating with the energy of our mission.

Leo pilots with the ease of a seasoned aviator, though James keeps a watchful eye.

The rugged landscape below unfolds in greens and browns, interspersed with the glinting silver of rivers.

Seated beside me, Sirena manages the details with calm efficiency despite the tension thrumming through all of us.

Her maps and documentation are spread out before us, but it's our memories that we'll rely on most. Every ridge, every valley, every shadow will be scrutinized for any sign of familiarity.

Three hours into the flight, my headspace is a tangled mess.

Is Wolf out there? Dead? Alive? Will we find him? What shape will he be in? My mind goes to a dark place.

I thought I was ready, but truthfully, I'll never be ready to see my brother's lifeless body. And that's precisely what we're looking for. His remains, scattered bits of him, pieces of clothing, footprints or DNA left behind by whoever took that photo.

We need to find the location where the picture was taken. It could point us to tracks from the tires of a plane touching down nearby. Or a helicopter. A snow machine. Some sort of vehicle was used to reach that gorge.

Amid the drone of the plane's engines and the hum of anticipation, Leo navigates with intense focus. Beside him,

James scans the landscape, waiting for his turn to take over the controls.

"You know..." Sirena turns those vulpine blue eyes on me, bending in and strangling my airway with her perfume. "Something about these missions really gets the blood pumping."

What are the rules about slapping a woman? Not a punch. Just a stinging, warning slap across the face?

I keep my eyes on the window as tension coils in my muscles.

Her long braid brushes against my arm. "You should let me take you out when we get back. Blow off some steam."

"Not interested." I glance at Leo, who clenches the yoke tighter than necessary.

He can hear us through the headset but doesn't look my way.

"So serious." She pokes my bicep. "A little fun wouldn't hurt."

"What did I fucking say about touching me?"

"Sirena," Leo cuts in, his voice a cold blade. "Focus on the mission."

A huff bursts from her nostrils, and she shakes her head, leaning back in her seat.

James's voice crackles over the headset. "Approaching the grid. Eyes open."

I scan the horizon, searching for any sign of recognition. How will we identify anything from this angle? I know the hills by scent, the feel of the land beneath my boots, and the sounds of water and ice.

Ten minutes later, the rugged terrain begins to look familiar, a patchwork of memories stitched together with pain and hope.

A river gorge catches my eye, a serpentine scar in the earth. Something about it stirs dread deep within me.

"There." I point at it. "That ridge looks familiar."

Leo nods, handing off the controls to focus on the landscape.

James guides the plane lower, circling until we find a

suitable spot to land.

The wheels touch down with a jolt, and we disembark into the crisp air.

August in the Arctic Circle offers a brief reprieve from the biting cold, the scenery awash in vibrant hues.

We spread out, methodically searching the area. The gorge's rocky walls rise around us, imposing and silent, just like I remembered. The river snakes through it, the water clear and refreshing, reflecting the sky's endless blue.

"Kody, look." Leo crouches by the riverbank, his head cocked, staring at the primrose.

And the Arctic Blue butterflies.

They flit around his face, their delicate wings both beautiful and haunting, conjuring memories of Wolf.

"I've seen them all over the Brooks Range." Sirena walks past, as oblivious to our pain as the butterflies. "Does anything look familiar?"

All of it.

None of it.

"Hard to tell." I scrutinize the area, the bend in the river, the jut of the cliffs, my eyes narrowing as I try to piece together fragments of memories. "Everything looks different in the summer."

"We need to cover as much ground as possible." James stands a few feet away, his gaze on the horizon. "Let's split up but stay within sight of each other."

"Want to partner up?" Sirena sidles up to Leo. "Two sets of eyes are better than one."

"Nope." Leo doesn't even look up.

She sighs dramatically, turning to me. "What about you, Kody?"

"Same answer."

With a shrug, she heads downriver with her equipment.

I share a look with Leo.

Don't turn your back on that one.

He nods and moves deeper into the gorge.

As the delicate wings of the butterflies flutter around me, I can almost see Wolf here, a ghost among the living.

Leo and I hike along the river, side by side, scenting the air and listening to the wind.

The midnight sun blurs the passage of time, its unrelenting light allowing us to push ourselves to the brink.

But as the hours pass and the miles drain the last of our energy, the landscape becomes increasingly unfamiliar. The initial sense of recognition fades, replaced by frustration and exhaustion.

No one has been here. No tracks. No signs of human life. Not in the past year. Maybe not ever.

"This isn't right." Leo pauses, tangling a hand in his hair. "None of this feels right."

I nod, the truth of his words settling in my gut. "This isn't our gorge."

James signals for us to regroup and gather our gear. As we make our way back to the plane, I take one last look at the river.

I knew it wouldn't be easy. But I didn't expect the first failure to sit so heavily in my chest.

That's what hope does. It crushes.

We wasted an entire day because of me. Because I picked the wrong fucking gorge.

How many more gorges will we hike? How many more days will we be separated from Frankie?

Too many.

Deep in my bones, I know this will take time, endurance, and patience.

Naturally, my mood is shit. The flight back to Fairbanks sucks, and luckily for Sirena, she has enough self-preservation to stay the fuck away from me.

We sleep in a cabin in Fairbanks, refueling the plane and our spirits, only to start again the next morning.

The search is relentless, and every day brings more of the same. A familiar landmark, hours of hiking, return to Fairbanks, rinse, and repeat.

Each night, we check in with Monty using the satellite equipment. The connection crackles, a lifeline to civilization we never had before. It's my favorite part of every day.

"Monty." I adjust the receiver. "Any updates on your end?"

"Nothing new here." His voice comes through, steady and composed. "Wilson is still narrowing down the suspect list. How's the search going?"

"Slow." I glance at Leo, who's pacing the small cabin. "The terrain is more challenging than we anticipated. But we're not giving up."

"Good. Keep pushing. I wish I were with you."

"How's she doing?"

"You can ask her yourself. Hang on." The sound of footsteps on wood flooring scrapes through the connection, followed by the creak of a door. "Frankie?"

A moment later, her soft lilt brushes my ears. "Kody? Is everything okay?"

"Yeah. We're safe. Just checking in."

Leo grabs the phone, his voice gentler than I've heard in days. "Hey, love. How are you holding up?" He listens, nods, and exchanges a glance with me. "We're doing everything we can. Just stay safe. We love you, too."

As the call ends, the cabin falls silent.

This feeling in my chest…I don't know how to process it or what to call it. The throbbing, twisting hollowness of it hits me the hardest at night after hearing Frankie's voice.

I think I'm homesick. I don't miss the island or Sitka or any specific place. I miss *her.*

"I'm ready to go home," I mutter. "Back to her."

"I know." He slumps beside me on the bed. "Me, too."

The next few days blur into a monotonous cycle of searching and refueling. Each day, we push ourselves further, scouring a new section of the grid under the glare of the endless midnight sun.

Despite our exhaustion, we take time each night to connect with Monty and Frankie before crashing into bone-tired sleep.

As the week draws to a close, our spirits are battered but unbroken.

We have yet to find anything. No trace of Wolf. No hint of Hoss. But the search isn't over. As long as the sun burns in the sky, we'll keep looking. For Wolf, for Frankie, for the answers that continue to elude us.

Finally, we return to Sitka. As I step off the plane, the island beckoning in the distance, I know one thing for certain.

We'll find him. We owe him that much and more.

The hunt isn't over. Not by a long shot.

The air-conditioning in the den blasts from the vents, chilling me to the bone and making me brittle.

Doyle leans forward in the chair, facing me, his eyes intense, magnetic, trying to draw me in, but I feel nothing.

I've learned to be wary of pretty faces and charming smiles.

Thank you, Denver.

"How are you feeling today?" He brushes his hand against mine. A fleeting touch, but it makes me shudder.

"Trapped," I admit. "It's been a month since Leo and Kody started searching for Wolf's body in the Arctic. Whenever they return to Sitka, I hardly see them. Kody's busy with the distillery, and Leo's finishing flight school. I feel so alone."

Doyle knows too much. More than he should. I've been seeing him for three months, and he's heard it all—every gruesome detail about my time with Denver, my relationship with Leo and Kody, Wolf's suicide, and the stalker.

The stalker who's been silent since we received Wolf's photo.

"You're not alone," he says. "You have me."

"For two hours a week." I laugh, hiding my discomfort.

"Rhett is still holding my job. I want to go back to work. I need to feel useful, to have a purpose."

"Your mental health is just as important as your physical safety. If going back to work makes you happy, you should do it. Even with the stalker threat, you can take security guards with you."

"I live with three men who would be absolutely furious to hear you say that. They want to protect me."

"Protect you? Or control you?"

"No one controls me."

Leo and Kody are my world, but their quests for closure and independence keep them from me. I understand, but it doesn't make the loneliness any easier.

They're somewhere in the Arctic Circle right now with Sirena. When they return, they'll be upset and worked up, their eyes haunted by another failed mission. And they'll direct that aggression at me.

They'll think of nothing else than luring me to be alone, putting their hands and mouths on me, pushing my clothes aside, and slacking their insatiable need.

I want them to feel how wet they make me while they whisper filthy words. Their touch, their growls, their scents, our connection—all of it compounds with mine, sparking like an overloaded electrical circuit.

The problem is they don't want me to leave the island, and I won't have sex with them under Monty's roof.

What kind of person would I be if I gave in and fucked them with Monty in the other room?

Cruel. That's what I would be. Fucking cruel.

Like it or not, I'm in a complicated love square, and until I figure it out, no one is getting laid.

It's torture.

So when Leo and Kody return, I'll continue to resist their advances with a crumbling willpower. It'll enrage them, and they'll storm off to Sitka and channel all that frustration into their dreams.

Kody pours his heart into the distillery, and I admire his drive. He'll be opening his bar to the public soon, and I couldn't be happier for him. But I miss him. So fucking much.

Leo remains focused on earning advanced pilot certificates. It's his way of gaining control, of proving to himself and the world that he'll never be helpless again. I love him for it, but I need him here, with me, to remind me that the present is just as important as the future. I need him to prove our connection is more than just sex.

Then there's Monty. He tries so hard to fill the gap, but I keep him at arm's length. Because I'm scared. I'm fucking terrified of my feelings for him. If I nurture those feelings...

It will ruin everything. My relationship with Leo and Kody. Monty's relationship with them. There's no scenario where the four of us can be together the way I want. I've thought about it. A lot.

"Every decision you make revolves around them," he says. "It's not healthy, Frankie."

"You're right." I rub my temples, conflicted and confused. "I don't know what to do."

"Maybe you should separate from them for a while. If they love you, they'll understand your need for independence."

Horror robs my breath as denial crashes over me, dragging me under where the light of reason cannot reach.

"No. Absolutely not. I love them."

"All three of them?" His eyes narrow, a flicker of something dark passing through them.

"Yes. I love them and can't imagine my life without them."

"We've talked about this, Frankie. You can't have three men. Especially three unstable men with aggression issues who refuse to see a therapist. You need to rewire your nervous system to gravitate toward healthy connections, enriching relationships, and meaningful intimacy. Not the toxic ones you're clinging to."

I bite my lip, my thoughts unraveling. He knows everything about me. Sharing my secrets with him and talking through the painful, triggering details has gone a long way in helping me manage the panic attacks. I haven't had an episode since I started opening up to him.

But something feels off today, like a discordant note in a familiar melody.

His suggestion to separate from the three people who will stop at nothing to keep me safe...that doesn't sit right. How could he even think I would do that? They're my lifeline, my family, the mates to my soul.

But he's right about one thing. I need to reclaim my purpose to feel alive again. Working at the hospital, helping others, it's not just a job. It's my calling.

If anyone is controlling me, it's the stalker. This unknown entity hovers over me like a dark cloud, keeping me trapped on this island. My mental health, my happiness, are worth fighting for. If I need security guards to achieve that, so be it. I won't be a prisoner in my own life anymore.

"You've been through so much." His expression softens, and he reaches out to gently touch my cheek, his touch warm, lingering, and more intimate than it should be. "Such a strong, magnificent woman. I want to see you heal and be happy again."

"You know what we haven't talked about?" I pull back, eyes hard. "Your unprofessional touching. It makes me uncomfortable."

"I'm sorry." He drops his hand, looking wounded. "My only intention is to help you."

Something in his tone sends another shiver through me. I want to believe him, to trust in his care and concern, but a growing part of me feels uneasy.

Maybe Monty was right. Maybe Doyle's intentions aren't benevolent.

"I appreciate your concern," I say, "but I need our relationship to remain professional. It's important for my healing."

"You're right. I overstepped." He adopts a soothing tone. "I thought you might need comfort, knowing how hard today must be for you."

"What?" My heart stops.

"You don't remember?" Pity draws his features as he scoots forward. "A year ago today, you were abducted."

Of course, I fucking remember. But I never told him the exact date.

"How do you know that?" I stand, backing away.

"You told me, Frankie." He smiles, but it doesn't reach his eyes. "Or maybe I saw it in the news."

I don't remember ever mentioning it. My mind races, trying to recall if I slipped, but nothing comes to mind. Suspicion coils in my gut and encases my skin in ice.

"I think we should end the session." Heart racing, I move toward the door. "In fact, I'll no longer be requiring your treatment."

"Your therapy isn't complete." He stands, his expression unreadable. "We're making progress, but you still have things to work through."

"I'll do it on my own." I grab the door handle, my palm slick with sweat as I wrench it open.

Monty leans against the opposite wall, hands in his pockets and blue eyes crashing into mine.

One look at me, and he shoves off the wall and storms forward. "What's wrong?"

"Doyle's leaving." Hugging my waist, I step to the side to let the man pass. "For good."

"If you change your mind," he says, exchanging a glare with Monty before turning to me, "I'm only a phone call away."

Sensing my discomfort, Monty shifts and puts his broad frame between us. "She won't be making that call." He raises his voice. "Jasper?"

Jasper steps from around the corner. "Sir?"

"Escort Dr. Whitaker off the island."

"Right away, Mr. Novak."

With Monty blocking my view, I don't know if Doyle glances back as he departs. I don't care. When the front door shuts behind him, I release a serrated breath.

"What happened?" Monty pivots, bending his knees and leveling his gaze with mine.

"Did you tell him what today is?"

"I didn't tell him anything."

"Was it in the news?"

"No." He blinks. "Not that I'm aware of. We kept dates and timelines out of the narrative. But a thorough journalist could've gleaned the details and posted it somewhere." His jaw flexes. "What did Doyle do?"

"He touched my face. I told him it was unprofessional, and he mentioned how today must be hard for me." A swallow sticks in my throat. "He must've spent some time looking for that date. But for what purpose?"

"He's at the top of the suspect list."

"I figured."

"He's not coming back."

"No. I fired him."

"Wilson will continue to keep an eye on him."

"He hasn't found anything?"

"No. Nothing to incriminate him or connect him to the stalker. Doyle hasn't taken a flight or left Sitka in the past year. But Wilson is still digging."

"Thank you." I tuck my hands in my pockets to stop myself from reaching for him. "For waiting out here, for always keeping me safe, and the letter..." I shift my weight. "Thank you for that."

I woke this morning with a note on my nightstand, scrawled in his meticulous penmanship.

Today is a reminder of your strength. I'm sorry for your pain, and I'm here with all my love.

I cried when I read it.

Leaving a note rather than smothering me all day with pity and concern was exactly what I needed.

"You're welcome," he says.

He's doing everything right, and it's slowly, painfully breaking me.

As I stare into his stern, overprotective eyes, I feel nothing but love.

Love for the man I married.

Love for the man he's become.

I love him.

He lost me, and that changed him. It ripped him open,

deepened him, and made him emotionally stronger.

Nothing is more breathtaking than a man who knows the salty taste of his own tears. A man who owns his mistakes as if they're tattooed on his bones with holy ink.

A year ago, I didn't believe he was my soul mate.

But the man standing before me with a broken heart and imperfect love in his eyes? He fits disturbingly, achingly, perfectly in my soul. And I'm in his. He never let me go.

"I'm sorry about Doyle." His hand twitches at his side. "I'll find you another therapist."

"I don't need another therapist. I need to go back to work."

"It's too dangerous." His eyes darken, flashing with anger. "You know that."

"I do, but I can't continue like this. I need to feel useful again, to have a purpose."

"What about your safety?"

"I don't know, Monty. You have all this security everywhere. You're rich and powerful and can destroy someone's life with the snap of your fingers."

"I don't do that."

"But you can. I'm going back to work. Snap your fingers and make it happen."

"Christ." He sighs quietly. "You're a pain in my ass."

"Thank you." I pat his jaw and stride away.

"Frankie."

"Hm?" I pause, glancing back.

"Are you happy?"

I pull in a breath and give him the truth. "No. I'm not. But I'm working on it."

"Put on that green dress. The one with the…" He gestures at his sternum.

"The low plunge halter? That's a fancy dress, Monty."

"I'm taking you to dinner."

"Off the island?"

When he inclines his head, a thrill jolts through me.

I haven't left the island since the night Leo and Kody were arrested.

Two months ago.

Before he can change his mind, I race off to the guest bedroom to prepare.

Sitka's priciest restaurant flaunts elegance and refined taste with a flair for luxury, much like the man sitting across from me.

Monty took care of everything, from the chauffeured ride here to the private dining room and the precise ordering of our meals.

His black tailored suit fits him like a glove, enhancing the sculpted contours of his lean, muscular body. The intensity of his blue eyes, set against the harsh angles of his shaved jawline and raven-black hair, captivates and intimidates.

At age fifty, his commanding demeanor and stern bearing make him a formidable presence, his wealth and influence casting a long shadow over the restaurant when we walked in.

Hell, that shadow stretches across the entire state of Alaska.

Flickering candles adorn the small table between us, the romantic setting too intimate for the state of our relationship.

The bourbon arrives first, just as I like it, with dark, juicy cherries. I quickly slug it down, the warmth of the alcohol soothing my nerves.

He watches me, those arctic eyes never leaving mine. Sharp

and penetrating, they reflect the icy waters surrounding his private island.

"You look stunning." His deep, velvety baritone strokes me in places it has no business stroking.

"Thank you. I feel like a haggard old sea witch next to you. Every woman in the restaurant drooled on their filet mignon when you stepped in the door. They're all going to go home tonight and watch billionaire porn until their fingers go numb."

He smirks. "I didn't notice them."

"Liar."

"In a crowd, my eyes always find you. No one else exists."

A thousand stupid butterflies take flight in my belly, winging toward certain death. "You can't say things like that."

"I can do whatever I want, darling."

"Whatever and *whomever*, apparently."

"I will *never* hurt you like that again."

"It was petty of me to bring it up. I've forgiven you."

"I haven't forgiven myself. I will apologize and grovel for the rest of my life."

"Please, don't." I stare down at my bourbon, the memory of that video playing in my mind. "After I saw the recording of you with her, I swore I would never love again. I would never trust another man."

"I know." His jaw tightens. "I hate myself for that."

"I don't. Despite my resentment, I fell in love again. Leo and Kody brought me back to life, gave me something to hold onto, and proved that I'm not broken."

He takes a deep breath, gearing up to say something, but the server enters with a delicate assortment of oysters, caviar, and lobster bisque.

Each bite is a luxurious experience, but I can barely taste it. My mind whirls with all the things unsaid between us.

We eat in silence.

His hand rests on the table next to mine, but he doesn't touch me. His eyes, however, caress every inch of my body, running up and down my green minidress. A dress that clings to my figure and reveals more than it conceals. The plunging neckline exposes my chest from throat to abdomen, my nipples barely hidden by the thin fabric.

I know he personally picked out this dress. He's always had a thing for my small boobs in green.

We move on to the main course, a perfectly cooked steak for him and a seared salmon for me, paired with an exquisite bottle of Bordeaux.

I try to keep the conversation casual, but my heart isn't cooperating. It pounds so hard I'm sure he can see it in my exposed chest.

"This is nice, Monty." I tip the wine to my lips. "You didn't have to go through all this trouble. I'm just glad to be off the island."

"I can't bear to see you unhappy." He sets his fork down and paws a hand through his hair. "It's killing me, Frankie. The guilt..."

"Guilt?"

"I'm responsible for your misery."

"What?" The salmon lodges in my throat, and I grab my water, gulping it down. "How?"

He presses his lips together, and for the first time since we arrived, he takes his eyes off me, darting them around the private dining room.

Two guards stand outside the door. Two more patrol the perimeter of the restaurant.

He's not worried about the security. He's stalling.

"You arranged an intimate dinner," I say. "If you have secrets to share, the moment is now."

He takes a long swig of his whiskey, drawing my attention to his thick throat, the way it jogs with each swallow. If I pressed my nose to his skin, I would smell traces of fine Italian leather and smoky vetiver beneath the sweet-earthy, musky-marine aroma of his aftershave.

I miss his scent.

"I helped Leo and Kody pursue their dreams to distract them." He meets my eyes. "I knew their careers would consume them and keep them busy. I knew it would keep them from you. I needed them out of the way so that I could win you back."

"You wanted to win me back by keeping me isolated?"

"I'm a monster. I knew what I was doing. I still know what I'm doing. I can't stop."

"Jesus." My heart flinches.

"Here's the kicker. You'll enjoy this part." He braces an elbow on the table. "I've grown to care about those guys on a level that fucks all my monstrous plans to hell. As it turns out, I actually want them to be happy." He huffs a self-deprecating laugh. "I bought boats for them last week."

"You what?"

"And motorcycles."

"Oh, God."

"It's a surprise. They're driving your shit cruiser back and forth to Sitka, and I'm worried it'll break down and leave them stranded. It's maddening. I'm supposed to hate them."

"No, you're not. They're your family."

"They're fucking my wife."

"I kept my promise. We haven't been intimate."

"You love them."

"Yeah. I do." I move my hand, lacing my fingers through his. "Sounds like you do, too."

"I love *you.*" He runs his thumb over my knuckles. "Let me in."

"You've always been *in.*" I stare at my plate. "In my thoughts, in my heart. I can't get you *out.*"

"Is that what you want? Would my absence make you happy?"

I pull my hand back, needing the distance to think clearly.

"If you have secrets to share," he murmurs, "the moment is now."

"I don't think you can handle hearing what I want."

"Try me."

"No."

"A year ago today, you had no problem telling me precisely what was on your mind. You wanted our baby, rightfully so, and you refused to take no for an answer. Where is that woman now?"

"I want the impossible."

"Nothing is impossible."

"I want the four of us to be together."

"We *are* together."

"Don't be daft, Monty."

"Spell it out."

"Fuck." I gulp, going for it. "I want the four of us to be in love and naked together for the rest of our lives."

His eyes darken, and he leans forward, his voice low and cold. "I will never fuck my brothers."

"Leo is your nephew."

"He's my blood."

"Monty." I haul in a calming breath. "Leo and Kody don't have sex with each other. They're weirded out if they accidentally touch. Well, mostly Leo. Kody's pretty open. But they keep a clear line between them. No contact during sex. No sword crossing."

"No double penetration?"

I don't get embarrassed easily, but as my cheeks burn with the fire of a hundred midnight suns, I realize I'm completely unprepared for this conversation.

I never imagined sharing the sexual details of my threesome with anyone, let alone with my estranged husband.

"Answer the question." He angles over the table, scorching me with those inescapable eyes.

"No double penetration."

"Because they're related?"

"That and..." I clear my throat. "The childhood abuse."

Leaning back, he rubs his hands over his face.

"Have you...?" I snatch my glass of wine and finish it off. "Have you ever shared a woman with another man?"

"No." He stares at me, eyes thinning to slits. "What do you want that you're not getting?"

"I already told you."

"What do you want in bed?" He rises, circles the table, and bends into my space. "Two dicks in one hole?" Twisting my chair to face him, he lowers his mouth to my cheek. "Three dicks in two holes?" He grazes those sinful lips across my other cheek. "All three holes stuffed at the same time?"

Tingling flames sweep up my neck and across my face.

Admitting my desires out loud feels like a betrayal to Leo and Kody.

I bite my tongue and avert my gaze.

"Say it." His tone hardens as he sets that cruel mouth against mine, barely touching, straight-up tormenting.

I shake my head.

"Fucking say it, Frankie." He cuffs my throat with a huge hand, the pressure gentle, sexual, and demanding.

"Monty..." My pulse accelerates, raising my body temperature. "Please."

"Use your words." He drags his teeth along my jawline, his breath hot and jagged and so damn hungry.

"Let me go." My legs part of their own volition as heat gathers between them.

This is wrong. It's so fucking wrong. We need to stop.

"Tell me your desires." With his grip on my throat, he brushes the knuckles of his free hand against my pebbled nipple, making me whimper. "Tell me what you crave, and I'll stop."

I want him to keep going. I want his tongue in my mouth and his gorgeous, hard cock between my legs.

But I'm with Leo and Kody.

So I give him the truth. "I crave *us.* You and them and me. I don't care about holes or positions or crossing swords. I just want the connection, the four of us bonded together in the most intimate way possible."

"Inside you."

"Yes."

"At the same time."

"Yes."

"Thank you." He abruptly releases me and returns to his seat, his features blank. "It would never work."

"Bullshit." A flustered exhale flutters past my lips. "You've had foursomes, fivesomes, and too-many-to-count-somes. Don't tell me it doesn't work."

"I know the sex works. I'm talking about the jealousy, the egos. You don't want a night of experimentation. You want a *relationship* with three possessive men. It would tear us all apart." He takes a breath. "I don't share. I'm selfish, and I won't apologize for it. I want you all to myself. That's *my* fantasy."

His words sting like a hard slap across the face. I know it's a pipe dream, but hearing his outright refusal makes it hurt that much more.

"Like I said. I want the impossible." I fiddle with the napkin. "I hate that loving them means hurting you and vice versa."

"You still love me." His expression softens, revealing the vulnerability he tries so hard to hide.

I don't respond, but that in itself is an answer.

"I wish there were an easy solution," he says.

"From where I'm sitting, there's *no* solution. I will never choose one of you over the others."

"Have you discussed this with them?"

"No."

"If you do..." He exhales sharply through his nose. "Let me know how that goes."

We continue our meal in silence, the food a blur of flavors and textures.

Whenever I glance up, I find him watching me with a look of awe, as if he's seeing me for the first time every time. That look reminds me of what we had and what we could still have.

If I chose him over Leo and Kody.

That will never happen.

I'll oppose it with every fiber of my being until my very last breath.

As the server clears away the plates and Monty pays the check, I play back our strange dinner conversation.

"Your plan to isolate me from Leo and Kody," I say, "is that still in the works?"

"No. It's making you miserable, and that's the last thing I want. I'll find another way to win you back."

There's only one way for us to be together, and he won't

consider it.

But I believe he truly wants me to be happy. He never stopped loving me, even after watching me have sex with Leo and Kody.

The more time I spend with him, the more he jeopardizes the effort I've put into scraping him out of my heart and erasing him from my mind.

Monty Novak was a billionaire playboy with a lot of secrets and even more pride.

Montgomery Strakh is a tortured soul in love, who admits his faults and fights for what he believes in.

He believes in me.

"Thank you for dinner." I shift my hand, grazing my fingers against his. "You're not a monster."

"Invite me back into your bed."

"Monty."

"Do it. Let me fuck you." In a blink, he captures my wrist and squeezes. "I'll render you powerless."

A throb hits my bloodstream, sending a frustrating rush of heat between my legs. I want to be held down and dominated by him again. I want his bruising kisses stuck in my teeth and his hand necklaces choking my air while he stretches my ass.

I just want...him.

If Leo or Kody had these thoughts about Sirena, it would gut me.

"Monty..." I stare at his fingers around my wrist.

"I have a surprise for you." He stands and moves to pull out my chair.

When he offers his hand, I take it, allowing him to lead me out of the restaurant.

With four security guards flanking us, we walk to his garage in silence. There, under the glow of overhead lights, he guides me toward a car resembling the batmobile. A red one.

"Get in." He opens the door for me, which rotates upward in a sweeping motion like a wing.

I lower into the bucket seat, enveloped by high-quality leather with detailed stitching.

The drive through town is a daze of lights and motion, the

car's engine a powerful roar. Security follows in the Range Rover, but it feels like we're the only two people in the world.

His long fingers grip the steering wheel with a command that quickens my pulse. When he shifts gears, I'm mesmerized by the fluidity of his movements, the way his knuckles flex and tendons tense.

There's something incredibly sexy about the precision with which he handles the hypercar. An effortless mastery. His jaw locks with concentration, but every so often, a smile plays at the corners of his lips.

He knows exactly the effect he has on me.

Heat radiates from his body, and I realize I've shifted too close to him, drawn to the scent of leather and aftershave. I want to touch him, feel the muscle and sinew beneath his shirt, and trace the ridges of power that define his physique.

But I don't. Because that would be cheating.

With my husband.

He crosses the bridge and parks in the hospital parking lot.

Confused, I turn to him. "What are we doing here?"

Without answering, he steps out, opens my door, and motions for me to follow.

Feeling self-conscious and exposed, I stand in the parking lot where I used to work and smooth down the minidress. It plunges daringly and barely covers my ass. Definitely not appropriate for a hospital.

"You're radiant. If I stare at you much longer, I won't be able to walk." He discreetly adjusts himself.

"Thank you." I grip his offered hand. "Why are we here?"

Again, no answer.

As he leads me to the entrance, I scan the lot, my eyes darting to the darkness at the edges.

Four security guards surround us, but the shadows writhe with menacing whispers, concealing watchful eyes and unknown dangers.

"Relax." He moves his hand to my lower back, adding firm pressure. "You're safe."

Inside, the familiar hum of the trauma unit greets us, a comforting chaos I've missed so much.

Dozens of familiar faces gather around the front desk as if expecting me. Dr. Simons, Nurse Letty, and Rhett stand among them, the warmth of their smiles quickening my gait and tugging me away from Monty's grip.

"Frankie." Rhett's face lights up when he sees me.

I rush to him and wrap my arms around his sturdy frame. As he hugs me back, I feel a weightlessness I haven't experienced in so long.

"I missed you," I whisper.

"We all missed you." He looks over my shoulder at Monty. "Good to see you, Monty."

Monty moves off to the side, hands clasped behind him, watching the reunion. For the next few minutes, I'm absorbed in the warm welcome of friends I haven't seen in a year. The chatter, the hugs, the familiar faces, it's overwhelming in the best way.

"You knew I was coming?" I ask Rhett.

"Monty called earlier. Said he'd bring you by to fill out the paperwork for your employment. As you can see..." He gestures at the crowd of nurses and doctors. "We're thrilled you're returning to work. It hasn't been the same without you."

Monty did this for me, knowing how much I needed it.

The backs of my eyes ache as I glance at him over my shoulder.

Thank you, I mouth.

He nods, his expression severe. But I see the love in his gaze, a devotion so deep it nearly topples me.

After I catch up with my friends, Rhett guides Monty and me to his office, where the paperwork awaits. I take a seat, my heart still racing as Monty sits beside me.

"All right." Rhett hands me a stack of forms. "Let's get you set up."

While I fill out the documents, Rhett steals glances at the guards in the hall.

"We need to talk about security." Monty straightens the cuffs of his sleeves, his tone all business.

I look up from the forms, my anxiety surging again.

"I know about the stalker." Rhett captures my gaze. "Monty explained the situation. We have protocols in place, but we'll adjust them to allow your personal security detail to remain with you at all times."

"How will that work? They can't come into patient rooms with me."

"No, but they can wait right outside the door like they're doing now." He looks at Monty. "I'll make it my priority to ensure her safety."

"As will my security team."

"I don't want to be a burden," I mutter.

"Not at all. We'll take care of everything," Rhett says. "Just focus on getting back into the swing of things."

As I make my way through the forms, Rhett and Monty step into the hall to discuss the logistics with the guards. They talk about shifts, security rotations, and the adjustments needed to ensure my safety without compromising patient care. It's a lot to worry about, but I'm grateful for their thoroughness.

Finally, the paperwork is done.

"I think that's everything." Rhett stacks the documents into a folder. "I'll add you into the rotation this week. Oh, and I'm heading to Seattle tomorrow."

"Still traveling for the new cardiac program?" I ask. "How's that coming along?"

"It's going great." His eyes sparkle. "But yeah, I'm out of town frequently to collaborate with other specialists and secure the necessary funding."

"What kind of travel are we talking about?" Monty leans against the doorframe, arms folded across his chest.

"Mostly to major cities. I've been working closely with top hospitals in Seattle, San Francisco, and New York. They're helping me develop protocols and training programs to bring our cardiac care to the next level."

I nod, understanding the importance of his work. "I'm so happy for you, Rhett."

"Thanks. I'm also considering partnerships with medical research institutions to conduct joint studies. That means more travel, but it's necessary to ensure we provide the best care possible."

"With all this travel, who manages things here in your

absence?" Monty narrows his eyes.

"I put together a solid team and trust them completely. Plus, the travel is temporary. Once the program is fully implemented and the initial phase ends, I'll spend more time here to oversee everything personally."

"You need to communicate the security situation to the entire trauma team here." Monty rubs his jaw, his expression pensive. "I want to be in daily contact with whoever is in charge while you're gone."

"I understand." Rhett nods.

"Thank you, both of you," I say, "for arranging the security measures."

"If you ever feel unsafe, please let us know." Rhett extends a hand. "Welcome back, Frankie."

I shake it, smiling through my nerves. "It's good to be back."

After a round of goodbyes with the hospital staff, Monty and I leave the hum of the trauma unit behind and step outside. The shadows in the parking lot hover in my periphery, but with Monty's hand on my back, I feel safe.

We return the hypercar to his garage and catch a ride with his chauffeur, Kai, back to the dock.

As Monty and I step onto the boardwalk leading to the yacht, an eerie silence blankets the night.

His hand remains firmly and reassuringly pressed to my lower back, but I can't shake the feeling that something is wrong.

My ears prick at every sound, my eyes darting in every direction. The feeling of being watched follows me all the way to the yacht.

The security guard stationed at the entrance stands at attention, his face impassive.

"All good, Stanley?" Monty asks as we board.

"Yes, Mr. Novak."

Monty quickly pulls the lines from the dock cleats and prepares to depart. I kick off my heels and lean against the taffrail, watching him work.

"I'll get the last one." As I bend down to free the line, I

glimpse something out of the corner of my eye. Something that shouldn't be there.

A dark blob sits on the dock beside the cleat.

My heart lurches.

"Wait." I spin toward Monty, grabbing his arm. "Do you see that?"

He follows my gaze, his eyes narrowing.

"What the—?" He motions for me to stay and takes off toward the gangway.

Fuck that.

I race after him, ignoring his glare as we approach the strange object.

A few feet away, my breath hitches.

The moonlight glints off something metallic.

A fillet knife.

Then the rest comes into view.

A severed human hand.

With the palm down and fingers splayed, a knife plunges through it, pinning it to the wooden dock.

Attached to the blade is a note, undoubtedly written to me.

Bile hits the back of my throat as my mind swims.

Whose fucking hand is that?

My first thought is Denver. The stalker already sent his heart. Maybe all the pieces of him will show up, bit by bloody bit.

Please let that be Denver's hand.

I inch forward for a closer inspection.

"Stay back." Monty's face hardens, his jaw clenched in fury.

When I take another step forward, he pulls me back, shielding me from the gruesome sight.

"Stanley!" he shouts.

The security guard rushes over, his eyes widening in shock. "I was here the whole time, sir. I didn't see or hear anything."

The rest of the guards spread out around us, securing the perimeter.

"We need to alert the authorities," Carl says, his voice steady.

Monty nods. "Do it. And get more men out here. Lock this place down."

"I need to see it." I push around him, crouching down. "I need to know."

He lowers to his haunches beside me, grabbing my arm, ready to yank me back as if I'll try to touch it.

I dug human bones out of the ashes at Hoss. But this is different. It still has skin and blood, and it's fucking fresh.

"It can't be Denver's," I whisper. "The fingers are too thin, too smooth. I know every scar on both of his hands. There were a lot of them. This one..."

"Doesn't have any distinguishing marks."

Except for the knife running through it.

Not just any knife. I recognize the faded wooden handle, cracked with use.

"That's the fillet knife." A gasp escapes me. "The one Denver used when he stabbed Kody's hand on the table."

"Are you sure?"

"I would never forget it. I had to wash it after Kody removed it."

"Are you okay?" His blue eyes search mine.

"I'm not panicking." *Not yet.* I pull out my phone and illuminate the grisly appendage with the flashlight.

"Here." He takes the device from me, shining the light. "Do you recognize the hand?"

"No. It doesn't belong to Leo or Kody."

I know their hands better than my own. But I'm desperate to call them, hear their voices, and confirm they're okay.

"Wolfson?" He chokes.

My vision blurs as I peer closer, trying to rule him out.

"It's a man's hand. Wolf didn't have scars on his. But he always had them covered in black ink." My chin quivers. "I don't know, Monty." My entire body trembles. "We need to see what the note says."

Grimly, he pulls it free from the blade, careful not to touch the hand. Unfolding it, he reads aloud, his voice low and tight with anger. "Happy anniversary, little girl. He will never touch you again."

frankie

An icy shiver runs down my spine, pooling dread in my stomach.

Who?

I meet Monty's eyes. "Who touched me?"

"A dozen different people at the hospital tonight."

"Rhett." I grab my phone from his grip. "I have to call him."

"And Doyle." Standing, he removes his device and turns to the waiting guard. "Is the yacht secure?"

"Yes." Carl steps forward. "You should wait there."

As Monty wraps an arm around me, guiding me back on board, the threat feels more real than ever, pressing in from all sides.

In the main cabin, I start to dial Rhett when a text comes in.

Unknown number: How will your date end? If you go to bed with the wolf, will the bear and the lion fuck the siren?

Every muscle in my body coils, ready to spring or flee. But I'm paralyzed.

I glance at Monty, but he's already looking at me, his eyes sharpening, seeing it all on my face.

He plucks the phone from my trembling hands.

Fleeting shadows dart across his expression as he reads before his features settle into a chilling, impenetrable calm.

When he types a reply, it bounces back with a *No longer in service* response.

Clutching my hand, he leads me to the cabinet where he stores the satellite phone.

"Talk to the guys." He presses numbers into the receiver and hands it to me. "I'll call Rhett and Doyle."

As the call connects, he steps a few feet away with his phone to his ear.

"Monty?" Leo answers on the first ring.

My knees buckle, and I slide down the cabinet to the floor. "It's me. Is Kody with you?"

"He's right here, love. What happened?"

"We received another delivery."

I tell them about the knife, the hand, the note, and text message. Then I have to explain why I was off the island, the dinner, the visit to the hospital, and the significance of the date. They didn't know today was the day Denver took me.

But Doyle knew.

By the time I finish answering their questions about my final therapy session with Doyle, Monty returns and sits on the floor beside me.

"Rhett is still at the hospital." A muscle in his jaw bounces. "Doyle isn't answering."

My chest collapses.

"Why the fuck did you leave the island?" Kody growls through the phone loud enough that Monty hears him.

He takes the receiver from me. "Calm your ass down."

They argue back and forth until Carl enters the cabin, announcing the local police are here.

"Listen to me," Monty says into the phone. "I'm taking her home and keeping her safe. Don't you dare try to fly back tonight. Wait until morning when it's safe to fly. Use your fucking head." He listens, nodding. "I know. We're not letting this bastard win. We'll find him." Another pause. "She'll call you when we're back on the island. Yeah, you, too."

He disconnects and turns his attention to me. "How are you doing?"

"Fantastic." I grit my teeth. "How did they get so close to the yacht without being seen?"

"He's been watching, waiting for the perfect moment."

"How do you know it's a *he*?"

"I don't. But that note...my gut tells me this nutjob isn't just an admirer. He's possessive and jealous and wants you for himself."

He will never touch you again.

What does that mean for Leo and Kody? And Monty, too? Will their body parts show up next?

"We'll get through this." Monty pulls me close, his arms banding around me in a protective embrace. "We'll end him. I promise."

Unless the stalker is Wolf.

frankie

Not all wounds bleed. Not all scars show. Some live beneath bones, cold and alone. In the chambers of frost, pain is my art.

Until we find his body, I'm not giving up on him.

Kodiak

FORTY-ONE

Longing.

Fierce, protective longing rages inside me. I stand at the taffrail beside Leo as Kai navigates Monty's yacht toward the island.

Toward Frankie.

Despite the midday heat, the arctic wilderness still clings to my bones. Another fruitless week spent searching for Wolf's body and the cabin.

Frustration sinks in its claws, shredding vital organs. Every time we leave Frankie alone with Monty, the anger coils tighter.

A stalker on the loose, a human heart, a severed hand, more texts, and disturbing threats...enough is enough.

My eyes land on the dock as we approach. Two small yachts sit there, their polished surfaces reflecting the low Alaskan sun. They look brand new and expensive. Typical Monty.

I shift my gaze, and there she is.

My heart stirs from hibernation and starts to beat again.

Long red hair tangles around her shoulders, her petite

frame dwarfed by the towering, imposing man at her side.

How will your date end? If you go to bed with the wolf, will the bear and the lion fuck the siren?

A hot dart of jealousy pierces my gut.

He took her on a date last night.

He took her on a fucking date.

Did he take her to bed after?

I understand why they went to dinner, the importance of the one-year mark. I'm even grateful he was there for her. She shouldn't be alone. At the same time, I resent every moment he spends with her.

Her ban on sex makes it harder to stomach.

It's been almost two months since we've been intimate. The distance isn't just physical. It's emotional, straining our bond like a thread pulled taut, ready to snap.

The yacht docks, and Leo and I disembark, our strides purposeful. She rushes toward us, and we envelop her in a crushing embrace, sandwiching her between our bodies.

Our relationship has become a cycle of farewells and hellos. The separations feel wrong, unnatural, like the gray zone between life and death.

But the reunions. Each time we meet again feels like I'm breathing for the first time.

"Missed you," I murmur against her hair, inhaling her scent.

She smells like everything I miss. Warm skin. Ripe cherries. Sultry, sweet sex. *Frankie.*

"I've been so fucking worried." Leo kisses her nose, her cheek, her lips. "Tell me you're okay."

"I'm okay." She stares up at us, green eyes shimmering. "Now that you're here. I'm so glad you're safe."

"Welcome home." Monty pats me on the shoulder. "We have much to discuss."

He turns, heading back to the estate.

Security guards stand among the tall pine trees lining the path. Their numbers have doubled.

I lengthen my strides to catch up with him. "What's with the yachts?"

He pauses, his jaw sharp enough to cut steel.

"They're yours." He reaches into his pocket and pulls out two sets of keys. "Congratulations." He hands a set to Leo. "You're only one exam away from finishing flight school." Pressing the other keyring into my palm, he briefly squeezes my hand. "Your distillery opens to the public next week. I wanted to celebrate your achievements."

Leo and I exchange stunned looks.

"You're kidding?" Voice gruff with disbelief, Leo stares back at the yachts.

"Not kidding. And there's more. Each keyring has an extra set of keys. There are BMW GS motorcycles waiting for you in my garage in Sitka. Consider them part of the gift."

The warmth in my face wars with the chill in my stomach. "We can't accept this. It's too much."

"We haven't earned it." Leo tries to hand back the keys.

"You've worked your asses off." Frankie sidles between us, pushing Leo's hand back. "Don't be rude. Giving you these gifts already makes Monty feel awkward." Her lips twitch. "And dangerously in touch with his feelings. Just accept that he loves you."

"Just take them." Monty sighs, his expression pinched with annoyance.

Silence follows. The significance of his gesture, the search in the Arctic, the work that still needs finishing at the distillery, the strain on our relationship with Frankie, and the stalker—it's all a powder keg waiting to explode.

"Thank you," I finally say. "This means more than you know."

Leo grips his nape, nodding, looking uncomfortable as fuck.

"You're welcome." Monty continues along the path and steps inside the entryway. "We're waiting for the hand to be analyzed. The authorities are involved now, which will slow down the investigation. But I'm still moving forward with Wilson."

"Wilson doesn't have any updates for us." Frankie lowers

onto the couch, tucking her legs beneath her. "But Doyle Whitaker is missing. After our therapy session yesterday, he never returned to his house in Sitka."

"He's either the stalker," Monty says.

"Or the victim." She rubs her chest, her brow furrowing in thought. "The security team sweeps this place for cameras every day. Someone is watching and listening as if they know us. As if they're one of us." She meets my eyes. "Sirena could be involved. She knows about Wolf and the cabin."

"No one has told her about Denver or the stalker," I say.

"What if she found the cabin long before you started helping her?" She squints at me. "She could've found Wolf, Denver, and that fillet knife."

"How did she deliver those things last night while she was in Fairbanks with us?" Leo shakes his head.

"With help." She shrugs. "The woman is resourceful. Is she still trying to fuck you?"

"Is *he* still trying to fuck *you*?" Leo thrusts a finger at Monty.

"Yes." Monty leans against the wall, legs crossed at the ankles. "Trying and failing. None of this is helping. We can't rule out Sirena. Her involvement doesn't seem plausible, but we must consider every angle."

Leo releases a snarling string of curses and paces the room.

"If we could just find that fucking cabin." I slump onto the couch beside her. "It's like it doesn't exist."

"We'll find it," Monty says with a confidence that I've come to admire. "When do you leave on the next scouting mission?"

"Not for a while. Leo needs to take his exam, and I have a distillery to open."

"Once it's open, finding time for anything else will be hard." She reaches for my hand, lacing our fingers.

"I'll make time."

I can see it in her face. The doubt. I haven't made time for her in weeks.

Once the distillery is running and the stalker is found, I'll dedicate the rest of my life to her. I'll give her the epilogue she wants.

With a lot of sex.

We spend the rest of the day scrutinizing the details of the investigation, looking for things we've missed, and ensuring we're all on the same page.

That night, Leo and Monty slip away to discuss Monty's proposal for the seaplane base.

Leo has decided to accept the offer. We've talked about it often over the past month, and he's grown past his distrust for Monty.

So have I.

"Let's go to bed." I lift her from the couch and carry her up the stairs to the room she sleeps alone in more often than not.

She doesn't try to wriggle free. Instead, she coils her arms around my shoulders and buries her face in my neck, telling me without words how much she missed me.

I don't need to wonder how her date ended last night. She would never betray Leo and me.

After we undress and wash away the day's stress, we turn off the light and climb under the covers.

"What are your plans tomorrow?" She drags her fingers through my hair, massaging my scalp.

"Going back to work."

The renovations are finished, but I'm still putting the final touches on my handcrafted vodka recipes. I retained most of the staff from *Tipsy Sailor*, but there's training to be done and so many little details to finalize.

I wish I could take her to work with me. She hasn't seen the renovated space. But it's too dangerous. I don't want her to leave the island.

"I'm going back to work, too." Her hand tightens in my hair.

"What?" I rear back.

"Shh." She pulls me back to the pillow. "Listen, you brute. I'm surrounded by security guards. Here. There. Every fucking where. Monty took me to the hospital last night to arrange the details for my safety. I'll be under constant watch with guards and cameras and hospital staff at all times. Kody, I need this." Her voice wavers, her eyes pleading. "I won't let this stalker control my life and keep me prisoner."

"Frankie..." My temples pound.

"And I'm going to the opening for your distillery." She sets her jaw. "I'm not missing it."

"Christ, woman." I bring our foreheads together. "You're going to take years off my life."

"You said that in the hills. We're still alive. Still fighting. This is what we do. We survive."

"I'm sorry about yesterday." My pulse thuds, heavy and sluggish. "I didn't know. I should've worked out the date."

"It's not a day I wanted to remember. But four days after I was abducted..." She dusts her mouth across mine. "I met three beautiful, feral men." She bites my lip. "I met you."

"That's a day to remember." I tug her hips against mine, fitting us together.

"Will there come a time when I tire of my compulsion to be touched and kissed by you?"

"Don't count on it."

Our tongues collide, and sparks fly across my skin. Our hands roam, each fingertip a brushstroke of electricity, singeing my nerve endings.

We kiss and touch and reconnect for the rest of the night. My cock throbs. My balls ache. But I don't break her rules. I promised I would wait.

Besides, my desire extends beyond sex. My all-consuming need for her is this. Our connection. The intimacy that exists between us.

I only need her to look at me, see me, and feel the temptation as I feel it with her.

And she does.

With a kiss that lasts hours.

With an embrace that doesn't break.

With a whisper of love on her lips that no one can take.

Three days later, Coast Guardsmen find a submerged boat in the Sitka Sound. The investigation concludes that a damaged hull caused the vessel to take on water, lose buoyancy, and capsize in rough waters.

The boat belonged to Doyle Whitaker.

No body has been recovered.

Doyle is still missing.

But the fingerprints on the dismembered hand confirm what we already suspected.

He will never touch you again.

Doyle's hand was hacked off with the fillet knife, messily, passionately, without precision or surgical training.

That doesn't rule out the medical staff at the hospital, but it makes my colleagues a little less suspect.

Of course, the men in my life don't agree.

Despite their roaring, chest-pounding, overprotective objections, I return to work.

Stepping into the trauma unit in my scrubs feels like emerging from a long, dark tunnel into the blinding light.

The familiar sterile scent of the hospital, the beeping

monitors, the hushed conversations of doctors and nurses, all greet me like old friends.

I've missed this. The routine, the purpose, the *distraction.*

The hospital staff welcomes me back warmly, even those I don't know outside the ER. But there's an undercurrent of curiosity and pity in their eyes. Everyone knows about my situation.

My captivity was all over the news. And the stalker...well, small towns like Sitka don't keep secrets.

Doesn't help that I have security stationed at every entry point and following me everywhere.

Now that we know the stalker dismembers people who touch me, I'm not the only one with personal guards. Leo, Kody, and Monty don't leave the house without their own armed shadows. Additionally, we all have GPS tracking on our phones and can monitor one another's whereabouts at all times.

Whispers and sympathetic gazes follow me through the hospital. I ignore it and focus on my tasks, relishing the sense of normalcy.

But normalcy is a fragile thing.

An hour into my shift, I'm standing at the nurses' station, updating patient records with my back to the door, when a gasp sounds beside me.

"Holy Thor." Nurse Letty claps a hand to her chest. "Did anyone else just lose their breath?"

I freeze.

Oh, no.

"I've died and gone to Valhalla," another nurse says. "I didn't know they made men like that anymore."

No, no, no.

I spin and come face to face with glowing, savage, mismatched eyes.

"What are you doing here?" I glance down the hall.

Every woman in the vicinity stares in our direction.

At him.

If they didn't have a Viking kink, they have one now. He's going to cause a damn riot.

frankie

Leonid Strakh stands under the fluorescent lights looking for all the world like Ragnar Lothbrok has arrived to conquer Britain.

If Britain was me.

Small, tight braids run from his temples, down behind his ears, and twist into a knot on the back of his head, leaving the rest of his hair tangled around his corded neck. Add the sculpted features, chiseled jawline, and leonine scowl, and the man epitomizes Viking savagery and warrior ethos.

When he notices all the female onlookers, he curls his lip like a carnivore, sending them stumbling back and gasping.

Some of them giggle.

I can't feel my legs.

A white T-shirt molds to his muscled frame. Those low-waisted jeans should be illegal on his powerful physique. But it's his eyes that strike terror in the trauma unit. One molten gold, the other icy blue, they burn and freeze simultaneously, exuding a dangerous aura that buzzes the air.

The women in the corridor can't help but stare. And swoon. If a heart monitor sounded right now, no one would respond. Even the men have fallen under his trance.

"Leo." Forcing a smile, I stride toward him, grab his wrist, and drag him around the corner. "You can't be here."

"Stay there." He jabs a finger at one of his personal guards and sweeps me into an empty cubicle, closing the curtain.

Pressing against me, he traps me with his body and weakens me with his scent. The dark, masculine aroma of motorcycle exhaust wraps around me, draws me in, makes my pulse quicken, and my breath catch.

And his face. Lord help me, he's beautiful and fierce. Godlike and predatory. High cheekbones, straight nose, and lips that could tempt the Virgin Queen of England.

My body betrays me, heat pooling low in my belly, a flush creeping up my neck. It takes everything in me to compose myself, to remember where I am and what I'm here to do.

My heart races, but I force a calm I don't feel, pulling away with practiced professionalism.

"This is ridiculous." He reaches for me again. "You're risking your life."

"So are you. I'm working." I stop him with a hand on his chest. "I have guards, and you're supposed to be studying for an exam."

"I don't need to study."

"I don't need you causing a scene in the ER. Go to the distillery and help Kody."

His gaze bores into mine, giving me the full force of his arctic animalism. It's too much, the intensity of those eyes, the way they strip me bare. But I stand my ground, meeting that primal expression head-on.

"It's my first day." I square my shoulders, trying to inject authority into my posture. "Don't fuck this up for me."

He doesn't move at first. Then, without warning, he clamps a hand around my nape, fingers tangling in my hair.

"Leo—"

His mouth crashes into mine, and he kisses me with the wild, feral anger that lives inside him. He kisses me like a man starved, as if he waited a lifetime for this moment. His lips demand and bruise, leaving no space for hesitation or second thoughts.

I should push him away, should remind him—and myself—this is neither the time nor the place. But the fire in his kiss consumes me, igniting the desperation between us. I climb his mountainous frame, fingers digging into the muscled slopes of his shoulders, losing myself in his vicious raid.

Time ceases to exist. There's only the heat of his mouth, the roughness of his touch, the taste of him—his danger and desire. I don't want this moment to end as he tears us apart and puts us back together again.

Too soon, he pulls back, leaving me breathless and aching. His hand lingers on my neck, fingers caressing my skin.

"Remember that." He steps back, grinning through his anger.

"Dammit, Leo." I touch my mouth and straighten my bun. "Does it look like I've been making out?"

"Yeah, love. Swollen lips for days."

With that, he turns and strides out, leaving me dizzy and trembling.

What was I thinking? I shouldn't have let him kiss me here.

Idiot.

The scent of him lingers, pissing me off as I try to gather the shattered pieces of my composure.

I'm here to do a job, a meaningful one. I can't afford to let him distract me.

But as I force myself back to my duties, the taste of him still on my lips, I know he didn't leave. I sense his eyes on me, a burning brand that both comforts and suffocates.

The trauma unit is a whirlwind of activity, but I slip back into my role with ease. My hands remember the motions, my mind the protocols. I'm a nurse, capable and competent, and no amount of time away can change that.

Even with Leo watching and following me like one of the guards.

I see him in the hallway, his eyes locked on me. It's distracting, infuriating. I can't do my job with him hovering like this.

Not to mention how often I jump when someone walks up behind me. I'm constantly looking over my shoulder, fighting random shivers, and trying to convince myself I'm not being watched.

But I *am* being watched. Not just by Leo and security. Someone is out there, a murderer, a stalker, monitoring everything I do.

Hours pass, and I'm engrossed in my tasks, but the atmosphere remains tense.

As I tend to a patient, I struggle with a tricky IV setup. The sterile packaging and intricate components feel foreign in my hands after so long.

Paul, a fellow nurse and an old friend, steps in. "Need help with that?"

"Please. It's been a while since I've used one of these." I pass him part of the kit.

As he quickly assists me, we exchange a brief smile, a

moment of camaraderie.

"Good to see you back, Frankie." He helps me finish the task, resting a hand on my arm for balance as he leans around me.

"Thanks." I turn to find Leo storming into the private cubicle.

"What are you talking to her about?" His eyes flare with possessive jealousy, his posture aggressive.

"Just work stuff, man." Paul steps back. "Chill."

Leo doesn't chill. He never chills. His fists clench, and steam rises from his ears. "Keep your hands off her."

I step between them, flattening a palm on Leo's chest. "Paul is my coworker, and you're not supposed to be in here."

"He's flirting with you," Leo snaps, his eyes never leaving the other man.

"Seriously?" Anger spikes, slamming my molars together.

I have a patient lying in the bed two feet away, for fuck's sake.

"Back off." Paul stands his ground, refusing to be intimidated. "You're overreacting."

The situation escalates in a blink.

Leo shoves Paul, sending him stumbling back. My heart races as the security guards spring into action, separating them and escorting Leo out of the hospital.

"Get your hands off me!" He roars, but the guards outnumber him.

"Leo, stop!" I shout, but it's too late.

As they drag him away, a cold, nauseous stab of pain pummels through me.

Every instinct urges me to run after him.

I don't want to send mixed signals, but dammit, I love him. He was thrust into a new world, and he's still adjusting and adapting. He deserves grace, and I need to find a way to give him that while standing my ground.

Following them outside, I ask the guards to give us space. When they step away, I reach for Leo's scowling face and guide his forehead down to mine.

"I love you," I whisper against his warm mouth. "Forever."

Instead of words, he responds with his body, sliding his arms around me and kissing my lips.

"I'm not going anywhere." I rake my fingers through his short beard and around to his nape. "I'll be right here. Safe with my guards."

"They don't protect you from all the drooling males in scrubs."

"Leo." I lean back to stare at him. "How can we have a healthy relationship if you can't trust me to work with men?"

He blinks, huffs a frustrated sound, and glances toward the hospital entrance. Turning back, he ensnares me with a look of such ferocious concentration that I take a step backward.

He stays with me.

The intimacy we share is so profound and overwhelming it robs me of breath. I see the same struggle in his gaze, the mutual desire and anguish.

"Frankie." A breathless whisper. Then he kisses me with a fierce, desperate hunger.

Through it all, our eyes remain open and connected.

"I'll try," he breathes against my mouth. "I'll do better."

"Me, too."

Reluctantly, he lets me go.

"Go help Kody at the distillery," I say.

He inclines his head, and I return to work.

My attempt at normalcy is fucked. The whispers and curious glances from my colleagues sting, but I push them aside and focus on my job.

The rest of the day passes in a blur. I go through the motions, but my mind is elsewhere, replaying the scene over and over. By the time my shift ends, I'm exhausted, physically and emotionally.

The cool night air hits my flushed face as I step outside with the guards. Scanning the lot, I'm not surprised to find Leo waiting for me in the shadows.

"How long has he been here?" I ask Jasper behind me.

"He never left."

I worked a twelve-hour shift, and he stood in the parking

lot.

His devotion makes my chest hurt, deeply and sorrowfully.

He looks as haggard as I feel, leaning against his BMW motorcycle. I wonder how many women passed out when they saw him on that thing.

"Will you be riding to the harbor with Mr. Strakh?" Jasper asks.

"Yeah."

"We'll follow you there."

"Give us a minute." I stride toward my infuriating snow cabin boy, reminding myself he's only been in the civilized world for four months.

We'll have setbacks, and we'll learn from them. It's part of the process.

But that fresh crease of pain on his forehead is my doing, and it breaks my heart.

"Leo." I sigh. "What are you doing?"

"I couldn't stay away. You're not safe here." He reaches for my hand. "I need to protect you."

"Protect me from working? We talked about this." My voice rises, drawing the attention of passersby. "I can't do my job under your constant surveillance."

"Do you know what it's like? This relentless, clawing fucking need to shackle you to my side and force you back to safety? It rides me, Frankie. Day and night, it rides me so fucking hard I can't sleep, can't think. I can't breathe without you in my sight."

"I know. I'm sorry." I pull in a ragged breath. "But you can get help with this. You can see a therapist."

He doesn't argue. He just watches me with those strange, haunted eyes as if he's losing me on a level that's making him crazed.

I understand their reluctance to talk to someone. Their childhood abuse is so deep and painful. Reliving it again, exposing it, and dissecting it is terrifying and traumatic. They won't even open up to me about it.

But until they confront it, their relationship with me will never be healthy.

"Let's go." He stuffs a helmet on my head and straddles the bike, firing it up.

I climb onto the seat and lock my arms around his muscled torso. The instant he takes off, I'm transported back to the hills. With the wind in my hair and his body vibrating between my legs, I'm on the snow machine again.

Despite my turmoil, I love it.

I love this man, with his untamed temper, his unconditional loyalty, and even his surly protectiveness.

But we need to find a balance.

Something has to give.

The days that follow are more of the same. I work back-to-back shifts, and Leo shows up at the start of every one, sometimes with Kody in tow.

Each time I step into the hospital, I brace myself for the inevitable confrontation. Leo's eyes track my every movement. He never seems to sleep, his vigilance unyielding. Kody is quieter but no less present, his brooding figure a shadow in the background.

As I step out for a break during my third shift, I find Monty in the lobby, talking to the head of security.

His icy blue eyes meet mine, and I sag.

What now?

I stride over, my voice tight with exhaustion. "What are you doing here?"

"Just checking on things." He clasps his hands behind him, his attire all business, from the crisp white shirt and suit jacket to the shiny expensive shoes. "Making sure everything's secure."

"Is that really necessary? I have enough security."

"Clearly, it is." He glances toward Leo and Kody, who stand a few feet away, glaring back. "I'm trying to keep the peace."

"This has to stop." I rub my temples. "I can't work with all this...drama. They're going to get me fired."

"I know." His expression softens. "I'm trying to help."

"You want to help? Make them leave. They won't listen to me."

"I can instruct security to escort them out and prevent them from entering again." He quirks a brow. "Is that what you want?"

I shake my head, though I'm not entirely certain. I want them to be able to visit during my breaks or stop by if they need something.

As I turn to head back to the ER, I catch a glimpse of them, their expressions dark and aggressive.

Changing directions, I make a beeline for them and stop just out of arm's reach.

"A mat placed outside an exterior door for wiping shoes before entering." I rest my fists on my hips, watching their features twist in confusion. "A person who is physically weak and ineffectual."

"I don't understand." Leo tilts his head.

"What is a doormat?"

"That's not—"

"Not me? You're walking all over me and treating me like I have no common sense, self-preservation, or opinions of my own."

"Keeping you protected," Kody growls, "does not turn you into a doormat."

"I love you both. So much. If you love me a fraction as much, please leave until the end of my shift. Or stay outside. I'm trying to do my job, and I'm asking you to respect that."

Without waiting, I return to the trauma unit.

They don't leave, and an hour before my shift ends, the tension finally boils over.

I'm in the middle of helping a patient when a brawl breaks out in the corridor. I race out of the room and find Kody pinning Paul against the wall.

"Say it again," Leo snarls in Paul's face.

"Get your hands off me." Paul struggles against Kody's grip.

"Let him go!" I charge toward them, balling my fists. "Kody!"

"Tell her what you said." Leo points angrily at me.

The guards rush forward, but I step in their path, holding up a hand.

"Wait. Let me try." I turn back to Paul. "What did you say?"

"I just said you're pretty, Frankie." He bucks against Kody, going nowhere. "It's true. Everyone knows it."

I close my eyes and count to three. Then I glare at Kody. "Let him go."

"He's been staring at your ass all day." Kody shoves him before releasing him. "I confronted him about it, and he commented on your looks."

"Inappropriate, Paul." I glower at him and shift my glare to Kody and Leo. "Go home."

They plant their boots and cross their arms.

I see red.

Pivoting on my heel, I stride to the nurses' station to transfer my patients to the next shift and wrap things up.

Then I leave.

I ride back to the island with the security guards in silence. My mind screams with accusations and ultimatums. But I wait until we're in the privacy of the estate.

Leo and Kody hover nearby all the way home, stewing in their own thoughts.

They got what they wanted. I left the hospital. I'm returning to my prison.

But I'm not giving up. I refuse to back down. I need to work, to live. And I won't let them stop me.

When we reach the house, I turn to them, my heart aching.

"This isn't working," I say quietly. "This…whatever we're doing, it's not healthy."

"What happened?" Monty steps into the sitting room, taking in the standoff.

I quickly update him on the recent drama and turn back to Leo and Kody. "We need to change."

"What are you saying?" Leo's jaw tightens.

"I'm saying you need help. Talk to someone. We can't keep going like this, smothering each other, fighting over me. It's tearing us apart."

"You're not safe." Kody's eyes harden. "Someone is out there, killing people and sending their body parts to you like trophies."

"Paul is not a murderer."

"You don't know that," Kody says. "I can't lose you."

"You're not losing me." I reach out to touch his fisted hand. "But we need to find a way to be together that doesn't destroy us."

"I don't know how to do that." Leo grips his nape.

"You do it by not assaulting every man who looks at or talks to me. You do it by seeking help. There's so much anger inside both of you, and maybe that kept you alive in the hills. But we're not in the hills anymore."

"We shouldn't have left." Kody strides from the room. "We don't belong here."

"You don't mean that."

Leo follows him out without a word, leaving me with Monty.

Turning to him, I don't expect his help. He's not here to solve my relationship problems with other men. More likely, he would use the situation to his advantage.

But as he watches me, his gaze deepens. The air thickens.

Our dinner conversation hangs between us. My fantasy. His knowing. That newfound connection pulls us closer and closer together, charged and breathless.

"They need more time," he says in a caressing tone, meant to soothe.

Because he loves me. He wants me to be happy.

"Time." I nod.

I'll hold onto that. I'll try to hold us all together, but it feels like we're unraveling too fast.

Every day is a battle, every moment a test of our bond.

I demand change, and they refuse to admit they need help.

They're a raging storm, wild and uncontrollable, their love for me a fierce, consuming fire.

I can't help the feeling that something bad is coming, that something terrible is barreling our way. Not just with the stalker.

With us.

My feelings for Monty...I didn't want to fall in love with

him again. I fought it. I clung to my anger for so long.

But I'm no longer angry.

I'm scared.

No matter how this ends, someone gets hurt.

Someone ends up alone.

Part of me wonders if I'm the terrible thing that's coming.

Am I the one who will tear us apart?

Can I fight my love for Monty? I haven't admitted it out loud. Not to him. Not to Leo and Kody.

But how does that help?

I don't know how long I can fight this battle alone.

Tonight is Kody's grand opening.

Anticipation thrums through me as I stand before the mirror.

The black knee-length cocktail dress fits perfectly, creating a sleek silhouette that flatters my small frame and modest chest. I styled my hair in red waves down my back, and my green eyes, accentuated by smoky makeup, gleam with excitement and nerves.

For the first time in a long while, I feel genuinely beautiful.

"Frankie!" Monty calls from downstairs. "We're going to be late."

"Coming!"

Kody left hours ago with his security team to oversee the final details. He's put so much into the distillery, pouring his passion into this dream.

I take a deep breath. Tonight is a big deal. The press will be present, as well as vodka critics from all over the world.

It's his chance to step out of the shadows of his past and into something new. Time to prove how far he's come and how much he's survived.

As I descend the grand staircase, the sound of hushed voices accompanies the click of my heels.

"You know what's bothering me?" Leo whispers. "Where the fuck is Doyle's body? He could've cut off his own hand. That's all I'm saying."

"Why would he remove his dominant hand?" Monty asks. "If he's going to cut one off, wouldn't it be the one he least used? For that matter, why not just send a finger? A whole hand seems like overkill."

"Lovely conversation, boys." I step into view and find them waiting for me at the bottom of the stairs.

My blood runs hot.

Damn.

Monty and Leo, standing side by side.

Double damn.

What a devastating pair of gorgeous, potent lady-killers.

I wince. Maybe *killer* isn't the word I should be thinking, but fuck them and their heart-attack-inducing sex appeal.

Monty looks every bit the regal billionaire mogul in a black tailored tuxedo that fits him like a second skin. With his stormy blue eyes, squared jawline, and arrogant demeanor, he's a paragon of refined masculinity.

As he holds my gaze, the one-year separation in our marriage fades away. In a fragile moment, I stand before my husband as we once were—devoted, happy, and deeply in love.

I know things about this man, secrets no one else knows.

I know he has a soft spot for classic romantic movies, but he only watches them late at night when he thinks no one's around.

I know he keeps a collection of vintage toy cars in a hidden cabinet in his office. Each vehicle represents a milestone in his career, and he talks to them as if they're old friends.

I know he insists on tucking me into bed whenever I fall asleep on the couch. Even now, after everything. Even if it means carrying me to the guest bedroom when Leo and Kody are out of town. It's a simple act of care and tenderness that he's never shown another person.

And I know he pines for me as much as I secretly pine for

him, and it's unfair. It's unfair to him. It's unfair to Leo and Kody, and I don't know what to do.

"Fucking hell, love." Leo's deep rumble grabs my attention. His gaze crawls over me, making my entire body twitch. "Look at you. Absolutely breathtaking."

"Breathtaking doesn't begin to cover it," Monty rasps. "I think she might be magic."

Heat rises in my cheeks. While they eat me alive with their eyes, I can't tear my attention away from Leo.

He's a revelation. I've never seen him dressed up, let alone dressed like this. I try to reconcile the wild, mechanic-scented, arctic Viking with the man standing before me in an expensive black tuxedo.

His shoulder-length brown hair, usually windblown and tangled, is meticulously braided and pulled back into a sexy, savage knot that accentuates his chiseled features.

I love the way his muscled frame fills out the tux. The contrast of those classy lines against his feral beauty is a stunning juxtaposition. He looks like a savage prince, draped in the finery of civilization while refusing to be tamed.

God knows I haven't tamed him. I would never try. I only want him to stay out of jail and not be so angry.

My relationship with him and Kody remains in discord. We kiss and touch and sleep in the same bed, but a gulf of unresolved shit churns between us, leaving a constant ache in my throat.

Not tonight. I'm not going to let it upset me tonight.

As I stride toward him, he anticipates what I want, leaning down so I can press my nose to his neck.

Delicious. Cedar, spice, and something sensual and primal swirls from his skin. My body responds with a powerful pull, tight and relentless, my nipples hardening beneath the dress.

"You both look so handsome." I clutch my throat, stepping back. "I'm incredibly fortunate to have you at my side tonight, even if it means fending off all the women vying for your attention. I'll be the envy of everyone there."

They exchange a glance and, quite possibly, a shared smile.

"Tonight, we're going to create something magical." Meeting their eyes, I take each of their hands in mine. "No fighting, no jealousy, no tempers flaring. We're setting aside our differences and showing up for Kody. You're his brothers. We're his greatest supporters."

They nod, and the air squeezes from my lungs. There are so many things I want to say but can't.

I love you both.

I love you emotionally, romantically, physically, eternally, in every way.

They're everything I've ever wanted, everything I've ever needed. And tonight, for just a few hours, all three of them are mine.

Monty offers his elbow, and I take it. Leo falls into step beside us, looping his arm around my back.

Then the three of us, bound by pain, blood, and marriage, make our way to the waiting yacht.

Halfway to the dock, something itches between my shoulder blades, compelling me to glance back at the house.

In the dining room window, a dark shape hovers. The outline of a man.

I squint, trying to make out his features.

"Monty." I pull on his arm, slowing his gait. "Did Oliver leave for the day?"

"I'm not sure." He stops, his brow furrowing in thought as he looks at Leo.

"I thought he left earlier." Leo toys with the ends of my hair. "Why?"

"He's watching us from the dining room," I say.

We all turn to look back at the house. But when we focus on the window, the shadow is gone.

"I must have been seeing things."

Monty's eyes linger on the house a moment longer before he nods. We continue on, the momentary disquiet dissolving as the anticipation of the evening takes over.

Thirty minutes later, we step onto the crowded sidewalk in front of the distillery. The first thing that strikes me is the sign on the building.

frankie

Strakh.

Kody kicked around a few ideas for the business name, but I'm glad he settled on this one. A name that carries such a dark history now has a chance to be redefined, to stand for something amazing and hopeful.

The turnout is more than we could've hoped. Lines of people snake out the door and around the block, their faces eager, the buzz of conversation and laughter charging the air. And more are coming, given the snarl of traffic that stretches down the street.

I'm so happy for him despite the knot of anxiety in my gut. The stalker could be anywhere, on the street, in the crowd, watching me. The thought bunches my shoulders around my ears.

A team of security guards flank us on all sides. They move with trained precision, securing the area as we approach the front entrance. The crowd parts for us, curious and admiring eyes following our progress.

I dig my nails into Monty's arm as Leo wraps his huge frame around my back. My guys press in even closer as we skip the line and push through the mob.

The guards at the entrance nod respectfully, allowing us to pass without hesitation.

We step inside. The noise and chaos of the outside world fade, replaced by a sprawling, welcoming space. Rich, dark woods and soft, ambient lighting set the tone. A large stone fireplace sits at the center. Plush leather chairs and fur throws invite visitors to sit and stay a while, to sink into comfort and let the experience wash over them.

Deep in my heart, I know this is just the beginning. Kody's dream has come to life, and for a moment, I forget my worries, basking in the glow of his success and the safety of those around me.

Leo and Monty have already seen the final renovations. I steal glances at them, my heart swelling. Leo catches my eye and grins, a roguish tilt to his lips. Monty squeezes my hand, his expression severe and vigilant as he leads us through the crowd.

The security guards discreetly position themselves to keep a watchful eye on us and the surroundings.

Everyone stares.

Walking between Monty and Leo, I've never felt so exposed and scrutinized. How do they deal with this level of attention everywhere they go?

And where's Kody?

Frantically searching the throngs of people, I let out a huge breath when I spot him behind the bar.

The bar itself is a work of art, hand-carved from a massive piece of timber and polished to a warm glow. And the owner...

He doesn't wear a tuxedo like Monty, Leo, and most other men here. No, he's dressed in starched jeans and a Henley, the fabric gripping his muscled frame in all the right places. His beard is gone, but the stubble on his jaw casts shadows over his striking features, giving him an air of rugged sophistication. This is dressed up for my caveman, a roughened, refined look that suits him perfectly.

He pours and serves drinks but is more than just a bartender. He's a storyteller, guiding guests through the rich history and intricate process of vodka making.

He looks up as we approach, and a galaxy of stars shines in his black eyes, transforming his broody expression into pure joy.

"Frankie." His dark drawl hitches my breath as he abandons his customers and prowls straight to me. "You made it."

"Wouldn't miss this for the world."

"Christ, woman." He steps into me, raking those predatory eyes up and down my body. "You're a goddamn meal."

His deep, slow words rumble, reverberating through sinew and bone. He's my comfort. My home.

"The place looks incredible." Monty grips Kody's neck and hauls him in for a hug, a rare display of affection that makes my pulse flutter. "Congratulations."

"Couldn't have done it without you." Kody leans back, resting a hand on Monty's jaw. "Thank you. For everything. I mean it."

"You're welcome." With a smirk, Monty scans the bustling, crowded establishment. "Looks like my investment is paying off."

"You've outdone yourself." Leo leans against the bar and hooks one of those muscle-packed arms around me, pulling me back into the safety of his body. "What's a guy gotta do around here to get a drink for his girl?"

"*Our* girl is getting a private tour by the owner." Kody turns, motioning over one of the female bartenders. "Hey, Sophie. Pour my brothers the good stuff. I'll be back."

Kody snatches my hand, steals me away from Leo, and tugs me through the crowd.

I glance back, snagging on Monty's unreadable eyes. He looks like he might chase us. Then he blinks and directs more guards to follow the two that already trail us.

An endless line of people stop Kody as we pass. Or they try anyway. He greets them with quick nods and rushed words without slowing. We breeze through intimate lounges and into a deep, long room.

"The tasting room." He waves a hand around and tugs me forward. "It's where you taste stuff."

Despite the number of people, the space feels like a well-orchestrated gathering. Clusters of guests form organic, fluid circles around the tasting tables. Employees scatter among them, encouraging the patrons to feel the grains and smell the fresh water sourced from nearby glacial streams.

A massive window offers a view of the distillery room, connecting guests to the process that brings their drinks to life.

I was hoping for a tour of that, but he drags me past it and into the kitchen.

The delicious aroma of cooking seeps into my lungs, and I laugh as he practically jogs past the chefs.

"Kody, slow down." I dig in my heels. "Walk me through the menu."

With a grunt—and seemingly great effort—he pauses and gestures at some of the prepared dishes. "Each dish is designed to enhance the flavors of the alcohol. The smoked salmon is served with a dill-infused vodka."

He rambles off a few more main courses and their vodka pairings, barely giving me time to absorb the rustic charm of the kitchen before tugging me toward the next room.

The distillery itself.

"Shiny room where magic happens." He moves quickly past the intricate equipment, not letting me linger. "It's shiny and magical."

"You're a terrible tour guide." I pause to admire the stills, only to be tugged forward again. "Worse than Wolf when he showed me Hoss."

I mean, I get it. He has a full house, hundreds of patrons waiting for his attention. I can tour his place anytime.

Once my life is safe again.

"We'll come back to that," he says when I slow down to admire the gleaming rows of vodka bottles with the *Strakh* logo.

I don't complain and let him haul me along, skipping the fascinating details and speeding through the heart of the distillery.

Finally, we reach a door at the back. I don't remember it being there when the renovations began.

One of his personal guards stands beside it, nodding at Kody as we approach.

"Is it secure?" Kody asks.

"Yes, Mr. Strakh."

Kody enters a code into the keypad and pulls me inside. "This is the highlight of the tour."

I glimpse a cozy studio apartment with a kitchenette, bathroom, and king-sized bed before he lifts me, hooks my legs around his waist, and pins me against the closed door.

Oh.

My.

Kodiak.

His mad dash was just an excuse to get us here, to this moment, so he can press his king-sized cock against me.

Lucky for him, there isn't a single bone in my body that will resist him. We're not under Monty's roof.

"The highlight?" Warm sparks tingle from my belly to my pussy as I dig my heels into the muscle of his ass.

"You, woman." He licks my throat, slowly dragging his tongue over my jaw and across my lips. "You're the highlight of the tour."

"You gonna fuck me right here against the door? Blink once for yes, twice for no."

He gives me one hard blink, setting me on fire.

"All those people are out there waiting for you." I bite his full, firm lips. "Better make it quick."

"Couldn't go slow if I tried." He sinks a hand between our bodies, quickly finding the crotch of my thong. "This fucking dress. I want to kill every man who sees you in it."

"Except your brothers."

He makes a sound in his throat. "Fifty-six days."

"What?"

"That's how long it's been since I've been inside you."

"We endured longer in the hills."

"We were *dying*. Physically dying from starvation. This is a different kind of death." He shoves the hem of my dress past my hips and releases the fly on his jeans. "I said I could wait, but...goddammit!"

As he frees his cock, I hang onto his shoulders, staring into those dark, pouty eyes, waiting for his command.

"Give me your mouth."

There it is.

I part my lips for him, and holy fucking shit, he invades. The instant our mouths touch, he goes mindless, the vicious thrust of his tongue showing me how quick and dirty the sex will be.

Lifting my hips over him, he pushes the thong aside and slots his monstrous erection at my entrance.

"Not even going to take my panties off?"

"Nope." Exhaling against my mouth, he pushes in.

Inch by inch, he works himself inside where we both need him to be.

Then he moves.

No grace. No technique. All feral power and unbearable tightness as he wall-bangs me through the door with his twelve-inch dick. Pretty sure I'll need stitches after this. But there's no stopping.

Gazes entwined, fusing deeper and deeper with each thrust, never letting go, we couldn't slow down to save our lives.

His mouth is a conqueror, plundering, devouring, taking over. He fucks me with the same brutality. The door creaks on its hinges, alerting the guard in the hall exactly what we're doing.

He has a whole party out there in his honor. So many people here to meet him. And he's with me. Eyes on me. Thoughts on me. Cock inside me.

He cares about nothing else.

His body tenses, coiling, and I know he's close.

"You need to come." He fucks into me like a man possessed. "Come, right now, woman."

He snarls and demands, and that's what sets me off.

Blinding, blasting, every color shimmers through my vision. Every nerve, every pore, every cell melts into the electrifying connection we share.

He continues to fuck me, claiming my pussy. Right now, it's his. He's the one impaling it, stretching it, ruining it, and filling it with come.

"Frankie!" He roars, staring into my eyes and spilling inside me. "Fuck. Fuck. So fucking good."

The kiss that follows is soft, nothing like the hard, demanding fuck against the door. But it was more than just a quickie. Words can't explain the depth of our bond. But his mouth can. His teeth, tongue, and cock can.

He licks my bottom lip and pulls back just enough to say, "I missed you."

"Missed you, too. Congratulations on *Strakh Vodka*." I palm his firm, bare ass then give it a hard slap. "Let's get you back. Your guests await."

FORTY-FOUR

Kody returns me to Leo and Monty with a lingering kiss on my brow. When he steps back, a breath of feelings whispers between us. Relief. Reconnection. Love.

He looks away first, a divot of a smile lifting the corner of his mouth. He's so damn beautiful.

As he returns to the bar to engage with the press, Monty and Leo converge on me from both sides.

Surrounded by vigilant security guards, the three of us stand tightly together at a high-top table in a private corner of the lounge.

From our position, we watch Kody behind the bar in his element. He moves with confidence, pouring drinks, answering questions, and talking passionately about his vodka. It's a side of him I've never seen.

"He looks so happy," I murmur.

"He deserves this." Monty's eyes soften. "He worked hard for it."

"He's going to be a worldwide sensation." Leo's hand brushes down my hip. "I'll fly him to all his engagements."

"When do you take your exam?" I lean against him.

"Took it this morning."

"You did?" My breath hikes. "I thought you were here with Kody this morning."

"I was here. Then I took the test." He lifts a shoulder. "I passed."

"You're a pilot." A feeling of breathlessness floats through me. "It's official. You did it."

"Yeah." His bicolored eyes shift to Monty. "And I own a seaplane base. Haven't decided what to do with it, but I'm leaning toward operating Alaskan tours."

"And flying Kody to his vodka engagements." I grin.

"Yeah."

We don't mention the search for the cabin and Wolf's body, but we're all thinking it. Now that Leo and Kody own their businesses, flying to the Arctic every week won't be possible.

I don't want them to put aside their dreams to chase the past. Monty will likely take over the search with Sirena, and I like that idea even less. He spent enough time with her when I was trapped in Hoss.

Monty excuses himself to use the bathroom, and Leo immediately takes advantage of the moment.

Eyes aflame with wicked thoughts, he pulls me into him and kisses me, unconcerned about witnesses.

My body responds instinctively, an insistent craving pulsing at my core. His kiss possesses, demands, as if trying to claim a part of me that's always been his.

"Kody took you to his apartment." He turns me toward the table, the high top hiding the movement of his hand as he reaches beneath my dress. "I smell him on you."

"Leo." Arousal puddles in my belly.

I look around, confirming that no one can see. I shouldn't let him grope me here, but everything feels so bumpy between us. This, our physical connection and chemistry, is always solid and steadfast.

So I let him touch me. I let him have this stolen moment. I want him to have it, to have all of me.

Pressing against my back, he uses his body to block prying

eyes as he runs his fingers up my inner thighs, past the soaked crotch of my thong, and deep inside me.

"Messy," he breathes at my ear. "Is this him? Or you?"

"Both." My knees wobble.

"Couldn't keep his dick in his pants."

"No."

"Bet he didn't last five minutes."

"There about." I clench my legs together, halting the movement of his hand. "Monty will be back any second."

"What will he do?" His voice takes on an angry edge. "Will he cause a scene if he finds me knuckles deep in his wife?"

"I'm yours, Leo." I twist, causing his hand to fall from beneath my dress. "I don't want to hurt him."

"I know."

The atmosphere shifts, and Monty emerges from the crowd, striding toward us.

Leo holds his uncle's gaze and lifts his hand, slipping his wet fingers into his mouth, one by one.

"Stop," I hiss under my breath.

Before he sucks the final digit, Monty grabs Leo's hand and sniffs it, his expression turning nuclear.

"That's not just her you smell." Leo grins a cruel grin and yanks his hand away. "Got some of your brother in there, too."

"Kody fucked you?" Monty jerks toward me, panting with the intensity of his emotions. "Here?"

My stomach bottoms out, and I open my mouth, not to apologize. I'm not sorry for giving Kody that release. It was a private moment between him and me, not meant to be turned into another jealous fight.

It wasn't meant to hurt anyone.

"We're not discussing this here." I force my eyes to Monty, then Leo.

"Hey." Rhett strolls up, his smile faltering when he realizes he walked in on a tense conversation.

"Hi, Rhett." I gather myself and motion at Leo. "You remember Leo?"

"Good to see you again." Rhett looks away, scanning the

room, clearly uncomfortable. "I'll...uh, grab a drink."

Before he can slip away, a server pops over and takes his order.

"Dr. Howell." Monty straightens the cuffs of his sleeves as he regards my boss steadily. "Glad you could make it."

"I didn't realize you were in town." I rarely see him out of scrubs.

Seeing him in a tuxedo leaves me at a loss for words.

Rhett has always exuded confidence and authority in the hospital, but tonight, he looks like he belongs on the cover of a fashion magazine. His neatly combed blond hair and light blue eyes have a new dimension of sophistication.

"We're ensuring top-notch security tonight," Monty says.

"I noticed." Rhett nods appreciatively, glancing around at the guards stationed discreetly. "It's impressive. Safety first, especially with such a crowd."

He doesn't ask Monty for an update on the stalker. This is neither the time nor the place. Not that Monty would share those details. There's an unspoken understanding that Monty doesn't trust anyone. From his perspective, everyone is a suspect, including Rhett.

We share a round of Kody's vodka, keeping the conversation on easy topics like the delicious drinks and the stunning turnout for the opening night.

Eventually, Monty and Leo amble to the bar to talk to Kody, leaving me with Rhett and a team of security.

As the crowd mingles and celebrates, Rhett turns his attention to me.

"I have to know..." He stares at the gorgeous Strakh men across the room, his pupils dilating. "Are you involved with all three of them?"

His question catches me off guard, and for a moment, I hesitate. But the alcohol in my bloodstream melts my walls and loosens my tongue.

"Yes. No. Kind of. Not exactly."

"I assume the truth is in there somewhere?"

They're mine.

I want to scream it so every woman here knows, but that

would be unhinged. So I settle on whispering it to the one person who asked. "I'm in love with them. All of them."

"Oh, shit." He chuckles, finding amusement in my predicament.

"Yeah. A huge, heaping pile of *oh, shit*."

"What's stopping you from being with all of them? Who says you have to choose?"

"Do they look like the kind of men who share?"

He looks at them. He hasn't taken his eyes off them. "No. But if anyone can change their minds, it's you."

"I love your confidence in me, but I already know how this will end."

"How?"

"They'll make me choose, and I can't do that." My ribs tighten. "I would shatter my own heart if it means keeping theirs intact."

"They might surprise you. Do you know how many times they've looked over here in the past five minutes?"

"They're possessive. All of them. Makes everything complicated."

"Life is complicated, Frankie. Sometimes the simplest answer is the most scandalous one."

As I ponder that response, Sirena saunters in.

"Fuck my life." I grab my vodka, tipping it to my lips.

Her attention homes in on the Strakh men as if they're the only three people in the room.

"Who is that?" Rhett braces an arm on the table, leaning forward.

"The bane of my existence."

Dark hair flows around her like a silken curtain, and her short, low-cut dress barely covers her ample chest and long, beautiful legs. She makes a beeline for them, for my entire world, her flirtatious demeanor on full display.

"She leads Monty's investigative team." I gnash my teeth.

"She has a laser focus on your boys."

"Thanks, Dr. Obvious."

"You're just going to sit here?"

"Yep."

I'm going to keep my ass right here and talk to my friend. Because, unlike Leo and Kody, I have self-control. I went to therapy. I journal when I feel angry and murderous.

I support women. I do *not* pick fights with them, no matter how badly I want to grab a fistful of that black hair, throw her to the ground, and punch her face until she bleeds.

Nope, I'm not doing that.

"Want me to beat her up for you?" Rhett grins.

"Stop it. You already know what I'm dealing with at the hospital with two of those barbarians."

"For the record, Paul was out of line and has been written up."

"I wish you wouldn't have done that. I'm trying to fit back into this life. The transition would be easier if I made friends instead of enemies."

"Hospital rules, Frankie. He commented on your looks."

As we continue our conversation about Leo and Kody and the shit they've stirred up in the trauma unit, my eyes bore holes in the back of Sirena's head.

Her goddamn hands are never idle. She strokes Leo's braids, touches Monty's shoulder, and her lips...

Did she just brush her mouth against Leo's ear?

A throb pounds behind my eyes.

He's so accustomed to her constant touching that he doesn't even push her away anymore. How far do they let her go when they're traveling together? She's been with them more than I have over the past month.

And I have a ban on sex.

She clearly does not.

"I hate to run, but I have an early surgery in the morning." He glances at his watch before meeting my eyes. "Here's some unsolicited advice. Go over there and claim your men openly and publicly in front of her and everyone."

With that, he squeezes my shoulder and leaves.

Claim my men.

Right.

What do I have to lose?

I'll just walk over there and kiss Monty on the lips in front of Leo and Kody.

Then I'll kiss Leo and Kody in front of Monty.

Sure.

That will go over wonderfully.

Not only would it end in a bloody brawl and ruin Kody's night, I would lose everything. All three of them. My entire world.

When Sirena finally steps away to use the restroom, I seize my chance.

With security guards on my heels, I follow her into the hall lined with single-user restrooms. Each door leads to a private commode. A gold standard for public bathrooms, especially at a bar. Kody went all out in his renovations.

I tell my bodyguards to wait outside as I reach the restroom she entered, catching the door before she can close it on me.

"Oh, hey, Frankie." She tries to block me from entering, her flirtatious confidence gone. "What are you doing?"

I hip-check the door and slip in with her, shutting us inside the small room together.

"Stop flirting with my men." I turn the lock and face her, stepping into her space. "Stay the fuck away from them."

"*Your* men?" She tries to smile, but it doesn't reach her eyes. "You have more than one?"

"Cut the crap," I snap, stepping closer. "You know damn well the Strakh men are mine."

"Do they know that?"

"Why are you so desperate? You come across like a scared, little, insecure girl, aching for attention. Who hurt you?"

The blood drains from her face, and she glances around the bathroom, her eyes darting from corner to corner as if expecting to find cameras or hidden microphones.

Her paranoia lifts the hairs on my nape, and I find myself scanning the space, too. "What are you—?"

She's on me in a blink, clapping a hand over my mouth and an arm around my back.

I struggle, but she's bigger, stronger, and Jesus fucking

Christ, I'm an idiot. I didn't think this through.

Coming in here without bodyguards...

Dumb, dumb, dumb!

She pushes me against the wall and closes in, her voice barely a whisper in my ear. "Someone hired me."

My heart stops, and my eyes go wide, searching hers.

"I don't know who or why." Her whisper trembles down my neck. "They paid me a lot, more than I could walk away from. I've never taken money from an anonymous client, but I needed it. It was a year ago, and my only task was to fuck Monty and help him find his missing wife."

A chill grips my spine as I peel her fingers off my mouth, keeping my voice low. "Did you report information back to this person? Details on the investigation?"

"Wasn't like that. I was only tasked to take the job as his team leader and get into his bed."

My mind races, connecting the dots.

The stalker. It has to be the stalker.

We haven't told her about the threats against me. She doesn't know.

Should I tell her? What if her life is in danger?

"I have a stalker." I grip her tightly, whispering directly into her ear. "A dangerous one."

"What?" Panic strangles her voice. "I have to go."

"Frankie?" Monty pounds on the door. "Everything okay in there?"

"Yep! Just a minute."

Turning back to Sirena, I feel a strange concern for her. "Have you been threatened?"

Her face goes white. "I was only supposed to fuck them, nothing more."

"Leo and Kody, too?"

She nods.

"The stalker is sending me body parts. People are *dying*." I grip her arm. "How is your client contacting you? Text? Phone call?"

She shakes her head, backing up, her fear palpable.

"Does Wilson know about this client?"

"No." Her head continues to shake. "He has nothing to do with this."

"Frankie!" The door handle rattles, followed by more pounding. "Open the door!"

She flings it open before I can stop her and bolts past Monty.

"Sirena, wait!" I crash into his chest, caught in the snare of his arms.

He's not alone. Leo and Kody crowd into the doorway, all bearing down on me as I try to track Sirena's escape.

"Stop her." Pushing against them, I glimpse a blur of her dark hair.

Then she's gone, melting into the throng of people near the front door.

"What did she do?" Leo's eyes blaze as he shoves into the bathroom.

"Nothing. She talked to me. But she knows things about the stalker. I think she's in danger. You need to stop her."

Monty quickly directs some guards to follow her before turning back to me. "What happened?"

"She confessed that someone hired her to fuck you." I take a deep breath, trying to steady my nerves. "All three of you. She doesn't know who. It was a year ago. She was supposed to help you find me, Monty. And get you into bed in the process."

"Why would someone hire her for that?" Kody grips the doorframe. "Doesn't make sense."

"I think it's the stalker," I say, my voice barely above a whisper.

"We'll figure it out." Monty pulls me into a protective embrace.

"We need to find her." I untangle from him and shoulder my way out of the restroom.

They stay with me, of course, forming a circle around me as we rejoin the crowd in the lounge.

Then we wait for the guards to return.

Minutes crawl by at a glacial speed. The streets around the distillery teem with so many people that she could disappear into the night, either by her own doing or the stalker.

Monty and Leo have been calling and texting her with no luck. Kody returns to the bar to entertain the crowds.

The security team discreetly sweeps the bathrooms for recording devices. Then they turn their attention to the distillery, looking for anything that might've been planted throughout the night.

They've also been instructed to watch the patrons, something they've been doing all night, but now on a closer, more suspicious level.

Everything is handled in the background, the guests oblivious to my confrontation with Sirena.

Finally, Carl returns, shaking his head in frustration. "There are too many people outside. She was able to slip away in the mob."

"And her apartment?" Monty's jaw tightens.

"She hasn't gone home, but I have a team stationed there and more combing the vicinity."

"Continue the hunt until she's located."

"Yes, sir."

"It's time to go home." Monty meets Leo's eyes, who nods and starts to stand.

"No. Not without Kody." I remain seated at the far end of the bar, watching him interact with his guests. "This is his night, and we're not bailing on him."

So we stay.

We sit at the bar and put on smiles while Kody sails through the opening of a shiny, promising future.

When we arrive on the island in the dead of night, Sirena is still missing.

monty

FORTY-FIVE

Three days later, the hunt for Sirena Fisher continues.

What a fucking nightmare.

My head pounds as I stand at the kitchen sink and guzzle water and aspirin.

Leo and Kody are in Sitka today. But not without their bodyguards. Kody needs to be at the distillery while they work through typical growing pains. Leo is meeting with contractors to do walk-throughs of his seaplane base, mapping out the water for landings and takeoffs, the appurtenant shore, hangars, and facilities. He has a lot of decisions to make over the next few weeks.

Frankie isn't scheduled to work at the hospital until next week and hasn't left the island since Sirena went missing.

Thank fuck for that.

As much as she resents Sirena, she's worried about her. My wife has become withdrawn, quiet, seemingly lost in her head.

All of this puts me on edge.

"What?" I brace my hands on the counter, refusing to meet the judgmental eyes at my back.

"You need to eat," Oliver says in an unruffled tone.

"That's not why you're here, digging your beady little eyes into my skin."

"So uptight. You need to get laid."

"Also, not why you're here."

"You're right." He drifts closer.

I don't hear him moving, but I feel him like a shadow creeping up my spine.

Peering over my shoulder, I don't find him there.

What the fuck?

I twist, glancing over my other shoulder.

When did he move to the other side of the kitchen island?

He glares at me with a carving knife poised in his hand.

Fucking creepy.

The blade drips with juices from the slab of meat he's cutting. While wearing a suit, no less. The gold watch chain glints under the soft kitchen lights as he studies me.

If I didn't know better, I would suspect him of sending morbid gifts to my wife. His hidden accent and old-world manners hint at a sophisticated yet dangerous past.

But over the years, I have dug and dug, trying to unearth dirt on Oliver Popov.

He's just an old Russian chef, who manages my diet and well-being with a precision that borders on obsessive.

"You should not have involved the police." He saws into the meat. "They will only slow things down."

"The police are our best chance of finding Sirena."

He sets down the knife, wiping his hands on a white towel, leaving streaks of blood. "The police are...bureaucratic. They follow procedures, protocols. If the woman I loved were threatened, I would cut down every person who looked at her. I would take matters into my own hands."

This old guy?

"What are you suggesting?" I narrow my eyes. "Should I cut you for looking at her?"

He shrugs.

Sitka authorities are only involved in part of the investigation. They don't know about the heart or threats to Frankie's phone. They don't know she murdered Denver.

I've been in contact with Wilson constantly, trying to glean the truth about Sirena. He swears she was fully vetted when he hired her a few years ago. He personally assigned her to my investigation when I was looking for Frankie.

He's as shocked as I am by her confession about the anonymous client. That's against his policy for obvious reasons. She may have compromised the entire investigation, my search for Frankie, and our ongoing hunt for the cabin.

"I'm saying..." Oliver meets my gaze, his wrinkled features cold and blank. "Sometimes direct action is more effective than lawful action. You have resources. Power. Use them."

"I'm not my father."

"No, you're not."

A chill runs over my scalp. There's something in his tone, something I'm missing.

He returns to his cooking.

Before I can question him further, movement snaps my gaze to the kitchen window.

Outside, Frankie steps onto the patio, dressed in her running gear.

With summer drawing to a close, she runs the trails every day. I join her when I'm not on the phone.

Other than me, only a few of the guards can keep up with her.

Bending closer to the window, I scrutinize the guards hovering nearby.

Nope. She'll outrun all of them.

Fuck.

I just came from the gym and still wear my workout clothes. I'm also exhausted and fighting a headache.

Doesn't stop me from racing out of the kitchen to join her.

"Coming with me?" She stretches her calf.

"Wouldn't miss it."

We take off, jogging along the trails through the trees.

Her petite frame moves with power and endurance, her legs pumping furiously, three times as fast to keep up with my long-legged strides.

With the muscled weight she's gained, her body is stronger and faster than ever, her figure both delicate and resilient.

She's more beautiful than I've ever seen her, and that beauty comes from within.

I love to run with her just to spend time with her, to stare at her like a love-sick fool. But I also appreciate the shared silence, the rhythm of our breaths syncing with the beat of our feet on the earth.

Ten minutes into the run, we round the corner of the dense forest, approaching the quiet side of the shoreline. The ocean waves murmur in the distance. It's a moment of peace, a rare oasis in the turmoil of our lives.

Before we reach the shore, something breaks the silence. A whirring mechanical sound that quickens my pulse.

"Do you hear that?" I slow my gait, reaching for her arm.

"What is it?" Her eyes widen as she looks around.

"It sounds like—"

The noise grows louder, more insistent, coming from above.

"Take cover!" Stanley shouts.

The guards leap into motion as I lunge, crashing into her and taking her to the ground. We roll off the path into the dense trees, landing with my frame covering her protectively.

The guards rush in, forming a wall around us as the buzzing object falls from the sky and slams onto the trail.

I brace for an explosion that doesn't come.

"Stay down." My heart thunders in my chest.

"What is it?" Her breath heats my neck, her body trembling beneath me.

"I don't know. Just stay still."

An agonizing minute ticks, ticks, ticks.

"It's a drone," Stanley says. "There's a box attached to it."

My stomach sinks as I stare down at her, at the wetness blurring her eyes.

"Open it." I hold her devastated gaze.

The sound of ripping cardboard rings like a death knell.

"Dry ice," Stanley announces. "And something in a plastic bag."

Her face crumples.

"Take it to the house. No police." Turning back to her, I cradle her head and hug her to me. "Can you stand?"

"Yeah."

The guards carry the box back to the house. We follow them into the kitchen, where Oliver prepares dinner.

His expression empties when he sees the box. "Another one?"

"Delivered by a drone." I don gloves, my fingers steady despite the dread fisting in my gut.

Then I open the box.

Sickening vapors of déjà vu rise from the dry ice. I pull out a frost-covered plastic bag, set it on the counter, and cut it open.

Not a heart.

Not a hand.

Blue irises stare up at me from a severed pair of eyes.

Frankie makes a strangled sound.

Nausea surges, and saliva fills my mouth as the image of Wolfson's blue eyes flash in my mind. Eyes that match my own.

I must've said his name, because she grips my arm, shaking her head, her voice a whisper of horror. "Sirena."

Sirena had blue eyes, too.

"There's a note." Oliver nods at the box.

Everything inside me recoils. I can't stomach another photo of my dead son.

Steeling my spine, I reach for it and read the handwritten words aloud. "*But whom to love? To trust and treasure? Who won't betray us in the end? And who'll be kind enough to measure our words and deeds as we intend?* This is for us, Frankie. It's all for you and me."

"Pushkin?" She hugs her waist, looking so scared and alone.

"Yeah." I remove the gloves and wrap her in my arms, meeting Oliver's cryptic gaze across the room.

Sometimes direct action is more effective than lawful action.

"No more police." I square my shoulders. "We're doing this

the Strakh way."

monty
FORTY-SIX

That night, I sit at my desk, the walls in my office closing in on me. Shelves and drawers overflow with paperwork, the detritus of a life spent in pursuit of power and control.

A life deliberately crafted to separate me from my father's crimes, to ensure I would never follow in his blood-soaked footsteps.

I followed my own path. University. Business degrees. Building a global consulting firm from the ground up. I've ensured every contract, deal, and interaction was aboveboard.

My reputation as the wealthiest man in Alaska rests on the foundation of lawful conduct and ethical business practices.

Yet none of it will protect the woman I love.

Frankie's face flashes in my mind—her wild red hair, green eyes that puncture my soul, and a heart of liquid fucking magic. She has so much love in her. The purest form of love in existence.

I can't rely on the slow gears of justice to save her. I must act decisively and ruthlessly.

Turning to my father's legacy goes against everything I've worked for, everything I believe in. Yet, as body parts continue to show up, I have no choice. I must tap into the very darkness I've spent my life avoiding.

Drawing a deep breath, I stand and walk to the hidden safe behind the Ivan Aivazovsky painting. My hands are steady as I input the combination.

The safe opens with a soft click, revealing a small black ledger, the one I took from my childhood home after my parents' deaths.

I hesitate, my fingers hovering over the worn leather cover. This ledger is a gateway to the criminal empire my father once controlled. I've kept it hidden, a reminder of the man I swore I would never become.

With a sigh that feels like surrender, I remove it from the safe and carry it to my desk. Sitting down, I flip open the cover, the musty scent of old paper invading my nose.

Names, numbers, and coded messages fill the pages, a network of power and corruption laid bare.

But I'm only interested in one.

The Ghost.

A notorious hitman and enforcer in the Russian underworld. Known for his brutal methods and unwavering loyalty, he's feared across Europe. Or was. He disappeared from my radar years ago.

When he was active, he ran a covert network of ex-spies and assassins who specialized in tracking and eliminating targets in high-risk operations.

No one knew his identity, not even my father.

I trace a finger over the inked entry, a potential ally, a necessary evil. He's probably dead.

Unbuttoning the collar of my shirt, I dial the number.

"Who is this?" a voice answers in heavy Russian. "How did you get this number?"

"I'm Montgomery Strakh, son of—"

"I know who you are. The Wolf is all grown up."

My childhood nickname.

I'm not surprised he knows it. He worked for my father and knows everything about me.

"I have a job for you," I say in Russian.

"I'm retired."

"Name your price. Money is no object."

"Money is always an object, boy. But for you, I'll require something more. A favor."

"What kind of favor?" My mouth dries.

"I'll call on you in the future, and you'll grant me whatever I need, whenever I need it."

Ice forms in my lungs.

This is the cost of the path I'm choosing. A debt to a man like The Ghost. A chain that could bind me forever.

But for Frankie, I'll do anything.

"Agreed."

"Good. What is the job?"

monty

FORTY-SEVEN

The following week limps by, the days blurring into a relentless, torturous cadence.

I sent the dismembered eyes to my forensics team in New York, and they confirmed a match.

Sirena Fisher.

After hearing the news, Kody and Leo haven't left Frankie's side.

Until this afternoon.

The weight of their responsibilities pulled them back to Sitka. Kody's distillery requires constant attention. He's needed there more than he's needed here.

Same with Leo. With his seaplane base taking shape, crucial decisions are hitting him at a breakneck pace.

But those aren't the only reasons they're gone tonight.

They're following up on leads, re-interviewing witnesses from the night Sirena disappeared, and interrogating people on our suspect list.

They're hunting.

When I told them I was going with them, they stared at me like I was speaking Russian. Then an argument ensued about who would stay with Frankie.

From everything I read in her journal, they had similar arguments in the hills each time they journeyed from the cabin.

But since they both have business to tend to in Sitka, it was an argument I couldn't win.

So here I am.

Frankie curls beside me on the couch, her body a fragile ribbon of warmth against the constant chill of danger.

As she sleeps, my mind races, a torrent of crashing and colliding thoughts.

After everything she's been through, who would do this? Who would go to such lengths to terrorize her?

Who knew about the flight logs in my father's cellar? Someone from my past? Denver's past?

Denver's heart, Doyle's hand, Sirena's eyes—it's a message. A gruesome, violent message. But from whom?

And who will be next?

The questions torment me, each one a blade carving into my sanity.

I haven't heard from The Ghost since I contacted him. And I won't. Not until the stalker is identified and exterminated.

The wait is another level of hell.

Only Frankie, Leo, and Kody know that I made that call. I told them in a hushed conversation in my office, away from guards and household staff, and reiterated the importance of discretion. I trust no one else with that information.

Even with The Ghost involved, I continue to work with Wilson, scour every piece of evidence, and pore over Pushkin's poems with an analytical microscope, looking for hidden meanings.

I won't give up.

Frankie stirs, her hand reaching for mine. She whimpers, caught in the throes of a dream, and I tighten my grip.

"Hey." I bring her fingers to my mouth, kissing them. "You're safe."

Her lashes flutter as she wakes, and she looks up at me with a raw, unguarded expression of love. I want to haul her to my bed—our bed—and remind her why we used to make love morning, noon, and night.

At this point, I would settle for one of the three.

When I'm not thinking about the stalker, I think about my marriage.

The issue with us isn't that she doesn't love me. The issue is that she loves two other men.

My brothers.

They should never leave her alone with me. My hunger for her is dangerous.

I ache to taste her on my lips. I crave her hands on my body. I want to call out her name when I enter her with a fervor I haven't felt in over a year. I long to look her in the eyes, pausing to savor the unwavering love and desire we share.

"I love you." I hold her palm against my cheek.

"I know." Her eyes dart between mine, and her breathing goes shallow. "I..."

"Don't say it." I let her slide her hand away. "Not until you're ready."

"I won't."

She's a tough one to crack. The past year of hell has made her nearly impregnable. If I win her back, a life with her won't be easy. Not with the trauma she carries. She has always talked back and stood up for herself. She's always been hardheaded and independent. Now she's all those things with anxiety and PTSD. After the shit she went through, she's learning how to love herself again and requires more patience and effort than she did before.

I love her enough for both of us.

She pushes up to a sitting position, folding her legs beneath her.

"I had a dream." She stares at her hands, then at me. "I dreamed they were still alive. Doyle, Sirena, Denver..." Her voice cracks. "Wolf."

"Denver can't live without his heart."

"He never had a heart." She releases a shaky breath. "I watched him die and felt his life leave his body. No coming back from that. But the others...what if Doyle and Sirena are being held somewhere? Tortured? Getting hands and eyes removed while they're still alive?"

Another result of her trauma...She overthinks everything and believes the worst-case scenario.

I want to lie to her and tell her it's not as bad as she thinks. But she needs me to be completely honest and straightforward with her at all times. She's not a fragile flower, and I won't treat her like one.

"Yeah." Resolve hardens in my chest. "It's possible, but we're doing everything we can to find them."

"I'm worried about Leo and Kody."

"Their bodyguards are with them." I point to my phone on the coffee table. "I'll be notified immediately if anything happens."

"Where are they now?"

I grab the phone and check the GPS tracker. "They both just returned to the distillery."

She nods. "Tell me about Kodiak Island. What was it like growing up in a crime family?"

With a sigh, I settle into the couch and tell her all the things I kept from her before she was taken. The stories about my father's assassins lurking around the estate, the closed-door meetings, and hushed phone calls. Then I tell her about Kody's mother and all our adventures on the island, such as fishing in the bay, making ridiculous dance videos, and exploring the caves.

As I walk through my memories, she listens raptly and shares her own childhood stories.

It's late when she finally announces, "I'm going to bed."

I grab our phones and follow her upstairs.

"What favor will The Ghost demand of you?" She pauses in the doorway of the guest bedroom. "Coach his son's little league team? Babysit his pet tiger? Maybe send him some feet pics?"

"Maybe." A smirk hitches the corner of my mouth as I set our phones in the room. "It will likely be along the lines of laundering large sums of money, providing a temporary safe haven, or marrying the virgin daughter of an enemy Russian mobster."

"What?" She chokes. "You're already married."

"I am." I step into her. "Say it again."

"You're married." She swallows, eyes fixed on mine.

"That's right, and my wife is ferocious. Strong. Gorgeous. Fearsome. She would never share me with another." I dust the backs of my fingers across her snowy white cheek. "I can't take my eyes off her. Every soft curve, every little dip and arch. I want to eat her."

I draw closer, backing her against the doorframe and gripping the jamb above her head. Then I trail my fingers down her breastbone oh-so softly.

"Monty." She shrinks back, drawing her bottom lip between her teeth.

"Those sharp little fangs nibbling on your lip...the sight makes me rock hard." Resting my thumb against her mouth, I tug the plump flesh free. "I'm so fucking hard for you."

A small sound escapes her throat, part whimper, part gasp.

"Put your hands on me." I bend in, dragging my nose through her hair. "Feel what you do to me."

A second passes. Then she lowers her gaze—we both do—to the jutting, swollen erection in my gray sweatpants.

The thin material doesn't confine or restrain my ravenous hunger. Instead, it reveals every stiff inch, every angry ridge, every twitch. My goddamn cock isn't idle. It throbs and drools and jumps like a rabid animal under her scrutiny.

Touch me. Put me out of my fucking misery.

Her chest rises and falls as she shifts her hand. Not to wrangle my dick. No, she hooks a finger under the hem of my T-shirt, gathers it, and tugs it upward.

I reach behind my shoulders, yank the garment over my head, and drop it.

"Damn." She swallows a breathy inhale. "You've always had the body of a thirty-year-old athlete. I miss looking at you. Touching you."

My lungs seize. My heart strokes out. I grip the doorframe above her head, angling closer, lower, until we're at eye level.

Fucking touch me.

Her gaze dips to my lips. Then she does. She puts those tiny, delicate hands on my chest and begins an exploration that draws up my balls, lengthens my hard-on, clenches my ass, and has my fingers gouging the wood doorframe.

She caresses the slab of my chest, traces each individual stomach muscle, and follows the trail of hair down, down, down...

And stops.

"Fuck!" I kick my hips, unable to control myself. "I need inside you."

Like a bomb, the moment shatters.

"Oh, God." She drops her hands, her eyes round with horror. "What have I done?"

"Frankie." Panic spikes as I cup her face and bring our foreheads together. "We've done nothing wrong. I'm your husband. I love you."

"Monty." She shakes her head. "We have to stop. You know why."

"I can't, darling." I kiss her pretty mouth, coaxing her to kiss me back. "I'll never stop loving you."

Why won't she kiss me back?

Something stirs in my periphery. Predatory movement without sound. Not the creak of a floorboard. Not the rustle of a breath. But feral energy singes my skin.

I pull my lips from hers, and we turn our heads toward the stairs.

My gaze locks with the two men I consider my brothers.

Their eyes blaze with primal, untamed fury. Their broad, taut postures promise pain. Their fists flex with pure, unadulterated destruction.

A noise reaches my ears. The low, lethal, guttural growl of something that isn't human reverberates through the hall, sending Frankie into a frenzy.

Shoving and twisting, she jolts out of my embrace and scrambles into the path of war.

"No!" Arms stretched out at her sides, she tries to make herself bigger, taller, a barrier between them and me.

Protecting me.

From them.

Leo prowls forward, jaw clamped, muscles bunched and ready to kill.

"Stop! Listen to me." She swings her hands forward, smacking her palms against his heaving chest. "Don't blame Monty. Blame me. Hate me."

"Move, woman." Kody advances, an animal on the hunt.

"Let them by." Adrenaline pumping, I push back my shoulders, prepared to face their wrath.

Every instinct urges me to go to her, to set her out of the way. But if I take one step forward, they'll attack, and she'll be caught in the fray.

So I keep my feet planted, my stance wide, and I wait.

"No!" She stands her ground. "I won't let you hurt him. I put myself in that situation. Me! I did this!"

"You chose him." Kody's black eyes turn blacker, pulsing with pain. "You chose him over us."

"You're wrong." Her voice shatters. "I'll never choose. I can't. I want all of you. I love all of you. I'm the problem." She pounds her chest. "I'm the monster. The toxic red flag."

Leo flinches, his eyes flickering with confusion and anger before he turns that battle back on me. "I'll kill you for this."

"I won't apologize for loving my wife." Engulfed in the flames of their territorial fury, I crack my neck. "Do your worst."

"No! Stop this!" Frankie jabs a finger at Monty and spins back to Leo and me. "Focus on me, not him."

I glare into her eyes, recognizing the desperation she holds for him, the fierce need to protect and defend him.

The betrayal I feel is a gaping, unbearable, soul-deep wound, and that look on her face pours salt into it.

"You love him," I whisper, my voice breaking.

"Yeah." Her chin trembles. "I love him. And you. And Leo."

Behind her, Monty's eyes soften immediately, and a subtle quiver sweeps across his mouth as if he's struggling to hold back a sappy declaration.

"For how long?" Leo pitches forward, bringing his face nearer to hers. "Have you been fucking around with him since we moved in?"

She flinches, curling in on herself as if he took a sledgehammer to her chest.

I snarl at him, baring my teeth.

Monty's face turns to stone.

With a deep inhale, she lowers her arms and squares her shoulders.

"I told you I loved him in the gym three months ago. My feelings for him have been shifting, returning, deepening into something new. But I never acted on them. I haven't so much as kissed him until tonight." Her chin dips. "I'm sorry."

"You didn't kiss me!" Monty swipes a hand through the air. "Don't apolog—"

"I never intended to hurt you." She presses the heel of her hand to her sternum. "I'm so fucking sorry for your pain, and I won't make excuses for my behavior. But I need to understand..." She aims her watery gaze at me. "You said I wasn't a possession, a thing to own. You shared me with Leo because you knew we would be happier together than divided. Why is this different?"

"I trust Monty with our safety, with our business deals, but not with this. Not with you." The pain in my chest intensifies. "Monty doesn't share. His obsession with you threatens everything we have."

"He's right." Monty inhales sharply. "I won't share."

"Shut the fuck up!" Leo roars. "You've caused enough damage."

"Stop yelling." She stands taller, fisting her hands at her sides. "Monty didn't cause this. I did. You want to fight? Fight me."

She's lost her mind. None of us would harm a hair on her head.

And fighting each other doesn't solve a damn thing.

Monty won't share her with us. Leo won't share her with Monty. I just want to be with her, but she's drawn a line in the sand. She won't choose between us.

There's no win here.

I won't live on this island and watch her fall deeper and deeper in love with a man who wants her for himself. They have a history, a marriage that Leo and I can't rival. We need to get her away from him.

"We can't stay here." Anger and hurt throb beneath my skin as I meet her eyes. "You're coming with us."

"You're not thinking rationally," Monty says. "There's a serial killer on the loose, and Frankie is the target."

"We'll take guards." Leo turns and storms down the hall, his footsteps echoing like thunder. "Let's go, Frankie."

"Don't do this." She chases him, reaching for him, trying to stop him. "Don't let this destroy everything we've built."

"Him or us." He whirls on her, catching her arms as she crashes into him. "Decide. Are you staying or going?"

"I won't stay here without you." She shakes her head rapidly, ignoring Monty's objections. "And I won't leave with you."

"That right?" Leo laughs coldly. "Well, those are your only two options, love."

"If you leave…" She juts her chin. "I leave. By myself."

"I forbid it." Monty's eyes flash.

"Where the fuck would you go?" I ask incredulously.

"The on-call room at the hospital has a bunk bed and bathroom." A tear splashes onto her cheek, and she slaps it away. "I'm the problem. I'm the one who needs to leave."

Her anguish cuts through me like a knife, twisting deeper into raw wounds.

"That's bullshit." Leo tangles a hand in his hair. "Either you're staying here or coming with us."

"I'm not going with you." She steps closer, her eyes pleading. "Stay with Monty. I choose all three of you. All three of you together, with or without me. I just want you to stay together and take care of one another."

"They can't be fixed," Monty mutters so quietly, so deliberately imperceptible by the ear.

He forgets I hear tones most humans can't.

"What the fuck did you say?" I lean toward him, a vein throbbing at my temple.

"You heard me." He lifts his chin, daring me to hit him.

So I rear back my fist and drive it straight into his throat.

The force of the strike doubles him over, shock flashing in his eyes as he grabs his gullet and coughs through the pain.

Sissy.

"Kody!" she gasps.

"He'll be fine." I back up and lean against the wall.

I barely throat-punched him. Just enough to stun him. He's already straightening, glaring at me like he wants another one.

But the look on *her* face...

Oh, shit.

She goes still, and a cold, dark shadow crosses her features.

"Out of line, Kodiak Strakh." Her tone is so calm it chills. "Out of fucking line."

"He deserved it."

"Then I deserve it, too."

I push off the wall. "I would never—"

"No. You know what? That's it." Turning, she paces off into the bedroom with Leo hot on her heels.

Monty and I stand with a stiff distance between us as our stares intertwine in a silent battle.

In the bedroom, I hear the sounds of drawers slamming and the rustling of bags being packed.

"You're not leaving on your own," Leo says.

The angry zip of a bag is the only response.

Monty opens his mouth to say something, but she charges out into the hall with two bags strapped over her shoulders.

She walks straight up to Monty and takes his face in her hands. "I would never force you into anything you don't want to do. I love you." Releasing him, she steps back, her eyes wet but determined. "The marriage between Frankie and Monty Novak ended a year ago. There is no you and me. There is only you, me, and them." She points a shaky finger at us. "You are Strakhs, and in my dream of the future, I share that last name with all of you."

"Frankie." Monty reaches for her.

She evades his hand and pivots toward Leo. "I love you, and I want the best for you. Your anger is too great, and your trauma is too deep. It worries me. That goes for all of you." She glances around at us and returns to Leo. "It affects you and your relationships. Seek help. If you won't do it for me, do it for each other."

"You're turning this around on me?" Leo narrows his eyes angrily. "Like this is my fault?"

"No. I take full responsibility for what happened tonight."

Her gaze shifts to me.

I watch with pounding agony as she swallows back a sob and tries to hold herself together.

"Woman..."

"Monty and Leo are your family. You will *never* raise your hand against them again." Her eyes harden with a fierceness that reminds me why I love her. "Promise me."

"I promise." My throat closes.

"I love you." Her expression wobbles as she hitches the straps on her shoulders and strides toward the stairs.

"You're not leaving without us." Leo prowls after her.

We all do.

We chase her through the house and into the misty rain, barking demands at her, shouting over one another, trying to make her see reason.

She keeps walking, eyes straight ahead and swimming in tears. But she doesn't cry. She doesn't make a sound.

By the time we reach the dock, reality sets in.

She's really fucking leaving.

How did this happen?

She betrayed us. And now she's leaving us?

Monty looks as stunned as I am. At least he has enough sense to remember her safety.

"You're taking guards." He directs four of them to board her cruiser.

"Yeah. I am." She meets his eyes, and something achy and lovesick passes between them.

That. That right there is why I want her away from him.

He'll steal her. He's been trying to steal her for five months.

She climbs into her boat and frees the lines.

"Explain this to me." Leo grips the taffrail as if he can stop the cruiser from leaving the dock. "He kissed you. Why are you punishing us for it?"

"I'm not punishing you. I'm punishing myself." Dewy rain clings to her face as she starts the engine.

"Why?" The heat of his frantic fury radiates off him as he yells at her over the motor. "What do you want?"

"I want the impossible." Her shoulders slump, and her eyes pool with tears. "I'm sorry."

She steers the cruiser into the drizzling fog, her four guards standing at attention around her.

Rain-soaked and numb, I watch her go, willing her to look back.

She doesn't.

Too soon, she fades into the dark mist. Gone.

In the stillness, the silence of her absence settles over the island, and I know that the bond among us all has been irrevocably shattered.

"Let's go." Leo boards one of our yachts.

Yachts that Monty gave us.

Monty stands alone in the gloom, wearing only a pair of sweatpants, feet bare, seemingly impervious to the cold night. But he's not bulletproof.

In the silent language of his remote expression, there's a complexity that affects me, a deep vulnerability he tries to conceal behind a veneer of stoicism. So many layers make up the man I've come to know as my brother, and right now, I know he's breaking inside.

He loves her, possibly as much as I do, and he's already lost her once.

Montgomery Strakh is a strong and powerful man, but I don't think he can survive without Frankie.

Our eyes connect, and I find something there I don't expect. Love. Concern. For Leo and me.

He blinks and quickly looks away to direct more guards to go with us.

Then he pivots and stalks back to the house.

Leo and I could stay. Monty's not making us leave. But none of us want Frankie out there alone.

Sending guards with her isn't enough.

Monty knows I'll keep an eye on her. *Stalk her.* It's what I do.

As Leo and I leave the island behind, the future feels more uncertain than ever.

For the next week, I pick up every shift available and throw myself into work.

When I'm not doing rounds in the trauma unit, I run on the treadmill in the PT wing, spill my guts to Rhett in his office, or hole up in the on-call room, reading everything I can find on Pushkin and his poems.

I'm scared to leave the hospital, even with my bodyguards. So I don't.

I traded one prison for another, and if I don't keep busy, I'll curl up in the corner and sob until I break.

Leaving my entire world on that dock felt so brave.

And self-condemning.

It was the hardest thing I've ever done. But what choice did I have?

If I stayed with Monty, it would've meant choosing him. If I went with Leo and Kody, it would've meant choosing them. Either option would've destroyed the fragile bond among the men I love.

My betrayal may have already done that.

I never intended to fall back in love with Monty.

So here I am, sitting on the bottom bunk in the tiny on-call room, hugging my knees to my chest, and fighting back tears for the hundredth time today.

I don't want to be alone. But more than that, I don't want *them* to be alone. I want them to be together.

So much of their lives has been taken from them. I can't fix our cracked past. But I can learn from it and help them create a better future. I can trust that they'll find their way back to one another.

As long as I'm not there to fuck it up.

A knock sounds on the door.

"Yeah?" I call out.

"It's Rhett."

"Come in."

It's his hospital, but he always knocks.

The door swings open, revealing my guards on the other side. They're on a regular rotation, but still. What a tedious assignment following me around the hospital all day and night.

Rhett strides in, clutching a greasy brown bag. The unmistakable aroma of burgers and fries follows him.

My mouth salivates.

"Didn't want you losing any more weight." He drops the bag on the bed beside me.

"Thank you." I dig into it. "You know, when Monty cheated on me, I stopped eating. On some fucked-up level, I was trying to vanish as a form of revenge." I shove a handful of fries into my mouth. "I'm not that woman anymore."

He knows all the ugly details of my life. Over the past week, I told him everything that happened from the moment I was abducted to the almost-kiss that led me here, seeking a safe place to sleep.

At first, I started spilling the tea just to see his reaction. I don't want to suspect my only friend, but at this point, I suspect everyone.

But I haven't sensed anything in his eyes, demeanor, or conversation to indicate malevolence.

He's the only person in my life who hasn't caused me pain over the past year.

"I'm losing weight because..." I chew off a huge bite of the burger. "Hospital food sucks."

"I told you to stay at my house. I'm never home, and there's a grocery store within walking distance."

"Thank you, but I won't endanger you. You're risking your life just by talking to me."

He glances around the cramped room. Metal bunk bed, bookshelf, desk—it reminds me of my university dorm room.

"Are your guards still checking for cameras?" he asks.

"Every day. I don't know how the stalker monitors my activity, but since I've left the island, I don't have that constant feeling of being watched."

"Good."

"Doesn't lower the risk, though. I'm serious, Rhett. You shouldn't be here."

When I suspected Doyle's motivations, he went missing. When I suspected Sirena, she went missing. I don't want to suspect Rhett, and I sure as hell don't want parts of his anatomy showing up.

I need to keep space between us for his safety.

"How long will you let this go on?" he asks.

"I'm just staying here until I figure things out." I finish off the burger and move on to the fries.

"You married a man with more money than God, and you're sleeping on threadbare sheets in a cold hospital. Alone. Your problems can be fixed, Frankie. But they won't fix themselves."

"My problems are cute little puppies in a pet shop window. I saw them and knew they were trouble. Then they licked my face and peed on my leg, and I just had to have them. I had to have all of them. I took them home, and they gained weight and became wolves and tried to kill one another. And I love them even more."

"Those men were never cute little puppies."

"And the cabin wasn't a pet shop. It's an allegory, Rhett. I'm trying to make a point."

"I get it." He steps toward the door. "Stay as long as you

want, but you and I both know you're safer with them." He pauses with his hand on the knob. "One of them is in the hospital as we speak."

I sigh. They've been showing up every day since I left. Monty pops in to double and triple-check my security. Kody's appearances are more stealthy. I never see him, but I know he's stalking me from the shadows. Leo always rolls in like a storm, vibrating with rage and ready to fight.

"Which one?" I ask.

"The Norse god of thunder."

I groan.

When Leo crashed into the trauma unit two days ago, he was aggressive, demanding, and refused to leave without me. I know he and Kody are staying in Kody's apartment at the distillery. I watch them through the tracking app on my phone only because I'm desperate to know if they're reconciling with Monty. Or getting help. Or doing anything to improve their situation.

Leaving them wasn't enough.

I must stay gone.

And that's where my big brave plan crashes and burns.

I'm so fucking lonely, scared, and sick with guilt. My eyes leak constantly, my remorse so strong they can scent it across the Sound. I ache everywhere—my teeth, my throat, my chest. God, the constricting pain in my chest makes it so hard to breathe. Every stab, every rib-cracking heartbeat urges me to go to them.

But who would I run to? Which one would I choose?

I can't. I won't do it.

I must train my heart to be the door, not the mat. Change the locks on it. Don't let them in unless they show up together, united.

I can do this. I have a room just my size. A head full of memories. A mind like a sharpie that draws thick, bold lines. A heart like a four-person bed, big enough to hold all of us. Except it has a hole in it the size of the Arctic, and it's cold. So fucking cold.

But I can do this. I must.

"I'll handle it." Standing, I brush the crumbs off my scrubs.

"He's injured."

"Injured how?" My breath sputters. "What happened?"

"Bar fight. He has a deep cut on his head and refuses to let anyone treat him. He's demanding that you do it."

"Where is he?"

"Exam room three." He opens the door. "Good luck."

"Thanks." Pulse racing, I follow him out and hurry to the ER.

Leo sits on the hospital bed, his intense gaze locking onto mine. I close the curtain, and the tension between us crackles, spitting static across my skin.

Blood trickles down his face from a deep gash along his hairline. He looks ferocious. Brutally beautiful.

Goosebumps spread across my flesh, awakening my senses.

He holds out his hand.

If I take it, he'll yank me between those powerful thighs and kiss me until I beg for his cock.

I'm not stupid.

"Frankie," he rumbles, low and demanding. "Come here."

"You need medical attention." I turn toward the supply cart.

"I need you," he snaps, frustration boiling over. "Just you."

"Lie down so I can clean that wound."

He obeys, lying back on the table with a wince. I gather the necessary supplies, my hands shaking as I approach him.

"Tell me what happened." I gently clean the wound, working quickly and efficiently despite the turmoil inside me.

His eyes burn, a pair of multicolored blades, tracking my every move. "I went to a bar."

"Kody's?"

"No."

"And?"

"The women wouldn't leave me in peace. So I voiced my thoughts about it."

"You did the growly thing and scared them?"

"Sure. Whatever. Some of the guys didn't like that. They

struck first, and I needed to blow off some steam."

"Is this gash from a beer bottle?" I finish cleaning the area.

"Yeah."

"What condition are they in?"

"Worse than me. And drunk."

"How are you not in jail?"

"Self-defense. Six against one. The cops let me walk."

"Are you hurt anywhere else?"

"No."

Six men attacked him? And he only has one cut?

Fuck.

As I prepare to give him a local anesthetic, he grips my arm.

"No numbing," he says. "I need to feel this."

"Why?"

"Need to feel your hands on me."

My chest squeezes and cracks.

With blurry, wet vision, I focus on the task. Neither of us speaks while I stitch the deep cut. But his eyes never leave mine. Not once.

Finished, I set the supplies aside. Then I give him what he really came here for.

I place my hands on the sharp edges of his face and slide them to his ears, his neck, and into his hair. Bending, I drag my nose along his and nuzzle him.

He loosens a rough exhale and wraps a muscled arm around me, hauling me onto the bed, right on top of his prone body.

So much for changing the locks on my heart.

Relaxing my weight, I rest my head on his shoulder and breathe in his manly garage and cedar scent.

When he says nothing, I go first.

"I'm sorry."

He waits, his silence uncharacteristically patient.

"I touched Monty's chest, his stomach, and he kissed me. I didn't kiss him back. I didn't push him away, either. I didn't stop him."

"You wanted to kiss him."

"Yes, but not without you. I don't want him without you,

and I don't want to exclude him." My throat burns. "In a perfect world, all four of us are together."

"That's *your* perfect world."

"How is it not yours? You have a relationship with him. It's not like your bond with Kody, but it can be. It can be whatever you let it be. I've seen the love among the three of you. I'm not asking you to share me with someone you despise. If you replay the past five months you've spent with him, is there any part you hated? Does he make you miserable? He put a roof over your head, helped you pursue your dreams, bought you yachts and motorcycles, and—"

"I know, Frankie." His jaw flexes against my head. "I fucking know. I owe him everything, but I will *not* give you up as payment."

"No one is asking you to do that."

"He is. Maybe not as payment, but that's what he wants."

"Change his mind."

He barks an incredulous laugh.

"Have you seen him?" I ask. "Talked to him?"

"We talk over text."

"About?"

"Your safety. The investigation. The search for the cabin."

The guards keep me updated on that. There's been no progress. No contact from my stalker or The Ghost. With Sirena's disappearance, the scouting mission in the Arctic has been put on hold.

"I'm sorry for what I said that night." He turns his head, pressing a kiss to my brow. "I know you haven't been fucking around with him. I know what we walked in on was an unintentional moment. Your hands were at your sides. Your back was to the wall. Your lips were closed. You weren't pursuing him. He was pursuing you."

"Don't villainize him. He never forced me, and I wanted to kiss him back."

"I know. He loves you. Who can blame him?"

I lift my head, my eyes achy with tears as I search his face.

"I'm lost without you, Frankie."

"And I'm lost without you. At least you have Kody. Monty's completely alone."

"So are you."

My mouth trembles. I don't want to cry. I need to be strong. Strong enough to support them through this.

But I'm not strong enough to stop his lips from lifting to mine. Not with his hand cradling my skull so lovingly.

It's not a kiss. There's no movement, no deepening. I hold still, giving him the same response I gave Monty. Just a touch of lips. An intimate moment of affection. A breath of love.

Then I pull back.

His hands fall away, and I feel an instant, harrowing sense of loss.

I want him closer. Of course I do. The tension in my thighs and the tightening in my core signal a unified craving, demanding I give in.

That's a problem.

I made a decision. I won't choose between them, and I won't waver.

Steeling my spine, I climb off the bed and meet his eyes.

He's breathless, angry, and staring back at me. "This isn't forever."

Forever without him?

The thought buckles my knees.

I grip the bed for support. "Family is forever. Find your way back to Monty. Talk to someone about your childhood abuse. Then come back to me."

"Those are your terms?"

"Yes."

His neck stiffens, and he looks away.

"Promise me, Leo. Promise me you'll take care of one another."

"I'll try." Standing, he leans in and presses a gentle kiss on my forehead.

I close my eyes, letting myself feel the depth of his love.

Too soon, he pulls away and walks out, leaving me standing alone in the empty room with a hollow ache in my chest and a lump in my throat.

Then I climb onto the bed, curl up in a ball, and cry.

Kodiak

FIFTY

No guards stand outside the on-call room, which means she's in the trauma unit. I'll find her. But first, I need to smell, lick, and indulge.

Inside the room where she sleeps, I close the door, grab a pair of her leggings from the chair, and bury my face in the crotch.

Groaning, my eyes roll back in my head.

I lick the inside, lapping at the swath of fabric that rubs against her cunt. It's not enough. Where are her panties?

Chewing on the garment, I scan the room, mindless, desperate.

She's been living in this space for two weeks. I can't sleep, can't think, can't fucking breathe without her and her intoxicating scent.

I drop the leggings and crawl onto the tiny bunk bed. My hands slide into the divot in the mattress left by her body. I inhale her sweat from the sheets and drag my face across her pillow.

Then I drop to my stomach and roll in her essence.

She would call me a caveman. But I'm more beast than

man. I'm a predator. An animal.

I'm hers.

I press my nose against every piece of her I can find. Her bras. Her earbuds. Her lip balm on the nightstand.

I suck on her hair tie and pace into the bathroom.

Grabbing her toothbrush, I pop it in my mouth and step into the shower. Droplets of water cling to the walls. I collect the moisture in my hand and rub it across my face.

As I return the toothbrush, I spot a laundry bag on the floor behind the door. A temptation I can't resist.

I spend some time in that bag, sniffing and gnawing on every enticing, Frankie-soaked pair of underwear.

Christ, I miss the taste of her, the sticky, wet feel of her against my mouth. I'm fucking starving without her.

With careful precision, I put the room back in order, returning everything where I found it.

Then I slip back into the hall and follow the scent of her trail.

The hills taught me the art of stalking, every movement calculated, every sense heightened. The biting cold honed my instincts, shaping me into the hunter I am.

Keeping to the shadows, I step silently, my footsteps muted against the hospital's tiled floors. The antiseptic air does nothing to diminish her lingering essence.

Her sweet, cherry aroma reaches my nose before I hear her voice.

My heart pounds. I stay hidden, muscles bunched. My eyes scan the corridor, catching a glimpse of her red hair through a gap in an exam room door.

She pauses, sensing something, and glances over her shoulder.

My breath hitches, but I remain unseen, a shadow among shadows.

Her guards know I'm here but don't bother to look my way. They're used to me lurking. I'm one of them, only better. I would die for her.

My fingers twitch, longing to reach out, to touch her, to pull her close. But she's working. I respect that and don't want to disturb her.

She exits the exam room and strides down the corridor, her steps quickening.

I follow, my senses attuned to every nuance. Her heartbeat, her fragrance, the sound of her breathing—they guide me.

She rounds a corner, and I prowl silently after her.

I can track her through a blizzard, through the densest forest, across the most treacherous terrain. Here, in the sterile, controlled environment of the hospital, it's too easy.

She stops again, her head turning slightly. She feels me. Our connection defies logic, an invisible thread that binds us together.

I miss her with a ferocity that borders on madness, my yearning a physical ache.

But I can endure pain, the scars on my back a constant reminder of that. Denver's cruelty knew no bounds, and it forged me into the man I am today.

That life, those lessons, they serve me now.

I move closer, the distance between us shrinking. She pauses to talk to someone, her soft lilt swirling over my skin.

Then she's on the move again, and I chase.

She's my prey, but more than that, she's my world. I'll never let her go.

I stay with her until her shift ends. When she shuts herself in her room, I approach her guards.

It's the same thing every day. They know what I'm going to demand before I open my mouth.

"We'll call you if she leaves or receives visitors," Stanley says.

I can storm in there, but she'll tell me the same thing she told Leo last week.

Find your way back to Monty. Talk to someone about your childhood abuse. Then come back to me.

If I want to fix it, the problem isn't in that room. It's out there with Leo and Monty.

With great effort, I turn away and leave the hospital.

Monty is waiting when I step outside, his presence as

commanding as ever.

He stands in the parking lot beside my motorcycle, cutting an imposing silhouette against the setting sun. But as I draw nearer, I see the unraveling.

His suit hangs in disarray, the once-immaculate fabric now rumpled and creased. His shirt is untucked, and his tie hangs loose around his neck. His hair looks finger-raked to hell, wild strands falling over his forehead.

His love for Frankie gouges new wrinkles on his face. Dark bruises shadow his eyes. Whiskers dust his chiseled jawline.

He misses her ruinously. It permeates from his very being.

But those arctic blue eyes haven't lost their sharpness. They meet mine, and I nod in acknowledgment.

We may not always see eye to eye, but we have a common goal—to protect Frankie.

"How is she?" he asks, his voice hoarse and controlled.

"Safe." I delete the final few feet to join him. "I won't let anything happen to her."

"Neither will I." A flicker of something unreadable crosses his face. "Are we going to talk about this?"

"Are you ready to talk about it?"

"No."

"Do you want to spend the rest of your miserable life without her?"

"That's out of the question."

"Then we're going to fucking talk about it." I straddle the bike. "Meet me at the distillery."

monty

FIFTY-ONE

The chill of drizzling rain soaks through my tailored suit as I step out of the Bugatti, gripping the wrapped picture frame in my hand.

After the conversation with Kody two days ago and the first session with my psychiatrist this morning, my thoughts are swirling up a storm, leaving no corner of my mind untouched.

But I push it all aside and focus on the task ahead.

The seaplane base sits before me, the dock, hangar, and facilities barely visible in the gloomy mist.

Leo's new venture.

Taking my advice, he decided to start his operation with a float plane service and was able to lease a few old planes to get him going.

It won't be long before he's operating tours out of Sitka and making a killing doing it.

Success runs in his blood.

My shoes crunch against the gravel as I weave around the buildings, peering into the windows. My bodyguards arrived in a separate car. I barely notice them as they spread out around me.

I find him in the hangar, busy with a task I can't quite make out.

"Give us a minute," I say to his guards and mine.

Everyone steps out, leaving me alone with him.

Standing on a ladder, he drills screws into the eaves. Buckets of water scatter the ground around him. He must be repairing leaks in the metal roof.

He moves with purpose and intensity, his muscles rippling beneath his oil-stained shirt as he works. The sight of him, so absorbed in his task, sends a pang of something—regret, maybe?—through me.

I step out of the rain and approach the ladder. He doesn't acknowledge me, but I know he senses me.

The tension between us lives and breathes, refusing to be ignored. It's been two weeks since our confrontation with Frankie, but the anger and hurt still simmer. We haven't seen each other, and our texts are limited to conversations about Frankie's security.

I'm here to change that.

"Leo," I call out.

He doesn't glance at me, his focus unwavering.

I step closer, the picture frame heavy in my hand.

He continues working, not even a twitch in my direction. That stubborn set of his jaw...it's fucking maddening. But I understand it. Hell, I feel it, too.

When he finally speaks, his voice is gruff and strained. "Do you have news on the investigation? Any word from Wilson or...the other thing?"

The Ghost. He knows not to say that name out loud.

"No updates. We're at a standstill. But Frankie's security is tight. No one can get to her at the hospital."

He pauses, glancing down at me.

His face is bruised, beard grown out, stitches crisscrossing his forehead. He's been in more bar fights than Frankie knows about, and it shows.

"What is that?" He nods at the wrapped frame in my hand.

"Something I wanted you to have." I set it against the wall and straighten the cuffs of my sleeves. "Look, I..."

I want to back away slowly and rethink this whole thing. I don't know what to say to him. I only know that I need to say something, do something, or I'm going to lose him.

I'm the patriarch of this family. It's my job to fix this. That's why I'm here. I'm going to fucking fix it.

But to do that, I must open myself up. Might as well take a knife to my chest and split the skin and bone. It would be less painful.

"Kody wants us to reconcile." I inwardly cringe, wishing I hadn't started with that.

"Reconcile?" He snorts, a bitter sound. "What does that look like? Will you invite me over for Christmas dinner? Will I be a third wheel on your date nights? When your kids are born, will I be Uncle Leo? Or Cousin Leo? Will you ask me to watch your house while you and Frankie travel the world together?"

"If you're going to be a dick, come down from there and be a dick to my face."

"I'm not trying to be a dick." He gathers his tools and descends the ladder. "I'm being realistic. You want her to be your wife, and you want Kody and I to be your family."

"You *are* my family."

"I know you talked to Kody. What's his stance on this?"

"He'll do anything to get Frankie back. I met with a therapist this morning. Kody starts his sessions tomorrow. We're trying to sort through our issues."

I pull Dr. Thurber's business card from my pocket and hand it to him.

He looks at it and tosses it on a nearby workbench. "I can't talk about my past, Monty. It's over. Done."

"What about your future? Will you talk about that? With me?"

"My future is with her." His blue and gold eyes bore into mine. "If we're not talking about that, we have nothing to discuss."

My pulse thrashes in my ears.

He wants to fuck my wife and expects me to go along with it.

How can I do that? It goes against every possessive, selfish fiber of my being.

Even if we could all agree to a polyamorous relationship—which I can't envision happening—how would it work?

I'm controlling, dominant, especially in the bedroom. An alpha doesn't share his bed with another alpha, let alone two.

I watched them fuck. They aren't bottoms.

And the bond she shares with them? It's stronger than her feelings for me. I know she loves me, but not the way she loves them.

I should walk away. Let them have her. That would be the selfless thing to do.

But I can't. I'll fight for her until my last breath.

Leo sees his future with her, and for me, that means a future of fighting and anguish.

"That's what I thought." He grabs the drill, climbs the ladder, and resumes his work with renewed vigor.

This was a mistake.

I stand there a moment longer, swaying beneath the enormity of everything left unsaid.

Then I turn away and walk back to my car with my guards.

Halfway there, the drizzle grows heavier, harder, intensifying into a downpour.

I came here to fix this.

I didn't even fucking try.

Fuck.

Halting in my tracks, I lift my face to the sky and let the cold rain wash over me.

Then I pivot and come face to face with Leo.

He stands a few feet away, arms at his sides, unblinking in the deluge.

"You look like shit," he says.

"So do you." I swipe a hand down my face, uselessly clearing away the rain.

"I appreciate you. Everything you've done for me. The support and encouragement, the opportunity to pursue my dreams, and every basic necessity I could ever need or want. I'm indebted to you."

"No, you're not."

"What did you come here to say to me?"

My chest tightens. My stomach hardens. My throat closes up.

One session with a psychiatrist, my first genuine attempt at trying, and I'm ready to puke my feelings all over the cement.

Here it goes.

"I'm scared." I rub my chest, and a shiver runs through me. "Scared of losing her for good. Scared of losing you and Kody."

"What are you going to do about it?" He crosses his arms, seemingly unfazed by the rain.

"You didn't want to share her with Kody. I read about all the fighting in her journal. What changed your mind?"

"Fear. She and Kody were gone for a month. I didn't know if they would return. The odds were against them, and I was in that cabin, alone and fucking terrified." He licks his rain-drenched lips. "Fear has a way of putting things in perspective. From where I'm standing, you're not scared enough."

"I don't solve my problems with fear. I take action, hire resources, and make plans. I execute."

"How's that working for you?"

"Are you willing to let me take the lead? Call the shots? Do this my way, no questions asked?"

He huffs a laugh. "Not in this lifetime."

"Then this will never work."

"Could've told you that." He turns and walks away, throwing a glare over his shoulder. "Good luck with those plans."

leonid

FIFTY-TWO

It takes me two hours to work up the nerve to open the package Monty left.

If it's a two-foot-tall, framed photo of Denver, I'll kill him.

I don't want a picture of my mother, either. I don't want that pain. I have enough in my life.

Maybe it's one of his expensive paintings.

I rip off the paper and stumble back.

A hand-sketched illustration.

Wolf's illustration of the Turbo Beaver's cockpit.

A hard knot forms in my throat, and I press a fist to my mouth, gulping down a pained breath.

In a sleek, modern frame, the sketch sits behind glass, its edges wrinkled with wear from being folded and unfolded countless times.

A barrage of memories pummels me. Wolf had broken into the plane and drawn this detailed diagram of the dashboard, our secret map for escape. We memorized it, studied it, and used it to fuel our hope in a dark time. Seeing it framed so carefully, a relic of our shared desperation, knocks my legs out from under me.

I drop to my knees, and a cry wrenches from my throat.

Fucking hell, I've tried so hard to keep this locked away. This deep well of misery and loss. I thought I had it sealed tight.

Tears spill from my eyes, and I squeeze them shut.

I miss Wolf so much it hurts. He left a dull, constant ache that I refuse to let myself grieve.

Grieving means confronting the past, and I can't do that. The abuse, the death—it's all buried deep, transformed into a simmering rage that I can no longer control.

Frankie's right. I've known it all along. I need help. But the thought of opening up, of breaking through that door and peering into the dark, dismal hell inside, paralyzes me. There's a terrible place within me, full of gruesome memories, a Pandora's box that shouldn't be touched.

If I don't do something, I'll end up in jail again. Or worse, I'll pick a fight with the wrong man and get myself shot.

I stare at the illustration for a long time, tracing a finger along the black ink, remembering Wolf's expressions as he wielded his sharpies with a skill that always awed me.

He's gone, but the memories he gave me remain.

So many memories. Good and bad. They all hurt.

In the silence of my grief, there lies another deep and yawning void.

Frankie.

What will I do to get her back?

Isn't the answer anything? Everything?

Are you willing to let me take the lead? Call the shots? Do this my way, no questions asked?

My ego kept me from accepting Monty's offer, if I can call it an offer.

He wants to run things. But hasn't he been doing that all this time? How would this be any different?

I didn't think to ask him if he was referring to sex or something else? Does he intend to control when, where, and how we fuck her?

The notion is ludicrous.

As I set the frame aside, I notice a note tucked in behind it.

My hands shake as I unfold the paper, revealing Monty's crisp handwriting.

Leo,

You're my family by blood and my brother by heart. I can't fathom my life without you. We'll get through this together. Please, don't shut me out.

Montgomery

The words are simple, but they hit with the force of a sucker punch.

He considers me a brother. He doesn't want his life without me.

The backs of my eyes burn. Goddamn him.

What will I do to get her back?

What will I do to get my family back?

Anything.

That's the answer, the only one I need.

I reach for the card Monty left and, with a shaky breath, dial Dr. Thurber's office.

In a clinical voice, the receptionist tells me the next available appointment is months out. When I mention Monty Novak, they miraculously have an opening this afternoon.

Fuck.

I'm not ready.

I'll never be ready.

But I'll do it for her.

I'll do it for *them.*

leonid

FIFTY-THREE

Two days later, I find myself crossing the Sitka Sound on my yacht, heading toward Monty's island.

Up ahead, the estate rises out of the fog, stately and lonesome.

I've felt anxiety before. Too many times to count. But never to the point that I want to puke.

Hanging my head over the side of the boat, I spit into the sea.

The nausea passes by the time I reach the island, but my nerves wreak havoc on my heart rate.

What if Monty and I can't work things out? I don't have a backup plan.

One therapy session isn't going to stop me from punching his lights out. That's exactly what I'll do if he doesn't cooperate.

I want my girl back.

Tonight.

Kody and I trimmed our beards, cleaned up our hair, and put on our best boxer-briefs this morning.

Yeah, we're fucking hopeful.

He got held up at the distillery but won't be too far behind me.

Oliver greets me at the door, his face expressionless. "He's upstairs."

I ascend the grand staircase, my heartbeat resounding with the echo of my footsteps.

I find Monty curled up in bed, looking worse than he did two days ago.

Sweatpants, shirtless, unshaved, and unwashed, he stares blankly at a black-and-white romance movie on TV.

"Is that Casablanca?" I walk in without knocking.

He glares at me.

"Is this your plan?" I gesture at the TV. "This is how you solve your problems?"

He continues to glare, the anger in his eyes burning through the shadows there. Then he turns his attention back to the screen.

"I started seeing your doctor." My palms slick with sweat.

"I know."

"Tracking my movements in the app? You fucking creeper."

"Yes."

"Then you knew I was coming here." I spot his phone on the nightstand.

He doesn't remove his eyes from the TV.

"You left me that package for a reason. The note..." I clutch my nape and shift my weight. "You wanted me to remember Wolf, to grieve him. Well, I'm here, and I'm grieving. But I can't do it alone. None of us can."

"That's not why you're here."

"Yeah. You're right. I'm grieving her, too. I miss her. I fucking need her." I feel my temper rising, the familiar heat licking at my insides. "The only way I'm getting her back is with you and Kody."

For a moment, I think he's going to tell me to leave. If he does, I'll have to break his face, and that would hurt Frankie.

He pushes to a sitting position and meets my eyes. "I'm not convinced."

"Convinced about what?"

"Your purpose here."

Christ, he's not making this easy.

I scrub my hands down my face and look him dead in the eye. "Like it or not, motherfucker, the four of us have been in a relationship for five months. We lived together. We ate our meals, worked out, pursued our dreams, learned to drive, cried, laughed, and fought together. We made all our decisions together as a team. Hell, we still do. The only thing the four of us haven't done together is fuck."

He doesn't even blink.

"What am I missing?" I cross my arms.

"I think you covered it." Powering off the TV, he shifts to the edge of the bed and clasps his hands between his knees. "But you brushed over some significant talking points."

"Such as?"

"Did you two get your shit worked out yet?" Kody strides into the room, his black hair soaked by the rain.

"No." I arch a brow at Monty. "Which points did I brush over?"

"If we share her, we'll face a slew of new challenges. Social stigma, time management, insecurity, jealousy, boundaries, legal and financial complications, pecking order..."

Kody grunts.

"What?" Monty squints at him. "I know you've had your share of complications with this already, but polygamy in the middle of fucking nowhere isn't the same as polygamy in modern society, where the world scrutinizes, judges, and interferes."

"You care what people think?" I ask.

"Not at all."

"You can make all the other shit go away with your money and influence." Kody snaps his fingers. "Like that."

"I can't make our internal obstacles go away. Strakh men are controlling, domineering, and stubborn as fuck. Put three of us in a bed together and what do you think will happen? I don't want to fight with you for the rest of my life."

"You're overthinking this." I lace my hands behind my

head. "Kody and I already sleep in the same bed. When we disagree, we work it out. We would do the same with you."

"We know a thing or two about overcoming obstacles." Kody leans against the dresser.

"Understatement," I mutter.

Monty taps his fingers together, studying me. "Why did it take you two days to come here?"

"Nerves." I brace a hand on my hip and chew my thumbnail. "Considering I turn every uncomfortable conversation into a brawl, I didn't want to fuck this up. Dr. Thurber taught me some breathing techniques, which I haven't used since I got here. I prepared a speech, which I forgot about until now. But I'm here. I came crawling back to you, willing to fucking beg, because I love her and refuse to spend one more night without her."

"Thank you for your honesty." His voice scratches, eyebrows furrowing.

"Why did I find you in bed, staring at the TV like you gave up on life?"

"Classic romantic movies are my comfort. I'm not giving up. Not even close." He lifts a shoulder. "I wanted to open myself up, let you see a part of me no one else does. This..." He stands, gesturing at his unkempt appearance, the bed, and the TV. "This is me when no one else is around."

"If you expect me to judge you for that, you got the wrong guy."

He nods and scratches his shirtless abs.

Then he squares his shoulders, and a transformation settles over him. The passive, chill, bed-rotting, classic-movie-watching guy vanishes, and the Monty I know stares back at me, his blue eyes sharp and icy.

His expression conveys a depth of intellect and unyielding will, but it's his dominating presence that makes me stand a little taller.

"If I'm in, I'm all in." He stalks into the bathroom. "That means equal parts in this relationship and our family. I'm your brother and her lover."

Kody and I exchange a look and follow him.

In one smooth motion, he strips his sweatpants and continues into the walk-in shower, fully naked.

"You said lover." I lean against the wall just outside the stall. "Not husband."

"If we do this, she's married to all of us, even if the law doesn't recognize it." He turns, facing us, with a hand on the faucet. "If we do this, we're giving her our last name."

A shudder runs through me, starting at the base of my spine and spreading like wildfire. It's not just a shiver. A cascade of electric excitement lights up every corner of my body. I feel it in my fingertips, tingling and alive. It courses through my legs, making my knees weak. My breath catches in my throat. My heart hammers in my chest.

This is her dream.

But not just hers.

It's mine.

And by the looks of it, Kody's, too.

He strides past me, crashes into Monty, and wraps him up in a chest-crushing, balls-slapping embrace that might've been awkward under other circumstances. Monty stands there, stark nude and uncertain, with his arms hovering at his sides.

Considering what we're about to do, about to spend the rest of our lives doing, a naked hug should be foreplay for those two.

"All in." Monty surrenders to the affection and squeezes his arms around Kody.

"All in." Kody steps back, breathing hard, and reaches for me.

We come together, our fists buried in each other's backs.

"We're going to get our girl," he whispers, hugging me tighter.

"Yeah, we fucking are." I smack a kiss on his cheek. "All in."

We pull apart, grinning and jittery.

"We're doing this my way." Monty turns on the shower and ducks his head under the spray. "I lead. Every step of the way. Understood?"

"Tonight only." I straighten, meeting his eyes. "We'll see

how you do. Then you can negotiate for more."

A smirk twitches his lips. "Deal."

I'm exhausted. The kind of bone-deep weariness that hollows out my insides. The trauma unit has a way of sucking the life out of me, one crisis at a time.

As I stand at the nurses' station, closing out my day on the computer, my thoughts gravitate to my guys. I try to stay busy enough not to let the despair consume me.

But I miss them.

I miss them with an intensity that tortures and slays.

It's been eighteen days since I left them on that dock. Eighteen days trapped in this hospital with nothing but loneliness and a broken heart to keep me company.

I've endured longer separations from them. But this time, it's different. There's no expiration date. It could take them months to reconcile.

It could take forever.

But I trust them. I have faith in their love. They'll pull their stubborn heads out of their asses eventually. They'll forgive one another. And maybe someday, they'll forgive me.

On the bright side, it seems the stalker lost track of me. Or hasn't found a way to torment me in the hospital. Makes me wonder how safe the island is. I often had the feeling someone was watching me there. Not to mention the man-shaped shadows in the windows.

I texted my concerns about this to Monty last week. He replied with, *The island is the safest place on Earth.*

Typical Monty.

Kody, on the other hand, continues to stalk me from the shadows here. He never lets me see him, but I know he comes every day. The guards confirm it when I ask.

He's probably creeping into my room and sniffing my undies.

"Oh, my lord." Nurse Letty runs up and shoves her arm under my nose. "Frankie, check my pulse. Hurry. I think I'm dying."

What now?

I glance at her, but she's not looking at me. Her mouth hangs open as she stares at something behind me.

Oh, no.

My neck stiffens, and I close my eyes. I don't have the strength to resist any of them tonight.

"The Viking?" I whisper.

"Mm-hmm." She grabs my elbow, drawing my gaze to her. "The Viking, the billionaire, *and* the caveman. Prepare yourself, honey. You're not ready."

I turn, and my heart stops.

Utterly stunned, I can't move. Can't breathe. The shock is so profound it takes a second for my mind to catch up with my body.

Standing there, together as a unified front, are Monty, Leo, and Kody. And they're smiling.

Three grins on three beautiful faces.

They're smiling and staring at me expectedly, and it's goddamn contagious.

This isn't real.

I'm hallucinating.

"Told you." Letty pushes my jaw closed. "Don't forget to breathe. Don't want you passing out."

She doesn't know the details of my breakup. She only

knows I've been sleeping in the on-call room while these three men try to drag me out.

She doesn't know what this means.

They're all here. Together.

Shimmery, sunshiny joy bursts through me. The grin on my face stretches so wide it hurts my cheeks. Tears of pure happiness blur my vision, but I don't care.

All I can do is laugh, and the sound startles me. I cover my mouth.

I can't believe it. After all this time, all the pain, the setbacks, the nights spent dreaming and hoping—it's finally happening.

The reality hits me with such force that I stagger back a step, needing a moment to steady myself.

I feel alive, more alive than I've ever felt, every sense heightened and vibrant.

This is it.

This is what it feels like to have a dream come true.

"Time to come home." Monty extends a hand, exuding enough authority to make my knees weak.

His perfectly styled hair, as black as a moonless night, frames his face with that square jawline I love so much. Goosebumps race across my skin as his arctic blue eyes lock onto mine. He's a fantasy brought to life in his fitted suit.

And he's waiting for me.

Here goes nothing.

I walk right up to him, bypassing his hand to lift on my tiptoes and press a kiss to his mouth. Chaste and quick. A kiss to test the waters.

He responds, his lips firm and commanding, a promise of things to come.

No growls from the other two.

No bloodshed.

Somebody pinch me.

I step back and move to Leo, spotting my bags on the floor behind him.

"We packed up all your things in the on-call room." His

beautifully unique eyes watch me intently.

Brown-blond braids tie back into a knot, adding a touch of the hills to his otherwise polished appearance. His surly temper is always close to the surface, but now there's a calm determination in his gaze.

"Do you forgive me?" I ask.

"What do I need to forgive, love?"

"The kiss?" My brows pull together. "At the house? The one you walked in on?"

"You'll be doing more than kissing him tonight. And every night ever after."

It's not just what he says but the dark, sensual way he says it that makes my core clench, and my heart beat faster.

I moisten my lips and whisper, "You got into another fight."

Faded bruises linger just beneath the skin around his eyes. Those weren't there when I stitched his head last week.

"Got into a few bar fights. But I'm working on that. Started seeing someone about it."

"Really?"

"All of us are." His hand comes up to cup my face, giving me the closeness I've missed so desperately. "We're seeing Dr. Thurber here in town. He's...kind."

My nose burns, and I blink rapidly, fighting back tears. "I'll be with you guys through the process. The four of us together make a damn good support system."

"I know."

I kiss him, tasting the fire and earthiness that is so uniquely him.

He pulls away, turning me toward Kody.

My broody lover stares down at me with animal magnetism, his black hair trimmed and finger-combed. His tanned complexion and muscled body have always reminded me of a dark Lycan prince. The way he looks at me is intoxicating, igniting a seductive fire that leaves me breathless, turned on, and a little afraid.

His carnal black eyes, which always hold a hint of sadness, now shine with something else.

Stars.

I throw myself into his arms, instantly enveloped by the scent of wood smoke and berry vodka. As our lips press together, I sink into his rugged tenderness. He's here, and he's not letting go.

"Let's go home." He lifts me against his chest and pivots toward the exit.

The brute is going to carry me out, and I won't fight him. I want this closeness. I need it.

Leo and Monty grab my bags and follow us amid an eruption of cheers and whistles. The entire trauma unit gathered to witness our reunion. If only Rhett were here to see it.

I'm going home. With them. I can barely process it.

Locking my arms around Kody's neck, I whisper, "Did you sneak into my room and sniff my underwear?"

"Yes."

Knew it!

"Did you jerk off on me while I slept?"

"Thought about it."

"Caveman."

"Call me whatever you want. I'm yours."

He carries me outside, where a chauffeured car is waiting. We all pile in, and I find myself sandwiched between Monty and Kody in the back seat.

"Keep your hands to yourself, on your lap." Monty shoots me a stern look. "Or I'll have you naked before we reach the dock."

Damn, he's intense.

I glance at Carl in the driver's seat, and my ears grow hot.

"Carl has been briefed on our new dynamic and is here to protect us," Monty says. "Nothing more."

The other guards follow in the car behind us. I'm used to the constant audience.

"Okay." I place my quivering hands on my lap.

"Good." Monty's fingers twitch on his thigh. "Now let's talk."

"Talk?"

"We have until we reach the island to say what needs to be said. The second we enter the house, we'll be using our lips for something other than words."

My mouth dries, and my nipples harden.

I haven't had sex with Monty in fourteen months. He's been celibate for over a year.

My body is ready. "What needs to be said?"

"I get that you've been in a polyamorous relationship for a while. But you haven't been in one with *me*."

"We're not setting rules." Leo twists in the front seat, staring back at us.

"I'll remember that when my dick comes in contact with yours." Monty grins.

Kinky, filthy bastard.

While Leo doesn't smile back, he doesn't recoil, either. He simply says, "All in."

Holy fucking shit.

This is happening.

"I take full responsibility for everything that happens from this point forward," Monty says. "All decisions go through me. Every concern. Every conflict. If something bothers you, come to me, and we'll work it out as a team."

"The self-proclaimed team leader." Leo arches a brow.

"Yes. We need one until we iron out the bumps in the road. And there will be bumps."

Pragmatic as always. He built a successful global enterprise with an iron fist. He'll apply that same ruthless control to ensure our relationship doesn't fail.

I nod with excitement, nervousness, and overwhelming happiness.

The drive to the dock is quick. We board Monty's yacht, and the no-touching rule remains firmly in place.

"Tell me what I missed. I want to hear everything." I curl up in the armchair in the cabin, hoping they'll all squeeze onto the couch.

To my delight, they do.

They sit side by side, manspreading, legs touching, completely at ease with Monty in the middle.

What life is this?

"We were slow to work things out." Monty stares at me, eyes burning as if he's thinking about later tonight rather than the present. "Kody initiated the first heart-to-heart. We talked. Really talked. Then I paid a visit to Leo and left the ball in his court."

"He framed Wolf's sketch of the cockpit," Leo says, his voice softer than usual.

Then he tells me the story.

Hearing him talk about his reaction to the gift breaks my heart and puts it back together again.

They explain how they worked things out maturely, and their reunion this afternoon fills me with a relief I can hardly describe.

It's everything I hoped for and more.

As they update me on the past few weeks, we don't bring up the stalker, the hired Russian mobster, or the failed attempts to find the cabin. We focus on the good things, their successes with their business ventures, and their sessions with Dr. Thurber.

"It's what you wanted." Kody's voice drops, rumbling through me. "For us to be together. We're doing it the right way."

"But is it what *you* want?" My hands curl on my lap. "Or are you only here because I gave an ultimatum and forced you into this."

"There's no forced participation here, darling." Monty smolders at me, his lids lowering. "Don't get it wrong. We are all consenting, and we'll spend all night proving it."

Perspiration beads on my skin. What's with this heat? I'm burning up.

Pulling the front of my scrubs away from my sweaty chest, I squeak, "Okay."

Monty sees right through me.

We stare at each other across the space until something shifts in his expression.

He glances at his watch, out the window, and back to me.

"Hand me that pillow." He motions at Kody.

A wordless conversation passes between them. Then Kody tugs the throw pillow from behind him and tosses it on the floor between Monty's feet.

A swallow lodges in my throat.

I know what Monty will say before he says it.

"Come here." He sits back, his baritone a silken caress.

Every nerve tingles with anticipation, charged with the electricity in his command. My heart thunders, breaths come faster, and heat rises through my skin.

Wetting my lips, I stand and walk to that pillow. "What about the no-touching rule?"

"Your clothes stay on until we reach the house."

"And yours?"

"Depends on what you want."

I start to lower my knees to the pillow, but he grabs my hips and pulls me onto his lap.

He stabs his hands into my hair, and God, I missed that commanding touch.

Guiding my face to his, he spears me with his eyes. The glacial depths ensnare me, like I'm stepping onto a frozen lake. Like the surface is cracking, and the danger is imminent. Because, of course, it is.

I'm about to be fucked by three Strakh men.

"Tell me what you want," he demands.

"I want the impossible."

"Nothing is impossible."

"I want the four of us to be together."

"We are together."

The exact same conversation we had in the restaurant.

"Spell it out." He lifts his hips beneath me, letting me feel the swollen state of his arousal. "I expect a more graphic answer this time."

I lean back to look at the impressive erection tenting his slacks. I sweep my gaze over Kody's lap, then Leo's. Both hard. Painfully so, given how their zippers strain to contain them.

"She wants three dicks." Kody shifts, adjusting himself.

"Let her answer," Monty says.

I glower at his chiseled jaw.

He's really going to make me say it.

Fine.

"I want three dicks. Double penetration. Don't care which holes as long as you fill me until my eyes water, and I don't know which way is up." I peek at each of them, encouraged by the hunger in their expressions. "Before we go to the house, I would love nothing more than to kneel on this pillow and watch all of you stroke your cocks while I suck each one dry. It's been a minute since you've had sex." I look at Monty when I say that. "Let me take the edge off before we go inside."

The yacht slows at the dock. We're already home.

But the guards don't enter the cabin. No one announces our arrival. Monty arranged everything.

"Was that graphic enough for you?" I ask.

"Yeah. It was fucking perfect." Reclining, he stretches his arms along the back of the couch behind Leo and Kody. "Now put that filthy mouth on me."

I'm still waiting for one of them to reach a breaking point and stop this before it starts.

But they don't.

As I slide off his lap and kneel on the pillow, the sound of zippers rends the air.

Dicks. So many beautiful, glorious dicks. I don't know where to look first.

Between Monty's legs, his erection juts from the open fly of his suit pants. Thick, veiny, and glistening with precome, it stands tall and imposing like the man himself.

I want it. I need it.

I need all of them.

My breath quickens, and my pussy squeezes, throbbing like a second heartbeat.

Leo and Kody grind their hands against their cocks. I try to watch them simultaneously, taking in the entire view.

"Focus on him, love." Leo drops his head back, watching me down the length of his nose as he pleasures himself. "We'll get our turn."

I can't believe this is happening.

We're together. Finally. And nothing is going to tear us apart again.

monty
FIFTY-FIVE

Seeing Frankie kneeling before me is a dream, one I fantasized about for fourteen months. Just looking at her excites me. Christ, I might come before she even touches me.

She licks her lips, igniting a fresh spike of need.

Stretching up my body, she goes to work on my shirt, frees each button, and spreads open the edges to expose my body to her rapacious gaze.

Biting her lip, she smooths her hands across my chest, caresses my twitching pecs, traces the valleys between my abdominal muscles, and follows the trail of hair to the base of my throbbing, leaking hard-on.

"Don't stop," I rasp.

Her eyes fly up to meet mine, her pupils blown and lips parted.

Then she wraps a hand around my cock.

Fucking God, she's doing it. She's fucking touching me.

I let my eyelids fall, isolating the glorious sensation.

She knows how to grip me, squeezing just beneath the head with perfect pressure, exactly how I like it.

Sinking deeper into the couch, I groan as she tugs and

strokes me from root to tip.

It's heaven. It's hell. I want to grab her head, shove into her mouth, and fuck her throat until I'm empty. But she's in a trance, a haze of mindless temptation, seduced by the heat of us, by the electric, molten reawakening of us.

The heavy breathing on either side of me grows louder, faster, as Leo and Kody watch. From what I read in her journal, this is Leo's kink. A voyeur's delight. He rubs his dick with vigor, his gaze glued to the motion of her hand as I leak all over her soft, delicate fingers.

Frankie is my kink. Everything about her makes me wildly, feverishly aroused.

Slowly, I bend forward, shaving away the gap between our mouths. I lean down. She leans up. We meet in the middle, and our lips collide, crashing like two powerful waves.

The kiss is sudden and intense, fire meeting gasoline, a hurricane making landfall. The earth shakes beneath us.

My hands possess her gorgeous figure, hauling her off the pillow and yanking her tightly against my chest. I gently clasp her graceful neck, gliding my thumb along her throat as her silky tongue chases and licks mine.

With her body draped between my legs and her hand around my cock, I thrust into her fist and shove my tongue in her mouth like a horny, inexperienced teenager.

And she moans for me.

Her desire elevates me. Her beauty humbles me. I bathe in her sensual radiance.

I grip her even closer, licking every recess and corner of her mouth, reacquainting myself with her sweet, sinful taste.

Easing back, she returns her knees to the pillow. Gripping the waistband of my briefs, she shimmies the fabric down my thighs until she has access to my heavy sac. Her hand cradles it, massaging my balls until I'm arching and lifting my hips with my cock bobbing in the air.

She captures me, her fingers curled around the root. Then she lowers her head and sucks the crown.

"Oh, fuck." I'm not going to last.

Two seconds of this, and I'll go off like a bomb and flood

her mouth.

"Frankie." I thrust against her tongue, growing thicker, hungrier, more frantic.

She pulls back, licking the tip. "Do you still have superhuman recovery time?"

"Don't know." I thread my fingers through her hair. "Spent the past year with my hand. It's been underwhelming."

"I'll make it worth the wait."

"I have no doubt."

She lowers her head and takes me to the back of her throat.

Scorching need surges through my veins, pulsing with maddening urgency.

Then she sucks me just like I remember, like her life depends on it. I groan wretchedly, my thighs shaking with the effort to last longer than a minute. I'm certain I'll black out before I climax.

I grind against her face, and she gags, breathes through it, and draws me even deeper down her throat.

"Jesus fucking Christ." I gasp, swelling in her mouth. "Take my cock. Choke on it."

She drags her fingernails beneath my balls, taint to sac, and laughs around me when I shudder violently.

Heat gathers at the base of my spine. I'm going to come.

"Wait, wait." I clasp her head, pulling myself from the merciless suction of her lips. "Give me a minute."

Beside me, the cushion dips beneath the press of Kody's knee as he leans across me and aims his porn-star dick at her mouth.

With a hand wrapped around my erection, she reaches for his.

The moment of truth.

I mentally prepared myself, envisioning all the ways they will be inside her and coating her with their seed. But watching it play out will be the real test of my possessive jealousy.

Her gaze locks onto mine as she leans toward him and swallows him down.

He groans, low and guttural, letting his head fall back on

his shoulders. With a boot planted on the floor and a knee on the couch, he grips my shoulder for support and kicks his hips.

Barely half of his length fits past her lips. It's a miracle she can take that much. But holy fuck, she looks drop-dead gorgeous with her mouth full of cock and drool dribbling down her chin.

I don't feel the usual testosterone-fueled jealousy clenching in my gut. Only happiness. Relief. Hunger.

She sucks our cocks in tandem, one after another. The short reprieves, when her mouth leaves me to go to him, are torture. Waiting for my turn—I thought that would be the hardest part. But the anticipation only heightens the pleasure when she draws me back into the tight heat of her throat.

Leo leaves the couch, his erection trapped behind the waistband of his briefs. As he lowers to his haunches behind her, he meets my eyes, daring me to stop him.

"Make her come." I grin.

"Gladly." He tugs her pants down and slides a hand between her legs, his nostrils flaring.

"How wet is she?" I groan at the feel of her tongue sliding over me.

He holds out his fingers, the digits soaked.

I grab his wrist and tug him closer. He bends over her back as I wrap my mouth around his finger and clean off her intoxicating flavor.

"Fuck." I lick the next finger and the next. "I wanted to do this at the distillery that night."

"I know." He smirks.

"Jesus, Monty. My heart wasn't ready for that." Frankie stares at me with hooded eyes, her lips swollen from sucking.

"You're swallowing two cocks, and that's what gives you pause?" Kody fists a hand in her hair. "We're going to fuck you until you're so full of dicks you can't breathe. Hope you're ready for *that*."

She laughs breathlessly until Leo shoves his tongue inside her. Her laughter dies on a strangled whimper.

He doesn't let up. He eats with the voraciousness of a feral creature, relentless until she screams his name and comes on his face.

She returns to Kody's cock, moaning and slurping with renewed intensity. A moment later, he groans through his release, digging his fingers into my shoulder and bucking his hips.

Then I'm back in her mouth, thrusting into the remnants that Kody left behind. I don't fucking care. She feels so damn good.

I stop worrying that I'm too rough and aggressive. After watching her swallow Kody's shameless monstrosity, I know she's up for it.

He and Leo switch places. As Kody buries his face between her legs, Leo stands a few feet back, watching her suck me with an intensity that leaves her breathless.

He fucks his hand, really getting into it, and within minutes, Kody makes her come again. He doesn't stop there. Going the distance, he digs in, determined to keep her screaming as she finishes me off.

Closing my eyes, I gulp deep breaths and concentrate on the feel of her hot, wet mouth.

My fingers sink into her lush red hair as I slide in to her throat. She moans around me, taking it like a champ. She's a goddess. Fucking enchanting.

She blew me every day for two years. But this right here? Best fucking blow job of my life.

Her mouth feels so impossibly warm and snug, and her tongue flicks with a precision that curls my toes.

She grips my thighs and bobs her head, smiling and humming her way through my undoing. I'm going to fucking come all over her.

"Fuck, you feel so good." I open my eyes and find her watching me.

In my periphery, Leo continues to jerk off, but it's her gaze that holds my rapt attention.

She has the deepest, most soul-binding eye contact I've ever experienced. It cleaves me open and exposes my insides.

I let her see me—my love, my vulnerability, and the

darkest corners of my soul.

She doesn't look away. She stares deeper, gives me a long, hard suck, and sends me careening over the edge.

"Frankie! Fuck, fuck, fuck!" I explode so violently it feels like I'm drowning her with my come.

She swallows rapidly, milking me of everything I have. Sweat drips down my nape as I gaze at her, those beautiful green eyes peering back.

When my cock is spent, she releases me with a pop of her lips and grins.

"Wicked woman." I slump into the couch, panting.

"That was so fucking hot." Leo steps up to her side, pumping his hand with a rhythm that tells me he's close. "Open your mouth."

She lifts her head and parts those beautiful lips.

"Now suck." Gripping the back of her head, he fucks her mouth.

Behind her, Kody thrusts his fingers and tongue between her legs, his eyes connected with Leo's.

They fall into perfect sync, timing the build-up with the skill of two men who have been sharing her for months. That knowledge used to eat me alive.

But as I watch them together now, it hits me. I don't want to return to how things were before I met them. While the implications of our foursome are unclear, the powerful emotions churning inside me keep me rooted in the present, anchored to them.

"Come." Leo cups her face and jerks his hips. "Come now."

Kody's mouth pushes her into a shattering orgasm as Leo roars to the rafters, announcing to every guard within a ten-mile radius that he's blowing his load.

I shake my head, a grin stretching across my lips. His mismatched eyes dart to mine, and the crazy fucker grins back.

"You guys are going to kill me." Frankie collapses over my lap.

"Tapping out already, love?" Leo tucks himself away and zips.

"Not a chance in hell." She laughs.

Kody gives her ass a light slap before straightening her pants and his.

"How's that refractory period?" She kisses my semi-hard cock, grinning as it swells with blood.

"Ready to go again."

Leo scoops her up and tucks her against his chest.

Rising to my feet, I straighten my clothes with steady hands. But I'm not steady.

This moment, this life-changing, profound moment, makes every moment before it feel unfinished. Halfway. A fragment of something greater.

It's no longer about the sex. It's about family, brotherhood, and mutual love for the woman who binds us.

It feels like I'm standing at the edge of a vast cliff, the unknown stretching before me, promising incredible possibilities and daunting challenges. The unsteadiness, excitement, hunger—all of it melds together, forming a sharper, more well-rounded version of myself.

As Leo carries Frankie off the yacht, Kody and I follow them. To our shared bedroom. To the consummation of our union.

To our future.

Together.

frankie

FIFTY-SIX

Leo sets me on Monty's bed, and the significance of that alone is surreal.

Tonight, all four of us will be in this bed. I imagined it—far too many times—but never thought it would actually happen.

It's fucking happening.

My hands tremble, and blood rushes in my ears, a steady drumbeat of nervous energy. It thrums everywhere—in the pit of my stomach, the pounding of my heart, and the shortness of my breath.

And it intensifies as Monty closes the door and prowls toward me.

"Remove your clothes." He pauses a few feet away and unbuttons the cuffs of his sleeves.

"I'd like to take a shower before we—"

Three resounding *nos* echo through the room.

"I've been working all day." I gesture at my scrubs.

"You'll be working all night." Leo toes off his boots.

"I love your scent." Kody takes my hand, pulling me to my feet and grazing his nose along my neck. "You're not washing that off."

Then he steps back and waits.

They all do.

My heart rate accelerates as I stand in the center, burning in the flames of their heated eyes.

"Where will we sleep?" I remove my shoes and socks with shaking hands.

"There." Monty motions at the bed that he and I once shared. "Objections?"

"Kody snores." Leo shucks off his shirt.

"So does Monty." Smiling, I remove my top and shove down my pants. "Did you sort out a pecking order?"

"The pecking order is this..." Monty empties his pockets and removes his watch, taking his damn time. "I haven't been inside you in over a year, so I'll be fucking you first." Wallet, watch, phone—he sets everything on the dresser and turns back to me. "After that, it's open season."

I shiver.

Every thought, every breath is magnified as I unclasp my bra and let it slide off my arms.

The world fades, narrowing to the rustle of fabric and the sounds of clothing falling to the floor.

They shed everything, baring themselves to me and one another. Not just their skin and scars and well-defined muscles. They stand before me, completely unguarded, with their hearts exposed. No walls. No secrets. No distrust.

My underwear is the last garment to drop. The instant it hits the floor, Kody snatches it up and presses it to his nose.

I laugh, my eyes watering.

"Look at you." Monty circles me slowly, his movements predatory. "A luscious, redheaded stunner with a filthy mind and a greedy pussy."

My knees wobble.

"The guys and I had a talk on the way to the hospital." He edges closer, naked and irresistible, making it hard to focus.

"About?"

"Limits." He stands so close his body heat cooks my skin, but he doesn't touch me. "Boundaries."

"And?"

"We have none."

"What?" My gaze flies to Leo and Kody. "Kody doesn't do anal, and for Leo, double-penetration is off the table."

They merely stare back with hooded eyes.

"Yeah, we're doing all of that. Tonight." Monty stands behind me and trails his fingers down my arm, quickening my pulse. "Anal and DP are unresolved hang-ups for them. Not limitations."

I check in with my guys again. Kody lowers his head, hungrily watching me from beneath dark brows. Leo, with his hand loosely curled around his semi-erection, winks at me.

Sweet Jesus.

Swoon.

I exhale a shaky breath.

"Look at me." The force of nature with sexy black hair steps around to my front, blocking my view.

I lift my eyes to his as his leather and ocean breeze scent envelops me.

Irresistibly intoxicating.

"In this room," Monty says, "we command, and you submit. You'll obey, surrender, and take what we give you until you can't breathe. Then you'll catch your breath and beg us to do it again. Understand?"

"Yes." I swallow.

"I've missed you." He cups my chin, his thumb brushing over my lips. "So fucking much."

"Missed you, too."

His breath warms my lips as he lowers his hand, trailing it down my neck, around my nipple, and along the shape of my waist and hip. Pausing, he leans back to stare down my body.

As I tremble beneath his scrutiny, a delicious, erotic frisson runs through me.

His penetrating blue eyes dart to mine as his fingertips continue downward, caressing my inner thigh and working their way up to my sensitive, wet pussy. Then slowly, oh-so fucking softly, he traces my slit and bends in to kiss the side of my neck.

Whimpering, I tilt my head and give him more access. I really need a wall or something to lean against. My knees keep buckling, and my legs feel like jelly.

As if reading my mind, Leo steps in behind me and slides his hands around my waist. His chest presses against my back, sandwiching me between two rigid cocks, the heat and scent of them overwhelming my senses.

Monty peppers kisses from my neck to my mouth while Leo's fingers begin a slow, torturous exploration of my body.

Kody lowers to his knees at my side and drags his nose up the back of my thigh. Then he nips and teases with those pouty lips, making my skin prickle and heat.

I have nowhere to go but to enjoy the sensations of their hands and mouths, melting into the submission.

Monty kisses me deeply, feverishly, groaning as he sinks two fingers between my legs.

"You're so wet, Frankie." He licks my tongue, panting. "So fucking wet. You're dripping down your thighs."

Our mouths fuse with frenetic energy. I match his hunger with my own need, clutching the back of his neck and pulling him closer as our tongues entwine, and our hips grind. Frantic, we devour each other, hands and lips fighting for as much contact as possible.

Behind me, Leo bites my neck, my jaw, and swirls his tongue around my ear. His fingers sink into my ass crack and slide down between my cheeks, lower, lower, joining Monty's hand between my legs.

Monty breaks the kiss, his eyes dark with desire as he looks at Leo over my shoulder. Then they both lower to their haunches.

Kody rises and lifts my fingers to his lips, kissing each one with a reverence that makes my heart ache. His touch is so damn tender, so at odds with his savage nature.

Then he takes my face and kisses me with the taste of vodka and wild berries on his tongue. His heavy cock curves upward, jabbing against my waist, the head glistening with precome and painting rivulets of wetness across my skin.

Leo coaxes my feet farther apart, and all at once, he and

Monty consume me with their mouths. With Monty in front and Leo behind me, they devour every inch of flesh between my legs. Tongues, teeth, and fingers slide everywhere, exploring, sucking, licking, and claiming.

While they torture me below the waist, Kody worships my upper half. With a hand kneading my breasts, he runs his nose up my bicep to the crease beneath. Lifting my arm, he presses his face in the ticklish hollow underneath and inhales my pheromones with a groan.

They inch closer and closer, kissing and touching and invading until there's no space left between us. The radiating ovens of their muscled bodies, the panting urgency of their breaths, and the steady thrum of their hearts—they smother me in the best way.

Together, a trinity of strength, passion, and love, they own me.

Kody's lips capture mine again, his kiss deep and possessive, while Monty and Leo spear their tongues and fingers into my holes, claiming me from the inside out.

Leo spreads my butt cheeks wider and spits on my rear entrance. Then he finger-fucks the sensitive knot while Monty does the same with my pussy.

"Goddamn, love. You're fucking perfection." Leo puts his lips where his hand is, sending me into a tailspin with that magical tongue.

"Her body is a work of art." Monty removes his fingers from my cunt and sucks them into his mouth. "Our horny girl is ready."

"Been ready." I gasp into Kody's mouth as he pinches my nipple.

"On the bed." Leo swats my rear and steps back, wiping his drenched grin with the back of his hand.

Monty stands, too, and all three of them retreat with their dicks in their hands, lightly stroking, impatiently waiting.

I climb onto the bed.

Before I can blink, Monty crawls up my body with his swollen dick between us. When his eyes align with mine, he inhales deeply, exhales, and feathers his fingertips along the side of my face.

"Dreamed about this for fourteen months." Resting his brow against mine, he reaches between us and notches himself at my opening. "Can't wait a second longer."

The hand beside my head closes around a fistful of my hair, and he pushes in, inch by agonizing inch. He doesn't breathe, doesn't blink as he stares into my eyes. The only part of us that moves is his hips, sinking, sinking, until he shoves in to the hilt.

He moans, his breath shuddering. I quiver and sigh beneath him.

"As tight as I remember." He grips my chin, peering so deeply into my eyes that I ache. "So warm. So soft and velvety around me. Squeeze my cock. Clamp that tight, little pussy around me like you'll never let it go."

"I'll never let you go."

"Christ." He braces his forearms on either side of my head and thrusts. "You're ours."

"Yours." At the edges of my vision, I see Kody and Leo approaching the bed.

"Wish you knew how significant this is for me." Monty grinds into me, circling his pelvis. "How long I've waited to feel you like this."

"Oh, Monty." I kiss his beautiful, vulnerable lips. "I do know."

"You feel like heaven around my dick." His timbre vibrates through my core, deep and husky. "Lips all swollen from sucking. A goddamn knockout."

His mouth crashes down on mine, and his pace quickens, driving into me with an intensity I expect from him. His girth stretches and stimulates, shooting pleasure to every corner of my body.

His brows furrow in concentration, his jaw locked tight as he slams in deep and goes nuts. All his precious restraint flies out the window. He loses control and fucks me like an animal.

Just when I think he's about to come, he goes still, gasping. Then he grips my hips and flips us.

I land on his chest, staring down into his dilated pupils. He's so undeniably gorgeous.

With my legs straddling him and his cock wedged inside me, he palms my rear with both hands and spreads me open.

"Kody." Monty fucks into me, little thrusts that make me wild. "Come on. Give our girl her fantasy."

I look over my shoulder, watching Kody's unnatural length bob against his abdomen.

"Uh..." I bite my lip.

There's no way. That bulging, swelling cock barely fits when it's just him inside me. I didn't think this through.

He and Monty together? They'll destroy my pussy.

"DP?" I ask, just to be sure. "Vaginal?"

"That a problem?" Kody kneels behind me, wielding his weapon of mass destruction.

"Lube," I squeak. "Lots of lube."

Monty bursts out laughing beneath me. "Darling, you're fucking soaked."

I want this. I've begged Kody and Leo for it. Time to own it.

"Okay." I turn back to Monty and clutch the pillow beneath his head. "Let's fucking go."

"Attagirl." He kisses me, his lips claiming mine with a fire that scorches my skin.

His hands mold around my breasts, pinching my nipples ruthlessly, distractingly, as Kody works himself into my already full pussy.

I arch into him, pushing, groaning, needing more.

Fucking hell, the burn. The friction. The glorious pleasure.

Kody continues to push, fitting his thickness alongside Monty's cock. Sweat drips. Chests heave. None of us move.

"Are you in?" I meet his black eyes over my shoulder and give a full-body tremble.

"You fucking serious?" He looks down at where we're joined.

"I kind of lost count after the first six inches."

"Woman." He puts his lethal lips at my ear. "You're so full of cock. How are you still breathing?"

My laugh is cut off when they start to move.

Oh, my poor pussy.

The first few thrusts are unbearable, but as they catch a rhythm, my inner walls relax and adjust around their invasion.

"How are you doing?" Monty caresses his hands down my body, his fingers brushing over inflamed skin.

"Is this real?" I melt into him, shaking with the need to come.

He answers me with his lips. My hands sink into his hair as he kisses and fucks me, his pace perfectly in sync with Kody's.

The bed dips beside us, snapping my head toward Leo.

Inching closer on his knees, he fists his erection and angles it toward my mouth.

"You're so beautiful." He spits on his fingers and presses them into the cleft of my ass, directly against my back hole. "Show me what you look like with all your openings filled."

I part my lips and swallow his cock.

Groaning, he pushes those wet fingers into my ass, his touch skilled and knowing. I cry out around his dick, my body arching into his hand, desperate for release.

Monty must have one helluva view, watching my throat work and tits jiggle as I take two cocks and suck on a third.

Evidently, he likes it because his hands clamp down on my hips, holding me in place as he fucks into his release.

With a broken shout, he throws his head back and comes with a wild, brutal shake of his body.

"Frankie!" He continues to thrust, spilling his seed all over Kody and me. "Fucking God. So fucking good."

Leo slips from my mouth and sits back on his heels, smirking. "The old man's still got it."

"I can out fuck you any day of the week." Monty flops an arm over his forehead, his gaze boring into mine. "She needs to come, and I don't want to pull out."

"You need to recover." Kody leans back, slowly stroking in and out of me. "We'll get her there."

"All right." Monty slaps him on the ass. "Flip over."

Kody wraps his arms around me and nuzzles my neck. "Ready?"

I nod, sinking into his embrace.

He rolls, pulling me off Monty and landing on his back.

Monty sits up and strokes my inner thigh, his eyes on Kody. "Scoot back. Sit against the headboard."

Kody hesitates.

"You're not going to hurt her." Monty pats Kody's hip. "She just took both of us at once. She's aroused and relaxed." He shifts his gaze to me. "Aren't you, Frankie?"

"One hundred percent."

If I'm reading the room right, Monty is coaxing Kody into anal.

I push up and ease off his cock. Then I crawl over his chest and look him dead in the eyes. "This is consensual. I'm willing. I want you in my ass because it feels good. Because I trust you. Because you will never fuck me to hurt me." I cup his beautiful, broody face. "If I want you to stop, I'll tell you."

"Okay." He licks his lips. Takes a deep breath. "Okay."

My heart flutters as we move into position. He sits against the headboard, looking so fucking sexy with all those stacked muscles, his pouty lips, and the enormous erection jutting from between his legs.

I crawl toward him, kissing the length of his powerful body and pausing to lick him from the base of his balls to the tip of his dick.

Then I take his face in my hands and kiss the breath out of him.

Once he's panting and flexing with mindless hunger, I twist and sit on his lap with my back to his chest.

Monty moves in, catching me around the waist and hovering me over Kody's hardness.

On my other side, Leo holds out a tube of lube.

Heart hammering, I let him squirt a dollop into my hand. Then I work the gel over Kody's length, relishing the grunts I pull from him.

I smear the rest between my cheeks, and Leo's there with a towel to clean my hand.

"You guys are spoiling me." I grip Monty's forearms, giving

him a nod. I'm ready.

"Slow and steady." Monty looks at Kody. "Let her adjust as you push in."

Kody grips my hips beneath Monty's hands, both of them supporting me as I relax, breathe, and arch into Kody's gentle drive upward.

It's an unhurried intrusion but a sudden, blinding onslaught of pleasure. I loosen a scream.

Kody starts to retreat.

"No! God, please, don't stop!" I reach down to touch myself.

But Leo's there, swatting my hand away. His mouth comes down on mine, and his fingers rub my clit.

With just a few strumming circles between my legs, I suck in a breath and come, grinding wildly against the pressure of his touch.

I liquefy against Kody's chest, staring wide-eyed at Leo and Monty as the orgasm rolls over me, clenching my empty pussy and emptying my lungs.

Kody fucks me through it, wrapping me up in his arms and pounding my ass.

"So tight, woman." He grunts and groans and drags his tongue along my neck. "Gonna come so fucking hard in you."

"Leo." Monty kneels beside us, pushing my legs wider. "Get in there."

Leo lowers his heated gaze to where Kody and I are joined and curls his lip in a snarl. "He's my brother."

Monty chuckles, wagging his head. "He's my brother, too."

Bending over our thighs, he puts his face between our legs, right where Kody impales my ass, and licks me from just above the base of Kody's cock to my clit, lapping up my juices.

Oh, my fucking God.

I'm so turned on I might lose my mind.

"Too brotherly for you?" He leans back and looks at Leo with an arch of his brow. "All in."

A dare. A challenge that Leo can't resist.

As Leo edges closer, Kody's thrusts grow wild and brutal. He's learning what I can handle, what I like, and letting himself go.

Even though I just came, I feel the tightening between my legs, the heavy pressure gathering again.

Leo rests his hands on my waist and brushes his lips against mine, his eyes burning with desire.

"You're exquisite." He licks my mouth. "You want us all in?"

"All in." I hold Leo's gaze.

Kody's tongue continues to torment my neck, his kisses gentle and soothing. "All in."

I see the moment he makes a decision. His breaths pick up, and his cock grows thicker and harder.

"We're going to fill you up." Kneeling between our legs, he guides himself to my pussy, rubbing the thick head against me.

Then he thrusts, entering me in one long stroke.

Ruthless. Intimate. Raw. That's my Viking.

"Fuck me." I gasp. "Be my feral lovers."

The chorus of sounds that break from them is guttural, animalistic, and not from this world.

Their hands fall all over me, gripping and bruising as they fuck and grunt and go wild. Monty's there with us, his long fingers tweaking my nipples and his lips traveling over every part of me he can reach.

The four of us together are filthy and sweaty, kinky and real.

"I'm so fucking full." I choke. "I can't breathe."

"Oh, fuck, Frankie." Kody bites down on my neck.

His entire body jerks. Deep in my ass, his monster cock explodes. He groans brokenly, thrusting shallowly as he dumps his release in powerful, hot liquid jets.

Before he can catch his breath, Leo pulls me off Kody, pivots, and falls on top of me, crushing me into the mattress with his body weight.

Our eyes meet, and I clench around his cock. That's all the encouragement he needs.

Of the three of them, he has the longest endurance. He can fuck for hours.

He sets out to prove it.

Monty and Kody eventually leave the bed to take showers. When they return, Leo is still pounding into me with the unhinged urgency of a madman.

He brings me to orgasm over and over.

I clutch tightly to his ass, to all that hard, flexing muscle, and hold him against me as he sinks deeper and finally, finally surrenders to his release.

He bellows so loudly the sound reverberates in my bones, setting me on fire and wrenching another orgasm from me.

We lie entangled in the bedding, breathing hard and staring softly. I love him when he's like this. Exhausted. Sated. Happy.

This is when I see his most vulnerable, unconcealed expressions. I see all the way into his soul, and I'm lost in it. Lost in his inner beauty, in his body's embrace, in the rough, unrefined perfection of it.

At some point, Monty and Kody leave to gather water and food.

Leo carries me to the shower.

After, the four of us have a picnic on the bed. We nap together. We fuck again. More showers.

And so it begins.

For the next three days, we don't leave the estate. I call into work sick. Kody leaves his distillery in the hands of his employees.

The stalker, Wolf's body, the cabin's location, and the dangers lurking outside our door—none of it exists in our bubble.

We spend three days naked and ravenous, learning, exploring, and understanding one another on the deepest, most intimate level. There's no part of them that hasn't been licked, touched, or deeply exposed by my mouth and hands.

The bonding between the three of them exceeds all expectations. They become so comfortable together that it's hard to imagine a time when Monty wasn't with them.

On the night of the third day, I lie in bed with Leo and Monty curled around me. They're hot and heavy on top of me, and I'm sore and bruised and bitten all over.

I've never felt such a deep sense of peace.

Moonlight seeps through the sheer curtains, casting an ethereal glow over our bedroom.

Water runs in the bathroom, shuts off, and Kody prowls back to bed.

He finds space. They always do. We've perfected the art of sleeping in piles.

Crawling up my legs, he pushes aside masculine limbs and squeezes in until his head rests on my stomach and his arms hook around my hips.

Sweet lord, my heart swells. It swells to bursting with the love I feel for each of them.

None of us are asleep, but we're close. We float in a state of blissful exhaustion that must be what heaven is like.

Slowly, I start to drift off until Monty's whisper snaps open my eyes.

"I didn't mean what I said." He stares at Kody, at his hand on Kody's welted back. His fingers feather over the crisscrossed scars that bubble Kody's flesh from neck to waist. "You don't need to be fixed. You're perfect just the way you are."

Kody shudders, his breath hitching as he tries to swallow his emotion.

A lump swells in my throat, and my fingers curl in the soft strands of his hair.

Monty turns to Leo, grazing his hand over the scar on Leo's stomach. "I'm sorry she did that to you. If I'd known the kind of person she was—"

"I would change nothing," Leo says in a gruff voice. "She gave us Wolf."

Monty nods, his face collapsing. "You're right. As much as I despise Denver, he gave us you. Having you here, standing strong, means everything to me. We've been through hell, but we'll always have each other. That's something Denver and Gretchen could never take from us. I'm proud of you."

Leo reaches for Monty, arms folding around him, and fuck, I can't breathe.

This is the fullness I wanted.

Acceptance.

Family.

Trust.

Love.

This is what I dreamed for them. Nothing is impossible.

I am theirs, and they are mine. For the first time in a long time, we're whole.

kodiak

FIFTY-SEVEN

The last three days have been the happiest in memory. I could spend the rest of my life in bed with Frankie and my brothers. I don't want to give it up. The world outside can wait.

But it seems the world has other plans.

Frankie's phone buzzes, the sound cutting through the tranquil morning. She answers it, and her expression changes, a collision of concern and determination hardening her features.

She hangs up, scrambles from our tangle of naked bodies, and hurries into the walk-in closet.

"A cruise ship docked in port," she shouts from behind the door. "Half of the passengers have the stomach flu." She breezes out, her mind on a mission as she drags on her scrubs mid-stride. "They didn't know they were infected until after they carried it into our town. The hospital is overrun, and they need all hands on deck. I have to go."

All three of us shoot up in the bed.

"Frankie, no." A knot tightens in my stomach.

"We just got you back." Leo climbs out and prowls toward her, shamelessly nude. "We're not letting you go."

He grabs her, buries his nose in her neck, and presses his hips against her.

"Put that thing away." She laughs, pushing against his stomach. "I'm serious."

Monty swings his legs over the side of the bed and braces his elbows on his knees.

Voice hard, he gives her his stoniest expression. "How do we change your mind?"

Her green eyes soften as she treads to him and cups his unshaven jaw. "You handsome devil, how many times have we argued about this over the years? How many times have I changed my mind?" She kisses the angry slash of his lips. "This is my career. My purpose outside of this room. I know you all understand that."

I do understand. I have my distillery, my own sense of purpose, and hard work. I never want to hold her back, but the fear of losing her is a snarling, rabid beast inside me.

"We'll go with you." Leo paces around her, flexing his hands.

"What part of *stomach flu* do you not understand? It's contagious." She pulls on her sneakers. "You're staying here, all of you, until this is under control."

I know we won't win this. Leaving the bed, I remove a pair of lounge pants from Monty's dresser and drag them on.

"What about you? You're exposing yourself to this thing." Leo walks through the room, gathering her hair ties, earbuds, coat, and purse.

"Risks of the job. But we wear PPE to minimize exposure." She takes his face in her hands, halting his movements. "I'll come back. I promise."

"Holding you to that, love." He helps her get ready in silent concentration, handling her gently as if she's flammable.

He's the one who's close to combustion. His tenderness disguises the Molotov cocktail blazing beneath his skin.

"You're not going alone." Monty snags a pair of sweatpants from the floor and hauls them on. "You'll take a security team."

She nods, knowing it's the only way we'll let her leave.

"This isn't going to wrap up in a day. I'll be there for a

while, working long shifts and taking naps when I can. Promise me you'll all stay here." She looks each of us in the eye. "Don't go into town and risk getting sick."

Monty stares at her, silent for a moment before nodding stiffly. "We'll stay. But you need to promise to stay safe, too."

"I promise." She kisses him then Leo. Then turns to me.

"I'll walk you out." I shove my feet into Monty's sliders.

With a small smile, she heads to the door.

"Frankie." Monty grabs her phone where she left it on the bed. "Forgetting something?"

"Shit." She spins back and takes it from him.

"This is a new phone," he says.

"It is?" She stares at it, eyebrows pinched. "Looks the same."

"Same model. After you left, I spent a lot of time thinking. How does the stalker know so much about you? It's like they can hear your conversations and see where you are."

Her eyes widen.

"I've been monitoring your phone for five months." He rests his hands on his hips. "I scan it for bugs and dig for hidden software constantly. But I'm not a forensics analyst. So while you were gone, I bought a new phone." He nods at the one in her hand.

"And you sent my other one to your forensics team?"

He nods.

"When?" she asks.

"The day after you returned. I swapped them out and shipped off the old one."

"Why didn't you tell me?"

"I was waiting until the analysis came back. Didn't want to worry you. But you're leaving with it and need to know. I manually installed everything on that one and might've missed something. I didn't want you to freak out if I didn't set it up correctly."

"This one has the GPS tracker, too?"

"Of course." He strokes his thumb across her cheekbone. "Come back to us, darling."

"I will."

I follow her out.

A perpetual drizzle mists our rainforest island in a fine sheen, clinging to my skin.

Our island.

Monty has spent the past three days pounding the concept of *all in* into our heads. Everything that belonged to him is now *ours.*

Frankie is *ours.*

I walk her to her cruiser, my heart heavy. She's going back into danger, and I fucking hate it.

Up ahead, the guards are already assembled on the dock.

"Your shoe is untied." I stop her with a hand on her back.

As she bends at the waist to lace the strings, I can't help it. I crouch behind her and shove my nose between her legs.

"Kody." She whisper-scolds through a laugh, only encouraging me to linger longer.

Inhaling deeply, I scent her through the fabric. It's not enough to hold me over, but my time is up. As she starts to stand, I sink my teeth into her muscled backside, biting hard enough to bruise.

She yelps, spinning toward me.

I rise to my full height and pull her close. The cherry aroma of her hair, the warmth of her body, everything about her is my oxygen, my nutrients, my lifeblood. "Come back to us."

"I will." She kisses me, a lingering, tender kiss that ends too soon.

She boards her boat with her bodyguards and blows me a kiss before steering it away and fading into the gloom.

I ache with loss. It feels wrong to let her go, but I have to trust her, trust she'll return to us.

An hour later, I sit with my brothers in the den, surrounded by maps, sticky notes, and diagrams. After Frankie's last session with Doyle, Monty turned this space into a war room. Clues, evidence, suspects, timelines—all the information we have is displayed on the wall in a complex diagram to help us focus and problem-solve.

"We don't have enough clues." Monty scans the wall of

sticky notes. "The stalker has been too quiet."

I lower onto the couch beside him. "Every message and morbid gift to Frankie puts this nutjob at risk of getting caught."

"Why send anything at all?" Leo rubs his head.

"Desire for control and power," Monty says. "By making us afraid of him, he can savor the perceived power he holds over us."

"He?" I raise my brows.

"Most serial killers are male," Monty argues.

"Okay, well, maybe these gifts are also a need for recognition." My throat works around painful memories. "Denver craved acknowledgment for all the *good work* he did. He believed he committed all those crimes for us and wanted recognition for it."

"Good point." Monty scowls. "It can also be a psychological thrill for this guy. The risk of getting caught is an adrenaline rush." He turns back to his notes on the wall. "I don't want more communication from him, but we need it. We need *something.* The investigation is going stagnant."

"What are we missing?" I lift the book of Pushkin poems. "Someone put this and the flight logs in Rurik's house, and the stalker knows about them. There's a connection we're not seeing."

"I agree." Monty rolls his lips. "I gave Wilson a list of everyone who's familiar with the estate on Kodiak Island and their connection to it. We need to retrace those threads, no matter how thin."

"Feels like we're always a step behind and looking in the wrong direction." Leo paces the room, chewing on his thumbnail. "It's like the bastard is dangling red herrings to distract us."

"He's toying with us." Monty looks up, his gaze steady. "We need to be thorough. Every detail matters."

"I want to hunt." My fingers flex and release.

"We tried that," Leo says. "We can't hunt until we know *who* we're hunting."

"I hate feeling useless." I let out a grunt of frustration. "Frankie's out there, risking her life, and we're stuck here chasing shadows."

"We're doing everything we can. We'll find him. Then we'll deal with him." Monty holds my gaze. "The Strakh way."

The conviction in his tone sets my shoulders. I can't fucking wait.

I just hope we're not too late.

We spend the rest of the day picking through clues, making phone calls, and touching base with Wilson. Monty is relentless, driven by the need to protect us all and find the answers.

"Someone out there has a motive." Monty slumps into the couch, exhaustion edging his voice. "A motive that set this into motion a long time ago."

Wilson has been painstakingly crosschecking the handwriting on Wolf's photo against the handwriting of those on our suspect list. So far, there have been no matches. But our suspect list is incomplete.

He's still pulling names from Rurik's incriminating ledger. Monty knew it would take an unreasonable amount of man-hours to scrub hundreds of pages of accounting entries, but it's been three months. It's taking too damn long.

"What about Alvis Duncan?" Leo leans over the table, reading through our list of suspects. "He kept tabs on Denver for decades. Maybe he knows more than he's let on."

"Wilson checked his handwriting, too. No match. And he hasn't left Whittier in years. He's a recluse." Monty frowns. "But we need to dig deeper. Maybe he can identify the stalker?"

"Tell Wilson to send photos of every person on our suspect list to Alvis Duncan. If one of our suspects collected the flight logs from him, he'll recognize their picture."

"You're right." Monty grabs his phone and makes the call.

It's late when we finally surrender to exhaustion, retreating to Monty's bed. It feels empty without Frankie. None of us can sleep, the chill of her absence tormenting us.

She sent us messages throughout the day, updating us on the chaos at the hospital. Her urgent demands to remain where we are only makes the fear more unbearable.

Sprawled on my back between them, I stare at the ceiling. "I miss her already."

"Me, too." Monty pats my stomach and leaves his hand resting there. "But she's strong. She'll be okay."

"She's a fighter," Leo mumbles.

In the middle of the night, Monty's phone rings.

He jolts up in bed and answers on speaker. "Wilson?"

"Alvis Duncan is missing."

"Missing how?" He tenses.

We all go still. No one breathes.

"Don't know yet," Wilson says. "I couldn't get a hold of him, so I sent James up there to Whittier. Alvis and his wife are gone. No signs of packing up. No indication of a struggle, either. But their dinner was still in the oven, burnt to a crisp by the time James arrived."

The news knocks the wind out of me, leaving me reeling.

Alvis never leaves Whittier. Maybe he had a family emergency.

Maybe he's the stalker.

Questions whirl through my mind, each one more troubling than the last.

The unease grows as we stare at Monty's phone in the dark. The connection is there, just out of reach, and we're running out of time to find it.

"And, Monty..." Wilson lowers his voice. "Frankie's phone had spyware on it."

frankie

FIFTY-EIGHT

The hum of fluorescent lights does little to ease the mayhem as the hospital teems with patients.

My heart pounds as I rush from one bed to the next, donning and doffing PPE and leaning into my training.

My bodyguards are never more than a few feet away, a constant reminder of the other danger lurking outside these sterile walls. When we arrived twenty hours ago, I tossed them masks, demanding they wear them. They didn't argue. They know better.

"Frankie, we've got another one!" Nurse Letty's voice slices through the frenzy.

I nod and head to the trauma unit, where a middle-aged woman struggles to breathe. Her skin is pallid. Sweat beads on her forehead, and fear shines in her eyes.

"BP's dropping. Get me more fluids!" I reach for the equipment, my gloved hands moving with practiced efficiency.

The past twenty hours have blurred together in a haze of feverish activity. Every bed is occupied, and we're running low on supplies. This stomach bug is aggressive, and our resources are stretched thin.

I can't let my emotions get the better of me. I focus on each patient, pouring every ounce of my energy into their care. We haven't lost one yet.

Eventually, fatigue drapes over me like a heavy blanket. I start fumbling with IVs and tripping over my own feet. But I can't go home. Not yet. I just need a few hours of sleep before I can continue.

After I scrub my hands for the millionth time today, I pull out my phone and send a group text to the guys, letting them know I'm okay and reiterating the importance of them staying on the island.

I hit send, my fingers trembling. I can't lose them. Not now, not ever.

"Take a break." Nurse Letty grips my arm as I sway against a doorframe. "You can barely stay upright."

"I'm fine."

"You already exceeded the max hours. You're going to start making mistakes." Her eyes harden above her mask. "Go get some sleep. Now."

She's right.

Dammit.

With a nod, I trudge toward the on-call room for a nap. At the door, I glance at my bodyguards, knowing they'll check the room before I go inside.

Carl precedes me, and I follow him in, my steps heavy, my mind foggy.

To my surprise, Rhett is sitting on the bed, a duffle bag at his feet.

"What are you doing here?" I collapse beside him and remove my mask. "I thought you went to Seattle?"

"I stayed to help with the emergency. I came in here to take a quick nap. But the bed is all yours now. Just need to pack my bag."

I glance at Carl, who stands at the door. "I'll sleep for a few hours. Don't let anyone disturb me."

"Six hours minimum," Rhett says to him and turns to me. "You should've stopped hours ago. You're going to run yourself into the ground."

Carl nods and closes the door behind him.

"When I got back into town yesterday, I was surprised to find this room empty." Rhett glances around. "You moved back in with Monty?"

"Yeah." I can't keep the smile from lifting my cheeks. "We *all* moved in with him."

"Wow. That's a big commitment. Are you sure about it?"

"Never been more sure in my life. We figured out a way to make it work."

"Would they die for you?"

That's a strange question, but the answer is easy. "Yes. Why?"

"I just don't want you to get hurt again." He bumps his shoulder against mine.

"I won't. I want to do this."

"Me, too," he whispers.

A sharp prick burns through my thigh.

I stare down at the syringe in my leg. The syringe that Rhett is holding in place.

Stunned, confused, I lift my eyes to him. My boss. My friend. The person I've trusted and relied on.

He's drugging me.

As the reality of what's happening crashes over me, the room tilts. My vision blurs. Panic sets in.

"What—what are you doing?" I slur, my tongue heavy.

I try to move, but my muscles refuse to cooperate. Every bone in my body quits, and I crumple onto the bed.

Rhett catches me, his face hovering over mine, distorted and smudgy. "I'm doing what's best for you, Frankie. You'll understand soon."

A scream swells inside me, an angry, punching fist full of horror and betrayal, and I'm falling. Falling in and out of the twisting, turning, empty pit in my stomach. I'm going to be sick.

"No," I say without sound, my strength draining away.

Please, don't.

He lifts me effortlessly, folding my body into his empty duffle bag. I feel my limbs being manipulated, my head lolling to the side.

"It's a good thing you're small." He strokes my hair. "I love you so much. It's time to go home."

The sound of the zipper closing the bag is the last thing I hear before darkness claims me.

monty

FIFTY-NINE

With an unsettling feeling in my stomach, I disconnect the call with Wilson and dial Frankie.

As the phone rings, I slide out of bed and grab something to wear.

Leo and Kody are already dragging on clothes, their jaws locked down and Adam's apples bobbing like buoys in a storm-tossed sea.

"She's not answering." I leave an urgent voice mail and call her head bodyguard.

"Mr. Novak?" Carl picks up on the first ring.

"Where is she?"

"In the on-call room. She worked twenty hours and needed rest. She advised me not to disturb her for six hours. She's been in there for forty-nine minutes."

"She's alone?"

"Yes. I checked the room. Dr. Howell was on his way out when we arrived. Is everything all right, sir?"

"There's another missing person. Do *not* leave that door. Do not fucking blink. Not for a second. And alert me the instant she wakes."

"Yes, sir."

I hang up and look at Leo and Kody. "She's asleep in the on-call room."

"Fuck that." Leo stabs his fingers in his hair. "Her guards need to bring her home right fucking now."

"Calm down." Kody shoves on his boots, his black eyes distant, hiding his inner turmoil. "She's safe in that room. Alvis Duncan could've had a family emergency, and the phone she has now doesn't have spyware because Monty just gave it to her. No reason to scare her until we have all the information."

I call Wilson on speaker.

"Monty," he answers.

"How was the spyware installed on her phone?"

"She clicked a link and inadvertently downloaded it."

"She knows not to click on unknown links."

"Not if she trusted the person who sent it to her."

"Can you find that link? Who the sender was?"

"Not easily. She deletes her texts and emails, but we're digging." Wilson clears his throat. "The spyware enabled the hacker to watch her through the camera, listen to her through the microphone, and track her movements through the phone's GPS."

My heart shoots into my throat, beating painfully.

They had access to her whenever she had her phone with her.

I wrack my brain, trying remember the conversation I had with her about The Ghost. We were in my office, and she was wearing sleep shorts and a tank top. No pockets. No phone with her.

Unless she slipped in another conversation with Leo and Kody, the stalker doesn't know about The Ghost.

Leo looks feral, his posture vibrating and breaths raging. Ready to kill.

"I received more potential persons of interest from your father's ledger," Wilson says. "The list is never-ending, but there's one entry I want you to see. I'll text a photo of it." A pause. "Just sent it."

I switch to the messaging app and open a photo of my

father's handwriting.

Renat Moroz

Age 12

"He filled a shelf with a small army of books and read and read; but none of it made sense. They were all subject to various cramping limitations: those of the past were outdated, and those of the present were obsessed with the past."

A chill runs over my scalp. "I don't recognize the name, but several things stand out."

"The Pushkin quote?" Wilson asks.

"Yes."

"It's the only Pushkin quote in the ledger. That's why I flagged it."

"The age..." I look at Leo and Kody, marking the horror in their eyes. "Is this one of Denver's victims?"

"Unconfirmed. But I found a Renat Moroz, who lived on Kodiak Island."

"Most of Denver's victims did. Where is he now?"

"He disappeared thirty years ago. Parents are deceased. No living family. The name doesn't ring any bells?"

"No, but Moroz is the Russian word for *frost*."

"Oh, fuck." Leo's eyes widen. "The text she received..."

Who am I? I think you know. We share the same heart of frost and scars.

"And Denver's riddle." Kody's voice drops to a deadly rumble. "In the chambers of frost, pain is my art."

"I think we have our stalker." My pulse quickens.

"Only problem is," Wilson says, "we don't know who or where he is."

"He would be using another name." I pace the bedroom, my mind swimming. "When Rurik paid off Denver's victims, he changed their names and moved them away so Denver couldn't find them."

"We'll find him." Wilson hardens his tone. "Now we know he's male, age forty-two..." He pauses. "Dr. Rhett Howell is forty-two."

Panic floods my chest. Adrenaline spikes, and the roar of thunder fills my ears.

But it's not thunder.

It's Leo.

He explodes out of the room with Kody on his heels. I disconnect the call and race after them, my exhales sharpening as fear bursts past my lips.

"Call her guards!" I shout at them and fly down the stairs, dialing The Ghost.

I catch up with Leo and Kody in the entryway, their phones held to their ears as they bark orders at the guards and sprint out the front door.

The pain in my chest is excruciating, threatening to bring me to my knees as the phone rings.

It rings in my ear at the same time an unfamiliar ringtone sounds behind me.

I freeze, the air leaving my lungs as something sharp flies past my head, grazes my scalp, and impales the doorframe before me.

Several strands of my hair fall from the blade of a fillet knife.

The fillet knife.

My heart stops. A cold sweat breaks out. Leo and Kody pause just beyond the open door, their expressions twisted with shock and confusion.

Slowly, I force myself to turn toward The Ghost.

And I come face to face with Oliver.

Holding his phone, he disconnects the call, his features unreadable as he says in Russian, "Let's have a little talk."

SIXTY

Consciousness returns slowly, dragging me from the depths of a dreamless void. Groggy and disoriented, I blink repeatedly, unable to clear the milky cloud that blurs my vision.

I lie on my back, legs extended. Wrapped in a soft cocoon of bedding, my body feels heavy and unresponsive, as if crushed beneath an unseen force.

Struggling to breathe, I sluggishly piece together flashes of memory.

The needle. The duffle bag. Rhett.

Panic flares, sharp and consuming, and I realize I can't flail. I can't move my limbs at all. My heart thunders, booming so hard it pressurizes in my ears. I try to scream, but my throat remains silent, my lips unmoving. I can't even gasp for air.

Complete muscle paralysis.

Don't freak out, Frankie. Don't let the fear take over. Stay calm. Find a way out.

I feel every sensation in my body, and that acute awareness dominates my thoughts. I focus on my heart rate, commanding it to slow. Sweat trickles down my forehead, pooling in the hollows of my eyes.

My eyelids respond, opening and closing. I encourage them, trying to regain my eyesight.

Slowly, the haze over my vision recedes, revealing a dimly lit room, the air cool and musty.

Familiar.

Horrifyingly familiar.

As my eyes adjust, recognition hits me like a white-out blizzard.

No, no, nononono!

Two-story windows, glossy wood floors, stone fireplace, curving staircase to a catwalk...

The cabin.

I'm back in Hoss.

My worst nightmare realized.

Panic spikes anew, my pulse vaulting into a war cry of terror. The cabin closes in on me, walls pressing nearer, air growing thinner.

A soft, rhythmic whirring sound buzzes from somewhere nearby. What is that?

I concentrate on the ceiling, counting the beams, desperately trying to anchor myself. But the sense of suffocation only grows. My breaths are too shallow, too rapid, each one fighting against the invisible weight on my chest.

Only my eyes move. I dart them side to side, frantic, searching for escape, for someone to assure me I'm not alone.

Lying on the couch in a sitting room full of memories, I'm swaddled in a blanket, the soft material tickling my skin. My bare skin.

Head to toe, I'm completely naked.

Where are my clothes?

Where's Rhett?

An IV line snakes in my peripheral vision, connected to my arm. The other end attaches to a fluid bag and small portable pump.

That explains the whirring sound.

I'm drugged.

Trapped.

A prisoner in my body.

In this cabin.

This hellish place.

Every crack in the wall, every shadow cast by the window light, brings back the fear, the endless night, the cold, the hunger, the abuse, the hopelessness. All of it lives in my bones.

Yet everything looks different.

During our final months here, we tore apart every wooden structure to fuel the hearth.

There's no trace of our struggle for survival. The destruction is gone, the wreckage swept away. New furniture fills the space. Repaired flooring. The cabin looks reborn, untouched by its haunted past.

The transformation is jarring, making my skin prickle and crawl.

Rhett has been traveling nonstop for the past five months.

Mostly to major cities. I've been working closely with top hospitals in Seattle, San Francisco, and New York.

I know Wilson investigated this. Rhett's flight plans checked out. But were all his flights confirmed? He must've been taking trips here, too.

How did he find Hoss? Leo and Kody searched and searched and couldn't locate it.

They don't know where I am.

They'll never find me.

I try to move again, but my limbs lay like dead things. I look down and study the IV drip in my arm.

My mind races. Whatever he's giving me only affects skeletal muscles. I feel every twitch, pulse, and breath in my body.

I can feel pain.

And wetness.

Wetness between my legs.

Did my bladder empty? Or is it something else?

Don't go there, Frankie. Don't think about it.

I'm wide awake. Fully aware. My brain is working, and I need to use it.

Rhett is my stalker.

He sent creepy messages and dismembered body parts to me.

Is he a serial killer? Or does he paralyze his victims the way he's paralyzing me? Does he keep them alive, trapped in their bodies, while he tortures them?

Is that what he intends to do to me?

Silent tears slip down my temples.

He has Wolf's body.

Tightness compresses my chest, my breath ramping into shallow puffs of air.

Sound comes from the arctic entryway. Doors open and close. Then Rhett appears, his expression unfamiliar, his eyes cold. Dead. I hardly recognize him.

"You're awake." He strides over in jeans and a thermal shirt, his hair windblown. Far removed from the heart surgeon I've known since my residency in Anchorage.

My only friend.

I glare at him with all the venom I can pour into my burning eyes.

You kidnapped me.

You're sick.

Let me go.

Please, don't do this.

The phone in his hand isn't a typical smartphone. The fat antenna and bulky size suggest it's a satellite phone.

It holds his attention as he approaches. When he reaches the couch, he shifts his gaze to me, a sad smile on his lips.

"Don't look at me like that, sweetheart." He sits on the couch beside my hip. "I've waited years for this. There's so much I need to tell you. So much you don't understand. But right now, all you need to know is that I love you. I've loved you since the day I met you in Anchorage." He glances at the phone again, watching something on the screen. "I saw you first, you know. Before any of the Strakh men knew you existed, you were mine."

He's insane. It's right there in his wide, unnervingly alert, deranged eyes.

As his stare fixes on me, it doesn't waver, as if he's in a

trance, lost in the fantasies of his obsession. The edges of his eyes twitch, a small, involuntary signal of the madness and chaos twisting beneath the surface.

He knows what I endured in this cabin. I confided in him, trusted him, and he listened with compassion.

All the while, he was stalking me and planning this.

He brought me back to the nightmare I fought so hard to escape.

On this day, of all days.

Exactly one year ago, I watched Denver rape Wolf. Then I walked down those stairs and made the devil's bargain.

Does Rhett understand the significance of this date?

Does he know winter is rapidly approaching? Does he know what that means in the hills of shivers and shadows?

Does he intend to keep me alive long enough to find out?

I direct my eyes to my unresponsive arm on my chest, narrowing my gaze on the IV port.

"Succinylcholine." He stares at his phone again. "It's temporary but necessary. The only way for you to stay calm and listen."

I'm not calm.

I'm the fucking opposite of calm.

Succinylcholine can be used to induce short-term paralysis. An injection wears off in ten or fifteen minutes. But he modified it, controlling the dose through the IV drip to extend its effects.

If he loved me, he would have a heart monitor set up, watching the spikes and ensuring the drug doesn't kill me.

My longevity is probably not part of his plan.

The horror of being trapped in my own body, aware of everything but unable to move or beg him for mercy, is more than I can withstand.

How did he pull this off? He sent creepy text messages to me while sitting beside me on the yacht. He has a successful career and a promising future. Why risk all that? What's his endgame?

I have so many questions and can't ask any of them.

My thoughts spin, drowning me in my own head. I need to get out of here, but how?

"I'm doing this for you. For us. You'll see." He leans down and kisses my forehead, the feel of his cold lips flooding me with nausea. "I'm not gay, Frankie. Never was."

His words slither ice down my spine.

No wonder he never married. I never saw him date or even touch another man. Come to think of it, he never outright said he was gay. Over the years, I assumed it based his comments about Monty's good looks when Monty and I started dating.

Mostly, I just thought Rhett was married to his job.

I'm so fucking stupid.

"I let you believe that because I needed you to feel safe around me." Another peek at his phone. "You *are* safe with me. I know it doesn't feel that way right now, but this will all make sense soon." He pulls in a breath. "They're almost here."

The shaking inside me goes still, paralyzed by a voltage of fear.

Monty, Leo, and Kody?

He must be watching them on his phone.

I search his indiscernible features, begging his blue eyes to tell me.

He shifts his position to run his gaze down the length of me. Holding his phone in one hand, he fists the blanket with his other. Then he drags it completely off me.

Cold air sweeps in, biting along my nude skin.

He leans closer, and I shrink inside my paralyzed body.

"Don't be shy." He reaches out, gently sliding a finger between my legs. "We've already been intimate."

My heart rate bursts into horrified tremors, and my stomach churns violently as he lifts a come-soaked finger and rubs it across my limp tongue.

"When I carried you out of the hospital in my duffle bag, I drove you to my bush plane at the Sitka airport, put you in the cargo hold, and..." He wags his head. "I couldn't wait. You weren't awake, but goddamn, you looked so beautiful and vulnerable, I had to have you before we took off."

He swipes the screen on his phone and turns it toward my

face.

A photo of me.

Naked, eyes closed, head lolled, legs spread, and a dick shoved up inside me. A dick with blond pubic hair.

My gaze flies to his blond head.

He raped me while I was unconscious.

Nausea surges, a stabbing, sickening agony that floods my mouth with saliva, compelling me to hurl. But even that simple reflex is denied to me. I can't retch. There's no relief from the roiling churn in my gut.

I scream in my head, sobbing and wailing without sound as my body ignores me, leaving me helpless and confined.

"You felt so fucking good, Frankie." He fingers my pussy, pressing his vile digits inside, molesting me until my mind fractures amid the shrieking screams of my trapped pain. "I sent that photo to the Strakhs."

No!

Oh, God, no! That would destroy them. It would cut them so deeply there will be no way to stop the bleeding.

And they're coming here?

Rhett must know that he'll have an army of bloodthirsty, murderous fiends charging in with claws and fangs unsheathed.

He would've prepared for that.

He's going to kill them.

I fight to control my thoughts, to quell the meltdown splitting my skull.

"I sent the photo to all of them with a link to the instructions to find you." He removes his hand from my body and returns his attention to his phone, swiping the screen. "When they opened the link, spyware downloaded to their devices. The instructions advised them I was watching and listening and included threats against their security team if they involved them. Threats against the lives of anyone they involved. They followed my instructions, made no phone calls, took the yacht to Sitka, boarded the bush plane I left for them, and smashed their phones when they took off."

They're alone. Walking into a trap.

"Once they were in the air," he says, "I sent the coordinates for the cabin to the avionics GPS in the plane. The communication system is disabled, but I can see where they are through the GPS system." He glances around the cabin. "This place is special. It's our safety from the world. Our home. I don't want anyone to find it."

Maybe they found a way around his instructions without his knowledge. His confidence in his plan makes my blood run cold, but Monty, Leo, and Kody are smart. They're survivors.

I have to believe they'll outsmart him.

"I've been watching them the entire way." He gestures at his phone. "They haven't deviated from the flight path. Haven't made any stops. They have no advantage. No way out unless they turn back in the next thirty minutes. If they do, I'll activate the bomb on board." He squints at me, his expression chilling. "Turns out you were right. They *are* willing to die for you."

The backs of my eyes catch fire as tears swarm my vision. I blink them away and shift my focus to the closed door. No help there.

Then I look at him and blink hard, two quick blinks, a desperate Morse code for no.

"No?" He brushes the hair from my face, sending a shiver along my dead limbs. "You don't want to see the men you worked so hard to unite? The men you love so much? They're my gifts to you. And there's more."

He stands and paces out of view. I track his footsteps into the kitchen. Straining my ears, I try to pick up any details, something that might help me as he moves around in the other room.

What did we leave behind when we escaped? Weapons in the armory. Knives in the kitchen. Scissors on the counter. None of that helps when I can't lift a finger.

My brain works frantically, formulating possibilities.

I will *not* let them die.

We survived this place once. We'll survive it again.

Think, Frankie. Fucking think.

I know the drug's effects are short-acting if not

continuously administered. If I can disrupt the IV, maybe I can regain control of my body.

Scanning the room, I look for anything within reach. The edge of a table, a zipper on the couch cushion, anything I can use to dislodge the IV. My mind whirls with desperation.

In extreme situations, a surge of adrenaline can sometimes help the body override paralysis. If I can just get a hand moving, maybe I can pinch or damage the IV line.

I shut my eyes, listening to his footsteps in the kitchen while willing my fingers to move, to close, to tear. Perspiration beads along my temples. Tears leak down my face. My insides tremble with the effort to unlock my joints.

The sound of his approach snaps my eyes open, the burst of energy quickly fading.

Not yet. But I can do this. I'll find a way.

He reenters the room, his demeanor calm. Too calm.

His blue eyes meet mine, and I hold his gaze in silent defiance.

"As much as I don't want to cover your gorgeous body, I don't want you to be cold." He kneels at my side, holding a velvety green robe. "I have something to show you. Something I've been collecting for you."

I don't want it. Please, don't show me anything.

He maneuvers my limbs, the IV fluid bag, and portable pump into the robe, ties the sash, and sets the bag on my stomach. Then he lifts me into his arms and carries my immobilized body into the kitchen.

While my arm dangles like a lead weight, my eyes are restless, frantically taking in each new angle.

I don't expect to find a table. It was one of the first things we burned in the hearth.

The scent of cold, damp earth merges with something sterile, something wrong. My heart rattles against my ribs, but there's nothing I can do.

Rhett carefully lays me on a new kitchen table.

A table surrounded by people.

People propped up in chairs, motionless.

No, not people.

Corpses.

My breath seizes, my eyes widening in terror as I take in the faces. I recognize them. Most of them.

Horror mauls my insides, turning everything to ice. Every muscle, every nerve screams for release, for escape, but I can't move. I can't fight back.

I can't escape this nightmare.

My nervous system riots with panic while my body remains silent, paralyzed, and compliant on the table of death.

Sirena's long black hair tangles around her shoulders, her eyes hollowed out, leaving dark voids where life once sparkled.

Doyle sits beside her, his handless arm on the table, the rest of him unnervingly still.

And Denver.

Holy fuck.

I inwardly recoil, unable to purge the bile in my throat.

Shirtless, he bears a gaping hole in his chest, his face beaten, disfigured, and partially decomposed, mostly as it was when I killed him. His eyes, open and glassy, have the same vacant stare as when he took his last breath.

There are two others on this side of the table that I don't recognize. An older man and woman. Their faces are unfamiliar but lifeless like the others.

I know another body sits behind me, but I can't turn my neck.

I don't want to turn it.

"That's Alvis Duncan and Thea, his wife." Rhett circles the table, approaching from above my head.

He leans over me, his face upside down, utterly unruffled, as if this grotesque scene is normal.

Alvis Duncan.

The man in Whittier who kept the flight logs, who watched Denver for decades.

But why? Why are they here? None of this makes sense.

It's a macabre dinner party with dead bodies arranged like guests around the table.

The trophies of a mass-murdering psychopath.

frankie

Numbness seeps into my bloodstream, dulling my senses. There's only so much a person can accept before the mind breaks.

I've reached my breaking point.

Or so I thought.

Rhett cups my face and turns my head to the other side of the table.

Wolf.

My Wolf.

The sight of him shatters what's left of my sanity.

My heart cracks open, and I try to roar, to howl in agony, but the chemical invasion in my veins imprisons me. All I can do is stare, helpless, my soul sobbing silently in a body that refuses to respond.

He looks exactly as he did when he jumped from the cliff.

Beautiful.

Broken.

His head hangs unnaturally on his shoulders, his hair draped across his face. His eyes are closed, his body unmoving.

Dead.

Just as dead as the others.

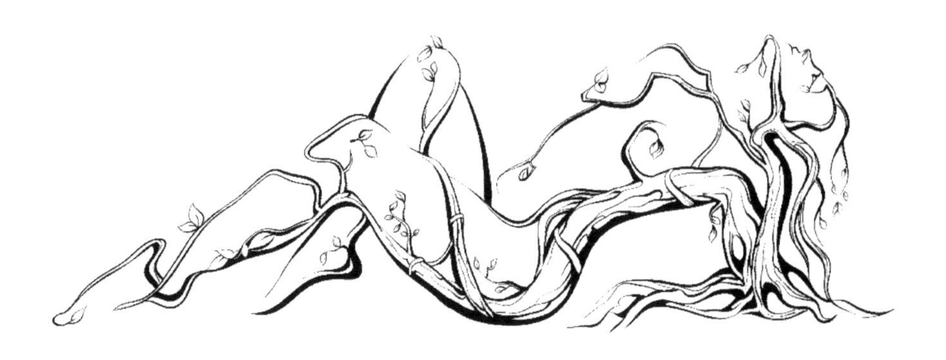

leonid

SIXTY-ONE

Rage.

That's too small a word to describe the thing inside me.

It's a war drum pounding in my ears, the blood vessels popping in my eyes, and the hellfire blazing through every nerve and tendon.

My fury is elemental, burning hot and violent, scorching reason and restraint into ash.

Hoss is the last place Frankie ever wanted to see again. The thought of her there, dragged back to her personal hell, locks my jaw tight enough to break my teeth. But I can't unclench it.

I fight to breathe, to remember the techniques. Inhale, count, exhale. But with each breath, I swallow glass. Each exhalation vomits fire.

My fingers curl around an invisible neck.

Rhett Howell.

I grip the armrest of my seat until my knuckles turn white.

Rhett is dead. He just doesn't know it yet. He doesn't know that the moment he touched Frankie, the moment he fucking raped her, he signed his death warrant.

We're his apex predators, his torturers, and his

executioners. Our wrath commands us. Our love for Frankie rules us.

Beside me, Monty pilots the bush plane with cold determination, his eyes focused on the horizon as if nothing else exists.

He thrives on control. He built his empire on it and ruled over others with it. But right now, the only control he's clinging to is the one keeping this plane in the air.

When we received the photo, I glimpsed what lies beneath his steely exterior, the brutality he's capable of inflicting. He destroyed the front room of the estate in under five seconds.

He won't hesitate to kill.

Rhett saw it, too. He watched us through our phones and listened to every word we said until we boarded this plane.

But we haven't spoken, not once since we received his instructions.

We don't need words to communicate. In the soundless language of our eye contact, the three of us made a plan, boarded this plane, and destroyed our phones.

The avionics communication system is disabled, but we know Rhett's tracking us through the plane's GPS system.

Behind me, Kody remains chillingly motionless. He's a shadow, dark and ominous, more animal than human. His eyes fix on something only he can see. He's our hunter, and tonight, he'll hunt something more than just flesh. He'll hunt for retribution, for justice, for the blood that was taken from us.

The anticipation of violence twitches through my muscles and prickles my skin.

I see her face behind my eyelids. Those green eyes hold my entire world in them. I hear her laugh, soft and sweet, like the whisper of snow on the wind.

Then I see her terror, the pain, the horror of that place, that cabin, and my control shatters. I want to tear something apart, crush and sunder until there's nothing left but a boneyard of vengeance.

The harness digs into my chest as I lean forward. The rampage inside me sharpens, becomes a blade, cold and deadly, ready to be unleashed.

leonid

The plane jolts as Monty dips low, skims the familiar ridge of a gorge, and follows the river that rushes between the cliffs.

He follows it north toward the hills on the horizon.

Our hills.

My breath catches in my throat.

The cabin, the nightmare, the place where Rhett has her—it's just ahead. I feel it, like a demon on the edge of my consciousness, a dark pull that draws me in, submersing me in bloodlust.

We followed Rhett's instructions.

Tell no one.

Arrive in the bush plane alone. Just the Strakhs.

Remove your clothes.

Enter the cabin, naked, with your hands in the air.

If you break these rules, I'll kill her.

He hasn't given us much wriggle room, but we have a plan.

It's simple.

We're going to butcher him, slowly and ruthlessly.

Wolf.

Oh, God, I loved him. I loved him so much, and he's gone.

Gone.

I feel it in my chest, in my stomach, in the way my insides tremble and convulse as if my body is trying to reject reality.

It's not just grief. It's a bottomless, excruciating pit, swallowing all light, all air, and all hope.

The drug keeps me locked in the empty darkness, my anguish trapped with no release. Tears pour from my eyes, hot and unending. And silent. I can't make a sound. I can't free my agony.

"You can keep them as long as you want." Rhett strokes my hair to comfort me, but it only deepens my horror. "They don't stink. I embalmed them and preserved them in chambers of frost. They're perfectly preserved for you, sweetheart."

Chambers of frost? Does he mean a morgue refrigerator? I strain my eyes toward the walk-in freezer in the kitchen. Did he keep them in there? How did he transport them here without getting caught?

And what gives him the impression I would want this?

Revulsion curls through me. He desecrated their bodies and turned them into morbid displays for his twisted pleasure.

He went through a lot of effort to set this up. Although, if he wanted to hide bodies, this is the place to do it.

I imagine he didn't have much time to prepare them. Some of their clothing must've been cut or partially removed to facilitate the embalming process.

Denver is shirtless. Sirena and Doyle wear the clothing I last saw them in. Same with Wolf. The bloodstained coat he borrowed from me hangs off his shoulders. The shirt beneath the coat appears dirty. Old.

He's been dead for ten months.

I'm going to die here, too. I'm going to die in the place I fought so hard to escape, surrounded by the corpses of those I loved and hated.

Why else would he lay me on the table like a sacrifice, positioning me among the dead?

I'm meant to join them.

"You'll be safe here." His soft voice chills my lungs. "I'll take care of you, just like I took care of them."

Denver knew.

He knew exactly what was coming for me.

There's another, lurking, yearning for you in a way far darker than my own affection.

I'm the silent ache, the shadow that lingers, the present from your past, the knife in your heart.

I want to scream and thrash and tear Rhett apart with my bare hands.

How could he do this?

How did he hide his evil from me all these years?

With my head turned toward Wolf's body, I can't pull my eyes from him. His face, once so expressive and adoring, droops with lifelessness, his beautiful blue eyes closed forever.

Rope digs into his chest, binding him to the chair in a cruel mockery of the man he was. Three empty chairs sit beside him, each with ropes already wound around the backs, waiting.

Waiting for Monty, Leo, and Kody.

Anguish, madness, soul-rending terror—it suffocates me

from within, crushing me breath by breath.

Rhett's going to put them in those chairs. He's going to kill them all, just like he killed the others.

And he'll make me watch.

I can't—I won't survive that.

The panic consumes, winding tighter and tighter with every second. I try to fight it, try to focus on anything other than the image of my men, dead and cold. But the thoughts keep crashing into me, one after the other, leaving me gasping for air I can't gulp.

Horror and helplessness strangle me, and there's nothing I can do but silently cry.

Rhett circles the table, his footfalls slow and deliberate, ticking through the kitchen like a countdown to the end of everything I love. I feel the vibrations of each step through the wood beneath me, through my bones, as if he's already started digging my grave.

My skin shudders, every nerve alight with fear as he comes around to my feet. I want to pull away, to kick him, to fight, but my body is useless. The only muscle that moves is my overworked heart.

His eyes roam over me, dark and hungry, and I know what's coming before he grips my ankles. His fingers dig into my skin as he tugs me toward him with a sharp jerk that clacks my teeth.

The movement sends my arm sliding off the table, and it falls limply onto Wolf's lap. The sight of my hand resting on the sleeve of his coat lodges a soundless scream in my unmoving throat.

The IV line connected to my hand pulls slightly, the fluid bag and portable pump on the table beside my hip. Seeing that clear liquid dripping steadily into my veins fills me with cold, helpless rage.

He's drugged me, drugged me so I can't fight, can't resist, can't do anything but lie here and endure whatever sick, twisted plans he has for me.

"I need you again," he murmurs, his voice sickeningly soft,

like a lover's whisper.

There's no love in what he does next.

Untying the sash on the robe, he spreads my legs, his hands rough and greedy.

I want to vomit. I want to die. I want to be anywhere but here.

He grunts as he enters me, using my body the way Denver did one year ago. Only this time, my suffering won't save Wolf.

It won't save Monty, Leo, or Kody.

Tears slip down my temples and into my hair.

The horror of each thrust is too much. I feel myself slipping, my mind fraying at the edges. I want to end this nightmare, but I can't even will myself to stop breathing. The drug keeps me alive, keeps me paralyzed, prolonging the torture.

Amid the despicable assault, I feel something.

It's faint, invisible, but it's there. Something warm against my hand, where it rests on Wolf's sleeve.

My heart stutters, wild hope kicking through my veins. I must be imagining it, some cruel trick of the mind.

But no. I feel it again. A pulse of heat, a flicker of life.

My eyes dart to Wolf, my vision smeared with tears. He looks dead, his face ashen, his lips pale, and his chest as still as a frozen lake.

Then I feel it again. A twitch. A spasm. A tiny movement under my hand, so small it could be nothing.

But it's not nothing. It's hope. It's life. It's warm, living flesh.

His arm shifts so subtly beneath my fingers, adjusting just enough to let me feel his hand, the microscopic movements, and the blood pumping under his skin.

Oh, my God.

He's not dead.

He's alive. He's fucking alive.

And he's trying to hold my hand.

The realization crashes over me, so powerful it overwhelms me. Relief, joy, disbelief—it all hits at once. If my throat worked, I would choke on the intensity of it.

But what if I'm wrong? What if it's just my mind, twisted by grief and fear, playing tricks on me?

I feel it again, and this time, there's no doubt. He's moving. He's alive.

The tears that fall now are different, still silent, but no longer just despair. There's something else in them. Hope. Desperate, fragile hope, but hope nonetheless.

Rhett finishes with a satisfied sigh, his breath hot and rancid against my chest.

He pulls my robe closed as if that can erase what he's done.

Stepping back, he straightens his clothes and checks his phone. "They're almost here."

His gaze goes distant, like he's already thinking ahead to the next atrocity he's going to commit. Then he strides out of the kitchen, his footsteps retreating toward the front room.

As soon as he's gone, the adrenaline hits me like a lightning bolt, searing through the fog of drugs and anguish.

Blood thrashes in my ears, and my heart hammers so fast I can hardly think.

Wolf is alive.

He's alive.

He's right here, with me, and we might have a chance. A slim one, but it's something. I can't lose him again. I can't lose any of them.

I focus on his face, willing him to open his eyes, to give me some sign that he's with me.

Is he unconscious? Drugged with a sedative, not a paralytic? I scan his body for any sign of an IV line or fluid bag, but I can't see anything. It might be under his coat.

Is he fighting it, just like I'm fighting the chemicals in my veins?

I pour every ounce of energy I have left into my hand, willing it to move, to press against his skin. It's agonizingly slow, my muscles straining against the drugs that hold them captive, but I keep pushing. I must. I must reach him.

Finally, after an eternity, I feel it. A twitch in my fingers. Just the tiniest movement, but it's enough.

I press harder, trying to feel over his hand, searching for anything that might help.

My thumb brushes against his wrist.

There.

The sticky edge of a plastic dressing holding something in place. The IV line. It's right there. So close.

I pick at the tape, my movements clumsy and weak, but I keep at it, scratching and pulling until I free one side.

My heart bangs so hard I'm afraid it'll stop, but I don't care. I have to save him.

But when I try to pull the line free, my fingers refuse to cooperate. I can't grip it hard enough, can't close my hand around it.

Panic spikes again, but I push it down.

Focus, Frankie. Keep trying.

Just as I'm about to lose hope, his wrist flicks beneath my fingers.

Oh, God, he's helping me. He's fighting, too.

I grip the line as best I can, and as he pulls his arm away, the IV slides free.

Holy fuck.

He's free of the drug.

If it's short-acting, he'll have full consciousness soon. We might have a chance.

The sound of a plane rumbles overhead, shaking the cabin and rattling the windows.

They're here.

My entire world.

The men Rhett plans to kill.

Maybe, just maybe, Wolf and I can stop him. Maybe we can save them, save each other, and end this nightmare once and for all.

Hope is a dangerous thing.

It crushes, darling.

Not this time, Wolf.

Hope is alive, a flicker of light in the darkness. And right now, it's all I have.

The strength in my fingers drains as quickly as it came, and my hand falls limp.

Footsteps sound, announcing Rhett's return.

Wolf's arm twitches again, moving, slipping back into the sleeve where it was, hiding the dislodged IV.

Rhett stops beside Wolf and stares down at my hand on Wolf's lap.

Please don't check his IV. Please don't look.

"He's not dead." Rhett tilts his head, searching my wide eyes. "I'm giving him Propofol."

He lifts the hem of Wolf's coat, revealing the bottom of the fluid bag beneath the zipper. The bag must be hanging from his neck to keep it upright.

He doesn't check the IV line under Wolf's sleeve.

Why would he? Neither of us can move.

Propofol is a sedative-hypnotic that typically wears off within five to ten minutes.

How long has it been?

"Wolfson, Kodiak, Leonid, and Montgomery." Rhett ticks their names off his fingers. "I kept the Strakh men alive and brought them here to test their strength and loyalty." He paces to the end of the table, standing above my head. "Wolf has been quite helpful over the past ten months, feeding me information about the family. Reluctantly, of course. It turns out he'll do anything to save your life, even if he did aim a gun at you in the end. He wouldn't have pulled that trigger. He doesn't have it in him."

He reaches behind him and removes a gun from his waistband. A pistol I recognize.

He found the armory.

"I have it in me." He lowers into the chair at the head of the table and presses the barrel of the gun to my skull. "Let's see how deep their loyalties run."

My mind is a hurricane of panic, spinning faster and faster, whipping thoughts through my head so violently I can't hold onto any of them. I can't think, can't focus, can't breathe, because all I see is Wolf, sitting there like a corpse.

That's exactly what his brothers and father will see when

they walk in.

"They followed my instructions," Rhett says. "I just watched them disembark the plane and remove their clothes. No one's with them. I'm impressed."

They won't cooperate. They're going to rage and lose control and get themselves shot.

I need to get a message to them, to let them know in about five minutes, Wolf will be fully conscious and ready to fight.

But I'm so utterly, completely trapped.

As the entryway door swings open, my heart explodes, slamming into my throat.

"Come in. Slowly. Hands where I can see them." Rhett digs the gun against my head.

As my beautiful, naked men approach the kitchen, a warm hand curls around my wrist.

Wolf's fingers move with strength and purpose, sliding under the sleeve of my robe. With one, smooth pull, he frees the IV line from my arm.

Fuck.

Yes.

Fifteen minutes.

I don't have a plan, but one thing is certain. We're going to fuck shit up.

Kodiak

SIXTY-THREE

I stalk into the cabin, holding up my hands, with Monty and Leo at my side. The familiar creak of the floors echoes in my ears, a sound I've heard a thousand times before.

But this time, it's different.

Everything is different.

The stench of death swamps the air, buzzing with the memories that haunt this place.

This is where I grew up. Where I was abused by a madman. Where I met Frankie.

It's changed since then.

I've changed...on the surface.

But my understructure remains the same. A feral animal still lives inside me. It helped me survive these hills, and those instincts guide me now.

As I follow Rhett's voice to the kitchen, heat trickles from the vents. He fixed the generator, repaired the floors, and cleared away the dust.

The cabin may look brighter and cleaner than we left it, but I see the shadows of what used to be here. I see the bloodstains of my childhood on the floor, the scars on the walls, the bones in the fire pit, and the danger lurking in Denver's bedroom down the hall.

And I see her.

Frankie, lying on the table, her robed body stock-still and her hair spread like a halo around her.

My heart stops, but I force myself to keep walking.

She's not restrained.

She's not moving, either.

An IV fluid bag sits on the table beside her hip. I follow the line to the opening in the sleeve of her robe, where her arm hangs on Wolf's lap.

Wolf.

He's here. Dead. And Frankie's drugged.

Horror cleaves through me.

Rhett sits at the head of the table, like a king on his throne. He holds a gun to Frankie's head, his finger resting on the trigger.

My blood turns to ice, my rage a cold, hard knot in my chest.

I'm going to eviscerate him. Remove his entrails with claws and teeth. But not yet. He has her, and as long as he holds that gun, I must wear my human skin and maintain my domesticated mask, the face I show in the civilized world.

No sudden moves. No growling or tensing. Nothing that might startle him into squeezing that trigger.

Beside me, Leo and Monty fight their own inner battles. They'll get their pound of flesh. But only if we remain calm, stall as long as we can, and give our plan time to play out.

A plan we never discussed. Not with words. That alone is goddamn unnerving.

Entering the kitchen, I stumble as my eyes dart from one corpse to the next. The two bodies I don't recognize must be Alvis Duncan and his wife. That would explain why they went missing.

Numb. I'm numb and frozen with rage at the sight of Frankie lying at the center of all this blood-chilling carnage.

Then my gaze lands on Wolf.

His lifeless body slumps against the rope that holds him in

the chair. I knew this was a possibility. I knew I might see the remains of the man I loved, but nothing could have prepared me for the reality of it.

My brother.

Monty's son.

I can't look at Monty and Leo. My own pain stabs too sharply, threatening to double me over as the knife of grief twists in my gut. I absorb it, bury the sorrow, and let it fuel my fury.

"Love what you've done with the place." Leo's lips curl into an arctic smile, a predator's grin. "Nice touch with the Mad Tea Party. Or is this The Last Supper? Do you fuck the guests before you eat them? Asking for a friend."

"You'll find out soon enough." Rhett gestures at the empty chairs. "After all, I saved a seat just for you."

"Oh, joy. I'm famished." Leo isn't just ready for this. He's fucking craving it.

Bloodlust inhabits every cell of his body, as much a part of him as his scars and his pain.

Nothing will stop us. Not the gun in Rhett's hand. Not the ghosts that haunt us.

Our demons are meaner, scarier, and they're fucking angry.

"They stink." Monty scowls at Denver's corpse.

"Impossible. I embalmed them." Rhett stands, his expression cold and detached, as he holds the gun to the top of Frankie's head. "There are bombs on both of those planes out there. I just activated them. Unless you know how to disarm a booby-trapped ignition bomb, it will detonate if you start either of those engines." He gestures at his fancy satellite phone. "Password protected."

Controlling those planes is his safety net, one we know too well. If we kill him, we're not leaving Hoss.

Or so he thinks.

"What is that?" His glare narrows on Monty's feet.

We're naked, vulnerable, and exposed—precisely how he wants us. Except for the slippers Monty donned on his way out of the house.

"I watched you demolish your home when you received the photo I sent." Rhett chews on his cheek, the gun unwavering on Frankie. "Those slippers came out of the box of mementos you hurled across the room. They mean something."

"A year ago today, Denver raped my son and my wife." Monty stands taller, an imposing pillar of confidence despite his nudity. "He raped them while wearing these slippers. The same slippers he stole from me the night he stole Frankie. If I die today, I thought it only fitting that I die wearing them."

Dramatic.

And effective.

"Sit at the table." Rhett directs his eyes at the empty seats. "Use the rope and tie yourselves to the chairs."

I'm already moving, a beast in human form, muscles tensed and focused. The time for bloodshedding is almost here.

I take a seat beside Wolf, and Leo sits on his other side, closest to Rhett. Monty lowers into the chair on my left near Frankie's feet.

We all stare at Frankie's motionless figure as we wrap the nylon restraints around our chests. Nothing within view indicates he intends to shackle our hands and feet.

A single rope around our torsos won't stop us from attacking him.

But the gun will.

Rhett holds all the cards right now, but that will change soon. We'll make sure he pays for every hair he harmed on Frankie's head.

We can't act yet. Not until she's safe, not until we can take him down without risking her life.

"Why isn't she moving?" Monty knots the rope around him. "What are you giving her?"

"The drug affects skeletal muscles. She can't move her mouth, but she's fully awake. It's safe. I'm a surgeon, after all."

"I know what and who you are, Renat Moroz." Monty cocks his head. "The hush money your family received from my father paid for your medical school and then some. You would've had millions left over. Is that how you funded this sick quest?"

We didn't have time to confirm that detail, but given Rhett's wide eyes, Monty's assumption is correct.

"At age twelve, you were assaulted by a pedophile." Monty directs his eyes at Denver's corpse. "My father moved you and your family to a location Denver couldn't find, changed your names, and paid you enough money to keep you quiet. You never forgave your parents for accepting that payoff. So you killed them years later. How am I doing so far?"

That part about his parents' murders is another assumption.

"How did you know that?" Rhett's brows pinch together. "No one knows that."

"I know the devastation that Denver left behind. Unfortunately, I learned about it too late." Monty hardens his voice. "Why is my son here? His body doesn't belong among these...*things.*"

"Oh, Wolfson isn't dead."

My head snaps toward Wolf, my heart exploding in my chest. He doesn't move. His torso doesn't lift with breath. Or does it? The bulky coat hides those subtle signs of life.

I start to reach for him.

"Don't touch him." Rhett stands, bringing my focus back to the gun trained on Frankie. "He's sedated. Unconscious."

As Rhett leans over her, her glare follows him, narrowing in determination. My throat tightens as she directs those green eyes at Wolf, then at me.

She blinks twice.

Blink once for yes, twice for no.

Why is she saying no? Wolf isn't unconscious?

"I wanted to surprise you," Rhett says. "He's been alive all these months."

He let us believe he was dead because he's a psychopath who thrives on breaking people, not just physically but emotionally and mentally. It satisfies his deep-rooted need for dominance and control.

I know because I was raised by a monster just like him.

This isn't just about killing us. He wants to flaunt his sense of superiority.

Denver abused him as a child, twisted him into this monster. Denver abused us in the same way, but we weren't alone. Leo, Wolf, and I had one another. We kept each other sane.

Somewhat.

I don't feel sane at the moment.

Rhett studies us as if probing for vulnerabilities. He's so focused on our faces, he doesn't notice Frankie's lips moving.

Ensnaring my gaze, she mouths, *Red flag*, and flicks her eyes to Wolf.

Red flag?

I glance at Leo. He saw it, too.

Didn't Rhett say she couldn't move her lips?

She must be fighting the drug. Unless...

I peek down at her hand on Wolf's lap. Their arms are hidden beneath their sleeves. But if Wolf is conscious, he could've discreetly removed her IV.

Leo and I exchange a knowing look as I recall a long-ago conversation with Wolf.

My red flag is I can tell you my red flag with a blank face.

He never clarified what he meant, but I assumed it was his way of saying he's self-aware and recognizes his problematic behaviors—*red flags*—without showing emotion—*a blank face*—which could itself be a red flag in relationships.

Is Frankie trying to tell us he's awake and faking it?

Only one way to find out.

As Rhett returns to his seat, I place my foot directly over Wolf's. He's also barefooted, and the cold toes beneath mine lift, responding to my touch.

Holy fucking shit.

It takes every ounce of strength to keep my face empty and my eyes on Rhett.

Wolf is alive.

He's alive and awake, and the only thing holding him in that chair is a measly rope around his chest and a gun leveled at Frankie's head.

He must've dislodged the IV line in her arm. How long ago?

Does she have full mobility? I don't know how long it takes the drug to leave her system.

My nerves riot, flooding my body with adrenaline.

One wrong move, and Frankie's dead.

What's Wolf's plan?

"After Rurik died..." Rhett's finger twitches against the trigger. "I returned to Kodiak Island, to that massive, ostentatious mansion on the cliff. I found the flight logs, the blueprints for this cabin, and those photos stuffed in a leather-bound copy of Pushkin's poems on his bookshelf." He looks at Monty. "You hadn't arrived yet to clean out the place. I took the book with the documents inside and followed the trail to Alvis Duncan."

My pulse sprints as I bump my foot against Monty's slipper. He's so engrossed in Rhett's story that he doesn't respond.

"I told Alvis I worked for Rurik Strakh." Rhett sighs. "It was so easy. He thought I was one of Rurik's henchmen and handed over the flight logs that tracked Denver's movements. And so it went. Over the years, I collected the logs, learned Denver's pattern, and tracked him when he flew in to gather supplies."

Keep talking, you crazy fuck. We need more time, and you're playing right into our hands.

I nudge Monty's slipper again, and this time, he nudges back. His gaze remains fixed on Rhett, narrowed on that fucking gun, as he slides his foot from his shoe and inches the slipper toward me.

"I don't remember you on Kodiak Island." Monty clears his throat, trying to hide any noise I might make.

It's not necessary. Silence and stealth are second nature to me.

"My father was Rurik's accountant for a short time." Rhett taps his thumb on the butt of the pistol. "He brought me to the estate only once. You weren't there. But Denver was."

"You were twelve, and Denver was..." Monty releases a breath. "Seventeen."

"Yes. While our fathers were holed up in Rurik's office all

night, Denver took me to the wine cellar, let me drink wine with him, and…"

"He raped you," Monty says bluntly. "And when you were old enough, you hunted him down to exact your revenge."

"At first, yes. I wanted to kill him. But as I watched him, I became…enamored. I wasn't that weak twelve-year-old boy anymore. Watching Denver hunt, stalk, and take Kaya and Kodiak without getting caught…" Rhett shakes his head. "He was brilliant. I wanted to be him. I guess you can say I developed a bit of hero worship."

And look at his hero now.

A pint-sized redhead with a ferocious heart took him down with a lead pipe.

Frankie stares at the ceiling, absorbing the information without moving a muscle. If she has full motion in her face, it would require incredible concentration to keep her expression slack.

I'm so fucking proud of her.

And terrified for her.

We need to keep Rhett talking.

Monty stares at our woman, his jaw grinding. "What's the meaning behind the Pushkin quotes?"

"When your father paid off my family and moved us out of state, he sent me a gift. An entire collection of books by Pushkin."

"Rurik was obsessed with the poet." Monty frowns.

"Yes. The book collection came with a handwritten note. Not signed. Just a quote. *He filled a shelf with a small army of books and read and read; but none of it made sense. They were all subject to various cramping limitations: those of the past were outdated.*"

"*And those of the present were obsessed with the past.*" Monty finishes.

"I guess Rurik knew I would become obsessed with the past."

"Whose handwriting is on the notes you sent?"

"I approached a homeless kid in San Francisco and paid him twenty bucks to write the words I gave him."

Jesus Christ. To what lengths will this whack job go?

"Did Denver know you were tracking him?" I ask.

"Yeah." Rhett inhales. "I don't know how, but he sensed me following him and showed up at my apartment in Anchorage one night. This was around the time I met Frankie."

"Why didn't he kill you?" Monty narrows his eyes.

"Same reason I didn't kill him. Mutual respect. I asked him to mentor me, and in exchange, he asked me to track down Gretchen Stolz. It was a test. One I passed."

Wolf doesn't respond to the mention of his mother. Not even the tiniest puff of air passes his lips.

Without moving a single muscle above my ankle, I slowly prod my foot into the slipper Monty passed to me. Size twelve. Same as me. Long enough to conceal a nine-inch fillet knife.

I don't know how Monty snatched it from the doorframe without Rhett spotting the movement through our cameras. Monty angled his body just right, slipped it beneath his clothes, and kept it hidden until we destroyed our phones.

Walking in here with it tucked inside his slipper was a risk.

But it paid off.

Curling my toes around the knife's handle, I carefully ease it out of the shoe and lower it to the floor beside Wolf's foot.

He feels it there, his toes twitching against mine.

My chest constricts, the tension unbearable, as I step down on the blade.

I hold the knife in place, my eyes on Rhett, as Wolf maneuvers the handle between his toes and grips it.

Transferring it from his foot to his hand will be the impossible part.

But he has it. The knife. The element of surprise.

Whatever his plan is, he's armed.

monty

SIXTY-FOUR

My hands fist so tightly on my naked lap that my knuckles crack.

The cabin reeks with the stench of decay despite Rhett's assurances that the bodies don't stink. They do. It's not a smell that lingers in the air but one that seeps into the soul. The kind of stink that rots the living from the inside out.

Frankie lies on the table before me, her eyes wide and body rigid with that damn drug pumping through her veins. She's supposed to be paralyzed, supposed to be helpless.

Yet I saw it. Just a twitch, but it was there. Her lips moved. She said something, but I didn't understand it.

In my periphery, Wolf sits between Kody and Leo. His head lolls on his shoulders, his hair dangling in his face. He looks dead.

But he's not.

My heart stutters, skipping beats as I try to wrap my mind around it. My son, who I thought I'd never meet, is here, breathing.

Knowing he's alive but not safe is a cruel twist of fate. I've been on a roller coaster since I saw him, thinking I'd lost him only to find out he's still lives.

The whirlwind of emotions hitting me one after another leaves me reeling and out of breath. But my expression remains composed, my hands frozen on my lap.

Kody has the knife now. I don't know what he'll do with it, but he's smart. Smart enough to know he can't make a move as long as Rhett holds that gun.

I just need to keep Rhett talking. Keep him distracted. Get answers.

He drones on in a sickening tone, vibrating with pride and madness as he explains everything that led up to this moment, how he meticulously planned it all, and how he orchestrated every move, with a detachment that makes my skin crawl.

He's in control, or so he thinks. He doesn't know Kody. He doesn't know what's coming.

"I saw Frankie first." He reaches out and strokes her hair, testing our willpower.

All three of us tense, ready to lunge across the table and drag the chairs with us.

Unable to hold back, Leo releases a dark, guttural sound.

"Denver promised he would help me take her." He scowls. "He said he would help me keep her without getting caught."

"You didn't think to ask her out on a date?" I growl. "Try to woo her the old-fashioned way?"

"She wasn't interested. She was focused on her career and put me in the friend zone."

"You told her you were gay," Leo spits, seething.

"I never told her that. She assumed, and I let her believe it. I wanted more than a one-night stand, and that's all she was willing to give anyone. Just one night."

"Until me." I meet her eyes.

She blinks once. *Yes.*

My chest fucking aches.

"You're the reason Denver and I had a falling out," Rhett says. "He mentored me for years. I no longer needed to collect flight logs from Alvis. Denver came to me on his own whenever he was in Anchorage. He taught me how to strategize, engineer bombs, utilize drones and spyware, and monitor Frankie undetected. He convinced me to be patient, to wait for the right moment. He promised that when the time was right, he would give me the coordinates to the cabin. He promised I could bring Frankie here, and we would have a life together."

"A life together? You intended to imprison her." My pulse accelerates, and my breathing turns shallow. "Just like you're doing now."

"I'm doing this for her." Rhett glowers. "She'll see that with time."

Kody loosens a harsh, inhuman sound. "Denver said the same thing."

"Denver was a liar. He wanted to ruin Montgomery's life and told me that if I helped her meet him, he would help me rip her away, break Montgomery's heart, and satisfy both our end goals. Then she would be mine."

Instead, Denver kept her for himself.

For Leo, Kody, and Wolf.

To use her in a twisted bargain with the devil.

"You came in with a dislocated kneecap." Rhett glares at me. "I assigned Frankie to you because I thought Denver would keep his word. For the next year, I didn't think you had a chance with her. Then you did. You and Frankie became inseparable, got married, and Denver cut ties with me. Just like that. I couldn't find him. I had stopped collecting the flight logs from Alvis and no longer had that connection. Denver evaded me. Used me. He saw me as a threat."

He saw you as the unhinged serial killer that you are, Dr. Howell.

Denver despised violence unless he was the one wielding it. He knew what Rhett would do to her. In his sick way, Denver protected her by bringing her to Hoss.

The crazy shit he spewed in his video is starting to make sense.

Look around you. Is your admirer there now? Watching? You were safe with me in the hills. Out here, no hills can save you.

"How did you find this cabin?" I ask.

"When Sirena started helping you search for Frankie, I contacted her anonymously and offered her more money than she could refuse. When she clicked on the link to receive the payment, it downloaded spyware to her phone. That enabled me to monitor your search every step of the way."

"Why did you return the flight logs and the book of Pushkin poems to Kodiak Island?" I grit my teeth.

"Your search went stale. I knew you would eventually look there and wanted to lead you to Alvis Duncan. Of course, I had to do it in a way that didn't feel suspicious." He pauses to squint at the illuminated chandelier over the table. "The blueprints for the cabin included instructions for the hydroelectric generator. I kept those instructions. That's how I got the power back on."

"Was it a missing circuit board?" Leo straightens.

"I'll never tell." He winks.

"Did you tell Sirena where to look for clues when we were searching Rurik's estate?" I ask.

"I may have given her a little direction."

That lying, traitorous bitch.

"Why did you tell her to seduce me?" I flex my hands.

"To test your loyalties. There's something about you." Rhett tips his head, studying all of us. "Something about the Strakh family that fascinates me. You're resilient, faithful, and extraordinarily strong, physically and mentally. I tried to break you apart with Sirena's propositions. I told her to seduce all of you." He glances at her corpse. "She was a beautiful woman, yet none of you surrendered. Not a weak bone among you. It's impressive."

Jesus fucking Christ. He wants to be part of this family. I see it in his crazed eyes. Talk about hero worship. I get the feeling we're here because he wants to take Denver's place and rule over us in these fucking hills.

"How did you find the cabin?" I ask again.

"I searched for it, same as you. While you and Sirena spent months flying over the Interior, I told her where to look, taking you off course while I narrowed down the grid. I found it the week Denver died. I was here when Leonid and Kodiak dragged Denver's body out into the tundra. I collected his remains the same day I pulled Wolf from the river."

He goes on to boast about his bravery in the arctic climate and the difficulty in landing a bush plane in torrential snow.

"Wolf," I say, cutting through his monologue. "Where has he been?"

He smiles. A twisted, self-satisfied smile that makes me want to saw his lips off his face with a dull knife. "That's where Alvis Duncan fits in."

My gaze shifts to the dead man across the table, and my stomach drops to my feet.

"That's right." Rhett pushes the gun against Frankie's head. "When you went to Whittier to interrogate Alvis, he was holding Wolfson in an old outbuilding on another property not far away. I knew I could trust Alvis. He collected those flight logs for decades, took money from a Russian mobster, and never told a soul. He feared for his family, and I put that same fear in him when I left Wolf in his care for ten months. He and Thea fed Wolfson and kept him safe. They also held Denver's body for me in one of their freezers." His smile fades, replaced by something darker, more sinister. "He was a loose end. You know how it is. I had to deal with that when I collected Denver and Wolf."

I want to roar, rage, leap across this table, and annihilate him. I can't stay still. The chair feels like it's confining me, suffocating me. I need to move, to act, to destroy.

I glance at Kody, and he meets my gaze, his expression broody and relaxed. But his eyes. The fire in them blazes with brutality.

"You're insane." I return to Rhett, my voice guttural. "You've done all this, killed all these people, for what? Some twisted sense of control? You think this makes you powerful?"

"It's not about power. It's about order. You and your family...you're chaos. You make a mess of everything. Someone had to bring us all together."

"Is that why we're all here? To be together?" I feel lightheaded. Queasy. *Anxious.*

"If you're willing." Rhett turns his attention to Leo and Kody. "After I saved Wolf, I returned to check on you."

"We saw you." Leo hisses a breath past his teeth. "We built an SOS signal."

"I know. But you were exactly where I wanted you. I went back to retrieve Monty. I was going to bring you all here. But I got sidetracked with the cardiac program at the hospital. It was my alibi for all the traveling, but I still had to run the damn thing."

"So you just left us here to die?" Kody snarls.

"You didn't die. You figured out how to fly. That really fucked up my plans." Rhett takes a breath. "I didn't expect Denver to warn you about me, either. That fucking riddle...it delayed this by five months. You locked down security and didn't leave the island. And when you did, you were always surrounded by guards. I had to get creative."

He knows about Denver's riddle, our security, every detail of our lives because he's been watching and listening through Frankie's phone.

"When did you put spyware on her phone?" I ask.

"When I sent her the information for Melanie Stokes."

Fuck.

That was the first fucking week.

"We searched for this cabin." Leo clenches his jaw. "With Sirena. Did you tell her where to search? Or where *not* to search?"

"Yes." Rhett's smile returns, cold and calculating, as he looks around the kitchen. "I was remodeling. I couldn't have you finding it. Not until you were all together. I encouraged Frankie to unite the three of you. As much as I want her for myself, let's face it. I don't know these hills. I can't survive here and keep her safe without you. But the six of us together? We'll be one big happy family."

He's insane. Certifiable. Fucking nuts.

And Denver knew it.

Not all wounds bleed. Not all scars show. Some live beneath bones, cold and alone. In the chambers of frost, pain is my art.

Denver knew he scarred this man irrevocably. He knew enough not to trust him. That's why he cut ties with him.

Denver created a monster more evil than himself.

"How did you text Frankie while sitting beside her on the yacht?" Leo asks.

"I scheduled it through a third-party service, using a fake number." Rhett wets his lips. "When I called her, I used another service to create the computerized voice."

"The phrase you used..." Kody inhales. "It sounded like something Wolf would say."

"That was intentional. I spent some time with Wolfson over the past ten months. He loves to quote movies. His humor is dry and inappropriate. He's hilarious." Rhett rakes his eyes over Wolf, making my entire body clench. "I led you to consider him a suspect to keep you from looking in my direction."

"Wolf was never a suspect," I snap. "But everyone else was, including you."

"Mm. I wasn't at the top of your list. Don't forget. I heard most of your conversations."

"Why would you risk your career and everything you've worked for to do this?" I ask.

"*This* is what I worked for. This is what I want. To unify the Strakhs and become part of your family. I'll lead you better than Denver did. I'm smarter and kinder. I killed for you." He nods at the row of corpses. "I waited for you to come together. I want you all to see that this is for the best. You'll thank me when it's over."

He's wrong. I'll never thank him. But I'll make sure he pays for every life he's taken, every horror he's inflicted on Frankie. I'll make sure he knows exactly who he's dealing with.

Because this family, this chaos he thinks he's controlling, we don't go down easy. We fight, and we win.

"Here's how this will go." Rhett stands and pulls three syringes from his pocket. The gun doesn't waver in his hand as he tosses the hypodermic needles onto the table in front of Leo. "This is the same paralytic I gave Frankie. Inject it into your arms. It's just one dose. It'll wear off in fifteen minutes."

My breath hitches. He can't be serious. But the look in his eyes tells me he's deadly serious.

Leo growls, the sound vibrating in his chest.

Fifteen minutes is a long time in hell. What does Rhett have planned during that time?

"I'm not injecting myself with that," I say, my voice hard as steel.

I won't make myself helpless. Fuck that.

"You don't get to decide." Rhett's expression darkens, his calm demeanor cracking. "You do it, or she dies. You all die."

The gun presses harder into Frankie's head, and a vise clamps around my lungs.

Why would he kill us after spending all this time collecting us?

I shift my eyes along the row of corpses on the other side of the table.

He's a serial killer.

If he doesn't kill us today. He'll kill us, eventually.

My mind spins, trying to find a way out. I'm not about to make myself vulnerable like that. Not with Frankie's life hanging by a thread.

I can't let this happen. We can't give him what he wants.

Before I can react, Leo reaches for the syringes and passes them down the table. "We'll do it."

Kody doesn't say a word, just grabs a needle and removes the cap. His eyes flick to mine, and in that brief glance, I see something. A message. A plan. But I can't decipher it. My mind is too clouded by fear, by the fury steaming from my ears.

"We want her to live," he says. "Trust me."

"You have two seconds to plunge those needles before I squeeze the trigger." Rhett meets my eyes.

I've never been one to back down, never been one to surrender control.

As I watch a stream of tears track down Frankie's temple, I know I don't have a choice. If I don't do this, she's dead. We're all dead.

Trust me.

I trust Kody and Leo with my life. And hers.

My pulse thunders as I snatch the syringe and flick off the cap.

monty

SIXTY-FIVE

I should be the one protecting them, protecting Frankie. Yet here we are, helpless and cornered by a madman.

My fingers tighten around the syringe. I flex my forearm, exposing the veins that lie beneath the skin.

My heart hammers in my chest, each beat echoing in my ears.

I've been through a lot of shit in my life, seen things that would make most men crumble. But this? This is fucked up.

This isn't a fight I can win with brute strength or cunning. This is surrender, pure and simple.

With a deep breath, I bring the needle to my arm, the sharp point hovering over my flesh. I hesitate, my mind screaming to fight back, to do anything but this.

I look at Leo and Kody.

They nod, holding their syringes.

Fuck.

Together, we push the needles into our veins.

The sharp sting barely registers as the drug enters my bloodstream.

A cold, creeping numbness that spreads from the injection

site, flowing through my veins like ice water. It's slow at first, almost gentle.

Then it hits like a freight train slamming into my chest.

My muscles start to fail, one by one. My fingers go limp, dropping the syringe to the floor with a dull clatter.

Beside me, their needles drop, too.

My legs buckle, and I slouch against the rope, the only thing keeping me upright.

The loss of control is immediate, terrifying, and absolute.

I feel everything. The panic rising in my chest. The frustration boiling over in my mind. But I can't move. I'm locked inside a shell of flesh and bone that no longer feels like mine.

This is what Frankie felt.

How many times did he rape her while she was unable to fight back?

My breaths come in shallow, labored gasps, each a struggle as my lungs refuse to cooperate. My vision blurs, and I try to focus on her, on the way her lips moved earlier, trying to make sense of it, trying to hold on to anything that might give me hope.

Leo and Kody crumple at the edge of my vision, silent and helpless.

I've always been in control. Always. But now I'm nothing but dead weight, slumped in the rope that binds me, ineffectual and vulnerable.

I can't even lift my head to look Kody or Leo in the eyes. All I can do is sit here, feeling the icy grip of paralysis tighten around me.

"Very good." With a relieved smile, Rhett leans down to Frankie, his eyes gleaming with sick pleasure as he kisses her brow. "Now we test them."

I roar, but there's no sound. There's nothing. No escape. No way to help her. Just the cold reality that we're at Rhett's mercy.

I've never felt so powerless in my entire life.

But even as the paralysis sinks in, even as I lose the last remnants of control, I cling to one thing.

Frankie's face. The determination I saw in her eyes when we arrived. The way her lips moved when they shouldn't have.

She's still fighting.

And so am I.

"Fifteen minutes." Rhett circles the table, passing behind us, sending a shudder through me. "During that time, you need to make a choice."

He pauses at Frankie's feet and sets the gun beside her leg.

Now would be a good time to use that fucking knife.

Except none of us can move.

He grips her ankles and slides his hands up her calves.

My heart collapses, and my insides shrivel.

No.

Fuck no.

"I'm going to make love to our girl while you watch." He parts her legs, and his hands inch higher. "When the drug wears off, you'll have two options. One, you accept this, accept me, and we make love to her together. Or two..." His gaze sharpens, and he pats the gun on the table. "You lose your shit, and I put a bullet in Frankie's head. Then I'll put one in each of you. I'll burn this cabin to the ground and return to my life in Sitka without you." He reaches for the sash on her robe. "What will it be? Are you all in, or are you all dead? You have fifteen minutes to make your decision."

Fury like I've never known rages through me. Muscles frozen, limbs heavy as lead, I'm a goddamn inferno.

My heart slams against my ribcage, each beat a bellow of rage ricocheting in my skull.

I can't move, can't twitch a finger, but inside, I rip myself apart, thrashing, bucking, and shredding my organs with a ferocity so intense it threatens to obliterate me from within.

Every molecule in my body is ablaze with it, this wrath that builds and builds with nowhere to go. It's a nuclear bomb scorching the walls of my mind, melting, destroying, burning me alive. I choke on it but can't release it. Can't let it out.

I want to grab Rhett by the throat, crush his windpipe until he's gasping for breath. Until his eyes pop out and his face turns blue. I want to slam my fists into his skull until there's nothing left but bone and blood. Until I've pounded every trace of his sick, twisted smile out of existence.

I strain with all my energy to move my muscles, but they don't respond. Not even the slightest twitch.

I don't have to see Leo and Kody to know they're in the same hell.

Rhett is going to rape her, and all we can do is sit here and burn.

I hate him with a force that defies comprehension. I hate him for what he's done to Frankie, to Wolf, to all of us. I hate him for what he's about to do. I hate him for taking away my ability to protect the people I love.

The depth of my hatred is a black hole, sucking in every last shred of light, every last piece of humanity, until all that's left is darkness and rage.

As Rhett opens Frankie's robe, something moves near her arm.

Out of the corner of my eye, I see...

Wolf.

He's awake.

And he's holding the knife Kody must have passed to him.

His hand moves fast, too fast to register. Before I fully comprehend what's happening, the blade flies through the air and sinks into the juncture between Rhett's chest and shoulder.

He stumbles back, staring down at the weapon in shock. Then he glares at Wolf with demonic eyes.

As he tries to yank the knife free, Frankie kicks the gun off the table with a burst of movement that defies everything Rhett thought he controlled.

The weapon clatters to the floor, skidding across the wood.

For a split second, everything is chaos. Rhett's face twists in fury as he dives for the gun, and Frankie lunges after him, her fingers clawing for it. The IV fluid bag and pump go flying, no longer connected to her.

Leo, Kody, and I are frozen in our seats, unable to move, to help, to do anything but watch as the scene unfolds before us.

Time slows, the seconds stretching into infinity as Frankie

and Rhett grapple on the floor. They scramble in and out of view, fighting to gain control of the gun.

I can't fucking move. I'm trapped in this useless body while the fire inside me rages unchecked, burning hotter and hotter with every second that passes. It's tearing me apart, this helplessness.

At the edge of my sight, Wolf struggles to free himself, to help, but he's fumbling. Still fighting the remnants of sedation.

Rhett's head pops up, the fillet knife still protruding from his shoulder. I see it in his eyes as his hand closes around the gun, the cold resolve of a man willing to do anything to win.

Frankie grabs it at the same time, and a shot rings out, deafening in the enclosed space of the cabin.

The sound echoes off the walls, bouncing around my skull and reverberating in my chest. Rhett and Frankie drop. I can't tell who fired the shot, can't see who has the gun, can't know who's been hit.

All I can do is sit here, helpless, as the world around me teeters on the brink of oblivion.

In the next breath, Oliver appears in my periphery.

The Ghost.

Thank fucking God. Finally.

He breezes toward Rhett and Frankie, a rifle in hand. He looks like he just stepped out of a war zone, his face streaked with dirt and his clothes torn from the descent. He wears a utility vest loaded with ammo and a parachute harness still half-attached to his back.

It was the only way we could bring him.

He sneaked onto the plane like a ghost, parachuted out of it as we approached the hills, and hiked as fast as he could into this hell.

Rhett rises to his feet, still fumbling with the gun, and I realize the fired shot came from Oliver.

Without a moment's hesitation, Oliver raises the rifle and fires again.

The sound of the shot cracks through the air, and the pistol flies out of Rhett's hand. He lets out a howl of pain, clutching his wrist as blood pours from his palm. His eyes widen as he stares at the gaping hole where his weapon once was.

Then his complexion pales with panic.

Tucking his bleeding hand under his arm, he turns to flee. His footsteps are frantic and staggering as he makes a desperate dash for the door.

Oliver is faster. He moves like a predator, his rifle trained on Rhett's back, finger hovering over the trigger, ready to end this once and for all.

But before he fires, Frankie jumps to her feet, her scream tearing through the cabin. "Don't shoot!"

Oliver freezes, his rifle still aimed at Rhett's retreating form.

Confusion contorts his face as he glances back at her, his brow furrowed. "He's getting away!"

Her lips curl into a crazed smile, and she laughs. It's a sound I've never heard from her. A sound more feral than human.

"There's no escaping Hoss." Her expression empties, and an eerie calmness settles over her. "Let him *run.*"

Oliver hesitates, clearly torn between his instincts and Frankie's cryptic command.

"The bombs," she says quickly.

"I will disarm them."

"Do *not* squeeze that trigger." Something in her eyes, something dark and knowing, makes him lower his rifle.

The front door slams shut as Rhett disappears into the night.

Frankie turns to look at us, her gaze sharp and intent. The air feels charged, electric, with the flames of something inevitable, something primal.

"My men want to hunt." She bares her teeth.

The room thickens with an unspoken understanding.

The night is far from over.

The drug still has me paralyzed, but inside, the fire burns hotter than ever. Because I know, deep in my bones, that this hunt won't end until Rhett pays for everything he's done.

And when that time comes, there won't be any mercy.

monty

SIXTY-SIX

A faint twitch buzzes in my finger, like a spark igniting in the dark.

The subtle tremor spreads quickly, and my body begins to awaken, each muscle shaking off the paralysis with a stabbing warmth.

Relief consumes my senses, but so does the fury that still simmers in my chest, ready to explode the moment I'm free.

"Oliver." Frankie tightens the sash on her robe, her green eyes ablaze with life. "I don't know how or why you're here—"

"I'm The Ghost."

"Oh." She makes a face like her head hurts. "I'm going to need to process that later. For now, will you go outside and watch for Rhett, keep him away from those planes, and maybe grab their clothes?" She motions at us.

"Of course." He inclines his head and turns away.

"Oliver?" She waits for him to glance back and says, "Thank you. For everything."

Another dip of his head, and he strides out of the cabin.

On the island, when he threw the fillet knife at me, his aim was deliberate, meant to grab my attention without harming me. With that single display of lethal precision, he proved he was The Ghost and solidified my trust in him.

He had about five seconds to promise me he would take down Frankie's stalker before that photo arrived on our devices.

By the time I clicked the link, The Ghost was gone, melted into the background. Rhett never saw him through our camera phones.

I didn't see him again until we boarded Rhett's plane in Sitka and destroyed our phones. He emerged on the tarmac, floated out of fucking nowhere, and slipped onto our plane wearing a goddamn parachute, rifle, and ammo vest.

He hid in the cargo hold and didn't speak to us on the way here. None of us spoke. We didn't know if Rhett had eyes and ears in the cabin. If he did, he would've seen The Ghost jump from the plane a few miles away.

It was a risk that terrified me until we walked in and saw Frankie alive.

I flex my fingers, testing the strength returning to them. It's agonizingly slow, but every second brings me closer to movement, closer to action. I breathe through the sensation, gritting my teeth as pins and needles stab at my limbs.

Wolf is the first to break free.

Shaking off the effects of the sedative, he finally regains enough energy to slip out of the rope and toss aside the IV fluid bag.

I can't believe he had the strength to fling that knife. And with such accuracy.

As he rises to his full towering height, my heart thumps with disbelief and overwhelming emotion.

My son.

Alive.

He's really here, flesh and blood, and he's fucking perfect.

Circling the table, he approaches Frankie with slow, cautious steps.

Something flashes in her eyes as she watches him, something dark and tumultuous I don't fully understand until she starts moving toward him.

Her face contorts with anger, grief, a violence that stuns me, even though I know the depth of what she's been through.

She charges at Wolf, her glare murderous.

Is she going to hurt him?

"Tinker Bell…" He backpedals, hands up, trying to calm her. "Hold up."

She doesn't stop. She barrels toward him, fury and sorrow propelling her forward.

He stumbles around the row of corpses and bumps into my chair, his body close enough that I feel his heat. But it's Frankie who holds my attention.

She's a storm unleashed, crashing into him, her fists pounding against his chest.

"We grieved you for ten months!" Her voice breaks as she screams, "You left us! You tried to die!"

"Hey, hey." He wrestles her swinging arms. "I changed my mind halfway down. I swear!"

"Why, Wolf?" She smacks his chest, losing steam. "Why?"

"I didn't want to die a virgin."

Her anger shatters, crumbling into sobbing wails that tear through the cabin. She breaks apart in front of us, and all I can do is watch as she releases everything she's kept bottled up for so long.

Wolf shushes her softly, wrapping his arms around her and holding her tight with his cheek pressed to her head.

My chest tightens. My soul aches. As Frankie sobs into his bloodstained coat, he hugs her, comforts her, and it's agony to witness. But it's also something else, something I haven't felt since Denver took Frankie.

Relief.

It's over.

After tonight, after we hunt our prey and bring down our ruthless, bloody vengeance, we'll go home.

No more searching.

No more stalkers.

No more death.

No more division.

We'll be safe. Together. Our family. Whole for the first time.

Frankie lifts her head, her hands gripping Wolf's face, her touch tender despite the tears streaming down her cheeks.

"Oh, Wolf." Her whisper trembles.

Then she kisses his jaw, nose, eyelids, and corners of his mouth, each press of her lips a plea, a question. "Are you real? Are you really here?"

"I'm really here, my little red wary berry." His blue eyes shine as he kisses her brow. "I'm right here."

He holds her close, his fingers running through her hair, comforting her.

I feel each touch like a physical ache in my chest, my heart threatening to burst. It's surreal to take in, seeing my son alive, seeing the way he loves Frankie, seeing the way she clings to him.

I've lost so much. I lost Frankie twice. I thought I lost Wolf.

But I haven't lost it all. Love lives and breathes. I feel it radiate from Kody and Leo at my side. I feel it wrap around us, fusing us together.

Frankie and Wolf pull apart, their breath coming in ragged gasps as they slowly turn to face me.

The air is thick and heavy as my muscles gradually come back online, allowing me to lift my head, to finally meet my son's gaze.

He stares, really stares at me, for the first time. I stare back, unable to tear my eyes away from the boy.

No, not a boy.

A tall, handsome man stands before me. It's like looking into a mirror and seeing my twenty-year-old self gaze back.

The connection between us kindles, an invisible thread of fire pulling us together, binding us in ways I never thought possible.

"I'm Wolf." His voice is steady, strong, but there's a hint of uncertainty he tries to cover with a cough. "I've heard so much about you."

"I've heard a lot about you, too." My throat tightens, and I fight to keep it together, to maintain my composure.

Oliver slips in with our clothes, passing them to Frankie before vanishing again.

She hurries toward us, dropping garments on our laps and untying the ropes that no longer need to hold us upright.

My muscles feel stiff, the drug still lingering. But I have the strength to pull on my pants.

Leo and Kody regain control, too, their limbs obeying sluggishly as they start to dress.

As I slide on my shirt, Frankie leans in and presses a deep, passionate kiss to my lips. It's a shock to my system, pulling me back to life.

I grip her beautiful, tear-stained face and kiss her back, pouring every ounce of my love, my relief, into that kiss.

She eases away and moves to Leo and Kody, repeating the same gesture, kissing them with the same fierce love.

My gaze locks with Wolf, and we meld into a silent exchange, our eyes saying what our mouths can't yet.

Father.

Son.

I'm sorry.

I love you.

Where do we start?

"I know everything about you." He lowers his head, his eyes boring into mine. "Rhett visited me. Kept me updated on Frankie, Leo, and Kody's escape from this place, on their transition into their new world." His lips twitch, almost a smile. "I know all the struggles you've faced. And I know the four of you are in a relationship."

There's no judgment in his voice, just an acknowledgment of the truth as if he's come to terms with the reality of it all.

"Congratulations." He shifts his weight.

I don't know what to say, unsure how to respond to this dreamlike moment.

I'm having a conversation with my son.

It's unreal.

Frankie watches us and starts to say something, an apology forming on her lips.

"No. Don't." Wolf stares at her. "I've had ten months to think. You were right. You're my sister. Without the dirty benefits." A grin spreads across his face. "And you're banging my dad."

A suffocating weight lifts off the room, the tension breaking apart with that simple, self-deprecating humor.

"I have a lot of healing to do." He lifts a shoulder. "A lot of soul searching. I need to master self-love like I mastered self-pleasure before dragging someone else into all this…" He motions at himself. "Sexy chaos."

His words hit me deep, the honesty of them, the maturity I never expected but should have.

He was held captive for ten months in an outbuilding, listening to stories about those he loved continuing on with their lives, pursuing happiness, and finding love without him.

The devastation he must've felt, the hopelessness. I can't fathom it.

I can't rewind the clock and take that pain from him, but I will be at his side, every day, for as long as he lets me.

Finished with my clothes, I push myself up from the chair, my legs shaky, clumsy, but I manage to stand.

Frankie steps back, giving me space as I take a few tentative steps around the table, my heart racing.

Wolf regards me for a moment. Then he starts moving, meeting me halfway.

When I reach him, we fall into each other's arms. The instant I feel his strong body against mine, I know I'm never letting go.

It's not just an embrace. It's everything we've lost, everything we've found, wrapped up in a hug. I hold him tight, my hands fisting in the back of his shirt. I feel him shaking, feel the emotion rolling off him.

Frankie's sobs shudder through the room, but I can't focus on anything other than my son, this miracle in my arms.

No words are needed. We just hold each other, father and son, united after so much pain, so much time lost.

My eyes burn with tears, hot and unstoppable.

When we finally pull back, I drag a knuckle across my wet

cheeks.

I can't believe this is real. I can't believe he's here.

Before I can process it, Leo and Kody crash into us, their arms wrapping around Wolf, lifting him off his feet in a tangle of limbs and laughter and grunts of deep emotion. It's pure chaos, pure joy, and I can't stop the tears from falling as I watch them—my son, my brothers, my family—together again.

My gaze finds Frankie, and I crook my finger.

She rushes forward, her hands framing my face as she pulls me down for another kiss, this one slow and sweet, filled with all the love I've been holding onto for her.

"I love you," she whispers against my lips. "I love you so much, Monty."

"Love you more." I deepen the kiss, fisting my hands in her hair, gripping hard. "I'm sorry. I didn't protect you. I didn't—"

"I'm okay. We're all okay. We survived." She glances at the corpses sitting at the table and grimaces. "We have some fucked-up trauma to unfuck. Lots of therapy. *All* the therapy. But we'll sort it out. We're going to have the happiest life together."

She leans back, her eyes glimmering with tears and glowing with a smile.

A hand smacks the back of my head, snapping my attention to Kody.

His lips curl back, flashing a chilling smile as he holds my gaze. "It's time to hunt."

Kodiak

SIXTY-SEVEN

In the armory, surrounded by tools of destruction, I feel the predator in me rising, taking over.

Tonight, we're not hunting to survive.

We're hunting to avenge.

Consuming rancor has eaten away my last shred of humanity. This thing inside me was born when Denver tore away my innocence. It grew with every lash he welted across my back.

It sucks on my bones, feeds on every thudding beat of my heart, and sets fire to the breath rasping through my lungs.

It's primal, animalistic, and it wants blood.

Tonight, I'm going to let it out.

Tonight, I'm going to unleash hell.

I pull weapons from the walls, my hands moving with deadly purpose. My favorite crossbow remains in Sitka, but there are a few spares here. I grab a quiver loaded with bolts designed to puncture through bone and sinew. Knives, sharp and wicked, each a promise of the pain I'll inflict. Ammo, gear, everything we need to turn this hunt into a slaughter.

Leo, Wolf, Monty, and Frankie are doing the same, their

faces stony, determined, darkened with the same violent hunger that drives me.

Suddenly, Oliver appears in the room without sound, making Frankie jump.

"Fuck!" She spins, staring wide-eyed. "How did you do that?"

He gives her a tight smile. "I disarmed the bombs on the planes."

"Okay, but question..." She holds up her hand. "On the island, I saw shit. Shadows. Silhouettes in the windows. We all saw things. Was that you?"

His smile stretches, twisting his features into a chilling mask.

Then his expression clears, and he turns away.

"Oliver." Monty slings a rifle over his shoulder, his eyes hard. "Will you stay here and guard Frankie?"

"I'll guard her with my life."

"Thank you."

"Let's get this party started." Wolf leans against the doorframe, flipping a knife in his hand. No guns. No ammo. Just a belt of sharp blades buckled around his waist. "He'll wear himself out before we catch him."

Frankie grabs a bear trap and places it in my hands.

"Butcher that monster until there's nothing left of him to bring back. I don't want to see any part of him again." Calm, controlled, and stunningly fierce, she's a force of nature.

But right now, she's holding it back, letting us take the lead, letting us be the animals we're meant to be.

"I love you." I kiss her lips, but my mind is elsewhere, already in the tundra, hunting Rhett down, imagining all the ways I'll carve him up.

She kisses the others and sends us off.

We step outside, the cold air biting into my cheeks. There were enough fur coats left behind to go around. It's good to see Wolf in pelts rather than that bloodstained thing he's had for ten months.

It's good to see Wolf. Period.

If Rhett hadn't pulled him from the river, we would've

found him. We would've had him with us this entire time.

Just one more reason to make Rhett pay.

I'm not angry. I'm beyond that. I'm something else entirely, something feral and savage that I've kept buried deep down for far too long.

The man I was before is gone, burned away by the fires of revenge. What's left is hellish, an unholy fiend that wants to rip and tear and kill.

We hike across the snow-covered terrain in silence, slipping into the frigid night like ghosts.

Born and bred in this frozen hell, we know these hills, this tundra, better than anyone. Every crevice, slope, and jagged boulder is part of us.

Rhett thinks he's running for his life, but he's just running deeper into our territory.

Leo, Wolf, and I keep a close eye on Monty. He could easily get lost out here, but he's tough. And he's *ours*. We won't let anything happen to him.

I breathe in deeply, and the scent of Rhett's blood hits me like a punch to the face, strong and metallic, hanging in the crisp air.

My pulse quickens. My muscles tighten, and my senses sharpen. He's bleeding out there, leaving a trail like a wounded animal, and I snarl with anticipation.

"Got him?" Wolf looks at me, his eyes dark with the same need to kill.

"That way." I lead them a mile into the hills before holding up a hand, stopping them. "Let's set the trap here."

Leo helps me place the bear trap in a clearing and carefully covers it with snow.

"We need to corral him near the river." His eyes glint in the starlight. "We'll play with him for a while. Then flush him into the trap."

"Which way?" Monty flexes his gloved hands.

My ears perk at the sound of stumbling footsteps in the distance, each one heavy and desperate.

"North." I prowl in that direction.

Rhett doesn't know the dangers that lie in wait, the trap we set, the wolves lurking just out of sight. He doesn't know he's being hunted by something far worse than any creature he could imagine.

Dark, violent energy pulses through my veins. The beast is free, and it wants blood. It wants to taste Rhett's fear, to tear him apart piece by piece, to make him scream for mercy and deny him over and over.

"He raped her," Wolf says, a gleaming blade dancing between his fingers. "I don't know how I pulled myself from unconsciousness, but I felt her there, her hand on my lap. I felt her pain, her horror, as he raped her on the table. Somehow, during the assault, she managed to dislodge my IV line. By the time you arrived, I had enough strength to remove hers, too."

A snarl rips through my chest, my hands tightening around the crossbow until my knuckles go white. Nothing compares to the searing fire that burns inside me. I'm wrath incarnate.

Beside me, Monty turns to ice. Cold. Expressionless. And just as lethal.

Leo seethes, too far gone for words, too consumed by the need for violence, for blood.

We catch up with Rhett quickly and make our presence known, stomping our boots and sending him scrambling toward the river.

It's instinctual, the way we move and work together. A pack of wolves closing in on our prey.

We spread out around the cliffs, melting into the shadows, not far from the fire pit.

I crouch low, my senses on high alert, listening to the sounds of the night, to the approaching thud of Rhett's staggering footsteps.

He's panicking, his breaths bursting fast and loud, his heart beating out of his chest. I hear and feel it all, and it only makes me hungrier.

Minutes later, he lurches into view, spinning in place, frantically scanning the massive boulders surrounding him.

He knows we're here, senses the danger, and it's too late to run.

We toy with him, flinging knives from the shadows, each hitting its mark with deadly accuracy. I aim for his limbs, for his flesh, not to kill him, but to hurt him. To make him scream. To make him suffer.

Each time a knife sinks into his skin, I relish the pained hitch of his breath. His steps falter. His head whips around as if he can't believe what's happening.

But he knows. Deep down, he knows this is the end.

I raise my crossbow, sight him through the scope, and fire. The bolt punches through his leg with a sickening thud.

His scream rips through the night, echoing off the hills.

Music to my ears.

I let loose another arrow, and it flies true, burying itself in the same leg.

Two more should do it.

I aim them at the same spot, the meaty part of his thigh. Even with his teetering, spinning motions, I nail the target.

Four bolts protrude from his leg, his scream a high-pitched wail that doesn't end.

He wobbles, whirling, driven by sheer terror, as he takes off toward the trap.

We give him a running start, making him suffer, dragging out his death.

Then we stalk after him, flanking him from all sides, herding him like a panicked animal.

He doesn't stand a chance, and we all know it. But that's not enough. We want him to know it, too. We want him to feel every ounce of the terror he inflicted on Frankie, on Wolf, on all of us.

His footsteps grow more frantic, the scent of his blood ripe in the air. It drives me wild. I want to dismember him, to feel his guts hot and wet on my hands, to watch him fall apart under our attack.

A few feet ahead, the bear trap snaps shut with a crunch that sends a shiver of satisfaction up my spine.

He goes down, screaming, thrashing as the metal teeth dig into his flesh, sawing through tendons and splintering bone.

Leo and I close in, circling him like predators ready to pounce on a wounded deer.

"P-please. Please, don't do this. I…I can help you! I can give you anything you want! Money…health care…anything. Please, just let me live!" His teeth clatter, his eyes wide, bloodshot with fear.

His words turn into frantic, incoherent pleas until they're swallowed by the pain, by the inevitability of what's to come.

But we're not done. Not even close.

leonid

SIXTY-EIGHT

Blood.

It's everywhere, seeping into the snow, staining it a deep, dark red.

Rhett will bleed out eventually, but it's not enough.

I want more. More blood. More pain.

We will drag this out and make every second a living hell for him.

The fillet knife is still buried in his shoulder. A dozen more knives stick out of his limbs, including four of Kody's arrows.

We were careful to avoid vital organs and arteries.

I crouch beside him, my eyes locked on his. I glimpse the fear there, the plea for mercy.

Gross.

Rearing back my arm, I slam my fist into his eye socket.

He howls, blubbering and thrashing in the bear trap.

"I didn't like the look on your face." I shrug. "Couldn't help myself."

"I was...I was just trying to save you! To save all of you!" he cries.

"You can't even save yourself." Monty plucks the fillet knife from Rhett's shoulder, making him cry harder. "Want the honors?" He offers it to Wolf.

"Does a bear shit in the woods?" He accepts the blade and kneels in the snow beside Rhett. "I think death by three hundred cuts is the right choice here. All in favor?"

"Why three hundred?" I ask.

"That's how many days he kept me away from you."

"Three hundred it is." Monty unsheathes his knife.

Kody and I follow suit.

Together, we descend on Rhett, slowly, ruthlessly, our blades gleaming in the starlight as we count.

Seventy-five cuts for each of us.

We don't hesitate. We don't flinch. We sink our knives into Rhett's flesh with excruciating slowness, dragging our blades across his skin, savoring every moment, every drop of blood that spills from the wounds.

We cut in tandem, extending his suffering, each slice going deeper and twisting harder than the last.

I make my incisions with a hacksaw motion, splitting skin and severing tendons.

Monty sticks him with plunging stabs, slow and methodical, pushing hard on his handle until he hits bone.

Kody focuses on the genitals. After cutting away the clothing, he castrates Rhett in pieces, taking his time, shortening Rhett's flaccid penis one slice at a time. Then he works on the balls, piercing them like pin cushions.

Wolf is just as diabolical. He wields the fillet knife as designed, cutting thin slices of fragile meat. He flays Rhett's flesh, peeling him with precision, layer by layer, and collects the pieces in a neat pile.

"You're not keeping that, Buffalo Bill." I meet his eyes.

"Tell that to Lorena Bobbitt over there." He points his knife at Kody.

Then he goes back to cutting and counting.

Rhett writhes in pain, his vocal cords blown as he stares at us, trying to reach out with his good hand, grasping at nothing.

Begging is futile.

There's no mercy to be found in the faces of those he

wronged.

There's no escape.

His screams ebb into whimpers, his body shaking with the effort to cling to life. But there's no life left in him. Just pain. Just terror. Just the cold, hard truth that he'll die here, in the place where he thought he could overpower us.

The relief that brings me borders on ecstasy.

As we near the three-hundredth cut, Rhett's breaths huff in wet, gurgling gasps, his chest heaving with the effort to stay alive. He won't live for long.

He's bleeding out, his body a mangled mess of wounds as he chokes on his blood, trying to speak.

No sound comes.

"The final cut." Monty meets Wolf's stare. "It's yours."

Wolf leans over Rhett, his hand gripping the handle of the fillet knife as he sinks it into Rhett's chest one last time, slowly, deliberately. The seconds tick by, and he continues to push that blade, millimeter by millimeter, while staring into Rhett's eyes.

Rhett jerks, a final spasm, before falling still. His eyes stare up at the stars, but there's nothing left in them.

We sit back and catch our breath.

There's no triumph. No joy. Just the knowledge that we did what we came here to do.

We leave his remains for the wolves, knowing they'll finish the job. Enough blood spilled in these hills tonight. It won't take them long to find us.

Backing far enough away, we wait.

Within the hour, the wolves fall upon the pieces of his body, their howls echoing through the hills.

A fitting end for a man who thought he could kill us.

I turn to my brothers, Wolf, Kody, and Monty, and see darkness in their eyes, the same primal violence that burns in me.

We crossed a line tonight, became something else, something more than human. But we did it together, and we'll carry this with us, this bond, this blood, for the rest of our lives.

We avenged Frankie.

It's early morning when we return to the cabin and find her waiting on the porch with Oliver.

She takes one look at our blood-soaked appearances and grimaces. "Showers for everyone."

We step into the cabin, bloodied, exhausted, and relieved.

The smell of death clings to the air, but it's fainter now, not as overwhelming as before.

I exchange a look with Kody. He notices it, too.

Drawn by the need to confirm my senses, I veer toward the kitchen, expecting to see the grotesque dinner party Rhett left behind. But the kitchen is empty. The bodies are gone.

Oliver appears before us, his eyes flat, kind of scary. "I moved the corpses into the walk-in freezer."

I blink, the answer almost too simple, too practical. He says it like it's nothing, just another task he had to check off his list.

Who am I to judge?

I just hacked up a heart surgeon without hesitation or regret.

Kody and Wolf head upstairs to shower in our old bathroom.

"Monty." Frankie brushes her fingers against his, drawing his attention. "Oliver wants to cash in his favor."

That was quick. The Ghost doesn't fuck around.

Monty stiffens, his brow furrowing as he turns to Oliver. "What do you want?"

"I want the cabin." Oliver doesn't smile, doesn't even blink. "This cabin."

"What for?" Monty's eyes widen with surprise.

Oliver gives him a blank look, the same inscrutable expression he's worn since we met him.

It's unsettling, the way he can make even the simplest requests feel like something darker, something that should be questioned.

Monty glances at me, then back at Oliver, and there's a sudden flash of worry in his eyes.

"Does that mean you're no longer my chef?" he asks, his voice lighter, but there's an edge to it. "No more Eggs Benedict?"

Silence.

Monty's unease grows as Oliver remains expressionless, giving no indication one way or another.

There's no negotiation here. Monty agreed to Oliver's terms when he hired him. Now Monty must pay it.

"Monty." Frankie's tone carries a quiet authority that we all instinctively respond to. "I intended to scorch this place to the ground when we leave. Oliver wants the cabin and the second plane, too. He'll stay behind and deal with the bodies."

"You can fly a plane?" Monty cocks a brow at Oliver.

"I can do many things."

He jumps out of planes, too. This dude has secrets.

"I have a bone to pick with you." Monty steps into Oliver's space.

"Interesting word choice," I mumble.

"When you learned my real name was Montgomery Strakh, you were a fucking dick. Leo was convinced you spit in my food."

"True." I nod.

"How do you know I don't spit in your food?" Oliver grins.

"Oliver..." Monty pinches the bridge of his nose. "You were pissed at me for not telling you my real name. Yet all this time, you kept *your* identity from me."

"Oliver is my real identity. The Ghost is an alias."

"Same difference."

"Not the same at all."

"Can you both forgive and forget?" Frankie anchors her hands on her hips. "It's time to move on."

Monty and Oliver incline their heads.

"The cabin is yours," I say to Oliver. "My brothers and I want nothing to do with it."

"We'll leave you the extra plane under two conditions." Monty steps back, returning to Frankie's side. "Contact me every time you're in town, so I know you're not trapped here. And you will not use this place to imprison, harm, or kill innocents. Agreed?"

"Agreed."

"Time for those showers." Frankie takes my hand.

Monty motions her forward, and she leads him and me down the hallway.

It feels like she's pulling me into a dark memory. The walls shiver, and the floors hum with whispers of everything that's happened here.

The door at the end of the hallway looms ahead. Denver's bedroom. We escaped this place. Fled for our lives. It doesn't feel right to enter this domain again.

She pushes the door open, the creak of the hinges shuddering through me.

"This is his room?" Monty peers inside.

"Was." She enters and flicks on the lights.

Lights that haven't had power since before Denver died.

I hesitate, my eyes locked on the nest of bedding still piled near the hearth.

"Looks like Rhett only remodeled the main rooms." She moves farther into the bedroom, her hand trailing along the mantle as she looks around, her expression unreadable.

Finally, she turns back to us, her eyes meeting Monty's with a look filled with something I can't quite name.

"Denver raped me in this room." She points at the bedding on the floor. "I slept there with Leo and Kody during the darkest months of my life. We made good memories and bad ones."

The tension in Monty's posture matches mine. I have my own memories of what was done here. I know exactly what this room represents.

"This is where it stops." She looks at both of us, her voice steady, resolute. "The pain, the abuse, the nightmares, it all stops here. We're going to step into that shower and wash it off. Then we're going to go home. We're going to take our Wolf home and never look back."

Without a word, Monty scoops her into his arms, his expression hard but his touch infinitely gentle as he cradles her against his chest.

The raw, unspoken need in the way he holds her is stunning. She's the most precious thing in the world, and he knows it.

He carries her into the bathroom and lowers her feet to the floor.

The sound of water rushing through the pipes tells me Kody and Wolf are still using the upstairs shower.

I turn on the faucet, setting the temperature on a warm, comforting stream. The kind of warmth that washes away the cold and the dark.

But inside, I'm still burning, coiled tight with a fury I can't shake. The bloodlust is still snarling and clawing, making it impossible to be anything other than rough.

Monty's hands move with care as he unties her robe, peeling the fabric away from her skin.

I step in to help, my fingers brushing against his as we work together to remove the last barrier between her and the water.

The robe falls to the floor, and I swallow hard, my chest tight as I take in the sight of her. She was bruised. Drugged. Raped. But she's still here, fighting.

Monty and I move in sync, shedding our clothes quickly, our eyes never leaving her.

My fingers are clumsy as I pull off my shirt, the fabric sticking to the dried blood smeared across my skin. I still feel the heat of the hunt, the violence we unleashed. It's hard to let it go and soften the edges when every part of me remains out there in the hills, killing with a vengeance.

The water hits my skin, washing away the blood, the dirt, the sweat, but it doesn't wash away the knowledge of what was done to her. I scrub at my skin, the movements harsh and punishing, as if I can force the darkness away and scrape off the layers of brutality.

Monty guides her under the spray, his touch so different from mine. Soothing, gentle, careful. He has that ability to be soft when the world is hard, to be calm when everything else is chaos. And right now, she needs that. She needs him.

Together, we wash the remnants of the assault from her body, rinsing away the violence that was forced upon her. I follow his lead, my touch firm but careful, doing what I can to help, even though I want to send my fists through the wall.

The water turns pink as it swirls down the drain, taking with it the stains of the night, but it doesn't take away the memories. It doesn't erase what was done to her, what she had to endure. But we do what we can. We clean her. We hold her. We let her know she's not alone.

When we're done, I grab a towel, wrapping it around my waist. Then I meet Monty's eyes.

He knows me well and understands the war inside me. He also knows that Frankie needs more than just a shower.

She needs affection, reassurance, a loving touch. I can't give her what she needs without fucking her into the wall.

Monty and I exchange a wordless understanding.

She sees it and nods. "You're on the right track, but I'll spell it out so we're all clear. I need you to erase his touch. Remove it. Replace it with yours." Her voice breaks, choked with emotion. "I need you inside me. Right now."

I lean against the vanity as he turns and wraps her in his arms, pulling her close, his lips finding hers in a kiss that's soft, tender, and flowing with love.

She melts, clinging to him as his hands move over her skin. With each touch, the tension in her body eases.

His lips trail over her cheeks, neck, and shoulders as if he can kiss away the bruises, the hurt, the memories.

He lifts her against the wall, his dick hard and ready. Then he makes love to her, gently, slowly, reminding her that she's loved, that she's safe, and that she's everything to us.

They're beautiful together, their bodies rocking beneath the cascade of water. The faint sounds of their breaths, the soft murmur of Monty's voice as he whispers to her, it's intimate, private, but not exclusive.

As they start to come, their eyes turn to me, inviting and wanting. I lean in and capture her mouth, kissing her as they climax together.

We find clean clothes we left behind in Denver's old room. By the time we emerge, I can breathe again, my heart slowing, my mind starting to clear.

I'm ready to go home and put the hills behind us.

leonid

An hour later, we board the bush plane.

The engines hum with a steady vibration as I check the instruments one last time.

The sky is calm and dark with the onset of polar night. No snow. No wind. Monty assures me it's safe for flying.

He sits beside me in the co-pilot's seat, his hands steady as they move over the controls.

Behind us, the cabin is quiet, save for the soft sound of breathing and the occasional creak of the plane's frame.

I glance back, checking on Frankie.

She grips the armrests tightly, but she's managing. Her chest rises and falls in measured breaths as she uses her techniques to keep the panic at bay.

Kody checks her seat belt for the hundredth time, his fingers moving over the buckle with teasing flicks.

"Dude." Wolf sighs. "The belt is latched."

"He's trying to get into my pants." Frankie smirks despite the tension in her shoulders.

"He needs to work on his technique."

Kody buckles himself in, his eyes never leaving her.

She's strong, and she's holding on. We all are.

Wolf returns his gaze to the window, his gaze distant, lost in thoughts I can't imagine.

I know Rhett transported him in planes, but Wolf was never conscious for it.

This is different.

He's here. He's awake, and it's all hitting him at once. The freedom, the reunion with his family, the introduction to his father, and the fact that he's truly escaping.

I remember that feeling.

I turn back to the controls.

This is it. We're finally leaving this place behind.

The engines roar to life, and the plane vibrates beneath us, eager to take off, to soar.

"Hey, Wolf." I twist in the seat and find his blue eyes staring back. "Have you heard the fairy tale about the lion, the bear, and the drag queen?"

"Uh...Maybe?" His lips twist.

"Well, it turns out that lions can fly. Bears make mighty fine vodka, and the Magic Kingdom will no longer be without its queen."

Wolf huffs out a laugh, and I turn back to the controls.

The plane lurches. The wheels bump over the terrain. Then we're off, lifting into the air, leaving the ground behind, leaving Hoss behind.

The sky opens up before us, vast and endless.

We're moving forward, together, as a family.

Four months later.

"Can't stop looking at you." Leo shifts us deeper into the velvet couch and tucks me tightly against his side. "You're fucking stunning, love."

I adore the way he looks at me.

It goes beyond mere attraction. He sees the anxiety, the scars, the bouts of madness and darkness, and instead of turning away, he embraces me with a stare so loving and deep it makes me feel cherished.

And claimed.

I belong to three men.

My gaze drifts across the lounge to Monty and Kody behind the bar, where they put on a show for the packed crowd in the distillery.

Kody's venue has become *the* destination spot in Alaska. Patrons book months in advance just to get in the door.

The owner's sexy, irresistible allure has a lot to do with that. The energy in the room thrums with excitement and desire.

Kody, with his dark, untamed aura, and Monty, the embodiment of billionaire porn, are the main event.

Bottles fly through the air, glasses slide across the bar, and the crowd cheers.

They compete with each other, tossing drinks back and forth, trying to outdo the other. It isn't just fun brotherly rivalry. It's proof that laughter can follow tragedy.

Life twisted them into violent, scarred warriors, but what they did in the hills doesn't define them. It made them stronger, closer.

The connection between the four Strakh men fills my soul.

Kody grunts as Monty flings a bottle toward him, catching it easily and spinning it behind his back before pouring the contents into a glass.

A smile tugs at the corner of Monty's lips as he slams a drink down in front of a customer with a flourish.

The crowd roars.

Leo shifts, feathering his fingers along my thighs beneath the hem of my dress, sending an electric thrill through me. The table hides our laps, providing some privacy in the packed room. But anyone looking can see the heat in his bedroom eyes.

"Monty's in rare form tonight." He brushes his warm lips along my neck, his hand slipping higher, fingers teasing the crease between my thighs.

"He's trying to impress you guys."

Monty's love for Leo, Kody, and Wolf is unflinching. It's a love that controls and smothers. A love born from fear.

Fear of losing us.

"He doesn't need to try so hard." Leo makes a hungry, rumbling sound as he nuzzles the spot beneath my ear. "We're not going anywhere."

Wolf's laughter rings out from across the room, drawing my attention to where he sits at the bar, surrounded by women who are all but draped over him.

A black, distressed leather jacket hugs his broad shoulders, the fabric abused and brought back to life like the man himself. Silver chains and metal accents adorn the leather, and the high collar is turned up, framing his face in shadows.

Underneath, a black lace shirt molds to his lean, muscled frame. Black jeans, ripped at the knees and thighs, reveal glimpses of skin and tuck into a pair of heavy combat boots.

As he leans against the bar with smoky makeup smudging his eyes, he looks like a fallen angel who's taken a wrong turn and ended up in a world of leather and shadows. Mysterious. Untouchable. Irresistibly beautiful.

And the women eat that up.

Like his father, he's the picture of confidence, his black hair falling in shaggy waves around his face, his ice-blue eyes glittering with mischief as he flirts shamelessly. He's come so far in such a short time, adapting to society with a speed that amazes me.

But beneath that cocky smirk is a deeply damaged man, haunted by demons he refuses to talk about. He goes to Dr. Thurber twice a week. We all do. Wolf says he opens up during his sessions. He just doesn't open up to us.

We don't need to know all the details of his captivity with Rhett, but some insight would help us through his panic attacks. He has PTSD, and the episodes are frequent. I have them, too, but not like his. He completely shuts down like he did when Denver stabbed Kody's hand the night I dumped bones on the kitchen table.

That memory torments me every time Wolf has a breakdown.

The good news is he's playing his saxophone again. Hearing his soulful melody drifting across the island comforts me on a visceral level.

I caress Leo's hard denim-clad thigh, noting the tension there.

He's still uneasy in large crowds. They all are. Doesn't stop us from taking full advantage of our freedom. Now that we're safe, we go out several times a week. Dinner and dancing. Motorcycle rides through the mountains. Yachting at sunset. Concerts and sightseeing in Anchorage.

Once Wolf is better adjusted and Kody and Leo's business ventures are more established, we'll start traveling outside

Alaska. Monty and I are dying to show them the world.

No amount of light can banish our past, but we're creating the brightest version of our future.

Leo's eyes trace the curve of my face, lingering on my lips as if memorizing every detail. Desire smolders from him, slowing down time and narrowing the room to just us.

"You're thinking too much." His tongue flicks my earlobe as he inches his hand closer to the heat between my thighs. "Christ, I love your body. These sexy fucking legs. And your ass. Fuck, you have a tight, perfect ass."

I shiver, and my nipples harden against the thin material of my dress.

"But the rest of you is so damn soft." His fingers reach the juncture between my legs, and he goes still. "Where are your panties?"

"Check Kody's pocket." I bite my lip.

"He fucked you before I got here? How? I was only five minutes behind you guys."

"He was hungry."

"He's always hungry. At least his apartment is getting some use."

It only gets used for sex. No one has slept here since our eighteen-day separation.

No matter how late Kody works, he always comes home to us.

"Now I'm picturing him fucking you." He groans and buries his face in my neck. "My goddamn cock is leaking in my pants."

With his body angled toward mine, he glides a finger along my wet slit, unconcerned about onlookers. No one can see his hand under the table, but it doesn't take a genius to know what he's doing.

He shoves two fingers inside me, and I gulp, eyes wide and cheeks on fire.

Across the room, Kody's dark eyes flash as he slides a drink toward Monty, who catches it with a grin, taking a long sip before giving Kody a nod of approval.

The crowd cheers, and I let out a moan. Leo mercilessly finger-fucks me.

"I'm about to put you on my lap." He licks my gaping lips. "Make you ride my dick in front of all these people."

"Recognize that bald man at the end of the bar?" I pant.

"That's the sheriff. He and I go way back. He won't arrest me for fucking my woman."

"He'll arrest you for public indecency."

"We're nowhere near indecent yet."

Before I can respond, Monty appears at our table, a drink in each hand. He sets them down in front of Leo and me, his attention narrowing on the movement beneath my dress.

A fresh surge of wetness seeps around the fingers inside me.

"Enjoying yourselves?" Monty has a predatory look in his eyes, a hunter staring down his prey.

"Couldn't ask for better entertainment." Leo grins, nodding at the bar. "The cocktail show isn't bad, either."

Monty's lips twitch, and he glances over at Kody, who's still behind the bar, expertly mixing drinks.

"He's a natural," Monty admits, pride evident in his tone.

Leo removes his fingers from me and stares at Monty. Then he proceeds to lick my arousal from his digits, grinning, taunting.

In a blur, Monty reaches out to snatch Leo's arm.

Leo dodges him, laughing. "Get your own." Then he returns those wet fingers under my dress.

Monty lowers into the space on my other side and leans in, grazing his lips along my neck.

There's a pause, a moment of eye contact. Then he says, "Open your legs."

Oh shit.

My chest flutters, and my pussy clenches as I part my thighs, stretching the skirt of my dress.

Monty's lips find mine in a slow, lingering kiss. And his fingers. Those long, skillful fingers join Leo's, and together, they rub and stroke and sink inside my soaked pussy.

The noise of the crowd, the weight of the past, all of it disappears in the heat of their hands and the taste of their lips as they take turns kissing me.

The orgasm comes swiftly and quietly. With their combined fingers inside me and their thumbs against my clit, they shatter me. I twitch and trap a deep, euphoric moan behind my pinched lips. Lips that Leo tries to pry open with his hot, demanding tongue.

I gasp, and he dives in, his dark laugh vibrating down my throat.

When he pulls back, I catch Monty sucking his fingers clean.

Animals. The whole lot of them.

There's a fire in his eyes, a promise of more to come. I know that tonight when we're alone, I'll be stuffed with so much cock I won't know which way is up.

Keeping up with the demanding libidos of three virile men is exhausting. And so fucking satisfying.

I'm in a perpetual state of orgasmic bliss.

Leo grabs his glass and raises it to Monty as if their fingers weren't just buried inside me. "Here's to surviving another day."

Monty's gaze softens as he clinks his glass against Leo's. "To surviving together."

My heart swells.

We're battered and scarred, but we're here. Happy and safe. No security guards. No pending investigations. We're no longer surviving.

We're living.

Dr. Rhett Howell is considered missing as the authorities continue to search for his body. They believe his plane crashed in the Interior, a trail that Oliver and Monty set into place. People go missing in Alaska all the time. Sometimes, they're never found.

Rhett, Doyle, Sirena, Alvis, Thea, Denver...they're all gone, never to be seen again.

I returned to my job at the hospital. Kody, Leo, and Monty have their businesses.

And Wolf...

My gaze shifts back to him at the bar.

Surrounded by a crowd of women, all hanging on his every word, he thrives on the attention, handling it with charm and aloofness that captivates.

A tall, statuesque blonde leans in close, her hand brushing his arm as she laughs at something he says. He gives her a crooked smile and leans back just enough to create a tantalizing distance between them.

It's a game to him, this flirtation, and he's playing it expertly, drawing them in without committing to any of their advances.

Then something shifts. His smile falters for a second, and his gaze drifts past the women, searching for something. Or someone.

When his eyes land on me, our connection fuses with sharp intensity. His playful smirk fades, replaced by something more intense, more raw. For a fleeting moment, I see the vulnerability beneath, the part of him that struggles.

Our stares intertwine, exchanging silent words. A quiet reminder. A need for reassurance. He's not alone. We see him. We love him.

I offer him a small, encouraging smile, telling him I'm here. We're all here. He doesn't have to face any of this alone.

His shoulders relax, and he gives me a subtle chin dip.

I blow him a kiss. He raises a hand, catches it, and puts it in his pocket.

Then, just as quickly as it came, the intensity in his gaze dissipates, and the playful smirk returns.

He says something to the blonde, making her giggle as he sips his drink, the flirtatious mask firmly back in place.

I turn back to Leo and Monty, my hand resting on Leo's leg. "Wolf has come a long way, but he's still struggling, even if he doesn't show it."

"He's always been good at putting on a show," Leo says quietly. "It's his red flag."

"We need to remind him he doesn't have to pretend." Monty traces small circles on my bare thigh. "Have you talked to him about his apprenticeship?"

"Yeah, we talked. He's really into it." Leo loosens a slow breath. "It's a good way for him to express his art and the owner of the tattoo shop...What's his name?"

"Declan," Monty says.

"Declan won't shut up about how crazy talented Wolf is. But..." Leo glances at me.

"You're worried." I squeeze his thigh. "Wolf's still dealing with so much. The nightmares, the blackouts...It's a lot."

We all visit him regularly at the shop. He's good when focused, but sometimes he checks out. Sometimes he stares at nothing like he's not even there.

"We'll get him through this." Monty's jaw tightens, his blue eyes narrowing with that protective intensity that never leaves him. "He'll never be alone again."

As we sit there, watching Wolf return to his playful banter with the women around him, I know his path ahead won't be easy. But we're a family, bound together by love, pain, and the ruthless ferocity to fight for a blinding bright future.

"Hey, Wolf." Kody leans across the bar, ruffling Wolf's hair.

Wolf swats him away, but there's a smile on his face, a genuine smile that shines through the dark Goth makeup.

Kody says something to him, and Wolf stands. They stride off through the crowd.

Stopping in the center of the lounge, Kody shoves two fingers in his mouth and releases a sharp whistle that cuts through the clamor of the distillery.

The commanding sound instantly silences the room. Every head turns toward him, followed by the faint clinking of glasses as people lower their drinks, eyes wide with curiosity.

A devilish grin appears on Wolf's face as he motions for Leo to join them. The crowd parts, and Leo rises, suspicion hardening his eyes as he makes his way toward Kody and Wolf.

Monty and I climb off the couch and follow him through the throng of people.

My pulse kicks up as curious gazes track our approach, and whispers of speculation ripple through the crowd.

When we reach Kody and Wolf, Kody throws an arm around Leo's shoulders, pulling him close with a proud smile.

"Ladies and gentlemen." Kody's voice rings out, deep and confident. "This is my brother, Leonid Strakh."

His brother. Not his nephew.

They were brothers first, and that's what they'll always be.

"I'm thrilled to announce that Leo just started his own float plane business, and it officially opens tomorrow. If you ever need a flight to anywhere, anytime, Leonid Strakh is your man."

The room erupts in cheers and applause.

Happiness shines in Leo's mismatched eyes as he looks at Monty, who gives him a nod, then at me, his gaze softening.

I rub a hand against my chest, leaning into Monty's side.

Kody raises his hand to quiet the crowd, and the noise dies down.

"I have one more announcement." Kody's hand sweeps out to point in my direction. "Please turn your attention to the stunning redhead."

What the hell?

My heart stutters, and my breath squeezes as hundreds of eyes zero in on me.

Heat rises in my cheeks, and I clasp my hands together, trying to steady myself. What is happening?

Just as the anxiety threatens to overwhelm me, Wolf steps up, his fingers slipping around mine, and the connection pulls me back from the brink.

He bends his knees to put us at eye level. "Don't you dare cry." He kisses my cheek. "If you start, I'll have to join in and ruin my fucking makeup."

"The horror." I laugh, a choked, nervous sound that breaks the tension in my chest.

He gives me a playful wink and shifts to my side as Leo, Monty, and Kody lower to one knee before me.

Three powerful, beautiful men kneel in front of me, and my heart feels like it might burst from my chest.

"Woman." Kody's black eyes melt with a softness usually hidden behind his brooding exterior. "Will you love us forever?"

I nod, unable to speak as the tears start to spill over, my vision blurring.

"Love." Leo smirks, his mismatched eyes glimmering. "Will you sleep with us forever?"

"Fuck yes." I laugh through my tears, ignoring the collective gasp that ripples through the crowd around us.

I don't care what they think. All I care about is the love pouring from my entire world.

Monty reaches into his pocket, pulling out a small velvet box. His eyes lock onto mine, and I'm transported to the night he proposed to me on his yacht.

We were different people then.

Everything is different.

He flips the box open, revealing a ring that makes my heart skip. It's my original diamond ring, the one he gave me that night. But it's been altered.

The solitaire diamond remains, but now it's flanked by two new rocks, one on either side.

Three diamonds.

Three husbands.

Three soul mates.

"Frankie," Monty says, his voice hoarse with emotion. "Will you take our last name and be Mrs. Strakh until death do us part?"

"Yes. One hundred percent, yes." A sob escapes me as he slides the ring onto my finger.

The weight of it feels perfect, like it's always belonged there. Three diamonds glitter brightly on my hand, and I know this is where I'm meant to be. With them. Forever.

The room erupts in applause and cheers, but all I can hear is the beating of my heart as my men reach into their pockets and remove three matching bands.

They slide the rings onto their fingers and gaze at me, smiling.

Goddammit, I'm crying again.

Monty rises, pulling me into his arms, his lips capturing mine in a kiss that seals the promise we just made. Leo and Kody are next, each kissing me with a tenderness that makes my chest ache even more.

When I finally pull back, Wolf is standing there with a crooked smile. A single tear carves a path through the dark makeup around his eyes.

"Look what you've done." He points at his face and wipes the wetness from my cheek with the pad of his thumb. "You're not getting rid of us now, sweet cherry fairy."

"Wouldn't dream of it," I whisper back.

"Looks like they're ready to get laid." He nods behind me.

I turn, finding three gorgeous men, my husbands, waiting expectantly with coats in their hands.

"I gotta know." He lowers his mouth to my ear. "When they're sword-fighting, how much dick kissing is involved?"

"Wolf."

"Three dicks. I can't even fathom the man mess you have to clean up."

"Stop." I press my hand over his mouth, laughing. "Are you coming with us?"

His eyes pop wide, and I instantly regret my word choice.

He shakes his head, dislodging my hand. "I don't want any part of that."

"I meant, are you coming home with us?"

"No. Leo left me the keys to his yacht. I have ideas burning in my head. I'm going to walk over to the shop and work on some sketches." He kisses my brow. "Don't wait up."

Given the three hooded stares in my direction, I'll be up all night.

"Make those dick kissers beg for it." Wolf takes my face in his hands and brings our foreheads together. "I love you."

"And I love you." I step back and glance at the women waiting for him at the bar. "Have fun stealing all the attention."

He shrugs, walking backward with a roguish gleam in his eyes. "Can't help it if the ladies love me."

When he pivots toward them, I clutch the ring on my finger and walk to our family, my husbands, my forever.

Kodiak

SEVENTY

The cool Alaskan breeze carries the scent of salt and pine as we step onto Monty's yacht. The deep velvet sky, studded with stars, reflects off the dark waters surrounding us.

The distillery sits behind us, the echoes of celebration still ringing in my ears. But here, the world feels smaller, more intimate.

Ours.

Frankie walks ahead, her red hair catching the moonlight, shimmering like fire in the dark. She glances back at us, her green eyes bright with emotion, her lips curved in a soft, inviting smile.

Monty's hand rests on the small of her back, guiding her forward. Leo drapes an arm over her shoulders, his thumb brushing the side of her neck.

I follow behind, watching them, madly in love with them, each in a different way.

We reach the main bedroom, a space that Monty warned us away from all those months ago.

So much has changed since then.

But not my obsession with her. That is unwavering.

She stands at the center of the room, her back to us, and for a moment, we just stare at her, taking in the woman at the heart of our fierce family.

Monty makes the first move, floating forward to wrap his arms around her from behind, his lips finding the curve of her neck. She melts into him, her eyes closing, a soft sigh escaping her lips.

Leo traces his fingers up her arm, brushing her hair over her shoulder. His lips meet hers, slow and teasing, and she responds with urgency, her hand cupping his jaw, pulling him closer.

She can't get enough.

I step forward, my heart speeding up as I close the distance between us. She turns her gaze to me, and our eyes lock.

Christ, she takes my breath away.

She reaches out to me, her hand finding mine, and she pulls me closer until I'm standing before her, close enough to feel the heat of her body, to hear the soft hitch in her breath.

I lean down, capturing her lips with mine. My hands frame her face as I pour my need for her into my kiss. Tongues rubbing, teeth clicking, lips bruising, we catch fire.

Monty finds the hem of her dress and slowly lifts it, revealing the soft, creamy skin beneath. Leo and I step back just long enough to help, and together, we undress her, our hands reverent as we reveal more and more of her to our hungry eyes.

She stands before us, bare and beautiful, the lamplight playing off her curves, making her glow.

I'm so fucking hard. My damn cock is trying to break through the zipper. But the moment I pull it out, tender time is over.

Monty guides her to the bed, positioning her sideways on the soft sheets, and we follow, finding our spots around her.

I stand near her head and bend down, bringing my lips to hers while Leo leans in to kiss her neck.

"Frankie." Monty caresses her round, little breasts. "We're going to try something different tonight."

She nods, her eyes gleaming with trust. "I'm all yours."

We talked about this. I don't know how it will work, but

Monty has it all mapped out. Of course, he does.

He meets my eyes and starts removing his suit.

We undress in a flurry, the sound of zippers and falling clothes ramping up my pulse.

When the last garment is shed, I stand over her, my cock bobbing above her face.

"Open that sweet mouth and suck me," I growl.

With her head hanging partially off the bed, she wraps her eager lips around me. I release a sound so loud and strangled that Leo laughs.

Fuck. The intensity of her mouth buckles my knees. I fall over her, catching myself with my hands braced on either side of her hips. The suction, the friction, and the depth she takes me is mind-blowing.

I thrust my hips, fucking into the warm, wet perfection of her mouth. Bent over her, the angle levels my face with her pretty, pink cunt. I bury my face in it, devouring her taste, her intoxicating scent, licking her until we both fall apart.

Monty and Leo take their turns next, fucking her mouth the same way.

Frankie loves to suck cock. She would do it all night if we let her. But this is just the appetizer.

As Leo chases his release in her mouth, my hand joins Monty's between her legs, our touches synchronized. Her cunt is so warm and soft around our fingers, her breath hitching as we explore her together, as we worship her with our hands and lips.

When Leo finishes, he leans down and kisses her forehead, his hand resting on her cheek. "We're not stopping until you can't breathe. You know that, right?"

"Bring it on, my Norse god." Her swollen lips curve in a wicked smile.

"Who's on the bottom?" Leo asks us.

"Me." I climb onto the bed, my dick throbbing and ready.

Frankie moves to the side as I lie on my back and gesture her over.

"Sit on my dick, woman." I grip it, angling it skyward. "Give me that ass."

Monty lubes up her hand, and she smears it over me and between her legs. Then she moves into position, facing my feet, and slowly lowers onto my cock, fitting me smoothly, wondrously into her ass.

She takes it in every hole, every day. Her body knows us, welcomes us, without hesitation or resistance.

My experience with anal sex before Frankie was traumatic and devastating. But I've talked through it in my sessions with Dr. Thurber and many late nights with Monty on this very boat while anchored in the Sitka Sound, drinking and stargazing.

Leo talks about his shit with Monty, too. Monty isn't just a problem solver. He's a damn good listener.

"How are you doing?" With my hands on her hips, I thrust in slow, measured strokes, letting her adjust to my size. "Ready for more?"

"If more means all of you…" She widens her legs, panting. "I was born ready."

"That's our girl." Monty nudges my thighs together and straddles them. Running his hands down her body, he brushes his fingers against mine and moves my grip to her tits. "You're ours, Mrs. Strakh. We're going to make you feel every bit of our love."

I hold still as his dick nudges against the base of mine. I don't know which hole he intends to fill until I feel him sliding in beside me.

"Holy fuck." I groan, shaking with the effort to remain motionless, not to let loose and start pounding. "Jesus fucking Christ."

Monty moans, a dark, guttural sound that vibrates through me. He takes his sweet-ass time pushing in, tormenting her and me with his goddamn control. He caresses her body, makes love to her mouth, and edges us both to the cusp of orgasm over and over.

"Fuck, Monty." She gives me her weight, lying back on my chest. "I need you to move, thrust, do something!"

He just laughs as his fingers work their magic on her clit, pushing her closer and closer to the edge.

When he finally bottoms out, sinking to the hilt, he finds my eyes over her shoulder.

Then we move.

Nothing compares to the sensation of his cock stroking alongside mine in her ass. The tightness, the ungodly friction, the intimacy...the pleasure overwhelms my senses, tightening my balls and spreading heat down my spine.

"I'm trying really fucking hard here not to blow my load." I cup her breasts and bury my teeth in her neck, clamping down.

"Don't you dare." Monty pauses, clenching his legs around mine. "Leo, let's go."

"Holy shit." Frankie gasps. "You guys are really doing this?"

Leo stands on the bed, stroking his dick a mile a minute. I'm surprised he hasn't come again.

He steps over us, climbing on between Monty and Frankie. Gripping the backs of her calves, he guides her feet toward her shoulders.

I wrap my hands around her ankles, holding her in the bent position.

"You okay?" Leo ducks his head, kissing her deeply.

When he leans back, she nods rapidly, eagerly.

Crouched over her with his ass pressed against Monty's abdomen, he angles himself at the opening of her cunt.

Then he impales her in one swift stroke, joining the four of us together.

Our groans echo through the room, a resounding chorus of shared pleasure.

Frankie and I face Leo and Monty. Three cocks. Two holes. She's officially stuffed.

"Look at you, taking everything we give you." I lick her neck, savoring the ravenous sounds of her breath. "You're so good for us. So beautiful. So fucking perfect."

"Every inch of you." Leo gives a small thrust, telling us to move. "Do you feel how hard we are? How much we want you?"

"Yeah. Yep." She gasps through a laugh. "Definitely feeling it."

We descend on her, rutting and huffing like a pack of wolves in mating season.

We fuck into her together, the three of us, filling her with our love, surrounding her with our devotion, until there's nothing left but the sound of our hearts slamming in unison and our breaths setting fire to the night.

She arches into us, her hand tangling in Leo's hair as she pulls him down for a kiss. Her other hand laces with Monty's, holding him close as he drives into her ass, setting the rhythm for us.

I watch them, my chest tight and my dick in heaven, getting the ride of my life.

We lose ourselves in one another, our gazes catching and clinging, our hands roaming, and our expressions twisted in ecstasy.

When we come, we fall together in a careening head-on collision. Shuddering, roaring, jerking, releasing, we explode in a mess of sticky, warm fluid, and it's fucking beautiful.

The sounds we make, the smiles we share, the blissful looks we exchange—this is us. Filthy, happy, and free.

When it's over, we lie together on the bed, our bodies entwined and sated. Frankie rests between us, her head on Monty's chest, her hand in my hair with my head on her stomach, and her legs hooked around Leo's.

"Ready to go again?" Leo bites her shoulder.

"Gonna need a minute," she slurs, halfway to sleep.

The warmth of her love, their love, surrounds me, filling me with an inner peace I've never known.

Her left hand drapes over Monty's hip, the ring glittering in the beam of moonlight. The three of us designed it together, and it couldn't be more perfect.

My thumb strokes the band on my finger. I'll never stop touching it.

We're married. Not in the legal sense. But in the only ways that matter.

In our hearts, where love is law.

In the hills, where we defeated the shivers and shadows.

In the bond we share, unbreakable and eternal.

kodiak

In the promises we made, now and forever.

monty

SEVENTY-ONE

We stand at the entrance to Disney World, the iconic Cinderella Castle rising in the distance, its turrets gleaming in the warm sunlight.

The place is a vibrant explosion of colors and sounds—families with excited children, lively music from hidden speakers, and the unmistakable scent of sweet treats in the air.

It's a place where magic happens, where joy is a living, breathing thing.

But nothing in this magical world compares to the look on Wolf's face right now.

His blue eyes stare in awe, his dark, rebellious demeanor gone, replaced by gobsmacked wonderment.

Black hair falls in messy waves around his face. He wears a black hoodie with Mickey Mouse ears embroidered on the front, paired with ripped jeans and red Converse. A faint smudge of black eyeliner darkens his eyes, a nod to his emo vibe.

I find myself smiling, caught up in his ridiculousness.

Frankie stands beside me, her hand warm in mine. We've both been here before, but never together, never like this.

This, standing here with our family. This is different. This is everything.

Leo and Kody flank us, their anticipation quieter but no less stunning. They've never been to Florida, let alone a theme park.

"What fresh hell is this?" Kody mumbles beside me, but I hear the smile in his voice.

"What's the plan, Wolf?" Leo rubs his neck, his gaze darting everywhere.

"We have to start with Space Mountain." Wolf studies his map with an enthusiasm he can't contain. "Then the Haunted Mansion, Pirates of the Caribbean, and The Tower of Terror. I want to see all the princesses. I'm doing them all. Probably at the same time. And the parade later. Followed by more princess banging and—"

"Wolf." Frankie taps a red-sequined sneaker against the back of his knee, making his leg buckle.

"What?"

"You're not banging the princesses."

"I saved myself for them."

"No." She crosses her arms.

"Evil queen." He flicks his fingers at her. "Let's go ride some rides."

She goes still, a strange quietness settling over her as her grip on my hand tightens.

There's a hesitation in her eyes, something unspoken that tugs at the edges of her joy.

"I can't do any rides that have swoops, drops, or forceful stop-and-go motions," she says suddenly, her voice soft but firm.

"Why not?" I turn, a frown of confusion twitching my forehead. "You loved them in the past."

She nods, her eyes locking onto mine. "I still love them, but..."

The corners of her lips lift in a mischievous expression as she reaches into her purse, pulls out something small and white, and holds it up between us.

It takes a second for my brain to register what it is, what it means, but when it does, the world stops spinning.

"Bumpy rides aren't safe for pregnancy." Her voice trembles.

Pregnancy.

The word echoes in my mind, reverberating through my entire being, shaking me to my very foundation.

A joy so profound, so intense, washes over me, trying to yank me to my knees.

I stare at the plastic stick in her hand, the two faint lines that change everything.

A baby.

Our baby.

My eyes find Leo and Kody.

They're just as blindsided as I am.

Blindsided in the best way.

A flood of emotions hits me all at once—love, gratitude, and an overwhelming sense of fulfillment.

Tears prick my eyes, and my throat tightens with the sheer magnitude of it.

I pull her into my arms, holding her close as my hand gently cradles the back of her head. Reaching out for Leo and Kody, I yank them in, swallowing her with our bodies.

I don't even care that we're standing in the middle of the busiest place on earth.

All that matters is this, us, the life we've created together.

"You're pregnant," Kody whispers, his voice choked, barely able to get the words out.

"Yeah." She nods against my chest, her tears wetting my shirt as she clings to us. "We're going to have a baby."

I lean back just enough to look into her eyes, my hands framing her face as I kiss her.

Around us, the world continues to move, the sounds of Disney World fading into the background. I'm lost in her, in this moment, in the knowledge that the four of us have created something beautiful and miraculous.

When we finally break apart, I take in the varying degrees of shock and happiness on their faces.

Leo's eyes shine with unshed tears. Kody's pouty lips split into a rare grin. And Wolf. His expression glows with wonder, a smile stretching as he steps closer.

"A baby?" he whispers, like he can't believe it. "We're going to have a baby?"

I nod, reaching out to pull him into our embrace, and he comes willingly, his arms wrapping around Frankie.

"Yeah, Wolf," she says. "We're going to have a baby."

"Best day ever." He pivots away and returns to his map with vigor. "We're going to do everything—rides, shows, parades—but first, we're getting ice cream. Baby Mama, you're eating for two now, so we're starting with ice cream. Then we're buying every single stuffed animal for the baby. Every. Single. One."

Together, the five of us stand at the entrance of Disney World.

As we step into the park, our smiles as bright as the sun, I know with absolute certainty that there's no place like home.

And for us, home is wherever we are together.

This concludes the Frozen Fate trilogy.
You may be wondering...
Will Wolf die a virgin?
You'll find out in his spin-off book.

OTHER BOOKS by PAM GODWIN

LOVE TRIANGLE ROMANCE
TANGLED LIES TRILOGY
One is a Promise
Two is a Lie
Three is a War

DARK ROMANCE / ANTIHEROES
DELIVER SERIES
Deliver (#1)
Vanquish (#2)
Disclaim (#3)
Devastate (#4)
Take (#5)
Manipulate (#6)
Unshackle (#7)
Dominate (#8)
Complicate (#9)

DARK COWBOY ROMANCE
TRAILS OF SIN
Knotted #1
Buckled #2
Booted #3

DARK PARANORMAL ROMANCE
TRILOGY OF EVE
Heart of Eve
Dead of Eve #1
Blood of Eve #2
Dawn of Eve #3

DARK HISTORICAL PIRATE ROMANCE

King of Libertines

Sea of Ruin

STUDENT-TEACHER / PRIEST

Lessons In Sin

STUDENT-TEACHER ROMANCE

Dark Notes

ROCK-STAR DARK ROMANCE

Beneath the Burn

ROMANTIC SUSPENSE

Dirty Ties

CELEBRITY ROMANCE

Incentive

New York Times, Wall Street Journal, and *USA Today* bestselling author, Pam Godwin, lives in the Midwest with her husband, cats, retired greyhounds, and an old, foul-mouthed parrot. She traveled the world for seven years, attended three universities, married the vocalist of her favorite rock band, and retired from her quantitative analyst career in 2014 to write full-time.

Her interests veer toward the unconventional: bourbon, full-body tattoos, and tragic villains. Equally peculiar are her aversions to sleeping, eating meat, and dolls with blinking eyes.

EMAIL: pamgodwinauthor@gmail.com